Christmas Tails

Other Books by Melody Carlson

Christmas Tails

STORIES OF OUR BELOVED FOUR-LEGGED FRIENDS

MELODY CARLSON

Revell

a division of Baker Publishing Group
Grand Rapids, Michigan

© 2009, 2012, 2014 by Melody Carlson

Published by Revell
a division of Baker Publishing Group
P.O. Box 6287, Grand Rapids, MI 49516-6287
www.revellbooks.com

Combined edition published 2015

ISBN 978-0-8007-0112-3

Previously published in three separate volumes:
The Christmas Dog © 2009
The Christmas Pony © 2012
The Christmas Cat © 2014

15   16   17   18   19   20   21   7   6   5   4   3   2   1

The Christmas Cat

Dedicated to Harry,
a very fine Maine Coon cat
who found us in the middle of a snowy winter
and won a place in all our hearts

1

Garrison Brown had been known to cross the street in order to avoid contact with a common house cat. As he hurried through the chilly Seattle air, he grimaced to see a black cat cut in front of him. With head down, the scrawny creature ducked into the alley behind a popular restaurant and disappeared into the mist. Garrison hated cats. Okay, *hate* was too strong a word. He simply wanted nothing to do with the furry little beasts.

During his missionary stint in Africa, his grandmother had lovingly teased him via email. *"Did you travel halfway across the globe just to escape my furry felines?"* For sure, domesticated cats were rare in Uganda, but it was not his cat allergies that had compelled him to leave the country—and Gram knew it.

As he went inside the apartment building where he'd secured temporary lodging with an old friend, Garrison reminded himself that cats could actually be rather amusing—from a safe distance anyway. He'd even enjoyed some of the hilarious YouTube videos that Gram had forwarded him over recent years. The one with the cat dressed as a shark riding a robot vacuum cleaner and pursuing a bird stood out in his mind.

It was impressive that his elderly grandmother had gotten so handy at technology, he thought as he scaled the first flight of creaky stairs. Equally amazing that the old girl had managed to accumulate so many cats during his nine years in Uganda. For some reason Gram had turned into a magnet for abandoned and abused cats. She called it her "St. Francis ministry," but he cringed to think of all those furry critters crawling about her home.

Garrison was well aware that Gram wasn't the only cat-loving person in this country. Unless it was his imagination, the country's cat population had hugely multiplied during his absence. He had no logical explanation for this phenomenon, but it seemed that everywhere he turned, including the ads on TV, there were cats, cats, cats. And he didn't mean the ones of the Broadway musical variety either!

He paused in the stairwell to dig his jangling phone from the depths of his coat pocket. Hoping it might be the director from the nonprofit agency he'd just interviewed with, he eagerly answered, "Hey, this is Garrison," with cheerful enthusiasm. His roommate had been encouraging him to sound younger and hipper—although Garrison was only thirty-four and not really ready to be put out to pasture. But according to Randall, Seattle was a youth-oriented town, and it seemed Garrison had some catching up to do—that is, if he wanted to fit in.

"Garrison Brown?" a deep voice asked.

"Yes, this is Garrison."

"I'm glad I could reach you, Garrison. Although I'm afraid I have some bad news."

Garrison's heart sank. The director had probably decided, like so many other personnel people, to politely decline him a job. Why was he even surprised? They didn't usually call back like this though.

"I'm Edward Miller," the man said. "I'm Lillian Brown's attorney and—"

"My *grandmother's* attorney?" Garrison interrupted. "Is something wrong?"

"Yes. I'm sorry to inform you that Mrs. Brown has passed away."

"*Oh* . . ." Garrison stopped climbing the stairs as a hard lump filled his throat. "Gram is dead?"

"Yes. She passed away this morning or maybe last night. A neighbor discovered her a few hours ago. I'm very sorry for your loss."

A heavy load of guilt pressed onto him. Garrison had truly meant to spend more time with his grandmother after returning from Uganda. He had *wanted* to. But with medical appointments to remedy his malaria . . . followed by job interviews to remedy his bank account . . . several months had passed and he'd only managed one visit down there so far and that was just one quick stop on a day trip with his roommate. He had planned to surprise her on Thanksgiving and spend the whole week with her. But now it was too late.

"What happened?" he asked weakly. "I mean, I realize she was in her late eighties, but she seemed in good health. I just talked with her a few days ago."

"I suspect it was her heart. Were you aware that she'd had some cardio problems?"

"No. She never mentioned it." He continued trudging up the last flight of stairs.

"Yes, well, she mentioned it to me late last summer. That's when she came in to make some changes regarding her estate. I suspect she knew that she wasn't long for this world."

"I had no idea. She always seemed so cheerful and energetic." Garrison felt tears filling his eyes as he pictured the old woman working in her garden . . . surrounded by her motley crew of castoff cats. He punched his fist against the door. Malaria or no malaria, why hadn't he spent more time with her right after he'd gotten home from Uganda?

"I'm sorry for your loss, Garrison. As I'm sure you must know, Mrs. Brown has designated you as her only heir."

Garrison sighed at the word *heir*. Poor Gram, like him, pretty much had nothing . . . besides her cats, that is. "Yes, well, Gram and I don't have many other relatives."

"So I'm hoping that you can come to Vancouver and help sort things—"

"Of course," Garrison agreed as he slid his key into the deadbolt of Randall's door. "I'll get down there as soon as possible. Maybe by tonight, if I can catch a bus in time."

"Tomorrow is soon enough." Mr. Miller gave some details regarding Gram's wishes for her funeral and interment. "I've already contacted her pastor. The service can be held next Monday at eleven, if you agree. But I'm sure there are some other details you'll want to attend to."

"Right." Garrison stepped into his friend's apartment, pausing to jot down some notes along with some phone numbers. "I'll call you when I get into town—probably tomorrow," he told the lawyer. They wrapped up the dismal conversation, then Garrison closed his phone and slumped into the well-worn leather recliner. Leaning forward with head in hands, he allowed his tears to flow. An old part of him felt ashamed—crying like this seemed unmanly. But then he remembered something a Ugandan friend once told him. "A real man is not afraid to shed tears." Besides, he reminded himself as he loudly blew his nose, this was Gram he was grieving.

Gram had been his rock after his parents were killed in a car wreck twenty-two years ago. She'd been recently widowed, but the older woman had shown real backbone by insisting on taking her bitter adolescent grandson into her home. She'd barely known Garrison at the time, and yet she had persistently loved him—through thick and thin. And there had been a lot of thin. But despite his deep-rooted rebelliousness and sassy back-talking habits, she refused to give up on him. She even forgave him when he nearly torched the nearby grade school. Her grace and diligence had eventually won him over—both to her and her faith. Without Gram he knew he would've gone down, or up, in flames.

And now she was gone and he couldn't even say goodbye.

"Hey, man." Garrison's roommate called out a greeting as he came into the apartment with a pair of grocery bags in his arms. "How'd the interview—" Randall's brow creased as he set a bag on the counter. "What's wrong?"

"My grandmother." Garrison sniffed and stood, squaring his shoulders, trying to act strong—manly. "Her lawyer just called. Gram passed away this morning."

"Oh, man, I'm so sorry." Randall sadly shook his head as he set down the other bag. "Your grandmother was one of the greats, you know. I've always had nothing but respect for that sweet woman. Too bad. But she had a good life. You know that, right?"

"Right." Garrison filled a glass with water, taking a big drink. "Gram was a real lady. I'm gonna miss her . . . a lot." He explained his plans to get a bus to Vancouver tomorrow morning.

"Or borrow my car," Randall said as he began unloading produce.

"Thanks. But I don't know how long I'll be down there. As far as I know, Gram never got rid of her old Pontiac. I'll just use that while I'm there."

"You're kidding. That car must be ancient by now."

"Yeah," Garrison agreed. "It was more than fifteen years old when the missions committee gave it to her after she came home from Kenya."

"Even so, it could really go. That was one big honking engine. Remember driving that car around when we were in high school?"

"Don't remind me." Garrison tried not to recall the times he'd driven too fast. "Anyway I'll just use it while I'm there—figuring stuff out." Garrison nodded to the array of foods that Randall was lining up along the counter. "What's up with all that?"

"I promised Rebecca I'd fix dinner tonight," Randall explained.

"Special occasion?"

Randall shrugged. "Nah. I just lost a bet."

"Well, I can make myself scarce if you two need to—"

"No way. You better stick around." His eyes lit up. "Besides, I'm making pad Thai. I know how much you like it."

Despite his gloom, Garrison's stomach rumbled. He

hadn't eaten since early this morning, and he remembered how Randall had worked his way through college cooking at a Vietnamese restaurant. His pad Thai was killer. "Need some help?" he offered.

"Sure." Randall handed him a bunch of green onions.

As they worked together, peeling and chopping, Garrison reminisced about Gram. "I remember when she took me in," he said. "She tried to hide it, but I could see that she was still grieving for my grandpa. He'd died just a few months earlier. That was a lot of sadness—losing her husband and her only son so close together like that. But she always seemed so strong. So faithful and optimistic."

"And hadn't she just come home from the mission field herself? My parents were on our church's mission committee at the time. I still remember them talking about this missionary widow and how everyone needed to help her feel at home in Vancouver."

"Yeah, she'd barely been moved back to the States. She'd wanted to stay in Kenya, to continue the work, but the mission board wouldn't allow it. Fortunately, for her and me too, my grandpa's parents had left that house to her."

"That was a good thing—for you and me both." Randall grinned as he poured some fish sauce into a measuring cup. "I remember when you guys moved into the neighborhood. I knew right away we were going to be best friends."

"Yeah. That was pretty cool." Garrison nodded as he scraped the chopped green onions into a metal bowl, then he sighed. "I still can't believe she's gone."

"At least you know she's in a better place."

Garrison sighed. "Yeah . . . but I wish I'd gone down to see her . . . I mean, before it was too late."

"Well, if anyone would understand, it would be your grandma. You gotta know she was really proud of you, man. Working in Uganda like you did. Helping to put all those wells into those villages." He grinned as he opened a jar of pepper paste. "She's probably up there in heaven, bragging on you right now."

Garrison made a weak half-smile as the doorbell rang and Randall hurried to answer it. Rebecca burst into the apartment, greeting Randall with her usual boisterous energy, exclaiming over the storm system that was pressing into the Sound. "Can you believe it was sixty degrees yesterday, but I heard a weather report saying we might have snow by Thanksgiving?" She waved at Garrison as she peeled off her parka.

Garrison had known Rebecca for nearly as long as he'd known Randall. They'd all gone to school together in Vancouver. But it was only recently that Randall and Rebecca had reconnected via social networking. They'd been dating steadily for nearly a month now. As a result, Garrison had begun to feel a bit like a third wheel around this place. Randall tried to play down the relationship, but Garrison felt certain that Rebecca was hearing wedding bells in her head. And seeing Randall greeting her with a kiss and whispering into her ear . . . Garrison knew it wasn't just Rebecca. Consequently, Garrison had been very focused on finding a job of late. He knew he needed to get out of here and onto his own two feet. The sooner the better for everyone. The problem was that the kind of jobs he was looking for were few and the applicants were many.

He dropped the last peeled carrot into the colander in the sink as he gave Rebecca an apologetic smile. "I didn't mean to crash your dinner party to—"

"You're *not* crashing," she declared as she came into the kitchen with sympathetic eyes. "Randall just told me about your grandmother." She gave him a warm hug. "I'm sorry, Garrison."

He just nodded. "Yeah. I know she was old and it sounds like she had some health problems, but I still can't believe she's gone."

"What will happen to all her cats?" Rebecca reached for a carrot, breaking it in half and taking a loud bite. "My aunt lives down the street from her house. Some of the neighbors—you know, the ones who don't know your grandma very well—they started calling her the Cat Lady. Rumor has it that she has like twenty cats now."

Garrison frowned. "Well, as far as I know, it was only seven at last count. No, make that six. Her oldest cat, Genevieve—that's the one she adopted right after I went to college—she died a couple months ago. I even sent Gram flowers. Genevieve was twenty-three years old."

"Seriously?" Randall took his place at the stove. "Cats really live that long?"

"I guess some do."

"They might call Gram the Cat Lady, but she definitely does not have twenty cats," Garrison clarified. "Well, unless she took in some other cats that I haven't heard about. Although we talked weekly. She never mentioned it."

"Well, six cats isn't so bad." Rebecca took another bite of carrot. "I saw this old woman on TV. She lived in Florida and had more than a hundred cats. All in one little house. Thankfully no one has invented smell-o-vision or I would've changed the channel. Seriously, it was disgusting."

Garrison shuddered. "Sounds nasty."

Rebecca laughed. "Yeah, especially for a cat-hater like you."

"Garrison doesn't *hate* cats," Randall said defensively. "It's just his allergies. I've seen him. A cat comes within ten feet of him and the poor guy starts sneezing and wheezing."

"I know, I know." Rebecca gave Garrison a contrite smile. "I just like to tease you."

The three of them chatted congenially as they worked together. Then they all sat down around a big bowl of pad Thai. After helping them clean up, Garrison excused himself to his room to make travel arrangements and pack some things. More than that, he wanted to be alone. And he was certain the couple wanted to be alone too. It seemed obvious that he didn't fit in here anymore. Sometimes he wondered if he fit in anywhere anymore. It was probably just a matter of time before those two decided to tie the knot. He really was happy for Randall. And Rebecca too. But he also felt like the odd man out. In so many ways.

Garrison wasn't really jealous. In fact, he was glad that Randall and Rebecca had found each other after all these years. They were all in their midthirties now. High time to settle down. If things had gone differently in Uganda, Garrison might've been married by this time too. But Leah had taken a different path—married someone else. And really, Garrison was over it. As Gram used to say, that was water under the bridge. He zipped up his packed duffle bag. No looking back.

Thinking of Gram again just brought all the sadness back. Why hadn't he gone home sooner? Were his excuses of job hunting and doctor visits really legitimate? Or had he secretly allowed a few old cats to keep him away? *Stupid cats!*

2

Rebecca had been right about the weather system pressing into the Seattle area. Ice-cold rain whipped against him as Garrison hurried to the bus station. It wasn't so much that he was unaccustomed to Washington's climate. But after the years in Uganda—and after suffering from malaria—he was having difficulty acclimating to the chilly, damp environment in the Northwest. Fortunately he'd had the forethought to layer on lots of clothes this morning. He probably looked like a refugee in his strange-looking ensemble. Not that he cared about fashion. Besides, for all practical purposes, he was homeless. Homeless, jobless, and alone.

He tried not to feel sorry for himself as the bus rumbled down I-5 toward Vancouver, Washington. Instead, he focused his thoughts on the sweet old house that he'd lived in from age twelve to graduation. It had been nothing like his parents' new home in a brand-new subdivision high on a hill. Gram's neighborhood, with old homes and tree-lined streets, had real personality. Sure the neighborhood had been a little run-down, but the people had been friendly. Of course, that could've changed by now. After all, he hadn't really spent time in that area during the past nine years. And his last visit, due to the cats, had been very brief. The truth was that Garrison hadn't really spent much time there since graduating from high school. That was more than sixteen years ago, and about the same time Gram had started taking in cats.

Garrison had understood when Gram had taken in her first cat. The big orange tabby she named Genevieve had seemed like good company for her. And Garrison knew that Gram had loved having cats as a child. He also knew that she grew very lonely when he left for college on the East Coast. He had actually been comforted to know she had Genevieve's companionship, and he'd told himself that he could simply take his allergy medicine whenever he came home. But over time his visits home grew rare. He claimed it was because of the cost of travel, but he knew it was also because of the cat. He learned quickly that visiting Gram for more than just a couple of hours put his health at risk. For her sake, though, he had tried to play it down. He never revealed to Gram that sometimes it felt as if she'd chosen the cat over him. He knew that would be selfish.

As Garrison walked from the downtown bus stop toward the old neighborhood, he noticed that some people were giving him curious glances. With his longish dark hair and layered clothes, beat-up duffle bag and backpack, he probably looked suspicious. The fact that he hadn't shaved probably didn't help much either. His plan was to drop off his bag, peel off some clothes, drive Gram's old Pontiac back to town for a quick bite, and then meet with the lawyer at two.

The neighborhood looked even more run-down than he remembered. Not only that, some of the trees had been cut down, giving it a stark and somewhat desolate appearance. And due to the chilly weather, no one was out and about. As he turned onto Gram's street, he wondered if she still kept a house key under the same flowerpot on the back porch. But if it wasn't there, he could always call on Ruby next door. Mr. Miller had mentioned she was seeing to Gram's cats, so Garrison knew she would have a key.

Gram's two-story white house still had the same sweet welcoming look at first glance, but as he got closer he could see that the paint was peeling and some of the shutters were sagging. He must've missed that when he'd dropped in with Randall several months ago. It had already been dusky when they'd arrived, and thanks to the cats, they hadn't stayed long.

He went to the back porch where he found a tarnished key beneath a wilted pot of geraniums. He dumped his bags on the porch steps and let himself inside, where he immediately started to sniffle and then sneeze. He'd taken allergy meds early this morning, but clearly they had worn off. He could smell the musty aroma of cats, but didn't see any, and without looking around—and hoping that perhaps they had all been carted off to some shelter—he held his breath as he opened the kitchen cupboard where Gram kept spare keys. Finding the set for the Pontiac, he hurried back outside, gasping to get a breath of fresh air.

But it was too late. As he went over to the small unattached garage, his eyes were already watering and his sneezing was getting louder. So much for his plan to change clothes at

Gram's house. He had no intention of remaining in that house for one moment longer than necessary.

"*Garrison? Is that you?*"

He paused from going into the garage. "*Ruby?*" He peered at the short, rounded woman. Her hair had turned snowy white, but her skin was still the color of an old copper penny and not nearly as wrinkled as he would've imagined.

"Land sakes!" she declared as she hurried over. "I heard all that sneezing and I thought it must be you." She threw her arms around him. "Welcome home, boy."

"Thank you, Ruby." He erupted into a new seizure of sneezing.

"You still have those allergies?"

"The cats"—he sneezed loudly—"triggered it." He reached into the pocket of his backpack for his allergy pills. "I need to take one of these."

"You need some water to wash it down?"

"Ye-yes." He sneezed again. "Please!"

"Come on." She tugged on his arm. "Let's get you inside where it's warm."

He didn't protest as she led him to her house, which was similar to Gram's only smaller. And it was still painted a cheerful yellow with white trim. "How have you been, Ruby?"

"Well, it was a blow to lose Lilly. Can't deny that. And you know my William passed on last spring." She opened the door, tugging him into her cozy kitchen where she quickly filled a glass of water and handed it to him. "Ain't easy gettin' old."

"I'm sorry about William." He popped a pill into his mouth and gulped the water.

"Thank you. I'm real sorry for your loss too, Garrison. Lilly was a fine woman." She pulled out a kitchen stool with a cracked plastic seat and pointed at him as if she expected him to sit.

He eased himself onto the stool, still sniffling.

"You want something else. Something to eat?"

"Sounds good, but I should probably be on my way soon."

"How 'bout some apple juice? Or a nice hot cup of tea? Cocoa?"

"You have cocoa?"

"Just the instant kind, but I—"

"That sounds perfect, Ruby. Walking from the bus stop made me feel chilled to the bone. I'm still not used to this climate. Uganda was so much warmer."

"And I know you got malaria while you were over there." She grimly shook her head as she turned the gas on beneath a cherry-red teakettle. "Thought you'd know better than that, young man. Lilly told me all about it. How you forgot to take your malaria medication and got yourself sicker than a dog." She made a tsking sound in her teeth. "Shame on you, Garrison."

Feeling like he was twelve again, he stared down at her plastic topped countertop—same old yellow-and-green daisies, only now it looked retro—straight out of the sixties, and it took him straight back to his childhood. "I know," he confessed. "I was really diligent about taking the anti-malarial meds at first. But time went by . . . things got busy . . . I suppose I got a little careless. Unfortunately the chances of contracting malaria increase. The longer you stay in the country the more likely you are to contract it."

She patted him on the back. "Well, never mind that. I shouldn't have chided you for it. What you did over there in Uganda—that was *angels'* work, Garrison. God bless you for doing it. Lilly was real proud of you too. How many wells did you dig over there anyway?"

"A lot of people helped with the digging, Ruby."

"Oh, I know that, boy. But you were the brains. I know how you managed to work with the government and plan for the digging and everything. So how many you think you got put in?"

He shrugged as he unzipped his jacket. "Truth is, I sort of lost count after thirty."

She slowly shook her head. "To think that all those villages got good clean water thanks to you, Garrison."

He grinned. "And thanks to you too, Ruby. I happen to know that you faithfully sent money to the project. Just like Gram and lots of other generous supporters. We never could've done what we did without all that financial support. Takes a team to make a well."

"Not to mention our prayers," she reminded him. "That must've helped too."

He nodded.

"So what'll you do with yourself now that you're home?" She turned to the whistling kettle. "Any big plans?"

He pressed his lips together, wondering how much to divulge to Ruby. Then he remembered that she was Gram's best friend and confidante. And he had fully intended to tell Gram about his most recent dream. Why not tell Ruby? "Well . . . you know what I really want to do?" he said slowly. "Something I haven't told anyone . . . yet."

Her eyes lit up as she stirred the hot water into the cocoa powder. "What is it, Garrison? I'd just love to hear about it." She set the steaming cup in front of him.

"I know I can't make this dream happen right away." He

paused to take a sip. "I realize I'll need to raise some funds first. But I'd really like to make a halfway house for young men."

"A halfway house?" She looked curious. "What is that?"

"A place for guys to get better," he explained. "You see, a friend of mine in Uganda told me about his younger brother Jacob. This poor kid really struggled with addiction in his teens. When he was twenty he completed a thirty-day treatment program, but he just couldn't seem to get his feet solidly under him. Jacob eventually fell back into his old ways . . . died of an overdose just last year. My friend was devastated."

"Oh my." She paused from dipping a tea bag in her own cup. "How tragic."

"Yeah. And, even though I haven't had an addiction problem myself, I can relate to feeling disconnected. Being forced to give up Uganda . . . not having a job or a home to speak of . . . well, I can kind of understand how discouraged a young man might get. I get how he might want a place to call home . . . a way to connect with others."

"That sounds like a good dream, Garrison. I hope you get to build your halfway house. I'm going to put it on my prayer list."

"I plan to call it Jacob's House," he confided.

"Good, solid name. And I can just imagine it, Garrison. A homey place where a young man can get free from his old drug connections." Her dark eyes grew sad. "My grandson Elliott could use a place like that."

"Really?" Garrison remembered when Ruby's daughter Saundra used to bring her little boy to visit with Ruby. "How old is he now?"

"Twenty-four . . . going on fourteen."

Garrison nodded sadly. "Too bad."

"The poor boy has had some real struggles." She took a sip of tea. "Don't like to dwell on it too much. Better to just pray instead. Maybe the good Lord knows how to fix Elliott. Because I sure don't." She looked hopefully at Garrison. "But maybe you'll build something that can help—Jacob's House. I like the sound of it."

"Well, it's just a dream at this stage . . . but God willing . . . who knows?"

"Maybe you could use Lilly's house," she suggested eagerly. "It's got those four bedrooms."

He sighed. "That would be nice, but Gram had a reverse mortgage on it. She did that to pay for my college tuition and to make ends meet. I had always hoped to pay her back by now, but then I went to Uganda instead. Not exactly a get-rich-quick scheme. I'm sure that all her equity is gone by now."

"Yes, well, don't feel bad about that. Putting you through college and seeing you going off to Africa to help folks there— that was *exactly* what Lilly wanted for you. And you know what she believed, Garrison, *the good Lord will provide*. She never worried one minute about money. You shouldn't either."

He forced a smile. For the most part, he agreed with Ruby. But sometimes that "not worrying" thing was easier said than done. As he finished his cocoa, he asked if he could use her bathroom. "I'd like to freshen up and change my clothes before I go to see Gram's lawyer. I'd do it at Gram's . . . but those cats."

"Of course. You just make yourself at home, Garrison. There are no cats in this house." She frowned. "But I've been growing quite attached to Viola."

"Viola?"

"One of Lilly's cats." Her eyes lit up. "She's a big, beautiful gray cat with the softest coat of fur. I think Lilly said she is a Russian Blue, and I've always admired her. I think she's about twelve years old. My William never wanted a cat in the house. But now that he's gone . . ." She sighed. "Anyway, if you need to find homes for those cats, I'd like to be the first in line for Viola."

"Yes, of course," he eagerly agreed. "I don't see any reason you couldn't have her. For all I care, you can have all of the cats, Ruby."

She chuckled. "No sirree. Thank you very much. I used to take care of them for Lilly when she was gone. Not that she was gone much—that many cats tie a body down. Believe you me, I know how much work they can be. Lilly might've liked a houseful of cats, but it's not for me. Besides that, I couldn't afford all the cat food or vet bills. I probably can't afford to take in Viola." Her smile faded a little. "But I sure would enjoy having her for company."

"Well, as far as I'm concerned, Viola is all yours, Ruby."

Garrison felt a bit more presentable by the time he walked into the law office at two. Mr. Miller firmly shook his hand and once again expressed his sympathy. "Have a seat," he said, and waved to a black leather chair across from his sleek desk.

"Thanks for taking time to meet with me," Garrison said as he sat. "I doubt there's much estate to deal with, but I want to do things right. And I'm aware that my grandmother had a reverse mortgage on her home. I assume what little equity she had has been eaten up with taxes by now. And besides her old car, which needs some work, and a few household goods, I doubt there is much to discuss."

Mr. Miller didn't respond to this as he opened a large file folder.

"Oh . . ." Garrison cringed. "Unless she had debts. I hadn't really considered that, but I suppose it's likely. I know my college tuition was costly. And she helped support me in Uganda. I hope she didn't incur debt as a result. Although I will pay it all back if she did. I mean, I'm currently unemployed, but as soon as I get a—"

"No, no, don't worry. Your grandmother had no debt, Garrison." Mr. Miller looked across his desk. "In fact, she paid back her reverse mortgage about seven years ago."

"What?" Garrison was shocked. "How on earth did she manage to do that? She had nothing beyond some skimpy Social Security. You're probably aware that my grandparents were missionaries. I know for a fact that my grandmother lived as frugally as a church mouse."

"That might be so," Mr. Miller said. "But she had money."

Garrison frowned. "How is that possible?"

"Did Mrs. Brown tell you much about her parents?"

He tried to remember. "Well, she mentioned that they were opposed to her marriage to my grandfather. They thought she was throwing her life away to become a missionary. So they were kind of estranged. That's about all I know."

"Apparently her parents were fairly well off. Your grandmother's father was involved in the early days of the airline industry. He passed away about twenty years ago, leaving everything to his second wife. Then she passed away while you were overseas. According to your great-grandfather's will, the remains of his estate went to your grandmother."

Garrison was trying to absorb this. "So Gram *wasn't* poor? She was rich?"

"She wasn't a millionaire. And, as you mentioned, she continued to live quite frugally. I suspect she was comfortable with her lifestyle." Mr. Miller held up what looked like a bank statement. "The most money she ever spent was in donations—primarily to the Uganda Water Project. Her records show that she sent in a generous check every single month since inheriting the money."

"The Uganda Water Project?" He studied Mr. Miller. "That was the mission group that I worked with. I know she donated to it. But I never thought she could afford to give very much."

"Well, according to this, her support was significant. It appears that her checks were funneled through the church, but it was definitely designated to the water project. Your grandmother obviously believed in it. She's even left a nice endowment for the project."

"Wow . . ." He slowly shook his head, trying to absorb this. "I had no idea."

Mr. Miller flipped through some papers. "I'd like to go over the details of her will, Garrison. It is, well, shall I say a bit unconventional."

"Okay." Garrison leaned forward to listen.

"As you know, Lilly was very fond of her cats. But she was also well aware that you have severe cat allergies. She knew that she couldn't expect you to take care of them after she was gone. So she has asked you to take guardianship of the cats until you can find them each a good home."

"Oh?" He nodded. "That shouldn't be hard. In fact, I think I already found one home already."

"Not so fast." Mr. Miller held up a page. "There are some very specific stipulations for the placement of the cats."

"Oh . . . okay. What kind of stipulations?"

"Your grandmother made a list. Naturally, I'll give you a copy of all this, but I did promise your grandmother that I'd go over the whole thing with you. She suspected you'd be a bit surprised. She wanted to be certain that you thoroughly understood and accepted her plans."

"That's fine. Go ahead."

Mr. Miller cleared his throat. "First of all, the cats can only be placed in approved families. Second, the adoptive families must live in Mrs. Brown's neighborhood."

"That sounds doable."

"And the adoptive families must have resided in that neighborhood for at least a year. Mrs. Brown wants to be assured they're not transient. And the homes must be approved. Meaning that they are clean and safe for pets. She's made another checklist for this."

"Seriously?" Garrison shook his head. "It sounds more like finding homes for children than for cats."

"Her cats were her children."

"Well . . . yeah . . . I know."

"Do you want to hear the rest?"

"Of course." Garrison leaned back.

"The adoptive homes must have at least one person in the house for the better part of the day so that the cats aren't left alone for long periods of time. And if the cats are placed with married couples, the marriage needs to be stable and solid."

Garrison frowned. "How am I supposed to know—"

"Mrs. Brown has a list for that too." Mr. Miller peered

over the top of the paper. "It's all in a packet for you. Shall I continue?"

Garrison just nodded.

"If the adoptive homes qualify, the cats will be placed for a two-week trial period. After that, the guardian of the cats will conduct one surprise visit to ensure that the cats are happily settled into their new homes. If anything is amiss, the cats shall be removed. Then, after the cat has spent three weeks in the adoptive home, the cat guardian shall return and—"

"Is it just me, or does this all sound a little crazy?" Had Gram been getting senile? She sounded so sensible on the phone . . . but maybe he'd missed something.

"As I told you, Garrison, it is a little unconventional. That's why I'm going over some of the details now."

"But I don't get it. I mean, how will I ever find people like this? Seriously, who in their right mind would ever agree to jump all these hurdles—surprise visits and home inspections and all that—just to adopt some old lady's cat?"

"I'm aware that most people would be put off by these things."

"Then why did Gram insist on all this?"

"Because she wanted to be certain that all her beloved cats would be well cared for after she was gone."

"But it feels like you're asking me to do the impossible." Garrison ran his fingers through his hair. "I mean, after all, they are just cats."

"Are you saying that you do not wish to be the guardian of the cats?"

"No . . . I'm not saying that. It just sounds extremely complicated and difficult."

"Well, there is one little surprise that will make it a bit

easier." Mr. Miller laid down the papers. "All the adoptive families will be given a check for ten thousand dollars after you have determined that all six cats are settled and happy."

"Ten thousand dollars for adopting a cat?"

He just nodded.

"That's sixty thousand dollars total!"

"That's correct."

Garrison let out a low whistle. Was this for real?

"So you need to decide, Garrison. Do you want to agree to this responsibility? It was your grandmother's last wishes that you do this for her. But she knew about your allergies and she realized you might refuse—"

"I'll do it," he said suddenly. "It was obviously important to her. How could I not do it?"

Mr. Miller smiled. "She would be happy to know this."

"So am I supposed to tell these adoptive families that they'll get ten grand just for taking in a cat? I mean, that would make it pretty easy to find homes. Just run an ad in the newspaper or online and I'll bet my phone would start ringing nonstop."

"You could do it that way." Mr. Miller frowned as he slid some paperwork into a large manila envelope. "But that would make it difficult to sift the suitable adoptive homes from the gold diggers."

Garrison nodded. "Good point."

"Basically, it's up to you—I mean, how you choose to handle this. Your grandmother's final wish was for her cats to find good homes and for the people who adopted them to be blessed in the process. She was well aware that some of her cats were older and might not be easily placed. The last thing she wanted was for them to go to a pet shelter or wind up on the streets or be euthanized."

"That's understandable."

"And she realized that it would take you some time to work out the details of her final wishes," he continued. "To that end, she's left you some living expenses. Enough for a month or two, depending on how you handle it." He slipped what looked like a cashier's check into the envelope.

"That was thoughtful." Garrison knew that his tone sounded flat and unenthusiastic, but it was the best he could muster. It wasn't easy discovering that one's grandmother was fonder of her cats than her own grandson. He knew that was selfish on his part, but Gram knew he had allergies when she started taking in felines.

"She also put details about the cats in here." Mr. Miller grinned. "Complete dossiers with photos and vet records and everything she thought might be needed in the case of her demise."

"Seems she thought of everything." Garrison felt slightly overwhelmed. Was he really about to become the keeper of the cats?

"I expect you'll want to remain in your grandmother's house while you're acting as guardian and handling the placement of the cats."

Garrison shook his head. "Not with my allergies."

"Right." Mr. Miller closed the thick envelope and slid it across his desk toward Garrison. "I'll admit that Mrs. Brown's plan seemed a bit eccentric to me at first, but the more I spoke with her, the more I realized that her heart was in the right place. She really loved her cats."

Garrison let out a long sigh. "Yeah . . . that seems obvious." He hated to think he envied a bunch of aging cats, but he couldn't help himself. Gram's estate was going directly to the felines. And really, why shouldn't she disperse her money as she saw fit? After all, those cats had been a bigger part of her life than Garrison . . . at least for the past sixteen years. In reality, Garrison had spent only six years under her roof. It was clear, those cats were her family.

3

As Garrison drove home, he was determined to carry out Gram's last wishes to the best of his ability—and as quickly as possible. For starters, he would give Viola to Ruby. Surely that would make Gram happy. As he pulled into the driveway, he checked his watch to see that he still had a couple of hours on his allergy medicine. Besides that precaution, he had stopped by the drugstore to pick up a pack of disposable allergy masks as well as some medical-grade disposable gloves. He knew this might be overkill, but he didn't care. If necessary, he would get a respirator and maybe even a hazmat suit too. One couldn't be too careful.

"How'd it go with the lawyer?" Ruby asked. She'd emerged from her house just as he was closing the garage door.

He weighed his words. "It was . . . uh . . . interesting."

"Oh." She frowned.

"Do you still want Viola?"

Her eyes brightened. "Oh yes, I'd love to have her."

"Well, I need to find homes for *all* the cats. As soon as possible. It'd be great if you could take Viola off my hands and—"

"You won't have to ask me twice." Ruby followed him to the back door. "Do you think she'll be happy at my house?"

"I'm sure she'll be most grateful." He unlocked the door.

"I don't have any cat goodies . . . like food dishes and litter boxes."

"I'm sure Gram had plenty of that sort of thing." He paused to secure the mask and pulled on the gloves.

"You look like you're about to perform surgery," she commented as they went inside.

"Well, I do plan to remove some cats," he joked. "But not surgically."

She pushed ahead of him, calling out for Viola. "Here, kitty-kitty," she cooed sweetly. And just like that a small herd of cats came rushing into the kitchen. "They probably think I'm going to feed them again," she explained as she bent down to scoop up the big Russian Blue. "There you are, Viola girl. You wanna go home with Ruby?"

Garrison froze in place as the cats swarmed around his feet. He didn't want to show how unsettling this was, but he could feel his heart racing and it was getting difficult to breathe. Or maybe that was the mask. "Go ahead and look around for what you need," he told Ruby. "Cat food or dishes or whatever. Take anything you like."

"Are you okay?" She peered curiously at him. "Even for a white boy, you look awful pale. Are you having a malaria attack?"

"No, no . . . it's—uh—just the allergy thing," he murmured.

"Looks like more than that to me." She tilted her head to one side as she rubbed the top of Viola's head, studying him closely.

"More than what?" He carefully stepped over a big furry cat that resembled a raccoon.

"Looks to me like you might have some kind of phobia, boy."

"Phobia—of what?"

"Cats." She pushed Viola up close to his face and he quickly jumped back, accidentally stepping on a cat tail or paw and causing one of the felines to let out a loud screech that made him jump even higher. Ruby laughed loudly. "I do believe I'm right. You have a cat phobia, Garrison."

"No, no . . ." He tried to calm himself. "It's just the allergies. I like to keep a safe distance from—"

"I saw it on a TV show not long ago. Maybe it was Dr. Phil. Anyway, they said the best way to conquer your fears was to face them head-on." She grinned wide, revealing a gold tooth. "I guess that's what you're doing right now."

"Right now, I'm going upstairs," he told her. "I want to see if there are any rooms that have been off-limits to the cats." Mostly he just needed a place to steady himself, a spot where he could close the door and catch his breath.

"Lilly always kept your room closed up tight," she called after him. "Hoping you'd come home to stay with her a while. It should be a cat-free zone." She chuckled. "Imagine a big strong-looking young man afraid of a pretty little kitty like you, Viola."

"*Imagine*," he muttered to himself as he scaled the stairs. He went down the hall and directly to his old room, quickly opening the door and stepping inside. Once again, he was pleasantly surprised to see that it looked exactly as he'd left it straight out of high school. It was like going into a comfortable time warp. Sure, the sports posters were curled at the edges and the plaid curtains and matching bedspread had faded some, but for the most part, nothing had changed. A little more at ease, he closed the door and leaned against it. Then he cautiously removed the face mask and, taking in a slow, deep breath, he felt himself beginning to relax.

Was Ruby right? Did he really have some kind of cat phobia? He peered at his image in the cloudy dresser mirror. His brow was furrowed and his hazel eyes looked worried, and even his pupils appeared smaller. Wasn't that a sign of fear? And yet, what did he have to be afraid of? He'd traveled the world, faced various forms of danger—everything from wild jungle animals to guerrilla warriors—and he had never felt unreasonably fearful of anything. And yet, it was undeniable, those silly old cats in the kitchen had just sent shivers down his spine. Maybe Ruby was right after all. It was possible that he was dealing with some kind of phobia. Perhaps he should take her advice (or the advice of that TV doctor she'd mentioned) and simply face his fears.

He looked around his old room, wondering if it might be possible to actually stay in Gram's house. It would certainly save him some hotel expenses. With this haven in his old room, he might be able to get by for a week or so. Hopefully it wouldn't take long to find homes for Gram's herd of felines. In the meantime, he'd attempt to take Ruby's advice by facing his fears and getting to know these cats better. At least he'd try.

"*Yoo-hoo?*" she called as she clumped up the stairs. "Are you okay, Garrison?"

He put his mask back on, adjusting it snugly against his

cheeks. It was one thing to face one's fears, something else altogether to expose oneself to disturbing allergens. "I'm coming," he called as he emerged from his room, carefully closing the door behind him.

"I found some cat supplies," she informed him. "Lilly had a whole closet just chock-full of kitty goodies. I helped myself, like you told me to—hope that's okay."

"It's more than okay," he assured her as they went down the stairs. "Anything to get you and Viola off to a good start in her new home." Bracing himself, he reached out to give the gray cat a quick rub on the head. Baby steps, he said to himself. One cat at a time. "I hope you two are very happy together," he told Ruby. "And, uh, well . . . I shouldn't say anything, Ruby, but my grandma has made some provisions for the, uh, for the folks that adopt her cats."

"Provisions?" Ruby's brows drew together. "What do you mean?"

"I don't really want to go into the details now. But if you and Viola settle in nicely and you decide you want to keep her—"

"I already *know* I want to keep her," Ruby declared. "No question about that."

"Well then you shouldn't worry too much about the expenses of cat food and litter and vet bills and such."

She gave him a puzzled look. "What're you talking about, boy?"

"Gram made some provisions for her cats' new homes."

"What do you mean *provisions*?" she asked again.

He made a mischievous grin. "I shouldn't have said anything."

"You got that right, young man. You tell Ruby something like that and then leave her hanging?"

He held up his purple-gloved hands. "I'm sorry, Ruby. But that's all I can say right now. Okay?"

"Hmm . . . I guess so." Her mouth twisted to one side. "Now, you better take care of yourself and your little cat phobia, young man. I set my cat things out on the back porch. I'd like to get Viola home now. And I'll be sure to let you know how she likes living at my place."

"Thanks," he told her as they went into the kitchen.

"You let me know if you need anything." She sounded like her old cheerful self again. "Or if these cats start a-worrying you, just give old Ruby a call. I'll come to your rescue."

"Thanks. Appreciate it."

"Or if you get hungry, you come on over. In fact, I've a mind to just whip up some chicken pot pie tonight." She gave him a sly look as she wrapped part of her coat over Viola. "Maybe I'll see if I can bribe you with food . . . get you to talk."

He chuckled. "Ruby, Ruby."

"Or maybe you don't like my pot pie like you used to?"

"I haven't had a good pot pie in years," he said eagerly.

"Alrighty then. My stomach don't like eating too late at night. Come five thirty, you get yourself over to Ruby's kitchen and don't you be late."

"Will do." He saluted her.

"And I assume you'll take over feeding the cats now."

"Yes, of course."

She pointed to the refrigerator where a laminated page was attached by a cat-shaped magnet. "That's Lilly's detailed instructions. She always kept it there for me. Sometimes if she had to be gone for a spell—never more'n a day at most—I'd see to the cats."

He glanced at the note. "Good to know." He opened the

door for her and seeing her box of cat goods, scooped them up and followed her over to her house.

"Thank you, son." She rewarded him with a wide smile.

"Thank you for taking Viola." He set the box on a chair inside her back door.

"See you at five thirty."

"You bet." He grinned to himself as he closed her door. *One cat gone, five to go.* Maybe this wasn't going to be so hard after all. And it warmed his heart to imagine Ruby's expression when he handed her a check for ten thousand dollars next month. By his calculations that should be a little before Christmas. *Nice!*

He retrieved the duffle bag he'd stashed in the Pontiac and carried it, along with the envelope from Mr. Miller, into the house. He wanted to read through the papers from Gram's attorney, but as soon as he got back into the kitchen, the cats began converging and meowing . . . as if they expected something from him. *What?* A glance at Gram's directions on the fridge revealed these cats were used to eating their dinner between four and five. And it was just a little past four.

Still wearing the particle mask and gloves, he removed Gram's instructions from the fridge and continued reading. He quickly realized this was more complicated than just filling a big bowl with Cat Chow. Each cat was listed individually. Even with Viola adopted by Ruby, there were still five different feline diets to contend with. Garrison had to read through it several times, condensing it down to this: Oreo had to be fed by himself in the laundry room with just a special low-fat dry food because he was overweight and would devour the other cats' foods if he got the chance; meanwhile, Spooky needed special drops in her canned food to prevent hairballs; Rusty had a special mix of both dry and canned food; and Muzzy needed to be fed a special gluten-free food. It seemed that the only cat without special dietary needs was Harry.

"God bless Harry," Garrison said as he laid the instruction sheet on the counter. Then he looked around at the cats clamoring around his feet. "Which one of you is Harry?"

The big raccoon-like cat seemed to look up expectantly, rubbing himself against Garrison's legs as if to confirm that he indeed was Harry. "Well, that's easy for you to say," Garrison told the friendly cat. "But I need more evidence." Now he remembered the "dossier" that Mr. Miller had described. Hadn't he mentioned photos?

He opened the envelope and dug through it until he found the section that described the cats. Seeing that it was rather lengthy, he decided to take it up to his room where he could read it without wearing his mask and gloves. "I'll be back soon," he promised the cats as he hurried away.

The top page was for Viola, but since she had already found a home, he barely skimmed it. However, he did discover that, besides being a Russian Blue, Viola was twelve years old and slightly moody. She was very attached to Gram and considered herself to be the top cat. "Viola will not do well in a house with children and noise or other pets," Gram had written. "She would prefer being re-homed with a mature single woman who is affectionate and can bestow on Viola the special attention that she craves."

Garrison chuckled. Well, Ruby should be just about perfect. Really, this wasn't so difficult. He sat down on his bed and flipped to the next page. A photo of a big orange short-haired cat grinned back at him. *Rusty.* Apparently this cat was ten years old, fairly easygoing, and got along with children. "Rusty is the clown cat," Gram had written. "He is playful and loving and would enjoy a home with a big family and lots of attention and even other cats. Rusty gets along well with others."

"Good old Rusty," Garrison said as he set that page aside.

Spooky, he soon discovered, was the calico, a seven-year-old female that Gram had taken in two years ago. She was also the least social of the cats and very moody. "Spooky is independent, but she still likes attention. She would probably do best in a home without other pets." Since he had three cats to go and he knew they were hungry, he didn't bother to read all the details about Spooky.

He saw the photo of the black-and-white cat. Naturally, that was Oreo. That was easy to remember. He was nine years old and had come to Gram as a kitten. He sounded easygoing enough.

The loud Siamese cat was Muzzy. She was eight years old and according to Gram, "somewhat demanding and talkative." Garrison set her page aside.

Finally he saw the page for Harry—and, as it turned out, he *was* the friendly cat that resembled a raccoon. Harry was a Maine Coon cat that had found his way into Gram's home and heart just a year ago. "Harry is a very special cat," she had written. "I don't like to say he's my favorite, but if I could only keep one cat—God forbid—I would choose Harry. He is five years old and the smartest one of the bunch."

Armed with this new information, Garrison put on his particle mask again and went down to the kitchen to feed the cats. Naturally, it wasn't as easy as he thought it should be, but eventually he got the cats figured out and situated and fed. By the time he finished up it was nearly five—and he felt exhausted.

Not only that, but his nose was starting to run and his eyes were watering and by the time he made it to his room, he was starting to sneeze again. How could caring for five felines be this difficult? And, seriously, if he couldn't manage a few silly old cats, how did he ever think he could run a halfway house for recovering addicts?

4

think what you're saying is that Lilly created some kind of endowment fund for her beloved kitties," Ruby said as she gave him a second helping of chicken pot pie.

"I said nothing of the sort." He kept his eyes fixed on his plate.

"You might not-a said the words." She sat back down. "But I can tell that's what you mean." She reached over and put her hand over his. "You can trust me, Garrison."

He looked up and grinned. "Well, you probably know that Gram was always a generous woman."

She nodded as she picked up her fork. "Especially when it came to the cats." She chuckled as she dug into her second helping. "Generous to a fault."

After stuffing himself on the delicious pot pie, Garrison went back home and barricaded himself against the cats.

Stowed away up in his boyhood room, sitting at the desk that was a couple inches too short for him, he opened up his laptop and proceeded to write out an ad for the local classifieds. He also planned to place it on Craigslist and some other local sites. No stone unturned. The sooner he found homes for these cats, the better for all.

> Five very special cats have lost their owner and are looking for new homes. Take your pick: a Siamese named Muzzy, a short-haired black-and-white named Oreo, an orange tiger named Rusty, a calico named Spooky, or a Maine Coon cat named Harry. All are well mannered and between five and twelve years old. All cats are fixed and in good health. Vet records available. "Adoptive" parents must meet certain qualifications and live in northeast Vancouver. Call for more information.

He reread the ad, then typed in the phone numbers and his email address. Satisfied with it, he went ahead and posted it on the internet and emailed it to the newspaper. He also planned to make some signs to post in the neighborhood. Hopefully he would start getting inquiries by tomorrow.

Morning came and neither his cell phone nor Gram's landline was ringing. And so, after feeding the hungry horde of cats, Garrison set about creating what he felt would be an attractive and compelling poster. Protected by his allergy medicine and a fresh particle mask, he spent about an hour taking various photos of the cats. Then, safely back in his room, he selected a photo of Oreo and Rusty and, with the help of his laptop, put together a poster. He was just putting on the finishing touches when his phone rang. Hoping it was someone calling to adopt a cat, he eagerly answered. But it was Gram's pastor, calling to express his sympathy and finalize some details regarding the memorial service.

"We could have held it Saturday," Pastor Barton told him. "But the women are having their harvest fair tomorrow. They always have it the weekend before Thanksgiving."

"Monday is fine," Garrison assured him.

"Your grandmother was very specific about the kind of service she wished to have," he said. "And, as you know, she chose cremation. Her plan was to keep everything sweet and simple. She even wrote her own very humble eulogy. She didn't want anyone to make her sound overly grand. So, anyway, it's all rather cut-and-dried. Well, I don't mean to sound like that. She actually planned a very nice service. And she hoped that you would want to speak, Garrison. In fact, I'm sure the congregation would enjoy that too."

"Of course," he promised. "I'm glad to."

They discussed it a bit more before Garrison told the pastor he'd see him on Monday and hung up. He wasn't surprised that Gram had handled everything so efficiently. She had always been a practical, no-nonsense sort of woman—in life . . . and in death. Well, except for the cats. It seemed like she'd thrown practicality out the window when she'd started taking them in.

Her whole house, he'd discovered, seemed dedicated to her fine, furry friends. There were cat basket beds in every room. Not that the cats seemed to use them. Most of the furnishings were covered in hair. There were cat toys scattered about, sometimes making the house seem like a minefield—especially when he wasn't paying close attention. And some rather inventive scratching posts were stuck here and there. One reached clear to the ceiling with several platforms as well as a crow's nest on top. However, the upholstered furniture must've been preferable to the cats because everything was scratched and threadbare. Apparently the cats didn't understand the rationale of "scratching posts." Except for Harry. Garrison caught Harry working over the giant post with great vigor as he headed out to get his cat posters printed.

"Good kitty," he said as he passed through the living room. Harry turned and peered at Garrison with intelligent green eyes, almost as if he understood. "Take care of things while I'm gone," he told the cat.

After getting a bite to eat and some posters printed, Garrison returned to Gram's neighborhood and began putting them up here and there.

"What's this?" a young woman on a bicycle asked him.

He smiled at her. "Free cats," he said cheerfully. "You interested?"

She got off the bicycle and studied the poster. "As a matter of fact, I've wanted a cat for years. And I've been promising myself to get one ever since I got settled in a real house."

"Are you settled in a 'real' house now?" he asked in a teasing tone.

She nodded. "I am."

"Well, I have a nice selection of cats to choose from." He explained about his grandmother and how the felines had been her beloved family.

"Was your grandma the Cat Lady?" Her brows rose.

"I suppose some people called her that." He gave the nail head one last whack then turned back to the girl. With her dark brown ponytail and expressive brown eyes, she was strikingly pretty. "Did you know my grandmother—the, uh, Cat Lady?"

"No, but I heard she had a lot of cats. Like twenty?"

"As far as I know, she only had seven—at the most. Although I'll admit that's more than enough."

"Oh, well . . . you know how rumors go," she said apologetically. "This is a pretty tight-knit neighborhood. People talk."

"Yeah. Anyway, my grandmother passed on last week. It's up to me to find good homes for her cats."

"I'm sorry for your loss." She looked genuinely sympathetic.

"Thanks. I realize my grandmother was old and she was probably ready to go . . . but I still miss her."

"Well, if these cats are as nice as you say, I might be interested in giving one a home," she proclaimed. "But I'd like to meet the cats first."

"No problem." He frowned and pointed to a bullet on the sign. "But you have to live in this neighborhood." He made an uncomfortable smile. "My grandma has a whole list of requirements for potential adoptive homes."

"Well, that's no problem. I live just a few blocks from here."

"Perfect."

She stuck out her hand. "I'm Cara Wilson," she told him.

"Garrison Brown," he said as he clasped her warm hand. "Pleased to meet you."

"So is this a good time to see your cats?" she asked hopefully.

"Absolutely," he said eagerly.

"Great. I'm taking my break. Not that I'm really locked into a schedule. You see, I mostly work from home. Except for once a week when I have to go in for planning meetings."

"Well, there's no time like the present." He grimaced to remember the condition of the house. "Although I should warn you my grandmother's place is, well, a little catty . . . if you know what I mean."

She chuckled as she tucked a long strand of shiny chestnut hair behind one ear. "That's okay. I had a great-aunt who used to keep cats. I totally understand."

After Garrison told her the address, she said she'd drop her bike at home and drive her car over. "Just in case I get to bring the cat back home with me."

As he hurried back to Gram's, he felt greatly encouraged on two levels. First of all, he might've just found a home for another cat. That took the cat population down to four! But secondly, and probably even more significant, this girl had really caught his eye. Not only was Cara very pretty, in a wholesome girl-next-door sort of way, there was something else too. He couldn't quite put his finger on it—maybe it was a mixture of kindness and spunk—but he was certain he wanted to get better acquainted with her.

As soon as he reached Gram's house, he automatically pulled on the particle mask. He'd given up the surgical gloves, except for kitty litter cleaning, which he'd already done this morning. But despite his allergy meds, he knew the mask was a true necessity. Without it he was a mess. However, due to wanting to impress his visitor, he was tempted to shove it back into his pocket. Except the image of him sneezing and wheezing and coughing all over the poor girl was truly alarming. Really, which was less attractive—impersonating a surgeon or having an allergic fit?

As he kicked some cat toys under the sofa, he wished he'd taken the time to straighten up some. Gram's house really could use a thorough cleaning and he fully intended to do that . . . but getting rid of these cats was his first priority. After that, he planned to empty most of the contents of the house—at least the items that were coated in fur or had been shredded by claws. Even the wall-to-wall carpeting needed to be removed.

The doorbell rang and he hurried to open it. "Welcome to the cat house," he told her, grinning from behind his white mask as he waved her inside.

"What's that?" She pointed to his face.

"I have severe cat allergies," he explained.

She frowned. "That must be rough . . . I mean, with all these cats."

"It's definitely a challenge." As she went over to where Rusty and Oreo were playing together on the sofa, he quickly explained about how he'd been out of the country for nine years. "My grandmother helped raise me, but after I left home, she was lonely. So she started to collect cats."

She was stroking Oreo's sleek coat and scratching Rusty's head. "You two are so sweet," she said. "You look just like the picture on the poster."

He told her their names. "They're the friendliest of the cats." Just then Harry strolled into the living room, rubbing himself against Garrison's legs. "Well, I guess Harry is friendly too."

Cara looked over and her eyes lit up. "That's a Maine Coon cat," she exclaimed.

"Yeah, I know."

"Those are very special cats." She came over and kneeled down, running her fingers through Harry's long silky coat. "Oh, he is really a beauty."

"I've never been fond of cats," Garrison confessed, "but I have to admit he's a nice one. He was Gram's favorite too."

"Oh, he's perfectly lovely." Cara scooped the big cat into her arms, carrying him over to the sofa. "You are a darling," she cooed at him. Harry seemed to be eating up the attention. "And those pale green eyes. I can see real intelligence in them."

"Yes," Garrison agreed. "I think he's very smart."

"How old is he?"

"He's the youngest of the cats. Just five," Garrison explained. "But according to Gram's notes, Maine Coon cats sort of rule the cat kingdom. And I've noticed it too. It's like he has this regal quality about him."

"I adore him. Honestly, I think I'm in love." Cara looked up with glowing eyes. "Can I *really* have him?"

Suddenly Garrison remembered the stipulations of Gram's will. "I, uh, I think so. But I have to ask you some questions first." He made a sheepish smile. "It was my grandmother's dying wish that these cats get placed in the right homes."

"Sure. I can understand that."

"Well, I already know that you live in the neighborhood. And you work from home."

"Yes. I write for a relatively new online travel magazine. The pay's not so fabulous . . . not yet anyway. But the magazine has huge potential. And I've been with them for almost five years now. The longest I've been at any job."

"That's great." He tried to remember the list. "Are you married?"

She frowned. "I have to be married?"

"No," he said quickly. "But if you're married, Gram wanted to be assured you're in a solid marriage."

She chuckled. "Well, I am solidly single."

He grinned. "Maybe I should get the list, so we can go over it. This is still kind of new turf for me."

"Why don't you do that?" She turned back to Harry, cooing at him as she continued to stroke his coat. "You are a truly lovely creature, Harry. Would you like to go home with me? Be my cat? We could be very happy together."

Garrison hurried to the kitchen where he'd left the large envelope, quickly extracting Gram's long list of requirements. "Here it is," he said as he reappeared in the living room. "Okay . . . you live in the neighborhood." He peered over the page at her, taking in her profile, the upturned nose, firm chin. "Have you been here at least a year?"

She looked up with concern. "At least a year?"

He nodded. "That's a stipulation."

"Well, no . . . I've only been here since August."

He frowned. "What?"

"But it's not like I'm going to leave."

Garrison scanned the list, seeing something else that Gram's attorney hadn't specifically mentioned. "Do you own your home?"

"I have to own my home?" She sounded slightly indignant. "No . . . I'm renting."

"Oh . . ." Garrison stared at the line stating "adoptive owners must be homeowners in the neighborhood." Homeowners, really?

"So are you saying I don't qualify?"

He felt really torn. "According to this . . . you don't."

She gently removed Harry from her lap, setting him next to her on the sofa. "You mean just because I don't own my home—haven't lived here a year—you aren't going to let me have Harry?" She looked close to tears, and Garrison felt like a real jerk.

"I would gladly give you Harry," he said meekly. "But this list—it was given to me by the lawyer—it's my grandmother's dying wish."

Cara slowly stood. "Well, I wish you the best of luck in finding homes for your *five* cats," she said a bit stiffly.

"I'm really sorry," he said as he followed her to the front door. "If I could do it differently, I would. I mean, I'm as eager as you are—"

"I feel like I've been the victim of a bait and switch." Her eyes narrowed with suspicion. "Like I've been tricked."

"I didn't mean to trick you. It's just that I have to—"

"Don't worry, Garrison." Her smile looked forced. "I'll get over it." She turned around to give Harry one last glance. "Take care, big boy. I hope you find the right home."

"I'm really sorry, Cara, but I have to respect my—"

"Never mind," she said abruptly. "I get it." And then she left.

Garrison sneezed beneath the mask, causing it to slip off his face. And now his eyes were watering up. He could tell his allergy meds were wearing off. Harry sauntered over and rubbed up against his legs, letting out a friendly meow.

"It's not your fault, old boy." Garrison sneezed again. "Man, I gotta get outta here."

By the morning of the memorial service on Monday, Garrison had not managed to find a home for a single cat. He'd gotten only one phone call and that was from a woman who lived downtown. But at least he'd learned something. Rule number one: go over the basic stipulations before talking about the available cats.

However, cats were the last thing on his mind as he drove to the church. First and foremost, his thoughts were with Gram, and he knew this service had been important to her. Even though she'd written her own eulogy, he knew it was only respectful to say a few words. He also knew that public speaking was not his forte. The truth was, he'd rather get a root canal than address a roomful of people. Although his jacket pocket bulged from the numerous index cards he'd scribbled on last night, he hoped he wouldn't need to pull them out and fumble through them. But whatever it took, he was determined to honor Gram's memory today.

"My grandmother took me in after my parents died," Garrison began when it was his turn to speak. "I didn't want to admit it at the time, since I was nearly twelve years old, but I was a little afraid of her when I first moved into her house. Or maybe I was just in awe of her. I'd grown up hearing my dad speak of his parents with a mixture of pride and almost fearful respect. I knew my grandparents were missionaries in Kenya. I knew that they'd lived through a lot of tough challenges. I'm sorry to say that I probably challenged Gram as much or more than her beloved villagers, the ones she was forced to leave behind when my grandfather died. But Gram never gave up on me. She was the first person in my life to teach me what real unconditional love was like. I will always be grateful to her for that." He sighed as he gazed over the nearly full sanctuary. Gram had more friends than he had realized.

"Gram taught me a lot of valuable things. Like telling the truth and persevering even when a situation looked like it was hopeless. She helped me to see the world as a bigger place than just what's within our borders. She taught me to have compassion for the less fortunate. Because of her I served in Uganda for nine years. Nine years that have changed my life forever—and have helped mold me into the person I am today. I feel like I owe all that to my grandmother. Without her influence on my life, I cannot imagine where I would be today." *Well, aside from being the caretaker for a houseful of cats*, he thought a bit grimly, but naturally, he didn't say this.

Instead he finished by telling a story about how Gram had discovered he'd stolen some tokens from a video arcade and how she'd made him go take them back and confess to the owner. "I was so ashamed," he told them. "But when we got home my grandmother simply opened her Bible and read a verse about Jesus forgiving someone. I can't even remember which verse it was. But Gram looked at me and said, 'It's no different with you. Confess your sins to our Lord and he will forgive you your sins. That's all there is to it.'" He smiled. "I have taken those words with me wherever I've gone. I always will."

After the service, he visited with old friends from the church. They seemed genuinely happy to see him, and Gram's good friend Mrs. Spangle even invited him to come and speak to their missions group. He gave her his phone number and promised to make himself available.

"And is there anything I can do for you?" she asked.

"If you know anyone who wants to adopt a cat," he said quickly. "Someone who lives in my grandmother's neighborhood."

"I do know of a good no-kill animal shelter. Perhaps you could—"

"No, no. It's my grandmother's last wish that I make sure they find good homes."

Her thin brows arched. "Oh, my. Well, I wish you luck with that. Last I heard there was an abundance of cats in the Northwest."

As Garrison drove home, he wondered if it was time to re-vamp his feline relocation plan. The attorney had discouraged him from letting the word out about the monetary reward that would go to adoptive homes. But perhaps he could drop some subtle hints in a revised classified ad. Sweeten the deal, so to speak.

5

The morning after Gram's memorial service, Garrison called Mr. Miller. "I have some questions I hadn't considered when I spoke to you last week," he told him.

"Yes, I expected you would. Any luck finding homes for the cats?"

"I placed one right next door." Then he explained about his ads and posters and how he'd almost found a home for another cat. "But the woman didn't fit Gram's criteria. She'd only lived in the neighborhood a few months. But she seemed like a good choice, I wish I could've given—"

"Sorry, Garrison. My job is to respect your grandmother's final wishes. I'm sure you can understand that."

"Yes, well, that's not really why I called. Mostly I wanted to know what's to become of my grandmother's house. I know she'd had that reverse mortgage on it. But since I'm kind of stuck here for a while—I mean, until I get the cats resettled—I hoped I could empty it out a little. Also, there are some family things I'd like to keep if that's all right."

"It's all yours, Garrison. Other than what your grandmother set aside for the cats, the remaining estate is yours. However, you won't officially inherit it until you get the cats successfully placed in new homes. It's all spelled out in the packet I gave you."

"Oh . . . yeah . . . I haven't read through the whole thing yet."

"So feel free to do as you like with the house. As I mentioned in my office, your grandmother paid off the reverse mortgage. The house is free and clear."

"Free and clear?"

"Absolutely. I have the title on file here. When your task is finished, it will be signed over to you."

"So this is *my* house?" Garrison looked around the cluttered and run-down kitchen with wonder as reality set in.

"It will be. When the cats are re-homed."

"Right." Garrison considered this. "That's really great. Thanks!"

"Thank your grandmother."

"Yeah, of course."

When Garrison hung up, he walked through the somewhat shabby four-bedroom house, taking it all in and suddenly seeing it with a fresh set of eyes. This place had real potential. If he fixed it up and sold it, he might get enough capital to start the halfway house he'd been dreaming of creating. He closed his eyes and sent a silent thank-you to his grandmother. She really hadn't forgotten him. Not at all.

For the rest of the day, Garrison threw himself into cleaning, sorting, repairing, and disposing. It was good therapy, and the results were making themselves visible by Wednesday.

"My goodness!" Ruby exclaimed when she came in to see what was happening. "I hardly recognize the place. What's going on?"

"It started with removing some of the furnishings that were beyond hope," he confessed.

"Yes, I saw the mess in the front yard."

"Sorry about that. I've got someone coming to pick them up on Friday." He adjusted his particle mask, wiping a streak of sweat from his upper lip. "After that I just kept going. One thing led to another." He glanced around the somewhat vacant living room. Other than the scratching posts and a couple pieces of furniture, the place looked stark. "I'm afraid I've upset some of the cats." He nodded to an old chair where Rusty and Oreo were nestled together. "I hauled this piece back inside so they'd have something familiar."

Ruby pointed over to where Spooky was sitting on the stairway, looking at them through the banister with what seemed a disgruntled expression. "That one does not look happy."

He shook his head. "Yeah. Spooky is pretty mad at me. And Muzzy has been very loudly expressing herself too. Harry's the only one who seems to still like me." He made a sheepish grin. "But I figure I'm doing them all a favor . . . making it easier for them to go."

"Any responses to your ads?"

"A couple of calls, but the people didn't fit Gram's criteria."

"Too bad. Viola is settling in very nicely at my place. She doesn't even seem to miss the other cats."

"Good to know." He considered mentioning the bonus Ruby would receive in a few weeks. "Any interest in taking on a second cat?"

"Oh, no. Viola is plenty of cat for me. And I do believe

she's happier having me all to herself." Ruby chuckled. "She's already decided that my bed is her bed and truth be told, I don't mind a bit."

"That's great. Well, I guess I should write up another ad for the cats. Maybe I can put some kind of Christmas spin on it. *Give your loved one a cat for Christmas*?"

Ruby looked uncertain. "Speaking of Christmas, I came over to invite you to Thanksgiving dinner tomorrow. Some single folks in the neighborhood are getting together to share potluck."

"Right, I almost forgot about Thanksgiving. That sounds great. What can I bring?"

"Nothing." She waved her hand. "I just saw the condition of your kitchen. Doesn't look like any real cooking is gonna happen in there."

"I'm getting ready to paint in there. But I could pick something up at the—"

"Never you mind. These old gals are already cooking up a storm."

"If they cook half as good as you, it should be delicious."

"Dinner is at two," she said as she was leaving. "You can drive us."

"It's not at your house?"

"No. But I have directions. We'll leave a little before two."

After working all Thursday morning, Garrison showered and shaved and dressed in his favorite black pullover sweater and tan cords. As he pulled on his jacket, he felt Harry rubbing himself against his legs. Realizing that he'd forgotten to put on a fresh particle mask after shaving, Garrison was surprised that he wasn't having another sneezing fit. Maybe his allergy meds were working better these days. Or maybe he was building some resistance. He bent down and scratched Harry's head. "You're a good old boy," he told him. "More like a dog than a cat."

Harry seemed to nod, almost as if he understood and agreed.

"Take care of things, buddy. I'll be back in a few hours." He chuckled. "I'm off to dine with—a bunch of old ladies."

Ruby directed Garrison several blocks away. "There, that's it. The little brown house with the gingerbread trim. Inviting, isn't it?"

"Unless there's a wicked witch living inside." He chuckled as he parked across the street.

Ruby snickered. "I don't think our hostess would appreciate that comment."

He carried Ruby's heavy basket of food, following her up the narrow brick walkway. "Lots of cars out here," he said as she rang the bell. "This house looks a little small. Think we'll all fit?"

"Cara insisted on having it here. It's the first time she's lived in a real house and she really wanted to host this gathering."

"*Cara?*" He suddenly remembered the pretty brown-haired girl on the bike. "Is this Cara, uh, elderly?"

Ruby laughed. "Not in the least."

He felt his face flushing as Cara opened the door. Wearing a garnet-colored knit dress and with her dark hair pinned up, she looked even prettier than he remembered. Suddenly he wished he'd thought to bring a hostess gift. Like a cat.

"Come in." She blinked in surprise as she opened the door wider.

Ruby started an introduction, but Cara stopped her. "Garrison and I have already met." She made a forced smile. "He refused to part with one of his precious cats."

Ruby frowned at him. "Oh . . . but Cara would make a wonderful pet owner. I would vouch for her. I've known her aunt for ages and—"

"Speaking of that, Aunt Myrtle is in the kitchen." Cara took their coats. "She and Gladys have taken over and I think they'd appreciate your help, Ruby. They both agree that you make the best gravy." Cara led Ruby back through the somewhat crowded house. Left to his own, Garrison proceeded to introduce himself to some of the other guests. Although a few were younger, most of them seemed to be closer to his grandmother's age. Before long, he found himself cornered by a pair of elderly sisters who had been good friends with Gram. Naturally, they wanted to hear all about him and what he'd been doing the past couple of decades.

After answering the Dorchester sisters' questions about Uganda and explaining how he'd contracted malaria, he used the opportunity to tell them about Gram's cats. "I'm looking for good homes," he told them. "Can I interest you ladies in adopting a cat or two?"

The older sister wrinkled her nose. "I'm sorry, Garrison, but I don't care much for cats."

"That's right," her sister agreed. "Winifred had a bad experience as a child. She abhors cats."

"To be honest, I'm not terribly fond of cats myself, but I'm trying to adapt to them. I tell myself it's mind over matter. I hope that if I don't think about it too much, it won't matter." He chuckled and then explained about his allergies. "If I forget to take my antihistamines I am a complete mess."

"You should eat ginger," the older sister said. "It helps with my hay fever."

"Really?" Garrison nodded at them as he glanced over to where Cara was welcoming an older man into her home, hugging him and taking his coat. The perfect hostess . . . to everyone else.

Garrison put great effort into acting natural and relaxed as he chatted and dined with his neighbors, but the whole while he felt uneasy. Plus he was distracted with keeping one eye on the pretty hostess. Partly because he couldn't help himself, and partly because he sensed that Cara was purposely avoiding him. She was never rude, but at the same time she never exchanged more than the briefest of conversation with him. Yet she remained friendly and warm and congenial to everyone else. It was unnerving.

For that reason, Garrison made an excuse to leave early—even before dessert was served. He knew it was bad manners as he abruptly thanked his hostess, but it was the best he could do under the circumstances. After being reassured that Ruby could get a ride home, he explained his need to see to his cats. Naturally, this led to some goodhearted teasing at his expense. Particularly from some of the younger guests that, due to the Dorchester sisters, he'd not had the opportunity to get acquainted with.

He forced a smile, waved goodbye, and tried to take the whole social fiasco in stride as he left. So what if they shared some laughs at his expense after he was gone. He was just relieved to get away from there. Not only had that "charming" little gingerbread house been overly small and overly crowded, it had literally felt as if the walls had been closing in on him.

As he drove home, he thought about Cara. She had looked so pretty in that deep-red dress. And she had such an engaging smile. An endearing laugh. Yet it was obvious that the girl was harboring a serious grudge against him. She must've taken it personally when he'd refused to hand over Harry. He wished he could explain the will dilemma to her again—to somehow make her understand—but really, what more could he say? Perhaps it was best to let sleeping dogs lie . . . or should he say *sleeping cats*?

Garrison knew that his heart was softening toward
Gram's small herd of cats. Okay, he didn't actually
like *all of* them. Muzzy's obnoxious Siamese howling
was truly disturbing and Spooky's moodiness was irritating,
but he attributed their bad manners to their general displea-
sure with him . . . and missing their previous owner. However,
Rusty and Oreo were fairly easy to get along with. And then
there was Harry . . . that big, slightly wild-looking animal had
the best feline manners, not to mention intelligence. Harry
was clearly his favorite. Even so Garrison knew he needed
to find homes for all five of them. Good homes. No regrets.

This was driven even more firmly home when his phone
rang on Friday morning. The man who had interviewed him
last week, the same day that Gram had died, was calling to
offer him the job. Garrison explained about his grandmother.
"So I really need to see to some things regarding her estate,"

he told him. "I might be able to tie it up in a week. Maybe two if I'm lucky."

"No problem. December is always a slow month for the foundation. Although I would like to get you in the office for some important meetings before Christmas." He listed some specific dates. "That's when we start planning for the upcoming year. We have a big fundraiser in February and I like getting tasks pinned down before Christmas. Makes January go smoother."

"I'm sure I can wrap this up in two weeks max," Garrison assured him. "I'll be there in time for those planning meetings. Thank you, sir."

"I look forward to working with you, son. I really liked your résumé and that you'd spent that much time in Uganda. I can tell you're a diligent young man, and that you take your responsibilities seriously and see things through. I know you'll be a real asset to the team, Garrison."

In the spirit of diligence, Garrison started constructing a new ad on Friday afternoon. It was obvious that his first ad had been ineffective. For the new ad, Garrison decided to lure interest by mentioning that the cats would come with a special "Christmas bonus." He was careful not to mention cash, but he did word it in a mysterious way that he hoped would garner some prospective pet owners' curiosity.

He was just editing the ad when the phone rang. "Hey, Garrison," a woman's voice said. "I heard you're looking for homes for your cats."

"That's right," he said eagerly. "Did you see my ad or—"

"Actually it was Cara who mentioned it. I was at her Thanksgiving dinner yesterday. We barely met. My name's Beth, and I was there with my daughter, Annabelle. Although Annabelle had her nose in her phone and hardly said a word to anyone."

"Oh yeah," he said. "I know who you are." He remembered the flashy, middle-aged redhead with too much makeup and the teen girl who looked like the poster child for post-Goth.

"Anyway, Cara told me you had cats to give away. And, ever since we moved here, I've been promising Annabelle that she could have a cat."

Garrison cringed to think of the strange-looking girl with multiple piercings taking home one of his cats. But then he chided himself for being too judgmental. After all, he'd gone through some rough teen years himself. "You say you just moved here?" he ventured.

"Oh, it's been a couple years now. I kept making up new excuses not to have a cat. But Annabelle's not letting me off the hook."

He explained a bit about Gram's will. "I know her requirements might sound extravagant to some people, but I have to respect her wishes. Do you mind if I ask a few questions?"

"Not at all." She giggled. "Imagine being interviewed to adopt a cat."

"I know." He pulled out Gram's list and went over the preliminaries, and all seemed to be in order. Beth was a solid candidate. "Sounds good," he told her. "But I'll still need to evaluate your house."

"For what?" she sounded worried.

"To make sure it's a safe, healthy place for a cat."

"Seriously?"

"Yeah, but don't worry. It's not like I'm inspecting your housekeeping."

"Well, like I said, I do hair from my home, so I did pass that inspection."

"That's great," he told her. "Mind if I come by for a quick look? And, trust me, I'm as eager to find homes for these cats as you are to have one of them."

She told him where she lived, and he asked when he should come by.

"Can you do it right now?" she said eagerly. "Annabelle is out and I'd rather she not know about this. I mean, just in case it doesn't work out."

"No problem."

As Garrison hurried the several blocks to Beth's house, he actually shot up a quick prayer for help that this adoption would work out. One less cat would be real progress. And if Beth and Annabelle did qualify, hopefully they wouldn't want Harry. Perhaps Garrison would put Harry out of sight.

Garrison did a quick tour through Beth's house. Although her house was a little messy and cluttered and her breakfast dishes were still in the sink, he felt that the place was just fine for a cat. Before he left, he explained the need for another visitation after a couple of weeks. "I can't tell you exactly what day it will be. It's supposed to be a surprise visitation."

"Are you kidding?" Beth scowled.

"I know it sounds nuts," he admitted. "But can I trust you with a secret?"

Her blue eyes grew wide. "Sure."

"Well, there's a little surprise that comes with the cats. My grandmother wanted to be sure they found good homes."

"And you can't tell me what kind of surprise?" Beth looked curious. "Is it a year's supply of cat food? That would be nice."

"Something like that," he assured her. "But I can't tell you until the cat's been happily homed for at least three weeks."

"I thought you said two weeks?"

He was just finishing his explanation when Annabelle walked in. "What's up?" she asked with a suspicious frown.

"You remember Garrison from Cara's?" Beth said.

Annabelle just nodded.

"He's offered to give you a cat," Beth announced.

Annabelle's face lit up. "Really? I can have a cat?"

"That's right." Beth glanced at Garrison. "I mean, we did fit the criteria, didn't we?"

"What criteria?" Annabelle asked.

"Take it from me," her mom told her. "These must be very special cats. Garrison does not just give them to anyone."

Annabelle seemed to appreciate this. "When do I get it?"

"Is now too soon?" Garrison asked.

"Not at all. Can I get a cat right now?" Annabelle asked her mom.

"Why don't you go home with Garrison? I've got a client coming in a few minutes. Be sure and bring back the pick of the litter."

As they were leaving, Garrison regretted it. This wouldn't give him time to hide Harry. What if Annabelle fell in love with Harry?

Garrison rattled the cat treat bag. Just as expected, the cats began to emerge from their favorite nooks and crannies. Before long he was introducing each feline by name. Annabelle went from cat to cat, carefully examining each of them. However, it was the moody calico that seemed to capture her attention. Annabelle offered Spooky some more cat treats and, to Garrison's surprise, she soon got the temperamental cat to eat right out of her hand.

"I want Spooky," she announced, still holding the cat—who seemed strangely content—in her arms. "Is that okay?"

"That's fine." He grinned. "That's perfect."

"I think she needs me," Annabelle said.

Garrison showed her to the cat pantry, inviting her to pick out some things she might need. He explained about the special drops Spooky needed in her food to prevent hairballs and even gave her a cat bed and a carrying case as well as a bag of kitty litter.

As he drove Annabelle home, Garrison tried to conceal how elated he felt to have the moody feline off his hands. But he was glad for both the girl and the cat—they seemed perfectly simpatico. As he helped Annabelle carry the cat things into her house, she thanked him profusely, acting as if he'd just given her the greatest treasure in the world.

"You're completely welcome," he told her. "Don't forget that I have to come by to check on the cat after two weeks, and then again after three weeks."

"You can come see Spooky whenever you like," she told him. "I can understand how you might miss her. But I promise I'll take really good care of her. Don't worry."

Garrison tried not to laugh as he went back to the car. Annabelle had no idea how relieved he felt. And he knew Gram would be delighted to see how much this young girl loved her new cat.

As Garrison was leaving the church on Sunday, he was approached by an older man. Wearing a worn sports jacket and a tweed driving cap, the man waved to Garrison as if he knew him. "I'm Vincent Peterson," he said eagerly. "We met briefly at Cara's Thanksgiving get-together last week."

"Oh yeah." Garrison nodded, ducking beneath a covered walkway to get out of the rain that was just starting to pelt down. "I thought you looked familiar."

"Cara mentioned that you're looking for homes for your grandmother's cats. I might be interested. That is if you still have any cats left."

"Definitely," Garrison assured him. "I have four."

Vincent looked relieved. "I had a cat named Gracie for years. A big orange cat that I was very attached to. But she got a kidney disease and passed away last winter. I told myself I wouldn't get another cat, but I suppose I'm having second thoughts now."

"Cats can be great companions," Garrison said positively as they moved closer to the wall to escape the windblown rain.

"Yes, I think you're right. And since I'm spending more time at home . . ." He grimly shook his head. "You see, I was forced into retirement last spring. So I find myself rambling around my house. Last week Cara was trying to convince me that I need a cat." He chuckled. "The more I think about it, the more I think she might be right."

Garrison quickly went over the preliminary questions and, convinced that Vincent was a good candidate, he explained about the need for a home visit. Although Vincent looked bewildered by this, he agreed. "Why don't you come over for coffee tomorrow morning," he suggested. "That'll give me a chance to straighten up some."

They agreed on the time and Vincent gave Garrison directions to his house. Garrison tried not to do the Snoopy happy dance as he hurried across the parking lot to the car. If Vincent took a cat, that would leave just three cats to place. And his new ad hadn't even been run in the local paper yet.

As he drove home, he pondered over the fact that Cara had sent two potential cat owners his way. Perhaps she didn't despise him as much as he'd imagined. Or perhaps she was just concerned for the cats in his care. Whatever her motives, he still owed her his gratitude.

On Monday morning, Garrison showed up at Vincent's house at ten o'clock sharp. It was a small, modest, midcentury home, but it was tidy and neat in a plain and simple sort of way.

"Do you mind having coffee in the kitchen?" Vincent asked apologetically. "I'm not used to entertaining much."

"The kitchen is perfect," Garrison told him.

"This isn't exactly how I planned for my life to go," Vincent said as he placed a coffee mug in front of Garrison.

"How so?"

"Well, I had hoped to retire with my wife by my side." He let out a sad sigh as he sat on the other side of the well-worn table. "Lynnette left me about ten years ago. Talk about being blindsided." He took a sip. "Sure didn't see that one coming."

"Sorry about that."

"And then there was my retirement." Another long sigh. "Thought I'd walk away with a nice little package and benefits, you know. Not a windfall, mind you, but enough to do a little traveling or maybe just fix up my little house."

"That didn't happen?"

Vincent let out a sarcastic laugh. "Not hardly. Seems the

economy is responsible for my loss. Anyway that's what I was told. Didn't even get a gold watch. But I guess that's not so unusual these days."

"That's too bad."

He shrugged. "I suppose I should consider myself lucky to still have this house." He glanced around. "I know it's not much, but at least it's mine. Just wish I could afford to do some improvements though. I'm pretty handy with hammer and nails."

"Well, the house looks sturdy enough," Garrison observed. Then he explained about how he was doing some much-needed repairs to Gram's house. "But I have to admit I don't really know what I'm doing."

Vincent's brows arched. "Well, if you need any help, just call."

"Really?" Garrison studied him, gauging if this offer was just casual friendliness or something he could depend upon.

He nodded. "You bet. At the very least I can give you some pointers and tips. And I've got lots of time."

"That'd be great, Vincent. I'll take you up on it." Garrison described some of the projects he wanted to complete before it was time to return to Seattle, and Vincent had some brilliant suggestions. He even pulled out some do-it-yourself books for Garrison to take with him. Then they arranged for Vincent to come over and see the cats in the afternoon.

"And maybe you can show me how to fix that door that sticks," Garrison said hopefully.

"You got it."

As Garrison drove home, he wondered if it would be selfish to hide Harry in the laundry room when Vincent came to view the cats. Yet, at the same time, he knew that was silly.

Besides that, Vincent seemed like a nice guy. He would probably provide a great home for a nice cat like Harry.

Vincent showed up around one, just as Garrison was finishing up painting a wall in the kitchen. He'd chosen a nice buttery yellow that really warmed the room up. It was the first time he'd ever painted anything, and he didn't want to admit it, but he felt pretty pleased with himself.

"That looks good," Vincent told him as Garrison showed him his work. "But it would be a lot quicker and easier if you used masking tape."

"Masking tape?" Garrison frowned.

Vincent explained how to tape off areas that weren't in need of paint. "Like that baseboard there."

Garrison laughed as he pulled out a brand-new roll of blue tape. "So that's why the guy at the paint store insisted I buy this. I could blame my ignorance on Uganda. I spent the last nine years there and sometimes I feel like I'm still catching up on American culture."

Vincent showed how to mask off the cabinets and a couple of other tricks.

"I'm going to have to put you on speed dial," Garrison said as he set his paintbrush aside. "Now would you like to meet the cats?"

"Absolutely."

Garrison led him into the living room where the cats usually hung out. Harry was the first one to approach them, rubbing himself affectionately against Garrison's legs. "This is Harry. He's a Maine Coon cat and, in my opinion, the pick of the litter." He chuckled as he bent down to scratch the top of Harry's head.

"Handsome fellow." Vincent nodded with approval.

"And this is Muzzy." Garrison pointed to the oversized Siamese who immediately began "talking" in loud meows. "She's very social. As you can see, she likes to talk."

"She's a pretty cat," Vincent said. "But I'm not overly fond of the Siamese breed." He went over to the chair where Rusty and Oreo were snuggled up together. "And these cats?"

"They're both males," Garrison said. "The black-and-white is Oreo. This one lives to eat and could probably get a lifetime membership in Overeaters Anonymous. He always thinks it's dinnertime. The orange one is Rusty. They both have wonderful dispositions. Good-natured and easygoing and friendly."

"Rusty?" Vincent picked up the big orange cat. "You're a big guy, Rusty," he said in a friendly tone.

Garrison could hear the cat purring happily. "Rusty is ten years old. No health problems. My grandmother took him in about six years ago."

"You want to go home with me, big boy? Leave your cat friends behind?"

"All his friends are relocating," Garrison reminded him. "That is, unless you'd like more than just one cat?"

"Oh no, I don't think so."

Garrison was highly tempted to tell Vincent about the cash prize that was attached to each cat. He suspected Vincent could really use the money. But at the same time, it seemed unfair to tip his hand like this. Perhaps it was better for people to make up their minds about the cats without any extra incentive. That was probably the way Gram had wanted it.

Vincent grinned down at Rusty. "I thought I wanted a female cat, but maybe I was wrong. You seem like a good pal to me."

Rusty looked perfectly content. In fact, unless it was Garrison's imagination, he almost seemed to be smiling. "Well, I think you've made a friend," Garrison said to both of them. He explained about the two- and four-week visitations. "I know it sounds a little goofy," he said quickly. "But my grandmother was really attached to her cats. They were like her children. She just wanted to ensure their future."

"I don't mind a bit," Vincent told him. "It's been a little lonely at my house. I'd welcome your visits. And, like I said, I'm available to help with your home improvements. Just give me a call."

Garrison led Vincent to the cat pantry. "Feel free to take some things for Rusty." He explained Rusty's dietary preferences, removing an eight-pack of cat food cans as well as some other things. "And there's a cat carrier out on the porch."

Before long, Vincent and Rusty were happily headed out the door. Garrison watched as Vincent drove the car away. "Three down, three to go," he said as he closed the door. "Not bad for just over a week."

As he returned to painting, he knew he really owed Cara one. Make that two, since both Spooky and Rusty had found homes thanks to her intervention. He wondered how he could express his gratitude to her without offending her. He also wondered if there was any way to win her friendship . . . short of handing over Harry. As willing as he was to do just that—really there was no one else he'd rather give Harry to—he knew he had to honor Gram's wishes.

7

Garrison finished up the walls in the kitchen. After giving the cats each a kitty treat and promising to be back soon, he cleaned himself up and drove Gram's old car to town. His goal was to get a nice bouquet of flowers for Cara. His way to thank her—both for Thanksgiving dinner and for her help finding homes for Rusty and Spooky.

At the florist, he looked long and hard at the arrangements. He didn't want to get anything too romantic—like roses—because he felt certain that would scare her off even more. He just wanted something pleasant and unassuming. Finally he decided on a sizeable pink poinsettia plant that was prettily potted in a large metallic green container. Very festive and Christmassy. It would look nice on her big, round dining table. He also found a card that he took the time to write inside. Nothing too familiar or presuming—but just casually friendly and grateful.

"I'm going to make it a hood," the saleswoman told him as he was pocketing his receipt.

"A hood?"

She pulled out a long strip of brown paper. "To protect it from the chilly air as you transport it to the car."

"Huh?" Sometimes he felt like an alien from a different planet. Since when did plants start wearing clothing?

"Poinsettias are very sensitive to the cold. Make sure you get it directly into the house. Otherwise the petals will fall off."

He blinked. "The petals will fall off?"

She nodded grimly. "Yes. And we have a no-return policy."

"Right . . ."

"Is it a gift?" she asked as she taped the "hood" loosely around the plant.

"Yes, as a matter of fact."

"Well, whatever you do, don't leave it by the front door. That would kill it for sure."

"Right." He hadn't realized a poinsettia was so temperamental.

"Does the person you're giving it to have pets or small children?"

"No."

"Good. Poinsettia leaves are poisonous if ingested."

"Yeah, well, I doubt she will eat it."

The woman laughed.

Garrison was tempted to tell the woman he had changed his mind. Who knew a simple plant could be such high maintenance? Almost as bad as a houseful of cats.

"Well, I hope she enjoys it. It's really a lovely gift."

Garrison carefully picked up the plant. "Thanks. I hope I can get it safely to her."

She waved her hand. "Don't worry. I probably made it sound worse than it is. Just be careful with the cold air."

He hurried the delicate plant out to his car and, fastening the seatbelt around it, he quickly started the car and cranked up the heat. As he drove to Cara's house, he wondered what he'd do if she wasn't home. At first he had hoped she would be gone so that he could leave it on her porch. Now he wasn't so sure. Perhaps he could leave it with a neighbor? Or else he could take it home with him. Except that it might poison the cats.

Feeling a bit silly and uneasy, Garrison pulled into her driveway and carefully extracted the plant from the car, hurrying to take it up to the front porch where he rang the doorbell. When no one answered, he looked down at the bundle in his arms. He longed to just leave it, but the image of Cara discovering a dead plant on her porch was definitely not a good one.

"Hello?" a male voice called from the house next door. "Are you looking for Cara?"

"Yes," Garrison said eagerly. "I have something for her, but she doesn't seem to be at home and I don't want to leave it on the porch."

"You can leave it with me if you like." The guy waved him over. "Cara and I are good friends. She's usually home, but Monday is her day to go into the office. If you like, I can take it over to her when she gets home."

"Great!" Garrison hurried over to the tan house next door. "I'd leave it on her porch, but the flowers can't handle the cold."

"Are you a delivery man from the florist?" The neighbor glanced over at the old Pontiac with interest. "That doesn't look like their usual van."

"No, I'm just a friend of Cara's." Okay, Garrison knew that was a stretch. "A relatively new acquaintance actually."

"I'm David Landers." He smiled as he extended his hand.

"I'm Garrison Brown. I live a few blocks from here."

"Nice to meet you, neighbor." David appeared to be about the same age as Garrison, but unlike Garrison, this guy oozed confidence.

"Yeah. Thanks." Garrison held out the plant. "And thanks for taking—"

"Why don't you come on in?" David opened the door wider.

"Okay." Garrison was pleasantly surprised at this unexpected hospitality. "I didn't realize poinsettias were so fragile when I bought this."

"No problem." David closed the door and pointed to a glass-topped table in the foyer. "Just set it there for now. I'll get it to Cara as soon as she gets home. Probably around five." He grinned. "I like having an excuse to run over and see her whenever I can. When she first moved in, she used to come over here a lot to borrow stuff. It's her first time living in a real house and she'd need a potato peeler or some basil or whatever. I didn't mind a bit. After she got settled, I missed her visits so I started making up reasons to pop in on her." He chuckled. "But we're beyond that now."

"Right . . ." For some reason Garrison felt uncomfortable hearing this.

"How do you know Cara?" David gave him an overly curious look.

Garrison gauged his answer. "We met on the street just last week. And then my neighbor took me over to Cara's for Thanksgiving—a get-together for the single folks in the neighborhood." He studied David closely, trying to calculate his age. Somewhere between thirty-five and forty, he would estimate. "I don't believe you were there." He glanced around the homey-looking room. "But maybe you're not single."

"I'm divorced. Three years last summer. And I would've gone to Cara's little shindig, but I had a previous commitment with my family in Spokane. My parents wanted to see Jackson."

"Jackson?"

"That's my son. I have full custody of the kid. Jackson just turned eight." He called over his shoulder. "Hey, Jackson? You still in the kitchen? Come on out here."

A young boy came shyly around a corner, peering into the living room.

"Say hello to Mr. Brown." David looked uncertainly at Garrison. "It was Brown, wasn't it?"

"Yes." Garrison smiled at the boy. "Hello, Jackson."

"He-hello," the boy said with uncertainty.

"Mr. Brown brought a plant over for Miss Wilson," David told his son.

Jackson just nodded as he moved toward the staircase, nervously grasping the banister with one hand. "I—uh—I'm going—to my room."

"Okay," David said easily.

"Nice to meet you, Jackson," Garrison called out as the boy scurried up the stairs.

David frowned. "I like to give him every opportunity I can to interact."

"Sure." Garrison pretended to understand, although he wasn't completely sure what David meant.

"Because, as you can probably see, Jackson has difficulty

conversing," David continued quietly. "They say he's got a social anxiety disorder. But things got worse when kids at school started teasing him. So I took him out. I don't mind homeschooling so much since I work from home anyway. And Jackson is really bright. But I do worry about his social interaction. I wish he had someone his own age to talk with."

Garrison nodded, realizing that he could probably relate more to David's insecure son than to the self-assured dad. "Yeah, that would probably be good for him."

"I'm thinking about getting him a dog for Christmas. Although I need to make sure our budget can handle it. It hasn't been exactly easy getting my home business up and running. And I know dogs can be expensive. But it might be worth it . . . for Jackson's sake. Not that a dog can carry on a conversation exactly." David pulled back a corner of the brown paper hood to peek in on the poinsettia. "Pretty."

"How about a cat?" Garrison said suddenly.

"Huh?" David's brow creased as he pushed the paper closed again. "A cat?"

Garrison quickly explained about Gram and her cats and the need to re-home them. "I still have this Seal Point Siamese. About eight years old. Nice and big. And she talks *all the time*."

"She *talks*?" David looked skeptical.

"I know it sounds crazy, but this cat *talks*. In cat language, of course, but she's really chatty. I have a feeling she carried on lengthy conversations with my grandmother." He shrugged. "Unfortunately, I'm not great at conversing with cats. I'm sure poor Muzzy is completely fed up with me."

"A Seal Point Siamese? I've seen pictures of those. Nice-looking cats."

"Muzzy is really pretty. Nice, sleek dark coat. Big blue eyes. And like I said, she loves to talk."

"Eight years? Is that very old? I mean, for a cat?"

"My grandmother had a cat named Genevieve that lived to be twenty-three."

"No kidding." David shook his head. "And Jackson is eight years old—just like Muzzy."

"No worries that she'll have kittens," Garrison assured him. "And she's in good health. I have the vet records."

David narrowed his eyes as if really considering this. "You really think this cat could encourage Jackson to talk more?"

"I'm almost certain of it. The cat really wants to engage with someone. She's a real chatterbox." He didn't add that she could drive a quiet person crazy. Let them discover this. Besides, it was clear that David liked to chat.

"And a cat wouldn't pass judgment on Jackson."

"Not at all. And she'd be a good companion for him too."

"I like this idea." David nodded. "I like it a lot."

Garrison told David a bit about his grandmother's will. "I know it sounds a little eccentric, but Gram's cats were her family. She had to make sure they got good homes."

"I don't blame her a bit." David invited Garrison to remove his coat and sit down to go over the details of Gram's slightly eccentric requirements.

It didn't take long for Garrison to realize that this would be a great home for Muzzy. "And I know my grandmother would be pleased to think that Muzzy could be an encouragement to your boy."

"I want to do this," David declared. "It makes perfect sense. Jackson isn't getting a dog for Christmas. He's getting a cat."

"Great." Garrison frowned. "But I hope you don't want to wait until Christmas."

"Why not?"

"Well, I'm trying to get things tied up before that. I actually hoped to get the cats placed this week. And then I have to head back to Seattle for a job. I'd been looking for months and finally got an offer. Can't afford to let it go."

"Sure." David nodded. "I can understand that. And, come to think of it, I've heard that you should never give pets right at Christmas. Too much going on. They can get stressed out . . . or sick."

"So would you be interested in getting Muzzy sooner then?"

"Sure. Why not?"

"I could bring her by anytime you want," Garrison offered. "Well, unless you'd like to meet her first. Or maybe you want to talk to Jackson—"

"No, I think I'd rather surprise him."

"I can show you a picture." Garrison pulled his phone from his pocket. "I've got photos of all the cats on here."

David peered over Garrison's shoulder as he flicked through the photos. "There's Muzzy." Garrison held up the phone.

"She is a pretty cat." David smiled with satisfaction. "And you mentioned the two-week policy . . . Can I assume it works both ways?"

"Both ways?"

"If Muzzy doesn't fit in here. If she and Jackson don't hit it off—I can send her back?"

Garrison considered this. "Sure, of course. I know that my grandmother would not want Muzzy placed in a home that didn't work for everyone."

David stuck out his hand. "Then it's a deal."

"Deal." Garrison grinned.

"When can we have her?"

"If you like I can bring her over tonight."

"That'd be great."

Garrison felt like letting out a victory yell as he hurried out to his car. Finding a home for Muzzy—a cat whose constant "talking" was driving him up the walls—was fantastic. And if she could help Jackson with his social anxiety—well, it was a real win-win situation. At home, he felt slightly guilty as he gathered up a generous supply of cat things for Muzzy. It wasn't that he disliked the loud Siamese so much. In fact, she'd actually grown on him the last few days. But at the same time, he knew she needed a good home. Just the right kind of home. And he felt fairly certain he had found it.

Using a special gluten-free kitty treat to entice Muzzy into a cat carrier, he assured her that she was going to a happy home with a young man who would adore her. With her safely away from the other cats, he took a moment to give the others their dinner. Then he packed a box with everything a new cat owner could possibly want, including a nearly full bag of her special cat food, and loaded it into the back of the Pontiac. With the cat carrier safely buckled into the seat next to him, he drove over to David's. Was it really possible he was down to just two cats? Not to mention they were two of the most congenial cats. Finding them homes should be a piece of cake.

Feeling hopeful and optimistic, Garrison toted the cat carrier up to the front door of the Landerses' house. From the corner of his eye, he noticed a car pulling into Cara's driveway. Glancing over, he watched as the sky-blue Volkswagen Bug parked. While knocking on the door, he watched Cara climb out of her car and look curiously in his direction. Smiling, he waved, then knocked on the door again. It opened a moment later.

"Is this her? Is this Muzzy?" David asked expectantly.

"Is that the cat?" Jackson asked from behind his dad.

"This is Muzzy," Garrison proclaimed.

"Here's your early Christmas present, Jackson." David took the carrier from Garrison and held it out in front of his son. "Your very own cat. Meet Muzzy."

"I'm going back to the car for some things," Garrison called out to them. As he turned away he could hear the happiness in Jackson's voice. The boy was clearly thrilled to be getting a cat. It was like Christmas had come early.

"What's going on over there?" Cara asked with a curious expression.

Garrison quickly explained about finding a home for a cat. Her brows arched. "Really? Which cat?"

"Muzzy," he said as he reached in for the box of cat supplies. "The Siamese."

Cara smiled stiffly. "Well, that's very nice." She took a shopping bag out of her car. "Nice to see you, Garrison." Then she turned and hurried up to her house. Friendly . . . but cool.

Garrison returned to the Landerses' house, depositing the box inside the door and going over some particulars about their new cat, including her need for a gluten-free diet. At least they wouldn't have to worry about her sneaking food from the other cats and getting sick. Muzzy was on her own here. And already she was comfortably seated in Jackson's lap, and he was happily stroking her sleek dark coat.

"I'll leave you to it." Garrison reached for the poinsettia plant, still on the foyer table.

"You're taking that back?" David looked concerned.

"Cara's home now," Garrison told him. "I'll just take it over."

"Oh . . . okay." David frowned. "But I'm happy to—"

"No problem," Garrison said lightly. "I already said hello to her. I'll just run it over while I'm here."

David just nodded, but he didn't seem overly pleased. He had probably been looking forward to another excuse to pop in on his neighbor. Maybe their relationship wasn't as solid as David had made it seem. Or maybe it was. Maybe he felt jealous of Garrison's interest in her now. Wouldn't that be a twist.

"Thanks so much for the cat." David shook his hand. "I really appreciate it."

"Yeah," Jackson said with glowing eyes. "Thanks, Mister, uh, Brown. Thanks a lot."

"You're more than welcome, Jackson. I think my grandmother would be really pleased to see that Muzzy has found such a good home. I hope you really enjoy each other."

As Garrison carried his paper-covered poinsettia plant over to Cara's he had a sense of real accomplishment. But at the same time he felt uneasy. Maybe it was a mistake trying to befriend Cara like this. She seemed to be making herself clear—she had no interest in being anything more than a cool and casual acquaintance with him. Maybe he should just take a hint.

8

For me?" Cara looked truly surprised as he handed her the hooded planter and card.

"Yes." He forced a nervous smile. "To show my gratitude."

"Gratitude for what?"

"For sharing Thanksgiving dinner with me," he said sheepishly, "although I suspect you hadn't really meant to have me in your home. More than that, it's to say thanks for encouraging your friends—Beth and Annabelle and Vincent—to adopt cats from me."

She shrugged. "Oh . . . well . . ."

"I really appreciate you connecting them to me."

"They just seemed like good candidates." She made a smirk at him. "Unlike me."

Garrison felt deflated.

"Sorry," she said quickly. "I didn't mean to go there." She

gave him a genuine smile. "Why don't you come inside? It's cold out here. And I'd like to see what's in this package."

He felt instantly at home inside her house. And he was amused to see that it was actually bigger than it had seemed on Thanksgiving. "You have a really nice place," he said as she set the package on a coffee table and opened the card.

"Thanks." She nodded, then held up the card. "And thanks for this too." She leaned over and peeled the hood from the plant. To Garrison's relief the delicate pink blossoms were all still intact. "Why, it's beautiful," she gushed. "But you really didn't have to—"

"I wanted to," he clarified. "I felt like we got off on the wrong foot. And, well, since we're neighbors and all. And you've been such an asset in finding homes for my cats. Even discovering your neighbor David today came as a result of trying to drop this plant by your house."

"And he really took a cat?" she said with interest.

Garrison explained about Muzzy's chattiness and how she seemed a good match for Jackson. "I thought Muzzy might get him to relax and talk more . . . you know?"

"That's brilliant!" She picked up the poinsettia plant, carried it to her dining area, and, just like Garrison had imagined, she placed it on the dark-stained table. "Perfect."

"I couldn't agree more." He smiled. "Now I should let you get back to whatever you were doing."

"Just putting away groceries," she said as she went into the kitchen. "There's this great natural food store down the street from my employer. And since I have to go into the office on Mondays, I usually stock up."

"David mentioned that you had meetings on Mondays." He didn't know what to do, so he followed her into the kitchen.

It was small and old-fashioned, similar to Gram's. Except that it was in better shape.

"Dear David," she said as she removed an acorn squash from her cloth shopping bag. "I'm so lucky to have him next door."

"He seems to feel the same," Garrison admitted.

She studied him as she took out a large red onion. "Yes, it's nice to have good neighbors . . . don't you think?"

"Absolutely. I adore Ruby."

"She is a dear."

"And it seems obvious that you've made lots of friends in the neighborhood." He watched as she set some really nice-looking tomatoes on the tile-topped counter.

"You mean for a newcomer?" she teased.

"Yes . . . well, you know what I mean."

"Uh-huh. I'd venture to say I know more people in this neighborhood than you do."

"I'm sure that's true. Although, at the rate I'm going—finding homes for these cats—I might catch up."

"Well, except that you must be nearly out of cats. How many do you have left?"

"Just two. Oreo and Harry."

"Right . . ."

"And in my opinion they are the best ones of the batch. They should be easy to place."

"No doubt." She set a pair of zucchinis on the counter and smiled. "Well, thanks so much for the lovely poinsettia. It really brightens up the place. Puts me in the Christmas spirit." She narrowed her eyes slightly. "Now if I could just find myself a good cat."

Garrison cringed. "Okay, I get the hint."

"Sorry . . ." She held up her hands. "I know I can be a terrible tease sometimes." She walked up close to him and looked directly into his eyes. "Really, no hard feelings. Okay?"

He tilted his head to one side as if unconvinced. "I don't know . . ."

"What?"

"I'm not so sure I can trust you, Cara. You seem intent on harboring resentments against me. I'm beginning to think you'll never forgive me."

"Of course, I forgive you, Garrison. I'm just giving you a hard time."

"I don't know about that," he said in a slightly taunting tone. "A guy could take it personally."

"Well, that's ridiculous. I was just jerking your chain. I'm completely over the whole business with the cat and—"

"I might need more convincing," he said.

"*Huh?*"

"If you've really forgiven me, Cara, how about if you . . . say . . . went out to dinner with me?" He cringed inwardly. Had he really just said that?

"What?" She frowned. "Is this some kind of dating blackmail?"

He grinned nervously. "Maybe. Although I've never resorted to blackmail dates before." The truth was that his dating experience was embarrassingly limited.

She looked at the produce spread over her counter. "When do you want to go for dinner?" she asked.

"You name it."

She gave him a doubtful look. "Tonight?"

He concealed his surprise. "Sure, tonight is great. No problem."

"Good." She folded the bag and nodded firmly. "Despite collecting all these yummy vegetables today, I really didn't feel like cooking. It's been a long day."

As they put on their coats, Garrison could not believe his luck. Cara had actually agreed to go to dinner with him. Okay, maybe she just didn't want to cook at home, but what difference did it make? This was his chance to get to know her better. And maybe this meant that she and her neighbor David weren't as involved as he had assumed they were. Maybe he really did have a chance. Now if he could just not blow it.

"Do you mind if we meet there?" she asked as they went outside.

He tried not to look disappointed. "Are you afraid of my grandmother's old Pontiac?" He tipped his head to David's driveway where his car was still parked. Suddenly he was more aware than ever of the dull green paint, the dent in the right fender. He knew a little paint and TLC could turn the car into a real gem, but right now she looked pretty forlorn—although the interior was in good shape.

"No. I just like feeling independent." Cara tilted her chin up. "I'll have my own wheels—just in case we both decide we can't stand each other after all."

He frowned. "You really think that's going to happen?"

"You never can tell." She gave him a cheesy grin as she opened her car door. "I mean, if I'm not good enough for your cat, how could I be good enough for you?"

"But you said you'd—"

"Meet you at Fowlers'," she called as she closed her door.

He nodded. Fowlers' Fish House? That's where she wanted to go on their "first date"? Okay, he reminded himself, maybe this wasn't really a date. Maybe it was more like two people getting better acquainted over fish and chips. An icy rain was coming down as he drove to town. A night not fit for man or beasts. But he was not going to back down due to bad weather. And by the time he parked in front of Fowlers', which did not look very busy, a steaming bowl of chowder was starting to sound pretty good.

He jogged through the rain and caught up with her as she was going in the door. The whole restaurant was glowing, both inside and outside, with hundreds of multi-colored Christmas lights. The sight of a gaudily decorated fake tree and the smell of fried fish greeted him as he went inside. Everywhere he looked were the bright trappings and trimmings of Christmas. As a child he would've loved this. As an adult, it was a little over the top. But at least it was warm in here. That was something.

"Festive," he told Cara as he peeled off his coat.

She pointed to a glossy pine picnic table next to the window. "That okay?"

"Sure." He followed her over to the table and sat down across from her. "I haven't been here in years," he confessed. "But I used to like this place when I was a kid."

"I consider Fowlers' as one of my guilty pleasures," she said as she unwound a bright red scarf from around her neck.

"Why a guilty pleasure?"

"I heard how many calories are in their fish basket." As she reached for a greasy menu, she wrinkled her nose. Totally endearing. "As a result, I try to limit myself to only once a week."

"Right." He nodded. "Although I'm not sure why you're

concerned about calories. Frankly, after seeing all that produce in your kitchen, I'm relieved you're not a vegetarian or vegan or something like that."

She laughed. "No, I tried being a vegan briefly after college, but my hair started to fall out. However, I do try to eat my vegetables." Her smile faded. "That's something my mom always tried to get me to do . . . when she was alive. I didn't do such a great job then, but I'm trying to make up for it now."

"I'm sorry." He peered at her. "Has she been gone for long?"

"I was in my second year at college when she was diagnosed." She pulled a napkin out of the container, using it to wipe wet raindrops from her face. "Just the age when I was really starting to appreciate my mom. She battled cancer for about three years. She made it to my graduation . . . but not long after that."

"That's hard," he said sadly. "I kind of know how you feel. I lost both of my parents when I was twelve."

"Really?" Her eyes widened. "I'm sorry. I had no idea."

"Yeah . . . my grandma took me in. I was quite a handful. But my grandma—she was a really special lady. I honestly don't know where I'd be without her."

Her brown eyes grew warmer and softer. "And that's why you want to honor her wishes with her cats."

He nodded soberly. "Even when it's not easy."

"Well, that's very respectable, Garrison. I'm sorry I was such a pill about Harry. I hope you find him the perfect home."

Garrison talked a little about the recent cat placements and how they all seemed to be working out perfectly. "Almost like

Gram is up there in heaven orchestrating the whole thing." He smiled at Cara. "Or like she sent me an angel to help out. Again, I have to thank you."

"I'm happy to be of help. And that reminds me. I have another friend and I think she might be perfect for a cat. In fact, she would probably fall in love with Harry."

He nodded, but felt a small wave of uncertainty. As badly as he wanted to be rid of the cats and to sell Gram's house and to be on his way, he knew he was getting attached to that big Maine Coon cat. "Who is that?" he asked carefully.

"Her name is Sabrina," Cara began. "She's a real sweetheart."

"And she lives in our neighborhood."

"Yes. That's how we met. She lives on the street behind me. We share the same backyard fence. Her yard is absolutely gorgeous and she's promised to give me gardening tips next spring."

"Sounds like a nice neighbor."

"Yes. Sabrina is one of those women who can do everything. I mean, she cooks and gardens and sews and does crafts—the works. She's been a real inspiration to me."

"Sounds like she's a busy woman. Does she have a job?"

"She works from her home. As a seamstress. She does alterations and things like that. Her husband, Riley, manages an appliance store. They are like this sweet, old-fashioned couple, but they're our age."

"Our age?"

"You know . . . thirty-something." She grinned. "Riley might be pushing forty. But Sabrina has to be midthirties."

"Yeah." He nodded. "And do they have a solid marriage? Or do you know?"

"Very solid. Their biggest problem is that they can't have kids. Sounds like they've spent lots of money trying to. Sabrina is trying to resign herself to it, but I know it's been hard on her. I've been telling her she should get some pets. But she doesn't like dogs."

"Does she like cats?"

Cara shrugged. "I'm not sure. All I know is that she does not like dogs. One of our neighbors has several and she sometimes complains about what they do to her yard."

They chatted on and on as they ate fish and chips and chowder. And by the time they were done, Garrison felt like he'd made real progress.

"Friends?" he said as they prepared to leave the restaurant.

"Friends," she declared as she held out her hand. He grasped it and shook it.

"That's a relief. I was afraid you were never going to get over losing Harry," he confessed.

Her dark eyes twinkled. "Well, I now have a plan for Harry's future. I'm hoping he'll become my neighbor and I'll get to spend lots of time with him."

"You talk to Sabrina and we'll see how it goes," he said as they stepped out into the cold.

"Thanks for dinner," she called out as she pulled her scarf over her head and got ready to dash through the rain.

"Thank *you*!" Garrison took off after her, waving as they parted ways at their cars. That had gone well. Really, really well. As he started the Pontiac's engine, he looked at the funky old fish house and grinned. What a perfect place for a first date! Cara had been a genius to choose it. Why had he been so doubtful? And Fowlers' looked really beautiful from the car. Against the blackness of a dark rainy night, dozens of strings of colorful lights were cheerfully reflected in the shining puddles, doubling the effects of the rainbows of light. Even the inflated vinyl Santa standing next to the giant anchor had a certain charm. For some reason everything looked better to him now.

9

The next morning, Garrison was surprised to hear someone knocking at the back door. It was barely seven.
He hurried past where Oreo and Harry were already
waiting for breakfast and pulled open the door. "Ruby?" he
peered curiously at his bathrobe-clad neighbor. "What are
you doing out this early?"

She held out what looked like a covered plate. "Breakfast,"
she told him with a wide grin.

"Seriously?" He moved back, welcoming her into the house.
"What did I do to deserve this?"

"Just being neighborly," she said as she set the oversized
plate on the kitchen table, proudly removing the cover. "Ham
and eggs. Biscuits and gravy. And grits."

His eyes opened wide and his mouth started to water.
"Grits?"

She nodded knowingly.

"I haven't had grits in years." He smiled at her. "Not since I lived here and used to sneak over to eat them from your table."

"That's what I figured." She pulled out a chair. "Go ahead, eat it while it's hot."

"Don't mind if I do." He sat down and she handed him silverware from the drawer.

"Dig in and enjoy, Garrison."

"What about your breakfast?" he asked as he stuck his spoon into the grits.

"I already ate. Don't mind me. I'll just make us some coffee."

"Why are you being so nice to me, Ruby?"

"Just being neighborly," she said again. "Neighbors helping neighbors. That's what we do around here."

"Uh-huh." He nodded as he chewed a bite of ham, watching her with suspicion. She was up to something and he knew it. But whatever it was, he didn't think he cared. He hadn't had a breakfast this good in—years!

He was just finishing up the grits when she set a mug of steaming coffee in front of him. She had a cup of her own and sat down with a humph across from him. "Well, how do you like it? Can Ruby still cook grits or not?"

"Oh yeah," he murmured contentedly. "No doubt about it. Ruby still can."

She chuckled, then sipped her coffee.

He was almost done with the biscuits and gravy when she cleared her throat. "Elliott came by last night."

"Your house?"

"Yeah. He spent the night. Still sleeping."

"Uh-huh?"

"I could hardly sleep myself last night. Fretting and worrying over that boy. He's broke with no place to go. Down and out. I just don't know what's to become of him." She sighed. "His clothes were filthy. I've already run them through the washer twice. Once last night. And again this morning. Don't know if they'll ever come clean."

"Clothes can be replaced." He pushed the empty plate aside and reached for his coffee.

"I *know* that." She gave him an exasperated look. "But grandsons cannot."

"Yeah." He nodded. "That's true."

"So I got myself to thinking . . . in the middle of the night . . . after I spent more'n an hour praying to the good Lord to do something about this. I got to thinking that maybe there's something we can do right here. Right under our noses."

"What would that be?"

"Well, I know you're working real hard to fix up Lilly's house. And I got to thinking maybe you could use a spare set of hands." She leaned forward. "Elliott's a strong boy. He can work hard when he sets his mind on it. I thought if he could come over here and help out, well, maybe it would do both you and him some good. What d'you think?"

He chuckled. "I think this breakfast was a bribe."

"Not a bribe exactly. But I thought it might get your un-divided attention." She pointed to the empty plate. "Looks like it did too."

"And I'm not complaining either." He smiled at her. "But you didn't need to bring me breakfast, Ruby. I'm happy to hire Elliott. I really could use some help. But I can't afford to pay him much right now."

"I don't want you to pay him at all."

"Why not?"

"Don't want that boy having any money in his pocket. The longer he's broke, the longer he'll stay put."

"I see."

"When it's time to pay him . . . I'll let you know."

"What will I tell him?"

"Don't you worry about that. I'll handle everything." She finished the last of her coffee. "I'll tell him that I'm his manager. If a boy can't trust his grandmother, who can he trust?"

"Good point."

"So . . . if I can get him up—and that might be like raising the dead—I'll get some food into him and send him over here."

"Great." He stood up and rinsed the plate, then handed it back to her. "And thanks for breakfast. I can't remember when I've had a better one."

She reached up and patted his cheek. "You're a sweet boy, Garrison. I sure have missed you."

A couple hours passed before Elliott showed up at the back door—wearing low-slung pants, a ripped T-shirt, a knitted black ski cap, and a suspicious dark scowl. He looked around the kitchen with narrowed eyes. "Just what am I supposed to do anyway?"

Garrison reintroduced himself to the sulky boy, then explained his basic plans for fixing up the house. "I've made a long list." He nodded to the fridge.

"This is all about cats."

"The *other* list. Anyway, right now I need you to help me in getting the living room ready to paint. I want to take the drapes down and mask off the woodwork. After that, you can attack the bathroom." Garrison pulled a fresh particle mask out of a drawer and slipped it on.

"What's that?" Elliott frowned. "We working with toxic stuff or something?"

"No. I just have cat allergies. I take meds, but the masks help too." He jangled another one. "You can wear one if you want, but they get pretty stuffy."

Elliott shook his head then rambled into the living room where the two of them started to remove the dusty drapes and drapery rods. Next Garrison showed Elliott how to mask off the wood, explaining how it was important to get it straight and seal it tight and smooth. Elliott acted nonchalant, but when he started doing it, he took the time to do it right. Garrison could tell this kid was smart. Okay, maybe he wasn't smart when it came to life choices, but he had brains.

"Nice work," he told Elliott when they finished prepping the living room.

Elliott just shrugged. "No big deal."

"Actually, it's a big deal to me," Garrison corrected. "A lot of guys wouldn't do it half as well. I can tell you're intelligent."

Elliott's eyes seemed to light up and then he frowned again. "You mean for a black kid?"

Garrison laughed. "No, that's not what I meant at all. Just take a compliment for what it's worth, okay?"

He shrugged again. "Okay."

"Now if you could go tape off the bathroom beneath the staircase"—he pointed to the door—"just like you did in here, I'd appreciate it."

As Elliott meandered toward the bathroom, Garrison noticed a strange car in front of the house. A pair of women emerged and he felt a surge of happiness to realize that one of them was Cara. The other was a petite blonde woman. "Come in," he called as he opened the front door.

Cara quickly introduced him to Sabrina. "As it turns out, she is interested in getting a cat," she told him. "I hope you don't mind that we popped in."

"Not at all. I'd offer you a chair, but you can see there's a shortage."

"We just came to see the cats," Sabrina said.

"Harry in particular," Cara added.

Garrison went for the bag of cat treats, rattling the plastic and calling until both Harry and Oreo magically appeared. Harry, as usual, rubbed against his legs, looking up with adoring green eyes. Garrison bent down to scratch his head and chin. "Just two boys left," he told Sabrina, "but if you ask me they're the best of the lot."

"Harry is a Maine Coon cat," Cara said with enthusiasm. She knelt down next to Garrison, stroking Harry's silky coat. "They are the best cats ever. Very smart and loyal and, in my opinion, gorgeous."

"He is pretty," Sabrina agreed as she petted the other cat. "But so are you, Oreo."

"Handsome Harry," Cara cooed. Then standing, she glanced around the room. "Are you painting?"

"Yeah." Garrison picked up the paint samples, fanning the colors out. "Now if I could just pick a color."

Cara grimaced. "I wouldn't know where to begin." She pointed to Sabrina, who had squatted down to examine the cats. "She's the real color expert. You should get her opinion." She glanced at her watch. "Now if you guys will excuse me, I have to get home for a conference call at ten. I'll just walk back."

"Thanks for coming with me." Sabrina stood and looked at the color cards in Garrison's hands. "You really want help with that?"

"I would be truly grateful." He handed them over to her and she began walking around the room, taking it all in.

"Is this carpet staying?"

"No way," he assured her. "I'm just leaving it in until I finish painting. Thought it might protect the floors. They're hardwood underneath. I took a peek yesterday and they appear to be in good shape. This house belonged to my grandfather's parents originally and finally to just my grandmother. But I think the carpet was installed back in the sixties." He went over to peel back the corner for her to see.

"Pretty," she said. "It's a lighter wood than I'd have expected. But it'll brighten it up in here. I really like this color." Sabrina pointed to a warm shade of gray. "It's neutral but sophisticated, and it looks really handsome against the dark woodwork. See?" She held it against the wall then handed it back to him.

Garrison studied the color. "I never would've picked that color, but I do like it." He left the card sticking out. "Want to help me with the other rooms?" he asked hopefully.

"Sure. It's the least I can do in exchange for a cat."

"Great. Did you decide on which one?"

She pointed to Oreo. "This guy had me from the get-go. I didn't want to hurt Cara's feelings. She was so set on me adopting Harry. But I had a cat that looked a lot like this one as a child. So if you don't mind, I'd like to have Oreo."

He grinned. "I don't mind at all."

Before Sabrina left, with Oreo happily tucked into a cat crate, she had helped Garrison pick out a nice, pale robin's-egg blue for the downstairs bath and a lighter shade of gray for the downstairs bedroom. She even made some great suggestions for the bath and bedrooms upstairs.

After a quick trip to the paint store, Garrison returned with the living room and bathroom paint. He'd arranged to pick up the other cans at the end of the day and had grabbed a couple of Subway sandwiches. He and Elliott had a quick lunch, then launched into painting. "You're really good at this," he told Elliott as he watched him dipping a roller into the paint. "Have you done it before?"

Elliott flashed him a surprising grin. "Yeah, as a matter of fact."

Garrison laughed. "Well, who knew I was hiring a pro."

"I never did it as a real job," Elliott said as he rolled the paint-filled roller down the wall. "But I did help a friend paint his house last summer. I worked for free rent. It was a pretty good deal . . . at first."

"Yeah, I guess that happens sometimes," Garrison said as he used a brush to paint around the front window. "Sometimes things seem good at first . . . but we learn the hard way that they weren't as good as we thought."

"Yeah. My grandmother's always telling me that I get most of my education at the school of hard knocks. I guess she's kinda right."

"You have to decide when you're ready to quit that school," Garrison said as he dipped his brush. "Then it's time to take your life by the horns and turn it in the direction you really want to go."

"Yeah, well, that might be easier said than done."

"I know," Garrison agreed. "And I think it helps when you have someone to go alongside you. It's rough going it alone."

"You got that right."

"Hello?" called a feminine voice from the kitchen. "Anybody home?"

"We're in here," Garrison called back.

"It's just me." Beth emerged from the kitchen. "Sorry to just barge in. I came in the back door." She giggled. "I left you a little something in the kitchen."

"Really?" Garrison climbed down from the stepladder he'd been using.

"Yes. A thank-you for giving us the cat." She grinned. "Cinnamon rolls."

"Cinnamon rolls?" He smacked his lips as he removed the particle mask. "You hear that, Elliott?" He took a moment to introduce Beth to his young helper.

"I just wanted to express my thanks for giving us Spooky," Beth gushed. "You wouldn't believe the change that cat has brought to my Annabelle. It's the most remarkable thing I've ever seen. Annabelle had been so moody and distant lately. I was worried that she and I were never going to have a normal conversation again. But it's like that cat brought some kind of miracle over her." Beth paused to look around the room. "Hey, what's going on here?"

"Just fixing the place up."

"I like that color." She nodded with approval. "Where's your furniture? In storage?"

"No. I don't really have furniture. Other than a few pieces I saved from my grandmother's stuff."

"No furniture?" She got a thoughtful look. "How would you like some?"

"Huh?"

She laughed. "Well, it's a long story. You see, after my divorce—I got everything just like I deserved—but I ended up losing my big house over on Sheridan Heights just the same. That's when Annabelle and I moved over here. Anyway, with the downsize and all, the furniture from my old basement wouldn't fit. It's good stuff though, so I put it in storage, thinking maybe I'd get a real salon someday and use it in there. I thought it'd look nice in the waiting area. But that's just not happening."

"Uh-huh?" He tried to appear more interested than he felt. Beth's chatter reminded him a bit of Muzzy. Only Beth was a little more upbeat.

"So, anyway, I've been paying for this storage unit ever since we moved. Just throwing money away. I held on to the furnishings thinking I could use them in my salon—not like that's going to happen anytime soon. Then I thought maybe I'd let my ex take them. After all, he picked them out. I thought I might use them to coerce him into paying child support, but the jerk is just a deadbeat loser. And I refuse to hand them over to him now. If it wasn't the middle of winter I'd set them in my front yard and sell them."

"There are online classifieds," he suggested.

"I don't have time for that. Besides, I don't even know how." She rubbed a long red fingernail beneath her chin. "But what if . . . what if I plunked them down here for a while?"

"Here?"

"It would look fabulous, Garrison. It really would."

"But I can't afford to buy anything right now."

"Well, maybe you could in time. And if not, maybe I could just sell it when summer comes. In the meantime you'll be saving me rent money and you'd have something to sit on." She smiled hopefully.

He shrugged. "Well, when you put it like that."

Suddenly she was writing down an address and some numbers and fishing out a key. "Pick it up as soon as you can, Garrison. The payment is due on the fifteenth and I'd really like to save that rent. I could get Annabelle something nice for Christmas."

"Okay." He pocketed the slip of paper. "I'll do that. Thanks!"

"Thank *you*." She was beaming now. "And thank you for Spooky. I know that cat's the reason that Annabelle has started talking to me more. She seems so much happier. I can't even explain it. Except that I'm so grateful—for everything." She threw her arms around him, planting a big kiss on his cheek. "Thanks!" She stepped back. "And I thought the cinnamon rolls might help too."

He sniffed the air. "I can smell them."

"They're yummy. Now I gotta run. I've got a two o'clock perm."

"Thanks again," he called as she went out the back door. But before she was even gone, there was someone knocking on the front door. "This place has turned into Grand Central Station," he told Elliott as he went to answer it. "Cara?" He smiled big as he opened the door wide. "Come on in."

"Was that Beth I just saw in here?" She looked at him with a furrowed brow.

"Yeah. She brought some cinnamon rolls. Want one?"

"No . . . thanks." She turned to the wall Elliott was working on. "Nice color."

"Yeah. Sabrina picked it out. You were right, she's got a good eye for color."

"Speaking of Sabrina, I heard the news."

"News?"

"She took Oreo instead of Harry."

He shrugged. "Yeah, well, she—"

"Did you talk her out of Harry?"

"No, not at all."

"Seriously? Because I got to thinking that maybe you were saving Harry for yourself." She tilted her head to one side with a slightly suspicious expression.

"I'll admit I've gotten fond of him." He smiled. "He's a good cat."

She pointed to the face mask still in his hand. "How are your allergies?"

"As long as I stay on the meds—and after cleaning out most of the cat hair stuff—they've gotten a little better."

"That's great. So are you keeping Harry then?"

"I—uh—I don't really know."

"Oh . . . ?" She narrowed her eyes slightly, as if adding him up.

"I guess I'm still trying to figure things out." He shrugged, trying to think of a way to prolong this encounter. But it was pointless—Cara abruptly announced she had to get back to work. After she left, Garrison and Elliott sampled the cinnamon rolls and then returned to painting. But as he painted, he wondered—was Cara more interested in Harry or in him? And what about her attentive neighbor? Garrison was fully aware that David had his eye on Cara. And why shouldn't he? But how did Cara feel about David? Garrison wished he knew. What he did know was that—based on personal experience—his skills at reading women were shaky at best. And making assumptions could get a guy into trouble.

10

By Tuesday afternoon, Garrison and Elliott had finished the painting in the downstairs. They'd also removed the nasty wall-to-wall carpeting to reveal some fairly decent oak floors. "Are you going to refinish them?" Vincent asked as he kneeled down to examine the grain. He'd come by to help with some plumbing questions and was just getting ready to go.

"I don't think so," Garrison told him. "They seem okay to me."

"Yeah." Vincent stood. "If it ain't broke, why fix it."

"Especially with so much else to do," Garrison told him. "Thanks for getting that bathroom running."

"No problem. And I showed Elliott a couple of tricks so when it's time to work on the upstairs one, he might know what to do. That kid's got a good head on his shoulders."

Garrison looked outside to where Elliott was still heaping the carpet into the Dumpster. "And strong too," he said.

"But he seems troubled."

Garrison nodded, confiding in the older gentleman about how he had dreamed of creating a halfway house. "For guys just like Elliott. To help them find their way in the world." He pointed at Vincent. "They need guys like you . . . to sort of mentor them."

Vincent pointed back at Garrison. "And guys like you too. Hey, why not use this place for something like that?"

"I've considered it," Garrison admitted. "But it'd take some start-up money, which I don't have. That's why I need to take that job in Seattle."

Vincent frowned. "It'll be a shame to see you go, son."

"Yeah . . . well, I keep going back and forth on it. Who knows?" He thought about Cara. If only he could figure her out. "Maybe I'll stick around."

On Wednesday morning, Garrison rented a small moving van for half a day. "Come on," he called to Elliott as he was masking the wall along the stairway. "We've got some furniture hauling to do."

It took three trips to get the pieces moved to his house, but eventually they were put into place. A long black leather couch against the wall and two charcoal-gray leather chairs across from it. "That is sick," Elliott said as they stepped back to look at it.

"Sick?" Garrison frowned. "I think it looks cool."

Elliott laughed. "Sick *is* cool, man. Where you been?"

"In Africa?"

Elliott laughed even louder. But Garrison was encouraged to see him looking happy. The kid had a great smile. "Well, since you lived in Africa, maybe you'd like to see the rug we left outside."

"Huh?"

"I took a peek." Elliott chuckled. "It's *zebra*."

"Zebra?"

Before long they had the large rug laid out in front of the couch. "What do you think?" Garrison asked Elliott.

"Sick." Elliott's chin bobbed up and down. *"For sure."*

Garrison was not so sure. "Well, it does warm the place up a little."

Elliott pointed at Harry, who was just making himself comfortable in a sunny spot. "He likes it. But then he kinda looks like a wild animal too."

Soon they had the metal-and-glass coffee table in place, as well as a tall, dark bookshelf and some end tables. "Not bad," Garrison said as they both flopped down onto the chairs.

"Comfy too." Elliott patted the armrest. "A man could get used to this."

Garrison thought about Beth's ex. Had he gotten used to it? And, if so, would he show up and want it all back? Not that it mattered really. "Okay, let's get back to work," he told Elliott. "You see if you can finish that stairway wall and I'll return the truck."

Toward the end of the workday Garrison started working on the second-floor rooms, sorting through stuff and getting them ready for paint. As he was emptying a spare-room closet, he discovered some boxes containing artifacts from his grandparents' time spent in Africa. There were shiny black carved wooden statuettes. Spears and knives, ceremonial masks and baskets and woven mats. All sorts of interesting things that he thought might look good on that big shelf in his living room. He was just carrying them down when his cell phone rang. It was about the seventh time it had rung today. Once again, it was about the classified ad for the cats. He'd done too good a job on it and suddenly everyone was in desperate need of a cat. He gave the man the same message he'd been giving all morning. "I'm sorry, all the cats have found homes, well, except for one. And I'm considering keeping that one myself." Then, despite the man's pleas, he told him he was busy and had to go.

"I think you could've given away Harry about ten times today alone," Elliott said as Garrison walked past him with a box of artifacts. "I thought you were allergic to cats and wanted them all gone. Why you holding on to him?"

"Because I *like* him." Garrison turned off his phone. "And I'm getting sick and tired of these calls. And I mean *sick*-sick. Not sick-cool. From now on, don't call me, I'll call you," he said to his phone as he tossed it to the couch.

Elliott watched with interest, asking questions, as Garrison started to arrange the artifacts on the big shelf. Garrison, to the best of his ability, began to describe what the pieces were for, telling Elliott a bit about his time in Uganda.

"That's pretty cool what you did over there," Elliott said as he set a ceremonial knife onto the shelf. "My grandmother told me about how you put in wells so the poor people could have clean drinking water."

"Yeah. It took a whole team. I didn't do it single-handedly."

"I figured that much. But the thing is, *you did it.* You weren't that much older than me when you went over there. That was pretty unselfish, you know?"

He shrugged. "I suppose it could look that way. Truth was I wanted to go. Wanted to see the world. And I wanted to please my grandmother. All that could be considered selfish . . . depending on your perspective."

"From my perspective it looks unselfish."

Garrison looked into Elliott's eyes. "You are always surprising me."

"Huh?"

Garrison tapped Elliott's forehead. "How smart you are. How come you haven't gone to college?"

Elliott laughed. "You mean besides HKU."

"What?"

"Hard Knocks University."

"Oh yeah."

By the time Elliott went home, Garrison was exhausted. He knew it was partly because he was trying to keep up with Elliott and partly because he was gnawing on something in his mind. As foolish as it seemed, he was really considering letting the Seattle job go. What if he stuck around here and tried to turn Gram's place into a halfway house? Would it work? Or would he regret it—finding out he'd bitten off more than he could chew? Harry jumped into his lap as he sat in the living room pondering these things. "What do you think, old boy? What would you do if you were in my shoes?"

Harry gave him that adoring look—the look that clearly said he wanted Garrison to stick around and be his owner. Garrison laughed. "Yes, of course, that's because I'm currently feeding you and petting you. If someone else came along to take my place, you'd fall in love with them too."

On Thursday afternoon, Cara stopped by again. "I made too much zucchini bread," she told him as she handed over a foil-wrapped loaf that still felt warm. "I thought maybe you could use some."

"Thank you. Can you come in?"

"Well, I was just taking my afternoon walk."

"Want any company?" He brushed the dust from his hands onto his jeans.

She glanced over his shoulder. "I hate to drag you away from your work."

"No problem. Elliott's in charge anyway." He called out to Elliott. "I'll be back in a little."

"Looks like you're making progress," she said as he closed the door.

"Oh, yeah, I should've given you the full tour. It's really coming along."

"Well, it'll be dusky soon. We better walk while we've still got some light."

"Yeah . . . I still forget how night comes so much earlier in the winter. Uganda wasn't like that."

As they walked she asked him about his time in Uganda. He started by giving his usual answers, explaining about the well projects, describing the people. But then as she pressed him harder, he talked more about himself. "I get tired of people acting like I was some kind of superhero to go over there," he confessed. "There were a lot of times when I hated being there. A lot of times I felt really sorry for myself."

"That's understandable. I mean, you were there nine years."

He nodded. "And most of the time I really loved it. It was the adventure of a lifetime. I still miss it."

"Why did you come back?"

He told her about contracting malaria. "It was really my own fault. I got slack about the anti-malarial medicine. It happens a lot. When people stay there for more than a year or two, they start thinking they're invincible." He laughed sadly. "Unfortunately, it only takes a tiny mosquito to remind them otherwise."

"So that's why you came back? The malaria?"

"Yeah. It got pretty bad. They sent me home for medical help. Probably a good thing."

"And you can't go back?"

"Not anytime soon." He told her about his more recent dreams, about creating a halfway house, and even a bit about Elliott. "It's really giving me hope."

"Do you think you might stay here? Make a halfway house in your grandmother's house?"

"I'm seriously considering it." He confessed to how lost he had felt these past few months. "It was like I couldn't find my way. Couldn't get my feet beneath me," he told her as the sky grew duskier. Something about this purple-gray light made him feel more comfortable talking about his feelings. It was kind of like being in a confessional—where you couldn't see a priest. Not that he was Catholic or had ever done that, but he could imagine. "I felt like I was an old man, all washed up at the ripe old age of thirty-four."

"I'm thirty-two," she said quietly. "I can't imagine feeling washed up in a couple of years."

"Well, that's how I felt. Like my best life was behind me. Like I gave all I had and had lost a lot of myself in the process." Or maybe he'd just never known himself to start with.

"How could you lose yourself?"

He shrugged. "Maybe it was my heart that I lost while I was over there."

"Your heart?" she said quietly.

"There was a girl that I thought I was in love with." He

sighed, wishing he hadn't mentioned this. But there it was—out there. His admission to failure in the romance arena.

"Oh?"

"Yeah. Her name was Leah and I was pretty sure that the sun and the moon rose because of her." He made a forced laugh. "For a while she even pretended to care for me."

"Pretended?"

"Yeah . . . I'm pretty sure it was an act. Turned out she had another guy on the line the whole while she was spending time with me. I think she actually used me to make him jealous. Anyway, they are happily married now. With a baby too. Really, I wish them no ill. But it did hurt. It took its toll."

"Yeah . . . I can imagine."

"But here's the deal," he said suddenly. "I'm starting to feel found again. Like I really am coming back to life. I know it's partly due to feeling healthier now. The malaria is under control. But there's something about being here. Something about working on Gram's house. Spending time with Elliott. Even hanging with Harry . . . it all feels *right*." He paused under the streetlight, turning to smile at her. She smiled back and suddenly he longed to take her hand in his. He wanted to tell her that she was a big part of the "rightness" that was happening in his life. But at the same time, he didn't want to scare her off. Already, he'd said much more than he'd intended.

Instead of making what could turn into an awkward declaration, and since it was now dark, he insisted on walking her home. As they walked down her street, he lightened the conversation by telling her more about Elliott and how he recognized some great potential in the young man. "Here we are," he said as they walked up to her door.

"But now I'll miss seeing the improvements in your house," she declared as they stood on the front porch together.

"Come by tomorrow," he told her. "I'll give you the full tour. I promise."

As he walked home, he wondered if he'd been presumptuous to escort her all the way up to her door. As if he'd thought they were on a date. The last thing he wanted was to overwhelm her. Especially considering how they'd gotten off on the wrong foot over Harry last week. And he knew that his dating skills, at best, were rusty. He needed to go carefully with this woman . . . pace himself. Just the same, his step lightened as he considered the progress they'd made this evening. And he would get to see her again tomorrow!

On Friday morning, as Garrison worked on the second-floor rooms, he got an idea. Rather, Harry gave him an idea. It seemed that whichever room Garrison was working on, Harry was determined to occupy. But as Garrison was talking to the cat, telling him to keep his tail out of the paint tray, it hit him. If he kept Harry, why couldn't he keep the ten grand that was supposed to go with Harry? Wouldn't that be fair? Or would Gram's attorney have objections because he didn't meet Gram's strict requirements? But that seemed ridiculous. After all, he was her grandson. Wouldn't she be delighted he'd gotten over his cat phobia and wanted one of her cats?

With that ten grand, Garrison could afford to pass on the Seattle job. He could buy himself time to figure things out here. Perhaps he could even start up the halfway house.

Maybe he could get the church to back him. After all, they had backed him with Uganda. Suddenly it all seemed very doable.

He went to search for his phone, turning it on to see there were even more messages now. It seemed everyone wanted a cat now. Ignoring the messages, he called Mr. Miller, but discovering he was out of town until Monday, he told the assistant he'd call back. But even as he turned off his phone again, he felt hopeful. This plan could work! However, he knew better than to call Seattle and burn that bridge. It had taken far too long to land that job. No way was he going to toss it aside without some kind of assurance from Mr. Miller.

The bulk of the work in the house was pretty much wrapped up by noon, and to celebrate, Garrison ordered pizza for Vincent and Elliott. "You guys are the best," Garrison said as he held up a slice of pizza like a toast. "I never would've accomplished all this without your help."

"I've enjoyed having a project to dig into," Vincent admitted. "Wish I could do some of these upgrades in my own house."

"Well, when your ship comes in and you're ready to do some renovations, don't forget that I owe you," Garrison told him. He wanted to add that, come Christmas Eve, Vincent would have some unexpected cash to work with.

"I'll remember that," Vincent said a bit doubtfully. "When my ship comes in." He pointed at Elliott. "And if that should happen, I'd like to hire you, young man. The three of us could really do some great things on my house."

"Just let me know," Elliott said as he reached for another slice.

They talked and joked about the work they'd done and Garrison could tell they were all a little sad to see it coming to an end. "But don't forget," he reminded them, "as soon as the weather starts warming up, I'll want to start working on the exterior of the house. We'll have a reunion tour in the spring."

The doorbell rang as they were cleaning up the pizza mess. As Garrison went to answer it, Vincent excused himself, and Elliott said he was going upstairs to put a final coat of paint on the bathroom baseboard.

Cara was at the door, smiling expectantly. "Is this an okay time for a tour?"

"Perfect." He welcomed her in, explaining how they were just finishing up. Then he led her around the house, taking her from room to room while she gushed over the progress he'd made.

"I never could've done it without Elliott and Vincent," he said. "We made a pretty great team."

"Well, you've really turned this house around," she declared as they came back to the living room.

"There are still lots of little things to do," he said. "But the big stuff is done."

"And you even have furniture." She made a puzzled frown as she sat on the leather couch. "Very manly too."

He laughed. "That's just temporary. Beth's ex-husband picked it out." He explained about the storage unit.

"Oh . . . so you're kind of storing it for her?"

"Something like that." He grinned. "Although Elliott thinks it's *sick*."

She smiled. "As in cool, right?"

"Yeah. You knew that already?"

She laughed. "Unlike some people I haven't been living under a rock."

He feigned a wounded expression. Unfortunately, she was right.

"Sorry," she said quickly. "I didn't mean—"

"No problem. Just jerking your chain." He grinned.

She laughed as she stood. "Well then, on that note, I think I should go."

"Did I scare you away?"

"No, I just have a lot to get done before quitting time."

"Speaking of quitting time . . ." He followed her to the door, trying to think of a clever way to ask her out. "I, uh, I've been meaning to invite you to dinner. I'd like to properly thank you for all your help in finding homes for the cats. Are you busy tonight?"

"I'm sorry," she said as she opened the door. "I, uh, I already have plans."

Garrison just nodded, trying to determine if this was her way of saying he'd just stepped over the line. "Yeah . . . well, that's okay." He shoved his hands into his pockets, trying to act nonchalant. But for some reason this felt like a brush-off. Like Cara was being insincere . . . just making an excuse not to go out with him. He followed her out to the porch—more to be polite than because he wanted to.

"Okay, I can tell you don't believe me," she said a bit contritely.

He shrugged. "Hey, if you don't want to go out with me, I understand. I'd just like to think you'd be honest with me." He looked directly into her eyes. "We are friends, *right*?"

"Of course," she declared. "But I am being honest. I really do have a previous engagement tonight. I promised David that I'd go to a Christmas party with him and there's—"

"Cara, you don't have to report to me," he said too abruptly. "I *said* I understand. No big deal. I get it."

"Well, okay then." She let out a frustrated sigh and he

knew that he'd hurt her, but how could he take it back? "I better go," she said quietly.

"Yeah . . . me too." As he went back inside, Garrison knew he was being immature. He knew that this wasn't how you treated people—friend or not. But hearing that Cara had a date with David—well, that just cut him to the core. Especially after some of the things he'd shared with her. Sure, he was being juvenile, but he just couldn't seem to help himself. As he continued washing paintbrushes in the laundry sink, he tried not to think about it. But in his mind's eye he kept seeing them together. Cara in her garnet-red knit dress or maybe even something more alluring. David in a suave dark suit. Together . . . laughing . . . dancing . . . falling in love.

"Hey, man, are you painting or cleaning brushes?" Elliott asked as he stuck his head in the laundry room.

Garrison forced a smile. "Caught me."

"Well, I gotta go. Promised my grandmother we'd take in a flick tonight." He made a face. "Hope I don't see anyone I know."

"If you do, just hold your head high. Show them that you're man enough to be seen in public with your grandmother. If they don't respect you, they don't deserve your respect."

Elliott nodded. "Yeah, man, I think you're right."

The next morning, despite feeling a bit like Scrooge, Garrison decided to take in the Christmas parade. As he walked to town, he remembered the last time he'd been here for a Christmas parade. He'd been playing trombone in the high school marching band and hoping to catch the eye of a pretty majorette named Jenny—who probably still didn't know his name. Had things really changed much since then?

As he turned his collar up against the morning chill, he decided a Christmas parade was just the ticket to cheer him up. On his way, he strolled past the staging area, looking on with amusement as he passed the homemade floats and marching band members tuning their instruments and trying not to appear nervous. He grinned at a group of costumed children from the school of dance, stomping their feet to stay warm. Everyone was anxiously awaiting the firehouse whistle to signal it was time to begin.

Feeling unexplainably giddy himself, he hurried past the staging area and on toward Main Street. Eager to find a good spot where he could watch the small-town spectacle, he wondered how he'd managed to celebrate Christmas all these years without a folksy parade to kick it off.

He was just going past the hardware store when he spied Cara. It wasn't exactly like he was looking for her, but it wasn't exactly like he wasn't. Plus she was easy to spot. Her bright red scarf wrapped carelessly around her neck seemed to set off her shining chestnut hair. "Hey, Cara," he said as he stepped up next to her.

"Garrison!" Her eyes sparkled with surprise—or perhaps pleasure?

Garrison noticed the boy on her other side. "Hey, Jackson," he said in a friendly tone. "What's up, my man?" Okay, he sounded like a bad imitation of Elliott, but he was only trying to be friendly . . . to fit in.

Jackson flashed him a crooked smile. "Not much."

"How's Muzzy doing?" Garrison asked, hoping to encourage the boy to engage like his dad wanted him to.

"She's fine." Jackson nodded eagerly. "She's a *good* cat."

"Is she talking your ear off yet?"

Jackson laughed. "Yeah."

"Garrison!" David exclaimed as he joined them. "How's it going?"

"Pretty good," Garrison said with a stiff smile. "How about you?"

"I'm great. Thanks." David, wearing a black fedora and walking coat, resembled an ad for a fashion magazine. In his gloved hands was a cardboard tray with three hot drinks balanced in it. But he was gazing intently at Garrison as if he was in the way somehow.

Garrison got it. Barely nodding, he stepped away from Cara's side. Like clockwork, David slid right into the same spot—like he belonged there. And maybe he did. Clearly the three of them had come together to watch the parade. In fact, they actually looked like a family. Even though he was obviously odd man out, Garrison stubbornly remained in place. Sure, he could admit it—at least to himself: he was as socially challenged as young Jackson.

David's blue eyes twinkled as he handed a cup to Cara. "Here you go, my lady. Your mocha—just how you like it—dash of cinnamon, splash of vanilla."

"Thanks," she murmured with downcast eyes. Was she playing the coquette or was she simply embarrassed by David's patronizing and somewhat territorial attention? And really, why was Garrison remaining stubbornly in place? It was clear that his presence wasn't welcome.

"And here's your cocoa, bud." David handed his son a cup, giving Garrison an apologetic look. "If I'd known you were here, old man, I'd have got you a coffee too."

"No problem." Garrison forced a smile. "I was just about to head over to the coffee shop myself."

David held out the cardboard tray to him. "Hey, then maybe you can take this back for me. Recycling—good for the earth you know." He grinned victoriously.

Garrison took the tray and, feeling dismissed, said a quick goodbye and continued on his way. He wanted to throw the tray to the ground and smash it beneath his boot, but he knew that would make him look like a jealous fool. Already he felt stupid enough. What difference should it make to him if Cara wanted to watch the parade with her neighbors? Why shouldn't she?

Garrison picked up a newspaper, then got in line for coffee, telling himself that the mature thing was to grab his beverage then go back and enjoy the Christmas festivities with the three of them. After all, they were neighbors—right?

But as he ordered his coffee he heard the firehouse whistle blow and by the time his coffee was ready, the parade was well on its way. Instead of going out to the street to watch it, he sat down at a small table by the window and watched the parade—by himself. He felt like the kid with his nose pressed against the toy store window—longing for something he could never have—hoping for Santa to do the impossible, yet knowing that Santa wasn't real.

Garrison knew he looked pathetic sitting there by himself, moping over his coffee while pretending to peruse the local paper, but it was the best he could manage. Why had he let Cara get under his skin like this? Hadn't he learned his lesson with Leah in Uganda? Would he ever learn?

The best thing to do is get on with your life, he chided himself. Quit moping around and wrap up Gram's business and get himself back to Seattle where a job—and who knew what else—awaited him. He pulled out his phone and, for the first time in days, turned it on. To his surprise there were thirty-three messages—and all from strange local numbers. That silly ad had really done the trick. Garrison had no doubt what these people wanted. He listened to a few of them just to confirm his suspicions. All of them were eager to adopt a cat—unexplainably eager. Yet the more pleas he listened to, the more he wanted to keep Harry for himself.

But he knew that was crazy and selfish. Harry would not be happy in Randall's apartment—left alone all day while Garrison was at work and stuck in a small apartment with no access to the outdoors. That wasn't fair or kind. And Gram would never have approved. Besides that, what about his allergies? Did he want to continue taking allergy meds nonstop around the clock? Did he want to be forced to wear particle masks?

He knew it wasn't just selfish to keep Harry for himself, it was plain wrong. Harry was a good cat. He deserved better. But if he had to part with Harry, he was determined to find him a really good home. As he walked back to Gram's house, he began responding to the messages, sifting through and eliminating the callers. For the first time he was really thankful for Gram's list.

12

By the time Garrison got home from the parade, he knew what had to be done. Even if it wasn't easy, it was the right thing to do. He solemnly dialed the Maxwells' number, inwardly hoping no one would answer.

"I'm so glad you called," Mr. Maxwell said after Garrison went over the usual preliminaries. "We lost a beloved family dog a few months ago. My children were completely devastated. I'm still getting over it myself. I never knew that an animal could steal my heart like Barnie did. So much so that I told myself I'd never get another pet." He made a loud sigh. "But my children don't agree. So I thought . . . why not get a cat?"

"Well, this is a very special cat," Garrison told him. "Almost like a dog."

"That sounds like my kind of cat."

"So . . ." Garrison stroked Harry's thick coat as they sat together on the sofa. "The only thing left is the home visit."

"Yeah, sure," the man said eagerly. "Anytime you want. My wife and kids are out right now. Christmas shopping. But I'm here . . . just watching the Steelers game."

Garrison looked out the window where, despite the cold temperature, the sun was shining. Gently sliding Harry off his lap, he slowly stood. "I'll be there in about ten minutes." Grabbing up his coat, he hurried out the door, hoping that the short walk to the address he'd just been given would help clear his head and remind him, once again, why Harry needed to be placed in a "real" home. It wasn't fair for him to try to hold on to Harry. In fact, it was just plain selfish. And he knew it.

The Maxwells' home was a well-maintained but modest ranch-style house. Mr. Maxwell, wearing jeans and a Steelers sweatshirt, answered the door with a big grin and introduced himself as Tom. He tipped his head into the house. "Come on in. Feel free to look around. Make yourself at home."

It didn't take long for Garrison to see that there was nothing wrong with what was obviously a family home. Personality seemed to ooze from every space. In some ways it seemed like the American dream—mom and dad and three kids. All they needed was a dog—or a cat. Garrison told Mr. Maxwell that he'd passed the home visit.

"But you'd probably like to meet Harry first," he said. "I mean, cats do have personalities and temperaments, and although Harry is the sweetest cat I've ever known, you can never tell whether it will work. You guys might not be compatible." Garrison felt silly for talking about a cat like it was a human. But in some ways Harry felt human. And lately he'd been Garrison's best friend.

"Okay. Let me record this game and I'll drive you home. Then if Harry and I hit it off, maybe I can bring him back with me. It'd be a great surprise for the wife and kids when they get home."

Garrison agreed and it wasn't long until he was enticing Harry into the last cat crate. But the look in Harry's eyes nearly broke Garrison's heart. It was as if Harry knew, as if he were saying, "How could you? I thought you loved me. I thought we were buddies. Don't you want me anymore? What did I do wrong?"

"See you around, pal," Garrison said with a husky voice, closing the door of the crate and latching it with a finality that broke his heart. Suppressing the stinging tears that were building in the back of his eyes, he handed the crate over to Tom. "Take good care of him. I'll be by to visit in two weeks. And then another week after that."

Tom's brow furrowed. "Your grandmother must've really liked her cats, huh?"

"You got that right." Garrison literally herded Tom and Harry toward the front door, practically pushing them out. "Take care," he called out as he firmly shut the door. He leaned against it, trying to catch his breath and calm himself. But it was too late. Tears were pouring down his face and his chest ached from the pain of trying to contain them.

"*What is wrong with me?*" he shouted as he went to the bathroom to splash cold water on his face. "I'm a grown man—bawling over a stupid cat!" He looked up at his pitiful image in the bathroom mirror. "Okay," he said in an attempt to get control. "This is obviously not just about the cat. This is about loss and heartache and heartbreak . . . This is about Uganda and Leah and Gram and Cara

. . . and—and—" A guttural sob escaped his throat. *"This is about Harry too!"*

Despite its improved appearance, the house felt sad and empty and lonely. And with the landline phone unplugged and Garrison's cell phone off—to avoid the barrage of cat inquiries still coming even though he'd canceled the ad—it was as quiet as a tomb. To distract himself, Garrison focused his attention on the real estate section of the local paper. One real estate company seemed to run more ads than any other, using big colored photos and great house descriptions. Garrison turned on his phone and, selecting the photo of an agent who looked to be around sixty, dialed the number.

"This is Barb Foster," a friendly female voice answered. "What can I do for you?"

Liking her tone, Garrison quickly explained his interest in listing his house. "Maybe I shouldn't have called you on the weekend," he said apologetically. "But I just saw your ad and I thought—"

"Haven't you heard that real estate agents work seven days a week?" she said cheerfully. "In fact, we expect to work even harder on the weekends. Now, tell me more about your house, Garrison."

He explained the recent improvements he'd made. "I'm not saying the place is perfect by any means. But it's a lot better. I'd try to sell it myself, but I really don't know a thing about real estate. I did some looking in the classifieds, but I have no idea where to begin. Plus I need to get back to Seattle for my job."

"Well, darling, you've called the right person. I've been

working in real estate for more than thirty-five years. There's not much I don't know about this business." She asked him some preliminary questions and eventually inquired about the address. "That's an interesting neighborhood," she told him. "It went downhill in the late nineties, but it's been making a nice little comeback lately. I'll do some comps and come up with a number for you."

"Comps?"

"Comparing house prices. I also look at tax records and some other things. We want to price the house just right. Not too high, not too low. *Right on the money.*" She chuckled. "And that brings you the money. Do you want me to start working on it for you?"

Garrison felt drawn to the warmth in her voice. She had an almost maternal sound. "Yes," he declared. "I want to move forward." He glanced around the lonely house. "As soon as possible."

"Well, you're in luck because I'm doing an open house today and it's been pretty slow on this side of town. I've got my iPad with me, and I'll start looking into your property right now. Then if you don't mind, I'll stop by around four and take a look at your property."

"That's fine. Great!"

By the time Barb showed up, Garrison felt so unbearably lonely that he rushed to open the door and invited her in with enthusiasm. Chattering at her nonstop—similar to what Muzzy used to do—Garrison showed Barb everything.

"The place looks good," she told him. "Like you said, it's not perfect. But it's clean and cleared out." She glanced around. "Almost too cleared out."

"Really?"

"But don't worry about that."

"So do you want to list it?" he asked hopefully. "I mean, I realize the holidays are coming. Maybe that's not a good time to—"

"Oh, you'd be surprised at the people who enjoy house shopping during the holidays. Folks are visiting relatives or just driving around to look at Christmas decorations." Her eyes lit up. "Say, we should put some nice, tasteful lights outside—really show the place off. And we should put a tree up and add a few Christmas touches." She pointed to the mantel. "Maybe some greens and candles and such."

He gave her a blank look. "I—uh—to be honest, I'm not really good at that sort of thing."

She laughed. "No, of course not." She pointed to the zebra rug. "Clearly this is a bachelor pad. But that's not what buyers want to see. Let me take care of that for you. You've done a great job already, darling, but we need to warm it up. My daughter-in-law is a magician at staging."

"Staging?"

Barb explained how houses sold more easily when the furnishings were arranged in a certain way. "Felicia will bring some things over—just on loan until your house sells. She'll get the place looking like something right out of a magazine."

"Really?"

"You bet. Like I said, this girl is a whiz. My guess is we'll have this place sold before the new year. How does that work for you?"

He forced a smile, realizing this was really it—the end of an era. It felt like a large stone had lodged itself in the bottom of his stomach. "Uh—yeah, sure. That sounds great."

She patted his hand. "I understand, son. This was your

grandmother's house, your childhood home. It's only natural you should feel some sadness."

He nodded. "Yeah, it's hard to give it up. But at the same time, I know it would be harder to stay." He looked around. "It's pretty lonely here."

As soon as Barb left, Garrison called Randall in Seattle, quickly explaining his job and a need to return. "Hopefully you won't be stuck with me too long," he said. "My plan is to get a place of my own as soon as possible." He told him about listing Gram's house.

"No problem," Randall said easily. *"Mi casa es su casa."*

"Thanks." Garrison let out a relieved sigh. "Can't wait to see you, bud."

After he hung up, Garrison decided to take a walk. Partly because he was restless, partly because he needed to get out of the house. It felt like the loneliness was eating him alive. The air was crisp and cold and since it was late in the day, the streets were vacant of foot traffic. Many of his neighbors' houses were lit up with strings of Christmas lights and cheerful decorations. But even the ones that weren't had the warm amber glow of lights flowing from windows, suggesting that the people inside were happily enjoying each other's company, maybe fixing meals together, sharing a laugh, watching a football game. For the second time today, he felt like the kid with his nose pressed against the window. He felt left out . . . lost, lonely, longing . . .

As the daylight faded he decided to venture over to Cara's street. Yes, he knew he might look like a stalker, but it wasn't like he was planning anything sinister. He just wanted one last look. Feeling somewhat concealed by the dusky light, he slowly strolled past Cara's house. She had put up Christmas lights too, making her sweet little home resemble a gingerbread house even more. David and Jackson's house had similar lights on it. Perhaps they had all worked together to put them up. Garrison could imagine the three of them with ladders and tangled strings of lights, laughing and drinking hot cocoa together, maybe even singing Christmas songs as they "decked their halls."

Feeling chilled to the bone, he turned the next corner and jogged back home, where the starkness of his bachelor pad greeted him like a glass of cold water tossed into his face. As he went to the kitchen to fix himself some dinner, he looked around, expecting one of his furry feline friends to appear—for Harry to rub up against his legs. Of course, that was not happening. "I've got to get out of here," he said as he opened the freezer, removing a microwavable meal. "The sooner the better."

13

W hy'd you give him away?" Elliott demanded on Sunday. "I thought you liked him—I thought you were gonna keep him?"

"I can't keep him," Garrison said for the second time. Elliott had popped in to say a friendly hello, but had grown increasingly irate after discovering that Harry had found a new home.

"Why not?"

"Because I have to get back to Seattle. My job starts—"

"*You're leaving?*"

"Well, yeah . . . I have to—"

"What about the halfway house? My grandmother said you might make this place into a halfway house for guys?"

"That was just a dream, Elliott. A dream that takes money."

"What about faith, man?" Elliott glared at him with dark eyes. "You been talking to me about being a man of faith? Where's your faith now?"

Garrison frowned, not wanting to admit that he hadn't even attended church this morning . . . that he'd barely been able to drag himself out of bed . . . where was the faith in that? "I still have faith," he muttered.

"Not enough faith to make this place work. You let Harry go. You just give up and leave. You're just like everyone else, man." Elliott pounded his fist onto the kitchen counter. "Well, I can leave too!"

"Wait!" Garrison called. "You don't understand."

But it was too late, Elliott was already storming out. And before the back door slammed shut, Garrison observed the real estate agent's car pulling into the driveway. Wearing a stylish navy pantsuit, Barb got out of her car and went around to the trunk. He watched as she removed something bulky. Of course, it was a For Sale sign. She leaned it against her car, then, carrying a packet of papers, walked up to the front door. *This is it*, he realized as he went to answer it. Now everyone in the neighborhood would know that he was leaving. Well, maybe that was just as well. The sooner they figured it out the better.

Garrison signed the agreement. Just as he finished helping Barb plant the sign in his front yard, he noticed a hefty figure wearing a purple woolen coat and a matching hat marching toward him. "That's my neighbor," he said quietly to Barb. "And she looks like she's on the warpath."

"What?" Barb looked up in alarm.

"I didn't tell her I was selling the place."

"Oh, well, I'll make myself scarce." She gave him a little finger wave then hurried back to her car.

"What in tarnation do you think you're doing?" Ruby demanded.

"Listen, Ruby, I wanted to tell—"

"*What are you doing?*"

"I have to go back to Seattle. I have a job there and—"

"What about your halfway house? What about Elliott?"

"It's a dream, Ruby. And sometimes dreams take time and—"

"*Yes!*" She shook her finger beneath his nose. "And you have to *give* them time, Garrison. You are not giving this enough time! You're running off like a scaredy-cat, boy. Your grandmother would be ashamed of you."

"How do you know that?" he demanded.

"Because I am ashamed of you."

"Just because I'm going to take a job in Seattle? Because I'm selling this house? Why should that make you ashamed?"

"Because it looks to me like you're giving up." She peered at him with misty-looking brown eyes. "In my heart, I feel that you just gave up. Like you let something whip you, and now you're running off with your tail tucked between your legs." She shook her head grimly. "I can't even explain it, but I just feel it inside here." She tapped her chest. "In my heart, I am sure that you are making a big mistake."

He didn't know what to say.

"What about Harry?" she asked with a smidgeon of hope in her eyes.

"I found him a home . . . yesterday." He held up his hands hopelessly. "You wouldn't believe how many people have called to adopt cats," he said quickly, hoping to change the subject. "I must have a hundred messages by now. It's uncanny."

She shrugged. "Well, that's because of the rumor."

"Rumor?"

"You haven't heard?"

"What do you mean?"

"The million-dollar-cat rumor. It's circulating around town."

"What are you talking about?"

"Somehow folks got it into their heads that one of Lilly's cats—or maybe all of them depending on who you listen to—is going to inherit a million dollars." She gave him a smirking look. "I know it's plum foolish, but that's what folks are saying. Everyone's talking about the million-dollar cat. I expect that's why you got so many calls." She gave him a suspicious look. "You did find Harry a good home, didn't you?"

Garrison nodded sadly. "Yeah. It's fine."

"Just tell me one thing," she began again. "Why can't you just stay here until Christmas?"

"Because I can't."

"Why not?" she pleaded.

"They need me on the job *now*," he said firmly. "I'm supposed to report on the tenth."

She took in a deep breath then pursed her lips. It looked like she wanted to explode all over again.

"I'm sorry, Ruby."

"I'm sorry too, Garrison. Sorry for you."

"But you'll forgive me, won't you?"

She narrowed her eyes. "As a Christian woman, I have to forgive you. But as your grandma's good friend, I do not have to like it." She turned to walk away. "No," she repeated, "I do *not* have to like it!"

After getting a new cell phone number the next morning, Garrison stopped by Mr. Miller's office, explaining his need to get to Seattle. "I promised to be on the job by the tenth and that's tomorrow. Is it okay if I do the two-week checkups today? It'll be a couple days early for some of them, but—"

"I don't think that's a problem. That is, if you feel confident you've found them all good homes."

"I honestly think I have. And if I can wrap this up, I'd really appreciate it." Then he remembered Harry. "Although one of the cats was only placed a couple days ago. That two-week check is a ways off and I'll be working in Seattle then."

"Hmm . . ." Mr. Miller wobbled a pencil back and forth between his fingers. "Maybe I could check on that one for you."

"Sure, I'd appreciate that." Garrison felt a wave of relief. The last thing he needed right now was to visit Harry and have that cat look longingly with those pale green eyes. He already missed Harry far more than he'd imagined possible. Almost as much as he missed Cara—although he was determined not to dwell on that. Onward and upward.

"The most important part of all this is the final visit. And that'll be up to you to do." Mr. Miller aimed his pencil at Garrison. "Only you can determine if the cats are properly settled—and it's your job to deliver the checks too."

"The deadline lands right before Christmas for five of the cats. Although Harry, the one I placed most recently . . . is later." Garrison frowned. "Does that mean I'll have to make a special trip from Seattle to check on him?"

"Hmm . . . I'm thinking out loud here . . . since that's the cat I'll be checking on next week, maybe we can bend the rules a little. If I decide that it's a good home, I'll recommend that you include that cat's final visit with the others. How's that sound?"

"That'd be great. That way everyone will get their bonuses before Christmas."

"Good. Now you email me your two-week report along with all the names and addresses of the new pet owners, and I'll have my assistant prepare a package for you. It'll be ready to pick up"—he paused to write this down—"on the twenty-fourth." He smiled at Garrison. "And you can have the pleasure of playing Santa Claus."

"Great."

"And just so you know I'll be leaving town on the twentieth. Taking the family on a ski vacation for Christmas. But Ellen will be here, although I told her she could leave early on Christmas Eve. So the sooner you get here, the sooner she can be on her way."

"I'll do what I can to leave work early that day," he assured him. Then they tied up a few more loose ends and, feeling satisfied that he was getting closer to having fulfilled his grandmother's final wishes, Garrison thanked the lawyer and left. Now all he needed to do was to make some quick visits to check on the cats.

He stopped by Vincent's house first. Vincent, wearing a checkered apron, was in his kitchen making cranberry-nut bread. Rusty was basking in the sunshine on a kitchen chair, watching his master it seemed.

"This is a recipe my wife liked to use," Vincent explained as he wiped his hands on the front of his apron. "I never tried it before myself, but for some reason I felt inspired today. Or maybe I was just hungry for it."

"How are you and Rusty getting along?" Garrison reached down to scratch the big orange cat's chin.

"Like a pair of old pals." Vincent grinned at the cat. "Two bachelors making the best of it."

"He appears happy and healthy." Garrison looked at

Vincent. "Also I wanted to let you know I'm heading back for Seattle this afternoon. Took the job there after all."

Vincent's smile faded. "You're leaving? So soon?"

"Yeah." He shrugged. "Gainful employment . . . so to speak."

"Well, you'll be missed around here."

Garrison nodded. "I really appreciate all the help you gave me on the house. Wish I could be around at payback time."

Vincent's brow creased. "No worries there. My finances aren't going to change."

Garrison wanted to disagree, but at the same time, he did not want to let the cat out of the bag. He smiled to himself at the appropriateness of that metaphor, then shook Vincent's hand and promised that he'd be back in time for Christmas.

Since Beth's house was only a few blocks away, he made that his next stop. Beth was in the midst of touching up an older woman's roots. Garrison, seeing that Spooky looked perfectly fine and was actually a bit more friendly than he recalled—or maybe Garrison's general opinion toward cats had changed—told Beth that he had no complaints. "Looks like Spooky has found herself a perfect home," he told her.

"I wish you could see Annabelle and Spooky together," Beth told him as he pulled his coat back on. "It's like they were made for each other." She smiled. "Thank you again!"

He told her about his house being on the market. "So if it sells, we'll have to figure out what to do with your furniture."

She waved her hand. "Who knows? Maybe the buyers will want to purchase the furnishings too. I wouldn't argue with that."

He told her he'd mention that to his agent, then promised to be back in touch shortly before Christmas.

Next he went to Riley and Sabrina's house to check on Oreo. He had no doubts that Oreo would be in good shape and, after Sabrina let him into the house, he knew the cat had fallen into a sweet little nest. "I just love him," she told Garrison as she cuddled the cat in her arms. "I don't know why I didn't think to get a cat ages ago." She rubbed her face into his. "Although I'm glad I waited for this one. He's really a darling."

Once again, Garrison made the speech about returning to do the final check at Christmastime, but before he got out the door, Sabrina stopped him. "I know it's none of my business," she said in a careful tone. "But I'm curious about what went wrong with you and Cara."

He gave her a puzzled look. "What do you mean?"

She shrugged. "I don't know . . . you guys just seemed like a good pair."

"Well . . . I . . . uh . . . I'm not sure what you're getting at."

"I just wondered what came between you two."

He frowned. "I guess it was David."

Her brows arched and he excused himself. "See you around Christmas," he called as he hurried out.

As he drove around the block to David's house he was curious. Why had Sabrina said that? Did she know something he didn't? And, if so, what was it? Glancing at Cara's house, he noticed the car missing from her driveway, then remembered how she worked in the city on Mondays. Probably for the best.

He tried to bury any resentment he felt toward David as he knocked on the door. This was not about Garrison—this was about a cat. Muzzy, to be specific. David was perfectly courteous and, once again, Garrison felt completely reassured that another cat had landed in the perfect home. Perfect for Muzzy and perfect for Jackson. And, unless Garrison was imagining things, Jackson's social skills were improving too. He thanked David and reminded him that he'd do the final check right before Christmas. As he got back into his car, he did not allow his eyes to wander over to the gingerbread house. Best not to look back.

The last one on his list was Viola, although he knew there was really no reason to check on that cat. She was perfectly happy with Ruby. However, he wanted a second chance to make things right with one of Gram's dearest friends—a woman who'd been like an aunt to him. But before he knocked on her back door, he made one last check on the house and put his bags into the back of the Pontiac. His plan was to be on the road by two.

Ruby scowled darkly as she let him into her kitchen. "I s'pose you're here to check on Viola," she said in a grumpy voice. "As if I don't know how to take care of my own cat by now."

"I had no doubts about that," he assured her. "I was more interested in seeing you. I'm sorry to find you in such bad spirits. Are you still mad at me?"

She rolled her eyes. "The world does not turn around you, Garrison Brown."

He blinked. "No, I didn't think it did."

"If you must know, I'm out of sorts over Elliott."

"Elliott? What's he done?"

"He's done left."

"Left?"

"That's right. Took off in the middle of the night. Not so much as a fare-thee-well from that ungrateful boy's lips."

"Ruby . . . I'm sorry." He put a hand on her shoulder.

"Oh, Garrison." She broke into sobs and he wrapped his arms around her. "I had such hopes for that boy. Seemed like he was really connecting with you."

"I'm sorry, Ruby." His voice choked. "I feel this is partly my fault."

She stepped back, fishing a tissue from her sleeve and wiping her nose. "No, no, that's not fair. I'm not blaming you for my grandson's bad choices." She looked intently into his eyes. "You are only responsible for your own bad choices, boy."

He nodded glumly. "That's true."

"You see to it that you don't make any more bad choices—you hear Ruby now?"

"Yes. I hear." He kissed her cheek. "And you and Viola take care. I'll see you at Christmas."

She brightened a little. "Oh yeah, that's right—you bringing me my million dollars to go with that cat, right?" She laughed like she knew that was never happening.

"I wish I could do that," he told her. "I'm sure you'd put it to good use."

Her chin bobbed up and down with strength. "You got that right. First of all I'd buy that house next door and turn it into a halfway house."

He grinned. "I'll bet you would."

As they hugged again, he promised to pray for Elliott and she promised to fix him another chicken pot pie the next time he came home. And then he got into the Pontiac and headed north to Seattle.

14

There had been a time when Garrison had loved being in Seattle. The photogenic landscape of mountains and water and sky had never failed to energize him, and the beat of the city had always filled him with enthusiasm and high expectations. But something had changed . . . and he didn't think it was Seattle.

To be fair, the grim, gray weather was not helping any. But Garrison tried to remain focused on his new job, his new boss, and the possibility of moving into a new apartment—when Gram's house sold. According to Barb, it could happen any day now.

"My first open house was a huge success," she'd told him shortly after he'd returned to Seattle. "I ran it on both Saturday and Sunday. And I had more than thirty people go through."

"Thirty?"

"Well, certainly some of them were Looky-Lous and some were just your curious neighbors wanting to see what you'd done with the place. But there were at least two families who were seriously shopping for a home. And, oh my, you should see how fabulous Felicia has made your house look. You probably wouldn't recognize it. I've got all the real estate agents in town coming through on Thursday. I wouldn't be surprised if we got an offer even before Christmas."

"Really?" He felt a mixture of anxiety and hope. On one hand, he wasn't ready to let go . . . on the other hand he had no choice.

By the end of his second week back in Seattle, Garrison felt so blue that he wondered if he was coming down with something. Or maybe his malaria was flaring up. But his temperature registered normal. And besides feeling gloomy and weary, he had no real symptoms. Telling himself it was simply the cold, wet weather getting him down, he jogged through the company parking lot and jumped into the Pontiac. Within minutes he was headed down the freeway. His hope was to reach the Miller law firm before three o'clock to pick up the packet. He knew that Mr. Miller had been out of the office most of the week and that his assistant planned to close early. Garrison had promised to get there before she locked up.

As he drove south, he tried not to think of what kind of a Christmas he would have this year—certainly not a traditional one. But, to be fair, his past nine Christmases in Uganda had not been traditional either. Yet they had been sweet . . . and genuine . . . filled with good-hearted people.

He turned the radio on, tuning to a station that was playing nothing but Christmas songs, and before long he started feeling cheery. After all, he was about to play Santa Claus in a very real sort of way. Handing out sizeable checks to some very decent folks—what could be better? He tried to imagine their surprised faces. Hopefully they'd be surprised. He remembered the million-dollar cat rumor that Ruby had mentioned. Surely no one had taken that seriously.

It was two-thirty when he pulled into the nearly empty parking lot in front of the law office. Pulling his trench coat over his head to block the rain, he ran up to the front door and, since it was locked, banged desperately on it. Surely the assistant hadn't gone home already.

"Sorry," she said as she let him into the foyer. "I'm supposed to lock the door when I'm the only one here." She thrust a large white envelope toward him. "The checks and everything are in here."

He thanked her and wished her Merry Christmas, then ran back out to his car. His plan was to go to Gram's house first. He'd dump his stuff, nuke a microwave meal, then be off to play Santa. But when he drove up to Gram's house, he almost didn't recognize it. First of all, the house was decorated with strings of delicate white lights. And in the front window stood a tall tree, which was lit up as well. Flanking the front door, which had been painted a nice brick red, was a pair of small evergreen trees in shiny red pots. They too were strung with white lights. On the door was a large evergreen wreath with a big plaid bow. Even though he knew that the house was vacant, he couldn't remember when it had ever looked this inviting. So inviting that he entered the house through the front door instead of the back.

Barb was right—he didn't recognize the place. And yet he did. It was the house he'd left behind, only better. It looked

so good that he suddenly felt ill at ease, like he was a tres-
passer. Perhaps he shouldn't be staying there. Just to be sure
he called Barb, interrupting her from what sounded like a
boisterous Christmas party. He quickly explained and she
just laughed.

"Of course you can stay there, darling! It's your house.
And, just so you know, most of the agents will be enjoying a
break for the next few days. So just make yourself at home and
don't worry about messing anything up. Felicia's people will
put it all back together. Just enjoy—and Merry Christmas!"

Feeling more relaxed, he dumped his bag in his room,
which had also had a facelift. Everything looked amazing.
And yet . . . something felt wrong. Something was missing. He
glanced around the living room as he headed to the kitchen.
Oh yeah . . . no cats. Of course, this simply reminded him
of the mission that lay ahead. After putting away a Hungry
Man meal, he opened the white envelope and discovered six
big checks held together with a paper clip. "Here comes Santa
Claus," he said as he slipped them into the inside pocket of
his trench coat. Then, feeling unexpectedly merry, he sang
the rest of the verse as he crossed the two driveways, hurrying
through what was turning into freezing rain, and knocked
on Ruby's back door.

"Come in, come in," she called out. "Get yourself outta
that cold."

"Merry Christmas, Ruby!" He hugged her tightly.

She returned the greeting, beaming up at him. "I got good
news for you."

"What's that?"

"Elliott came back."

"He's here?"

"Not right this minute. He just took off to the store for me. But I expect him back soon." Her face lit up with a huge smile. "Thank you for praying for him. I know you did."

He nodded, reaching into his pocket for the envelope he'd stuck in front. "I sure did. And now I have something for you. Merry Christmas, Ruby."

She fingered the long white envelope with a twinkle in her eye.

"It's not a million dollars," he said quickly.

She laughed. "I didn't think it was."

"But it's from my grandmother. It's for adopting Viola." He glanced around. "How is she?"

Ruby led him to her living room where she had a nice fire burning in the fireplace. "Queen Viola," she proclaimed as she pointed to the beautiful gray cat curled up on a purple velvet cushion. Viola looked up at him with languid green eyes.

He chuckled. "She does look like a queen."

Ruby was opening the envelope. He waited anxiously, hoping that she wouldn't be disappointed. That whole million-dollar-cat story was irritating. But Ruby let out a shriek of delight. "What in tarnation!" She stared at him with big brown eyes. "Is this for real, Garrison Brown? Surely you wouldn't jest with an old woman!"

"It's for real. Merry Christmas. And thanks for taking such good care of Viola."

She hugged him again. "God bless your grandma, Garrison. And God bless you!"

"Now I have some more deliveries to make."

She looked shocked. "Every cat is getting a check?"

He pressed his forefinger to his lips. "Mum's the word, okay?"

She nodded solemnly. He kissed her cheek and patted Viola's head, then made a quick exit. Chuckling to himself, he got into the car. This wasn't so bad!

Next stop was Beth and Annabelle's house. Hopefully they were still home since Beth had mentioned a party they were invited to. He'd called ahead earlier in the week, careful not to tip his hand, but letting them know he would be in town and wanted to make his final visit today. To his relief they were both home and, after checking on Spooky, who seemed perfectly content, he presented them both with the check. The house was filled with squeals of happiness as mother and daughter hugged each other—and then him—dancing around like they'd won the lottery.

Annabelle had Spooky in her arms as he was leaving, gently stroking her. She spoke soothingly in an attempt to calm the cat, who'd been startled by the uproar.

"Merry Christmas," he called out again. "God bless!"

As he got into the car, he realized that the freezing rain was turning into snow. If this kept up they might actually have a white Christmas. Or at least a whitish Christmas. With wipers running, and remembering how unpredictable the Pontiac could be on slick surfaces, he carefully turned the corner and drove down the street to Vincent's house.

To Garrison's surprise and relief, Vincent was not alone on Christmas Eve. "Come in, my friend," Vincent said merrily. Dressed in a cheerful red vest, he nodded toward the living room where several people his age were visiting. "A few of my other friends are here." He held up a small silver cup. "Can I interest you in some eggnog?"

"That sounds good." Garrison slipped off his coat and shook off the snow. "Did you know it's snowing outside?"

"Snow!" Vincent called out to his friends and they let out a cheer.

"How is Rusty?" Garrison asked.

"He's the life of the party." Vincent handed him a cup, nodding toward the living room where a gray-haired woman had the cat on her lap. "He's eating it up." Vincent chuckled. "And how are you? How is Seattle?"

Garrison forced a smile. "Okay." He held out the envelope. "This is a little thank-you from my grandmother—for giving Rusty such a nice home."

Vincent's brows drew together. "What?"

"Open it."

Vincent slowly opened the envelope and removed the check. With wide eyes, he looked at Garrison. "Is this for real?"

Garrison nodded. "Maybe it'll help you with some of those household repairs you've been putting off."

"Oh, my." Vincent's eyes were filled with tears. "I don't know what to say."

"How about *Merry Christmas*?" Garrison set his empty eggnog cup on the dining table and smiled. "Now, if you'll excuse me, I've got a few more deliveries to make before we're all snowed in."

Vincent continued thanking him as he walked him to the door, finally insisting on embracing Garrison before he could leave. Warmed by the eggnog and the gratitude, Garrison proceeded on through the storm. Who knew Christmas could be this much fun? Next stop was Riley and Sabrina's house. Riley answered the door, welcoming him into the house. "What a night, eh?"

"Yeah." Garrison could see that the couple was all dressed up. "Looks like you two are going out?"

Melody Carlson

"A party at my sister's," Sabrina said with a frown. "Don't get me wrong—I love my sister dearly."

"It's just that she's got three kids under the age of four," Riley explained. "It gets pretty loud."

"Especially tonight." Sabrina pointed to a couple of heaping bags by the door. They were filled with brightly wrapped gifts. "My family always opens on Christmas Eve. It'll be a madhouse."

"At least we can leave," Riley reminded her.

She nodded with a relieved expression. "I know you want to check on Oreo." She glanced over her shoulder. "Last I saw him he was playing with his jingle-bell mouse in the kitchen." She called out, "Here, kitty-kitty," and the black-and-white cat came running. "There's my baby." She bent down to scoop him up. "Mommy and Daddy won't be gone long, sweetheart," she cooed into his happy-looking face. "Be thankful we're not taking you with us. Bentley would probably just jerk you by the tail." She made an exasperated look. "My sister's middle child is in his terrible twos."

Garrison reached over to stroke Oreo's head then reached into his coat pocket. "This is a little thank-you from my grandmother," he told them as he handed it to Riley. "For giving Oreo such a good home."

"What?" Sabrina's eyes grew wide. "Don't tell me that rumor about the million-dollar cat is true?"

Garrison laughed. "No. That is only a rumor. Sorry." He nodded to Riley. "Go ahead and open it."

"Ten thousand dollars?" Riley looked genuinely shocked. "Am I being punked?"

"No." Garrison laughed harder. "This is real. Merry Christmas."

155

"For taking in a cat?" Riley said. "For real?"

"Not just any cat," Sabrina reminded him. "This is a very special cat."

Riley grinned at her. "I'll say. He is one very special cat." He vigorously shook Garrison's hand. "Thanks, bro!"

Garrison made his exit and then, bracing himself for the next stop, he drove toward David and Jackson's house. The reason he was dreading this visit was because of Cara. He was determined not to look at her house. Just deliver the check and continue on his way. End of story.

Jackson answered the door. "Dad's in the kitchen," he said without too much discomfort.

"How about Muzzy?" Garrison asked. "Where's she?"

"In here." Jackson led Garrison into the living room where Muzzy was sitting beneath a tall, glittering Christmas tree. "She likes to whack the ornaments. I put the ones that break up high so she can't reach."

"Good for you." Garrison kneeled down to pet Muzzy. "You're still a gorgeous girl," he said. She let out several loud meows as if to confirm this.

"Are you staying for Christmas?" Jackson asked.

"No. I just came to drop something by for your dad."

"Garrison," David exclaimed as he came into the living room. "How are you doing?"

"Great." Garrison stood and shook his hand. "Looks like Muzzy is just fine."

David nodded. "Yep. No problems."

Garrison reached into his pocket for the envelope, handing it to David. "This is a thank-you from my grandmother—for taking in Muzzy."

"Huh?" David studied the envelope.

"Go ahead," Garrison encouraged. Reaching over to ruffle Jackson's curly hair, he added, "It's for both of you."

"No way." David held the check in the air. "Are you kidding me?"

Garrison shook his head.

"Wow." David stared at the check. "I'm stunned."

"Merry Christmas," Garrison said, turning to leave.

"So do you have plans for Christmas?" David asked suddenly.

"Well, I—"

"Dad is cooking turkey," Jackson said with enthusiasm. "Cara is coming too."

At the name *Cara*, Garrison froze. "I need to go see someone," he said awkwardly. "But thanks for the invite."

"Sure." David still looked shocked as he held the check in his hand. "And thanks for this."

Garrison gulped in the cold air outside, trying to forget what they'd just said . . . that Cara was spending Christmas with them. Well, of course, she was. Why shouldn't she? Without looking over toward the gingerbread house, he climbed back into the Pontiac. One last stop—and it was only a few blocks away—and then he could go home . . . to his lovely but lonely house.

15

The Maxwells' place was easy to spot—even from a couple blocks away. With so many strings of lights on their house, Garrison hated to imagine their electric bill next month. Maybe this check would help. His plan was to get in and get out ASAP. The less interaction with Handsome Harry, the better. Just the thought of looking into those pale green eyes was unnerving. In and out—and then go home.

"Hello?" A tall, sandy-haired woman answered the door. Behind her was the sound of jarring music, a video game that was turned too loud, and, in Garrison's opinion, total turmoil. "Can I help you?"

"Are you Mrs. Maxwell?" he asked, hoping that he'd come to the wrong house.

"Yes. Do I know you?"

He quickly introduced himself. "I'm the one who gave Harry to your husband a few weeks ago."

"Harry?" she said absently.

"*A large Maine Coon cat*," he said with growing concern. "About three weeks ago."

"Oh, you mean Snoop-Cat."

"Snoop-Cat?" Garrison was confused—and irritated.

"Well, his name was Harry when he got here," she said. "But TJ—that's my oldest—he decided to name him Snoop-Cat. Cute huh?"

Controlling himself, he made a stiff smile. "So, is he—is Snoop-Cat here?"

She gave him a puzzled look. "Sorry, he's not."

"He's not here?"

"No." She grimly shook her head. "Truth is we haven't seen him for—TJ," she yelled loudly, "when was the last time you saw Snoop-Cat?"

A preadolescent boy wearing braces came to the door, examining Garrison with a dull expression. "Huh?"

"Snoop-Cat. When did you last see him?"

"I dunno. Awhile back. Last week maybe."

"Last week?" Garrison felt a wave of panic. "Where did he go?"

"Who knows?" She tipped her head to the chaos going on behind her. "I can barely keep track of these kids—and then their friends come over—honestly, does this look like a house that could keep track of a cat?"

"So you have no idea where Harry went?" Garrison demanded.

The woman rolled her eyes. "God only knows why Tom thought we needed a cat. I thought he'd lost his mind."

"Dad got us the cat to get the money," TJ told her. "Remember?"

She laughed sarcastically. "Oh yeah. That's right. Tommy Boy got it into his head that he was taking in a million-dollar cat." She fixed her eyes on Garrison with an alarmed expression. "That wasn't true, was it?"

"No, no, of course not. Please, excuse me," he said quickly. "I've got to go."

"Wait a minute—was it true?" She followed him out to the porch. "Please, tell me it wasn't true." As Garrison hurried through the fast-falling snow, he could still hear the woman yelling, telling her son how she was going to "kill Tom when he got home."

Inside the protection of the car, Garrison thought about Harry. Good grief, who could blame the poor cat from running away from that madhouse? Garrison would've hit the trail too. But where would Harry have run to? He hadn't gone home. Garrison was sure of that. He'd been through the house. And he'd been to see Ruby—surely she would have told him if Harry had come back.

Garrison put down all the windows of his car, slowly cruising through the neighborhood, calling out Harry's name over and over. Okay, he knew this was ridiculous. How likely was it that Harry would be out roaming the streets in weather like this? Or would he? Garrison drove all around, going down every street and even a few alleys until he got worried that he might be disturbing some of the neighbors.

Fearful that Harry had been injured somehow, he pulled over and got out his phone, dialing information and getting the numbers of the local veterinarians. He called each of them, inquiring about missing Maine Coon cats whenever a live person answered and leaving a message with his number when they didn't. Wherever Harry was—Garrison was determined to find him.

With the windows open, snow had blown into the car and, despite the heater running full bore, Garrison was chilled to the bone. "Oh, Harry," he said desperately as he turned toward Gram's house, "please, come home, old boy. I'm sorry I gave you to those horrid people. I didn't know they were like that." And then, although he knew some would declare it wrong to pray for an animal—he didn't care what they thought—he shot up an earnest prayer on Harry's behalf. He made no apologies as he begged God to keep his furry friend safe and to bring him home.

He parked the Pontiac in the driveway and cranked up all the windows. Then, since he was already cold and wet, he did a quick trip around the perimeter of the house, calling out Harry's name. He even checked in Gram's garden shed. But no Harry.

Feeling like he'd lost his best friend, Garrison went back into the house and peeled off his wet coat, hanging it by the kitchen door. Then, remembering the check, he removed it from his coat pocket. It would need to be returned to Mr. Miller.

Thinking of Gram's MIA attorney was troubling. How was it possible that Mr. Miller had totally forgotten the "surprise visit" to the Maxwells'? Garrison knew that if Mr. Miller had gone as promised, he never would have approved that family. Indeed, if he'd gone, he likely would have discovered Harry was missing back then.

Garrison was just putting the check back in the large white envelope when he realized there was a slender folder inside. He pulled it out to discover it contained the title to the house and a couple of envelopes. He recognized Gram's lacy handwriting on the first envelope. Feeling a lump in his throat—and as if he'd let her down—he slowly opened it, removing several pages of fine stationery.

Dear Garrison,

If you are reading this, I must be departed to my heavenly home. I felt rather certain that my time was near. For that reason I've met with Mr. Miller, but you must know that by now. First of all, my dear boy, I want to tell you how much I love you. I fear that you may temporarily misinterpret my devotion to you because of my desire to find my cats good homes. So I want you to know that, along with my dear husband and son, you have been one of the loves of my life. You may not know how lost I felt when you came to me. I was grieving for your grandfather and for leaving Kenya. And then I was grieving for your father. But you brought life back to me. Your youth and energy forced me to participate in the community. I got involved in your school and church and the neighborhood. You, my dear boy, brought me back to life.

But when you went back east to college, I felt a bit lost again. I missed you more than you will ever know and I did not want you to know. That is when I got a cat. Genevieve was a wonderful companion to me. I was aware of your allergies and I knew I'd willingly find the dear cat a new home if you chose to come back, but I suspected that you would not. Then, when you went to Uganda (which made me so happy) I got another cat. Well, you know how this story goes. One good cat led to another. But I never went out looking for them. No, they came to me. And while you were so far away, they were my family.

Because you are reading this I know that you have successfully found good homes for all six of my "children." I thank you for that, Garrison. You may have guessed that one part of my plan was to keep you in your old neighborhood for a spell. I hoped that you might reconnect and perhaps even discover where it is the Good Lord is leading you next. I have to say that you've sounded a bit lost in our phone conversations. But I understand that. I felt lost too.

Now, lest you think I loved my cats more than I loved you, you will find another envelope in this package that Mr. Miller has prepared in the event of my demise. In that package you will find the title to my house and a check for the remainder of my inheritance. As you can see, you are receiving a much greater portion than the kitties. I know that you will use the money wisely—to help yourself and your fellow man. I pray that it will be a blessing and not a curse. Most of all I pray that you will find someone as dear to you as your grandfather was to me. It is hard to go this life alone. But if you must, perhaps you should get yourself a dog.

Always remember that your heavenly Father and your grandmother are watching over you, dear Garrison.

All my love,
Gram

With tears in his eyes, Garrison opened up the last envelope and removed a cashier's check. He stared at the figure, then, blinking to clear his eyes, he looked again. No, he was not a millionaire, but it was more money than Garrison could possibly earn in ten years. He shook his head in disbelief. But as he slid the check back into the envelope he felt unworthy of it. After all, it was his fault that one of Gram's beloved cats was missing. Sure, he knew she would understand and forgive him. She'd have to forgive her attorney too. As did Garrison.

Even so, Garrison wasn't sure he could forgive himself. How had he been so shortsighted? Why hadn't he investigated the Maxwells more carefully on that first day? And why had he left Harry—of all the cats—with what appeared to be a "gold digging" family? Poor Harry!

Still feeling chilled and blue, he went into the living room, and seeing that some birch logs were laid in the fireplace, probably for show, he struck a long match to light them, watching as the papery bark slowly caught fire. And not wanting to turn on the lights, he decided to light the candles along the mantel as well. It seemed a little silly to light candles with no one else around to enjoy them, but he hoped that it would put him in a better Christmas spirit.

In an attempt to distract himself from obsessing over Harry, he tried to focus his attention on the changes Barb had made to the house. Really, it was amazing, and perfect for Christmas, even if it was an illusion. The house truly looked festive—as if it should be hosting friends gathering around food with Christmas tunes playing in the background. He wished he could feel as festive as his surroundings looked.

He tried to recall the happy faces he'd witnessed while delivering the unexpected checks around the neighborhood. Surely his stint as "Santa" should be enough to erase the

Christmas Scrooge feelings that were darkening his heart. He reminded himself of his own check. Anyone else receiving a windfall like that would probably be over the moon.

He held his hands over the crackling flames, remembering Gram's sweet letter and how she'd wanted him to know how much she loved him. Okay, that warmed his heart. No denying it. But thinking of Gram reminded him of the cats . . . and how he'd let her down. How he'd let Harry down. Suddenly he felt blue again.

He could hear car doors closing out front. Glancing out, he watched as several people got out and hurried up to Ruby's house. She always hosted Christmas for her relatives, packing them into her little house and stuffing them with all the good foods she'd been preparing for days. Ruby had always included Gram and him as well, and he knew he would be welcome there tonight. He also knew he was in no condition to put on his game face and make small talk. Better to just lay low.

If he got hungry, he could nuke another microwave meal. He'd probably go to bed early and try to sleep. Perhaps he'd hear from one of the veterinarians tomorrow. If not, he would post "missing cat" signs all over town. He'd even offer a generous reward. That should help stir things up.

He was just heading for the kitchen when he heard the doorbell. Had one of Ruby's guests mistaken this house for hers? He hurried to open it, ready to redirect them next door, when to his surprise he saw Cara. With her bright red scarf circling her neck and white lacy flakes falling on her dark hair, she was truly a vision. For a moment he almost thought he was halucinating. But it was what she held in her arms that made him blink twice. Was this for real?

"Harry!" he exclaimed, reaching for the long-lost cat. "It's you!"

"Hello, Garrison," Cara said with an uneasy expression.

"Cara, hello! You found Harry!"

"Yes."

"Harry, old boy." Garrison held the cat close, looking down into his face. "I was so worried about you. I looked all over the neighborhood. I'm so glad you're okay." Suddenly he looked back at Cara. "I'm sorry. Do you want to come in?"

"Sure, if you don't mind."

"Not at all." He opened the door wide. "Come in and get warm. I even made a fire." He closed the door and set Harry down, then took her coat and led her to the fireplace.

"The house looks great," she said quietly.

"Yeah. Do you want to see the whole thing? I can turn the lights on and—"

"I've actually seen it already," she confessed. "I slipped in while your real estate agent was doing the open house."

"Right . . ." Garrison bent down and picked up Harry again. "I can't believe you found him, Cara. How did you? Where did you? When did you?"

"One question at a time," she said patiently. "I was on one of my regular afternoon walks several days ago. I was passing a vacant house on Washington Street—you know that old Victorian that's in really bad shape?"

"Yeah. The old Brinson place."

"Anyway I thought I saw a cat on the porch. I thought that was weird since no one lived there. And, as you know, I've been wanting a cat. As I walked up to the porch, I thought it was probably a feral cat because it looked kind of matted and straggly and wet, but it had been raining. I called out 'here, kitty-kitty' and it came running toward me. At first I was kind of worried—what if it had rabies or something? Then I looked into those green eyes and I thought it looked just like Harry, but I didn't think that was possible."

"Wow . . . amazing . . ."

"Anyway I took him home and dried him off and fed him. He was really hungry." She shrugged. "He's been with me ever since."

"When did you figure out it was Harry?"

"I tried to tell myself it wasn't really Harry," she said a bit sheepishly. "Like maybe he was Harry's long-lost brother, you know?"

"Uh-huh . . ." He scratched Harry's chin.

"But then I called him by his name—Harry." She made a sad smile. "And he came running. I knew then."

"Really? He came to you, just like that?"

"I tried to call you, Garrison. I tried your cell phone and the phone here at the house. But they were both out of service."

He explained that he'd changed numbers.

"And the reason I sneaked into the open house was to ask your agent how to reach you. But she was talking with a couple who looked like serious buyers and I didn't want to distract her." She frowned. "I was pretty disappointed when I saw the For Sale sign, Garrison. Didn't see that one coming."

"I'm thinking about taking that sign down," he confessed.

She looked surprised. "Anyway, when I went over to David's tonight, I heard that you'd been by. Heard about the check you gave him." She smiled. "That was really generous. He can use it right now. Starting his home business has been a challenge."

"Well, that was my grandmother's doing. I was just the delivery boy."

"Anyway, I thought I'd better get Harry back to you."

"Thank you!" He explained about the Maxwells.

"That's terrible."

"Yeah. I would much rather have given Harry to you." He reminded her of the conditions of Gram's will. "If I could've I would've, Cara."

"That's okay. I understand." She pointed at him. "Hey, what about your allergies? Or have you already taken some medicine?"

He looked down at Harry. "No, I haven't taken anything today. But, you're right, I don't seem to be sneezing . . . yet . . ."

They both just stood by the crackling fire without speaking. Garrison didn't know what to say. But he wished he could think of a reason to entice her to stay. "Sorry I can't offer you any Christmas goodies . . . I haven't even been to the store yet."

"That's okay. I should get back to David's. Besides, you probably have something to do . . . I mean, for Christmas Eve."

"No, no, not really." He could feel Harry getting restless in his arms and so he set him back down, watching as the handsome cat sauntered around, exploring the room with feline interest.

"But, um, before I go," she spoke slowly, "I'd like to ask you a question."

"Go for it." He folded his arms across his chest, studying her closely. He wanted to memorize the curve of her cheek, the way her dark eyes sparkled in the firelight, the fullness of her lips, the way she tipped her head to one side as she spoke.

"Okay . . . so I just want to know, Garrison Brown—why didn't you tell me goodbye?"

"Goodbye?"

"Yeah, you left here without even telling me you were going. And, call me stupid, but I thought we were friends."

"We were friends," he declared. "I mean, we *are* friends. Aren't we?"

"I guess. But, well . . . I just thought we had, uh, maybe something more. *You know?*" Her eyes narrowed with uncertainty. "But I must've been wrong. Otherwise you wouldn't have taken off like that—without a word."

"I thought you and David were a couple," he said abruptly.

"Me and David?" Her brow creased. *"Seriously?"*

"Yeah." He nodded sincerely. "You went to that Christmas party with him and—"

"I had agreed to do that a couple weeks before I even knew you, Garrison. In fact, I'm pretty sure I told you about it. David had this big fancy work-related party to attend and he didn't want to go stag. It was nothing. Absolutely nothing."

"What about the Christmas parade? You and David and Jackson together—you all looked pretty cozy, just like a happy little family."

She let out an exasperated sigh. "I had offered to take Jackson to the parade because David couldn't. It was going to be just Jackson and me and Santa Claus. David was tied up with a client coming by his house to look at something. Then his client was a no-show and David surprised me with coffee. You were there, you saw it."

"I saw it . . . but I guess I misunderstood," he admitted. Had he really been that off base, that thickheaded—to put a completely wrong spin on everything? "But what about tonight?" he said suddenly.

"Tonight?" She ran her hands down the sides of her dress,

a crinkly, cranberry-colored velveteen that was very pretty on her. She slipped her hands into pockets, waiting for him to explain himself.

"You're going to spend Christmas Eve with David and Jackson. I know it because they both told me. David is cooking a turkey. And you should probably be there with them right now." He proclaimed this like *"Aha, I got you!"* Although he'd never wanted anything less.

"Yes, I probably should be there right now," she confessed. "Along with a couple dozen other people."

"A couple dozen?" Garrison felt an irrational rush of hope. "So David's having a dinner party?"

"That's right. A potluck actually. Mostly people from the neighborhood. Some that you know as a matter of fact. Beth and Annabelle are coming. So are Sabrina and Riley—as soon as she can extract herself from her sister's house."

"Interesting . . ." Really interesting.

"So do you want to go with me or not?" she demanded playfully. "The food should be good—a lot better than your microwave meal. I made a big ol' pan of real mac and cheese—used three cheeses."

"Yeah, sure. Sounds great." He nodded in disbelief. "But, by *going with you* . . . do you mean kind of like a date?"

Her eyes twinkled merrily. "Kinda like that."

"Okay!"

"But not so fast, Mr. Brown." She pulled what looked like a small piece of a plant from her pocket. Was it from the poinsettia? She dangled it in front of him.

"What's that?" he asked.

She held it over her head. "Mistletoe."

He grinned with realization. "You mean . . . ?"

"Oh yeah . . ." She leaned forward with an expectant expression.

Garrison took in a quick breath, then leaned down toward her and, gazing into her eyes, he kissed her—and she definitely kissed him back! When they finally stepped away, he could feel the room spinning around him.

"Merry Christmas, Garrison," she whispered.

"Yeah," he said in a husky voice. *"Merry Christmas!"*

The Christmas Dog

1

As Betty Kowalski drove home from church on Sunday, she realized she was guilty of two sins. First of all, she felt envious—perhaps even lustful—of Marsha Deerwood's new leather jacket. But, in Betty's defense, the coat was exquisite. A three-quarter-length jacket, it was beautifully cut, constructed of a dove-gray lambskin, and softer than homemade butter. Betty knew this for a fact since she had touched the sleeve of Marsha's jacket and audibly sighed just as Pastor Gordon had invited the congregation to rise and bow their heads in prayer.

"It's an early anniversary present from Jim," Marsha had whispered after the pastor proclaimed a hearty "Amen." As usual, the two old friends sat together in the third pew from the front. On Marsha's other side, next to the aisle so he could help with the collection plates, sat Marsha's husband, James Deerwood, a recently retired physician and respected member of the congregation.

Naturally Betty didn't show even the slightest sign of jealousy. Years of practice made this small performance no great challenge. Instead, Betty simply smiled, complimented Marsha on the lovely garment, and pretended not to notice the worn cuffs of her own winter coat, a charcoal-colored

Harris Tweed that had served her well for several decades now. Still, it was classic and timeless, and a new silk scarf or a pair of sleek leather gloves might dress it up a bit. Not that she could afford such little luxuries right now. Besides, she did not care to dwell on such superficialities (especially during the service). Nor would she want anyone to suspect how thoughts such as these distracted her while Pastor Gordon preached with such fiery intensity about the necessity of loving one's neighbors today. He even pounded his fist on the pulpit a couple of times, something the congregation rarely witnessed in their small, dignified church.

But now, as Betty drove her old car toward her neighborhood, she was mindful of Pastor Gordon's words. And thus she became cognizant of her second sin. Not only did Betty *not* love her neighbor, she was afraid that she hated him wholeheartedly. But then again, she reminded herself, it wasn't as if Jack Jones lived *right* next to her. He wasn't her *next-door* neighbor. Not that it made much difference, since only a decrepit cedar fence separated their backyards. It was, in fact, that rotten old fence that had started their dispute in the first place.

"This fence is encroaching on my property," Jack had said to her in October. She'd been peacefully minding her own business, enjoying the crisp sunny day as she raked leaves in her backyard.

"What do you mean?" She set her bamboo rake aside and went over to hear him better, which wasn't easy since his music, as usual, was blaring.

"I mean I've studied the property lines in our neighborhood, and that fence is at least eight feet into my yard," he said.

"That fence is on your property line, fair and square." She looked him straight in the eyes. "It's the public access strip that's—"

"No way!" He pointed toward the neighboring yards where the public access strip had been split right down the middle. "See what I mean? Your yard has encroached over the whole public access strip and—"

"Excuse me," she said, shaking her finger at him like he was in grade school. "But the original owners agreed to build that fence right where it is. No one has encroached on anyone."

He rubbed his hand through his straggly dark hair, jutted out his unshaved chin, narrowed his eyes. "It's over the line, lady."

Betty did not like being called "lady." But instead of losing her temper, she pressed her lips together tightly and mentally counted to ten.

"And it's falling down," he added.

"Well," she retorted, "since it's on your property, I suggest you fix it." As she turned and walked away, she felt certain that he increased the volume on his music just to spite her. It seemed clear the battle lines were drawn.

Fortunately, the weather turned cold after that. Consequently, Betty no longer cared to spend time in her backyard, and her windows remained tightly closed to shut out Jack's noise and music.

Now Betty tightened her grip on the steering wheel, keeping her gaze straight ahead as she drove down Persimmon

Lane, the street on which Jack lived. She did not want that insufferable young man to observe her looking his way. Although it was hard *not* to stare at the run-down house with the filthy red pickup truck parked right on the front lawn. Obviously, the old vehicle couldn't be parked in the driveway. That space was buried in a mountain of junk covered with ugly blue tarps, which were anchored with old plastic milk bottles. She assumed the bottles were filled with dirty water, although another neighbor (who suspected their young neighbor was up to no good) had suggested the mysterious brown liquid in the containers might be a toxic chemical used in the manufacturing of some kind of illegal drugs.

Betty sighed and continued her attempt to avert her gaze as she slowed down for the intersection of her street, Nutmeg Lane. But despite her resolve, she glanced sideways and let out a loud groan. Oh, to think that the Spencer house had once been the prettiest home in the neighborhood!

As she turned the corner, she remembered how that house used to look. For years it had been painted a lovely sky blue with clean white trim, and the weed-free lawn had always been neatly cut and perfectly edged. The flower beds had bloomed profusely with annuals and perennials, and Gladys Spencer's roses had even won prizes at the county fair. Who ever would've guessed it would come to this?

The original owners, Al and Gladys Spencer, had taken great pride in their home. And they had been excellent neighbors and wonderful friends for decades. But over the past five years, the elderly couple had suffered a variety of serious health problems. Gladys had gone into a nursing home, then

Al had followed her, and eventually they both passed away within months of each other. The house had sat vacant for a few years.

Then, out of the blue, this Jack character had shown up and taken over. Without saying a word to anyone, he began tearing into the house as if he was intent on destroying it. And even when well-meaning neighbors tried to meet him or find out who he was, he made it perfectly clear that he had absolutely no interest in speaking to any of them. He was a rude young man and didn't care who knew it.

As Betty pulled into her own driveway, she wondered not for the first time if Jack Jones actually owned that house. No one had ever seen a For Sale sign go up. And no one had witnessed a moving van arrive. Her secret suspicion was that Jack Jones was a squatter.

It had been late last summer when this obnoxious upstart took occupancy of the house, and according to Penny Horton, the retired schoolteacher who lived next door, the scruffy character had brought only a duffle bag and three large plastic crates with him. But the next day, without so much as a howdy-do, he began tearing the house apart. Penny, who was currently in Costa Rica, was the one who informed Betty of the young man's name, and only because she discovered a piece of his mail that had been delivered mistakenly to her mailbox. "It looked like something official," Penny had confided to Betty. "It seemed to be from the government. Do you suppose he's in the witness protection program?" *Or perhaps he's out on parole*, Betty had wanted to suggest, but had kept these thoughts to herself.

Out of concern, Betty had attempted to reach the Spencers' daughter, Donna, by calling the old number that was still in her little blue address book. But apparently that number had been changed, and the man who answered the phone had never heard of anyone by that name. Even when Betty called information, citing the last town she knew Donna had lived in, she came up empty-handed. So she gave up.

Betty frowned as she bent to open her old garage door. The wind was blowing bitter and cold now, and she had forgotten her wool gloves in the car but didn't want to go back for them. She didn't usually park in the garage, but the weatherman had predicted unusually low temperatures, and her car's battery was getting old. She gripped the cold metal handle on the single-car garage door and, not for the first time, longed for a garage-door opener—like the one Marsha and Jim had on their triple-car garage. One simply pushed the remote's button and the door magically went up, and once the car was inside, down the door went again. How she wished for one now.

Her grandmother's old saying went through her head as she struggled to hoist up the stubborn door. "If wishes were fishes, we'd all have a fry." Oh, yes, wouldn't she!

Betty shivered as she got back into her car. She still couldn't get that obnoxious neighbor out of her head—all thanks to this morning's sermon! But what was she supposed to do? How could she love someone so despicable? How was it even possible? Oh, she'd heard that with God all things were possible . . . but this?

She decided to commit the dilemma to prayer. She bowed

her head until it thumped the top of the steering wheel, asking God to help her love her loathsome neighbor and to give her the strength she lacked. "Amen," she said. Then she tried to focus her full attention on carefully navigating her old Buick forward into the snug garage, although she was still thinking about that thoughtless Jack Jones—if that was his real name.

The next thing she knew, she heard a loud scratching sound and realized she'd gotten too close to the right side of the garage door. She took in a sharp breath and quickly backed up, readjusted the wheel, and went forward again, but when she turned off her engine, she knew it was too late. The damage was done. And, really, wasn't this also Jack Jones's fault? He was a bad egg—and had probably been one from the very beginning.

As Betty sat there, unwilling to get out and see what the scrape on her car looked like, she replayed the man's list of faults. And they were many. Right from the start, he'd stepped on people's toes. With absolutely no consideration for his neighbors' ears or sleeping habits, he had used his noisy power tools in the middle of the night and played his music loudly during the day. Of course, these habits weren't quite so obnoxious when winter came and everyone kept their windows shut. But how many times had Betty gotten up for her late-night glass of milk only to observe strange lights and flashes going on behind Jack's closed blinds? Sometimes she worried that Jack's house was about to go up in flames, and perhaps the whole neighborhood along with it. She would ponder over what that madman could possibly be doing. And why did he need to do it at night? What if it was something immoral or illegal? For all she knew, Jack Jones could be a wanted felon who was creating bombs to blow up things like the county courthouse or even the grade school.

Betty removed her keys from the ignition and reached for her purse and Bible. She slowly got out of the car, and out of habit ever since that notorious Jack Jones had moved into the neighborhood, she securely locked her car's doors. Then she sat her purse and Bible on the hood of the car and peeked around the right side to see the front fender. The horizontal gash was about a foot long with a hook on one end, causing it, strangely enough, to resemble the letter J. Betty just shook her head. It figured . . . *J* for Jack.

So she continued to obsess over him—and over today's sermon and her futile prayer. How *was* it possible to love someone so completely disagreeable and inconsiderate and downright evil? She grunted as she struggled to lower the garage door. *Really*, she thought as she stood up straight, *even Pastor Gordon would be singing a different tune if he was forced to live next to Jack Jones.*

Betty let herself into the house, turning the deadbolt behind her—another habit she had never felt the need to do before Jack Jones had entered the picture. She set her purse and Bible on the kitchen table, then went to the sink and just stood there. She gazed blankly out the window. It was a bleak time of year with bare trees, browning grass, dead leaves—all in sepia tones. A nice coat of snow would make it look much prettier.

But she wasn't looking at her own yard. Her eyes were

fixed on her neighbor's backyard. As usual, it looked more like a dump site than a delightful place where flowers once flourished and children once played. The dilapidated deck was heaped with black plastic trash bags filled with only God knew what. And as if that were not bad enough, there were pieces of rubbish and rubble strewn about. But the item that caught Betty's eye today, the thing that made her blink, was the pink toilet!

Betty recognized this toilet as the one that had once graced Gladys Spencer's prized guest bathroom. It had been a small, tidy bathroom with pink and black tiles, a pink sink, and a matching toilet. Betty had used it many a time when she'd joined Gladys and their friends for bridge club or baby showers or just a neighborly cup of coffee. Gladys had always taken great pride in her dainty pink guest soaps and her pink fingertip towels with a monogrammed *S* in silver metallic thread.

As Betty stared at that toilet, so forlorn and out of place in the scruffy backyard, she realized that time had definitely moved on. Betty could relate to that toilet on many levels. She too was old and outdated. She too felt unnecessary . . . and perhaps even unwanted.

Betty shook her head in an attempt to get rid of those negative thoughts. Then she frowned to see that last night's high winds must've pushed the deteriorating fence even further over into what once had been the Spencers' yard. Jack Jones would not be the least bit pleased about that. Not that she cared particularly.

Betty had long since decided that the fence, whether it was

her responsibility or his, could wait until next summer to resolve. But if she could have her way, she would erect a tall, impenetrable stone wall between the two properties.

She filled her old stainless teakettle and tried to remember happier days—a time when she'd been happy to live in her house. She thought back to when Chuck was still alive and when they'd just moved into their new house in Gary Meadows. It had seemed like a dream come true. Finally, after renting and saving for eight years, they were able to afford a home of their own. And it was brand-new!

Al and Gladys Spencer had immediately befriended Chuck and Betty as well as their two small children with a dinner of burgers and baked beans. And that's when the two men began making plans to build a fence. "Good fences make good neighbors," Al said. Since Chuck and Betty's children were still young, whereas Al and Gladys had only one child still at home who was about to graduate, it was decided that they'd put the fence directly on the Spencers' property line, allowing the Kowalskis the slightly larger yard. "And less mowing for me," Al joked. And since the city had no plans to use the public access strip, and there was no alley, it had all been settled quite simply and congenially. That is, until Jack Jones moved in.

Not for the first time, Betty thought she should consider selling her house. Depressed market or not, she didn't need this much space. Besides that, the neighborhood seemed to be spiraling downward steadily. Perhaps this was related to tenants like Jack Jones, or simply the fact that people were stretched too thin these days, and as a result, home maintenance chores got neglected. Whatever the case, there seemed to be a noticeable decline in neighborhood morale and general friendliness.

It didn't help matters that both her middle-aged children, Susan and Gary, lived hundreds of miles away. They were busy with their own lives, careers, and families and consequently rarely visited anymore. These days they preferred to send her airline tickets to come and spend time with them. But every time she went away, she felt a bit more concerned about leaving her home unattended—and with Jack Jones on the other side of the fence, she would worry even more now. Perhaps she should cancel her visit to Susan's next month. She usually spent most of January down there in the warm Florida sun, but who knew what kind of stunts that crazy neighbor might pull in her absence? And who would call her to let her know if anything was amiss? There could be a fire or a burglary or vandalism, and she probably wouldn't hear about it until she returned. A sad state of affairs indeed.

The shrill sound of the teakettle's whistle made her jump, and she knocked her favorite porcelain tea mug off the counter, where it promptly shattered into pieces on the faded yellow linoleum floor. "Oh, bother!" She turned off the stove, then went to fetch the broom and dustpan and clean up her mess. She had never been this edgy before—at least not before Jack Jones had moved into the neighborhood. And she was supposed to love her neighbor?

2

Betty opened an Earl Grey teabag and dropped it in a porcelain mug that was still in one piece. As she poured the steaming water over it, she just shook her head. "Love your neighbor, bah humbug," she muttered as she went to the dining room. This was the spot where she normally enjoyed her afternoon cup of tea and looked out into her yard as the afternoon light came through the branches of the old maple tree. But she had barely sat down by the sliding glass door when she glimpsed a streak of blackish fur darting across her backyard like a hairy little demon. She blinked, then stood to peer out the window. "What in tarnation?"

There, hoisting his leg next to her beloved dogwood tree, a tree she'd nurtured and babied for years in a shady corner of her yard, was a scruffy-looking blackish-brown dog. At least she thought it was a dog. But it was a very ugly dog and not one she'd seen in the neighborhood before, although she couldn't be certain that it was a stray. With each passing year, it became harder and harder to keep track of people and pets.

She opened the sliding door and stepped out. "Shoo, shoo!" she called out. The dog looked at her with startled eyes as he lowered his leg, but he didn't run. "Go away," she yelled, waving her arms to scare him out of her yard. "Go home, you bad dog!" She clapped her hands and stomped her feet, and she was just about to either give up or throw something (perhaps the stupid dog was deaf and *very* dumb) when he took off running. He made a beeline straight for the fallen-down fence, neatly squeezing beneath the gap where fence boards had broken off, and escaped into Jack Jones's yard—just like he lived there!

"Well, of course," she said as she shut the door, locked it, and pulled her drapes closed. She picked up her teacup and went into the living room. "A mongrel dog for a mongrel man. Why should that surprise me in the least?"

She sat down in her favorite rocker-recliner and pondered her situation. What could possibly be done? How could she manage to survive not merely her loutish neighbor but his nasty little dog as well? It almost seemed as if Jack had sent the dog her way just to torture her some more. If a person couldn't feel comfortable and at home in their own house, what was the point of staying? What was keeping her here?

It was as if the writing were on the wall—a day of reckoning. Betty knew what she would do. She would sell her house and move away. That was the only way out of this dilemma. She wondered why she hadn't considered this solution last summer, back when Jack had first taken occupancy in the Spencer home. Didn't houses sell better in the warmer months? But perhaps it didn't matter. Still, she wasn't sure it made much sense to put up a For Sale sign during the holidays. Who would be out house shopping with less than two weeks before Christmas?

"Christmas . . ." She sighed, then sipped her lukewarm tea. How could it possibly be that time of year again? And what did she need to do in preparation for it? Or perhaps she didn't need to do anything. Who would really care if she baked cookies or not? Who would even notice if she didn't get out her old decorations? Christmas seemed like much ado about nothing. Oh, she didn't think the birth of Christ was nothing. But all the hullabaloo and overspending and commercialism that seemed to come with the holiday these days . . . When had it gone from being a wholesome family celebration to a stressful, jam-packed holiday that left everyone totally exhausted and up to their eyeballs in debt when it was over and done?

Betty used to love Christmastime. She would begin planning for it long in advance. Even the year that Chuck had died suddenly and unexpectedly just two days after Thanksgiving, Betty had somehow mustered the strength to give her children a fairly merry Christmas. They'd been grade schoolers at the time and felt just as confused and bereaved as she had. Still, she had known it was up to her to put forth her best effort. And so, shortly after the funeral, Betty had worn a brave smile and climbed up the rickety ladder to hang colorful strings of Christmas lights on the eaves of the house, "just like Daddy used to do." And then she got and decorated a six-foot fir tree, baked some cookies, wrapped a few gifts . . . all for the sake of her children. Somehow they made it through Christmas that year. And the Christmases thereafter.

When her son Gary was old enough (and taller than Betty), he eagerly took over the task of hanging lights on the house.

And Susan happily took over the trimming of the tree. Each year the three of them would gather in the kitchen to bake all sorts of goodies, and then they would deliver festive cookie platters to everyone in the neighborhood. It became an expected tradition. And always their threesome family was lovingly welcomed into neighbors' homes, often with hot cocoa and glad tidings.

But times had changed since then. Betty had taken cookie platters to only a couple of neighbors last year. And perhaps this year she would take none. What difference would it make?

Betty set her empty tea mug aside and leaned back in her recliner. She reached down to pull out the footrest and soon felt herself drifting to sleep. She wished that she, like Rip Van Winkle, could simply close her eyes and sleep, sleep, sleep. She'd be perfectly happy if she were able to sleep right through Christmas. And then January would come, and she would figure out a way to sell this house and get out of this neighborhood. She would escape that horrid Jack Jones as well as the ugly mutt that most likely intended to turn her backyard into a doggy dump site.

3

A little before seven on Monday morning, Betty woke to the sound of someone trying to break into her house. At least that was what it sounded like to her. She got out of bed and pulled on her old chenille robe, then reached for the cordless phone as she shoved her feet into her slippers. Some people, like her friend Marsha, would've been scared to death by something like this, but Betty had lived alone for so many years that she'd long since given up panic attacks. Besides, they weren't good for one's blood pressure.

But the screen door banged again, and she knew that someone was definitely on her porch. And so she shuffled out of her bedroom and peered through the peephole on the front door. But try as she might, she saw no one. Then she heard a whimpering sound and knew that it was an animal. Perhaps a raccoon or a possum, which often wandered into the neighborhood. She knew it could be dangerous, so she cautiously opened the front door. She quickly reached out to hook the screen door firmly before she looked down to see that it wasn't a raccoon or possum. It was that scruffy dog again. Jack Jones's mongrel. The dog crouched down, whimpering, and despite Betty's bitter feelings toward her neighbor, she felt a tinge of pity for the poor, dirty animal. And Betty didn't even like dogs.

"Go home, you foolish thing," she said. "Go bother your owner."

The dog just whined.

Betty knelt down with the screen still between her and the dog. "Go home," she said again. "Shoo!"

But the dog didn't budge. And now Betty didn't know what to do. So she closed the door and just stood there. If she knew Jack's phone number, she would call him and complain. But she didn't. She suspected the dog was hungry and cold, but she had no intention of letting the mongrel into her house. He looked as if he'd been rolling in the mud, and she'd just cleaned her floors on Saturday. But perhaps it wouldn't hurt to feed him a bit. Who knew when Jack had last given him a meal?

She went to look in her refrigerator, trying to determine what a hungry dog might eat. Finally, she decided on lunch meat. She peeled off several slices of processed turkey, then cautiously unlocked and opened the screen door just wide enough for her hand to slip out and toss the slices onto the porch. The dog was on them in seconds.

Betty went to her bedroom and took her time getting dressed, hoping that Jack's mutt would be gone by the time she finished. Perhaps he would beg food from another neighbor. But when she went to check her porch, he was still there. So she went to the laundry room and found a piece of clothesline to use as a leash.

"I hope you're friendly," she said. She bent over, hoping to tie the cord to the mutt's collar. But the dog had no collar.

Instead he had a piece of string tied tightly around his neck. What kind of cruel gesture was that? She broke the dirty string and fashioned a looser sort of collar from the clothesline cord, looping it around his neck. To her relief, the mutt didn't make it difficult, didn't growl, didn't pull away. He simply looked up at her with sad brown eyes.

She stepped down from the porch and said, "Come!" The dog obeyed, walking obediently beside her. "Well, at least Jack has taught you some obedience," she said as she headed down the footpath to the sidewalk. "I'm taking you home now." Then she turned and marched down the sidewalk toward Jack's house. But now she wasn't so sure. What if this *wasn't* Jack's dog?

"Hello, Betty," Katie Gilmore called out. She stepped away from where the school bus had just picked up her twin girls. "How are you today?"

Betty smiled. "I'm fine, thank you."

Katie frowned down at the dog, then lowered her voice. "Does that dog belong to, uh, Jack Jones?"

"That's what I assume," Betty said. "I saw him in Jack's backyard yesterday."

"Yes, I noticed him over there too." Katie looked uneasy. "I hadn't known Jack had a dog. I hope he's friendly."

"I'm sure there's a lot we don't know about Jack." Betty forced a wry smile as she looked down at the dog. "But the dog seems to be friendly enough."

Katie frowned at the animal. "Poor thing."

Betty suspected Katie meant "poor thing" in relation to having Jack Jones as an owner. Everyone knew that Katie's husband, Martin, had experienced a bit of go-around with Jack last summer. Quiet Martin Gilmore had walked over and politely asked Jack to turn down his music one day. But according to Penny Horton, who'd been home at the time, Martin had been answered with a raised power tool and some rough language.

"Are you taking the dog to Jack's house?" Katie glanced over her shoulder toward the shabby-looking house.

"Yes. And I intend to give him a piece of my mind too."

Katie's brows arched. "Oh . . ." Then she reached in her coat pocket and pulled out a cell phone. "Want me to stick around, just in case?"

Betty wanted to dismiss Katie's offer as unnecessary, but then reconsidered. "I suppose that's not a bad idea."

"He can be a little unpredictable," Katie said quietly. "That's the main reason I've been making sure the girls get safely on and off the school bus these days."

Betty nodded. "I see."

"I'll just wait here," Katie said. "I'll keep an eye on you while you return the dog." She shook her head. "It looks neglected . . . and like it needs a bath."

Betty thought that wasn't the only thing the dog needed, and she intended to say as much to Jack Jones. Naturally, she would control her temper, but she would also let him know that organizations like the Humane Society or ASPCA would not be the least bit impressed with Jack's dog-owner skills.

When she got to Jack's house and knocked on the door, no one answered. However, his pickup was still parked in the front yard, so she suspected he was home and knocked again, louder this time. But still no answer. Finally, she didn't know what to do, so she simply tied the makeshift leash to a rickety-looking porch railing and left.

"He didn't answer the door?" Katie asked when Betty rejoined her.

"No." Betty turned and scowled at Jack's house. "I've a mind to call the Humane Society."

"It seems cruel to leave the dog tied to the porch," Katie said.

Betty shrugged. "I don't know what else to do."

"Well, I can see Jack's porch from my house. I'll keep an eye on the dog, and if Jack doesn't come out and let the dog inside or care for it, I'll give you a call."

Betty wanted to protest this idea. After all, why should that dog be her concern or responsibility? But she knew that would sound heartless and mean, so she just thanked Katie.

"Martin and I just don't know what to do about him," Katie said as she walked Betty back to her house. "I'll admit we didn't get off on the best foot with him, but we've tried to be friendly since then, and he just shuts us down."

"I know," Betty said. "He shuts everyone down."

"Now Martin is talking about moving. He's worried about the girls. He even did one of those police checks on Jack—you know, where you go online to see if the person has a record for being a sexual predator."

Betty's eyes opened wide. "Did he discover anything?"

"No." Katie looked dismal. "But now Martin is worried that Jack Jones might not be his real name."

Betty nodded. "The thought crossed my mind too."

"So what do you do about something like this?" Katie's tone was desperate now. "Do you simply allow some nutcase to ruin your neighborhood and drive you out of your home? Do you just give in?"

Betty sighed as she paused in front of her house. "I don't know what to tell you, Katie. I wish I did. And even though I've lived in this neighborhood for nearly forty years, I really don't have any answers. The truth is, I'm considering moving myself."

Katie shook her head. "That's just not fair."

"Well, I'm getting old." Betty forced a weak smile. "My house and yard are a lot of work for me, and the winters are long. Really, it might be for the best."

"Maybe so. But I have to say that Jack Jones has put a real damper on the holidays for me. The girls' last day of school is Wednesday, and I told Martin that I'm thinking about taking them to my mother's for all of winter break. Martin wasn't happy about that. He still has to work and isn't looking forward to coming home to an empty house while we're gone. But I told him that I didn't look forward to two weeks of being home with the girls with someone like Jack next door."

"That's too bad."

"I'll say. It's too bad that we don't feel safe or comfortable in our home."

Betty just shook her head. What was this neighborhood coming to?

"Anyway, I'll let you know how it goes with that poor dog," Katie said. And then they said good-bye and went their separate ways.

Once inside her house, Betty decided to call her daughter. Susan had always been sensible, not to mention a strong Christian woman. Plus she was a family counselor with a practice in her home. Surely she would have some words of wisdom to share. Some sage advice for her poor old mother. Betty planned to explain the situation in a calm and controlled manner, but once they got past the perfunctory greetings, Betty simply blurted out her plan to sell her home as soon as possible.

"When did you think you'd list it?" Susan sounded a little concerned.

"I'd like to put up a sign right now. But it probably makes more sense to wait until after the New Year."

"So . . . in January?"

"Yes. I didn't think anyone would want to buy a house right before Christmas."

"But you're coming here in January."

"Yes, I know. I'll put my house up for sale and leave."

"But the market is so low right now, Mom."

"I don't care."

"And I'll bet you haven't fixed anything up, have you?"

"I'll sell it as is."

"Yes . . . you could do that."

But Betty could hear the doubtful tone in Susan's voice growing stronger. "You think it's a bad idea, don't you?"

"I don't think it's a bad idea to sell your house. But I suppose I'm just questioning your timing. January isn't a good time to sell a house. The market is low right now. And I know you have some deferred maintenance issues to deal with and—"

"You think I should wait?"

"I think waiting until summer would be smarter."

"Oh."

"Why are you in this sudden rush, Mom?"

Betty felt silly now. To admit that it was her rude neighbor sounded so childish. And yet it was the truth. So she spilled the whole story, clear down to the scratch on her car, the broken tea mug, and the dirty dog.

Susan actually laughed.

"It is *not* funny."

"I'm sorry, Mom. I'm sure it's not funny to you. But hearing you tell it, well . . ." She chortled again. "It is kind of humorous."

"Humph."

"What kind of a dog was it?"

"What *kind* of a dog?" Betty frowned. "Good grief, how would I know? It was a mutt, a mongrel, a filthy dog that I would never allow inside my house. I can only imagine what Jack Jones's house must look like inside. It's a dump site outside. Did you know that there is a pink toilet in his backyard right this moment?" Betty went on to tell her daughter that Katie Gilmore was considering evacuating for Christmas and that Martin had actually done a criminal check on Jack.

"Oh dear," Susan said. "Do you think he's dangerous?"

"I don't know about that, but I do know he's very rude and inconsiderate and strange. I can only imagine what he's doing to the Spencer house. For all I know, he might even be a squatter or an escapee from the nut hatch, hiding out until the men in white coats show up to cart him away."

"Seriously?"

"Oh, I don't know."

"Have you even given him a chance, Mom? Maybe he's just lonely."

"Of course he's lonely. He pushes everyone away from him."

"But it sounds as if everyone is being confrontational."

"He invites confrontation!"

"Have you tried being kind to him?"

Betty didn't answer.

"I remember how we used to take cookies to our neighbors . . ."

Betty laughed now, but it was edged with bitterness. "I do not think Jack Jones would appreciate cookies, Susan. You don't understand the situation at all."

"Maybe not. But I do remember that my mother once told me that kindness builds bridges."

"All I want to build is a tall brick wall between Jack's house and mine." Betty mentioned the falling-down fence and disputed property line.

"See, that's just one more reason why it's not time to sell right now, Mom. You need to resolve those issues first."

"Maybe so."

Then Susan changed the subject by talking about the grandsons. Seth was still on a church missions trip, where they were putting in wells and septic systems in Africa.

"He just loves what he's doing there," Susan said, "and he loves the people. In fact, he's extended his stay until March now."

"And what about Marcus?" Betty asked. "How's school?"

"School is going fine. I think this is finals week. And, oh yeah, he has a girlfriend."

"A girlfriend? Have you met her?"

"No. But it sounds like he may be going to her house for Christmas."

"So you and Tim will be alone for Christmas?" Betty had booked her flight to Florida months ago, but now she considered changing the dates so that she could be with her daughter during the holidays too. Why hadn't she thought of that sooner? Oh yes, she remembered—her commitment to help with the Deerwood anniversary party just days before Christmas.

"Not exactly alone . . ." Susan explained how Tim had put together a plan to share the expenses of a small yacht with some other couples while they toured the Florida Keys together during the holidays.

"That sounds like fun." Betty frowned out the back window. Jack's dog was in her backyard again!

"I wasn't sure at first, but I'm getting excited now."

"Well, I'm excited too," Betty said in an angry voice. "That mongrel dog has sneaked into my backyard again!" The mutt was making a doggy deposit right next to her beloved dogwood tree! Did the mongrel think that because it was a *dog*wood tree, it was open season for dogs? "That horrible animal! I think I'll take a broom to him."

"Oh, Mom!" Susan sounded disappointed. "That's so mean. You've never been mean like that before."

"Are you suggesting it's not mean for Jack to force me to

clean up after his dog? To remove nasty dog piles from my own backyard?"

"That's not the dog's fault, Mom. You said yourself that the fence is falling apart. What do you expect?"

"I expect the owner to take some responsibility for his animal. Maybe I should go throw something at the nasty dog."

"What happened to the sweet Christian woman I used to know?" Susan asked.

"Jack Jones is making her lose her mind."

"Oh, Mother, you can do better than that. Remember what you used to tell me when I was young and I'd get so angry that I'd feel like killing someone?"

"What?" Betty felt a headache coming on.

"You'd say, 'Why don't you kill them with kindness, Susan?'"

Betty rubbed her forehead as she remembered her own words.

"So, why don't you do that now, Mom? Why don't you kill Jack Jones with kindness?"

"And his little dog too?"

"Yes. And his little dog too."

Betty promised her daughter that she'd consider the challenge, and she was just about to say good-bye when Susan said quickly, "Hey, I almost forgot to tell you."

"What's that?"

"Have you heard from Gary lately?"

Suddenly Betty felt worried. She could tell by Susan's voice that something was wrong. Surely no harm had come to her son. "No . . . I haven't spoken to him since Thanksgiving. Is everything okay?"

"Well, I wasn't supposed to say anything to you . . ."

"Anything about what?" Betty was really concerned now.

"It's Avery."

"Oh." Avery was Gary's stepdaughter. She was in her mid-twenties and still acted like an adolescent. "What's happened with Avery?"

"She's gone missing."

"Missing?"

"Gary called awhile back and told me they haven't heard from her since October."

"October?" Betty considered this. "Gary didn't mention this when he called me at Thanksgiving."

"He probably didn't want to worry you."

"I see."

"But they're starting to get concerned. I mean, Avery's been known to take off and do some irresponsible things before, but not for this long. And she usually checks in from time to time."

"And she hasn't checked in?"

"No." Susan sighed. "Apparently Avery got into a big fight with Stephanie."

Stephanie was Avery's mom, Gary's second wife. She was an intelligent woman and very beautiful, but her temper was a little volatile, and this sometimes worried Betty. "When was the fight?" Betty asked.

"Mid-October."

"Naturally, Avery's been missing since then?"

"Pretty much so."

"Oh dear, that's quite a while. I hope she's okay."

"I'm sure she's fine. Avery probably just wants to teach her mom a lesson. Anyway, I've really been praying for her, and I thought you might want to also."

"Yes, of course I'll be praying for her."

"And I'll assume you're praying for your neighbor too?" Susan's voice sounded a tiny bit sarcastic now.

"I'm *trying* to pray for him," Betty said. "But it's not easy."

"Well, I'll start praying for him too, Mom. Keep me posted."

"And you keep me posted on Avery."

"Sure, just don't let Gary know that I mentioned it. And in the meantime, remember what I told you."

"What's that?" Now Betty felt confused. They'd talked of so much—to sell or not to sell the house, Avery's disappearance.

"You know, take your own advice—kill him with kindness."

Betty looked out at her backyard only to see that the stupid dog was now digging in her favorite tulip bed. "I'll kill him, all right," she snapped.

"Mom!"

"Yes, yes, like you said, with kindness. I have to go now, dear." But after she hung up and went outside, Betty did not have kindness in her heart. And when she saw that someone—and it could only be Jack—had hammered a board over the opening in the fence, on his side of the fence, she felt outraged.

Had he allowed his dog to pass through and then sealed off the doggy escape route? What was wrong with that man?

She marched out to the woodshed and got an old ax. The dog followed her, watching as she took the ax to the fence and chopped an even bigger hole. Fortunately, the fence was so rotten that it wasn't much of a challenge. The challenge came with getting the dumb dog to pass back through the hole onto his own side of the fence. She went back to the house and utilized another piece of lunch meat to entice the mutt into Jack's yard. Once he was there, she shoved several pieces of firewood in the hole to block the new opening of the fence.

She let out a tired sigh as she looked across the sagging and now somewhat ravaged-looking fence. The dog just sat there in the yard and looked at her with those sad brown eyes.

"I'm sorry," she said. "Dogs don't get to pick their masters, just like I don't get to pick my neighbors. We both need to make the best of it."

But as she walked away, she felt guilty on several levels. And the expression on the poor mutt's face seemed to be imprinted in her mind. When had she become so mean?

4

Betty finally had to pull the drapes on the windows that faced her backyard because she could still see the dog sitting out there in the bitter cold just staring toward her house in the most pitiful way. She picked up the phone and considered calling information for the number of the Humane Society. Why shouldn't she turn Jack Jones in for dog neglect? He deserved it. But then she remembered her daughter's words. And so she replaced the phone and decided to go to the grocery store instead.

With Susan's challenge running through her mind, Betty decided she would give this her best attempt. She would do all she could to "kill Jack and his dog with kindness." And, although she normally lived on a fairly frugal grocery budget, today she would throw caution to the wind. So, along with her normal groceries, Betty also gathered up the ingredients for cookies and fudge. After that she stopped in the pet aisle, where she added to her shopping cart a red nylon collar and matching leash, some dog shampoo, a couple of cans of dog food, and even a red and green plaid bed.

"Looks like somebody is getting a dog for Christmas." The cashier winked at her as he bagged up her purchases.

"Looks that way, doesn't it?"

"Or maybe the family pooch is getting something from Santa?" he asked.

She just gave him a stiff smile and paid in cash from her envelope. This was a habit she'd developed years ago when the children still lived at home. But today's shopping had used up the remainder of her December grocery budget. The month was only half over, and she usually went shopping once a week. But perhaps it would be worth it. Perhaps this was how she would buy peace. And, if the kindness plan didn't work, she would simply sell her house, and she might even toss budgeting out the window. Maybe she'd do like Susan— board a boat and just sail away into the sunset. Why not?

But as Betty loaded her unusual purchases into her car, trying to ignore the J-shaped gash on the front right fender, she felt rather foolish. What on earth was she doing with this doggy paraphernalia anyway? As she closed her trunk, she feared she might be getting senile. Or maybe she had simply lost her mind. Had Jack Jones driven her mad?

To distract herself from Jack, she focused her attention on praying for Avery. Although they weren't related by blood, Avery had started calling Betty "Grandma" shortly after her mother married Betty's son Gary a dozen years ago. And Betty had adopted Avery into her heart as a granddaughter.

Betty remembered the first time she'd met the quiet, pre-adolescent girl. It had been shortly before the wedding, and Betty had suspected that Avery wasn't too pleased with her mother's marriage. But during the reception, Betty and Avery seemed to bond, which was a good thing since Betty was to keep Avery while Gary and Stephanie honeymooned in the

Caribbean. Naturally, Avery had been reluctant to be away from her friends, and Betty had been a bit apprehensive about caring for a girl she barely knew, but by the end of the two weeks, they'd become fast friends. Avery had even cried when it was time to go home.

Over the following few years, Avery usually spent at least two weeks of her summer vacation at Betty's home. And sometimes spring break as well. But everything seemed to change when Avery turned sixteen. That was when, according to Betty's son, Avery became a "wild child." And Gary worried that his stepdaughter's strong will would be too much for his aging mother. Just the same, Betty missed those visits, and over the years she continued to send Avery cards and gifts, and occasionally money, for birthdays, holidays, and graduation. Betty seldom got a thank-you in return, but she figured young people weren't trained in the social graces very much these days.

As Betty pulled into her driveway, then carefully parked her car in the garage again, her thoughts returned to Jack Jones. Suddenly she wondered just how she planned to present her eccentric "gifts" to her neighbor. More than that, she wondered how he would receive them. Besides being rude and inconsiderate and painfully private, Jack Jones struck her as being an extremely proud young man, and stubborn too. For all she knew, he might throw her silly purchases right back in her face. Really, it was a crazy idea—what had she been thinking? Perhaps the best plan would be to simply forget the whole thing and take the items back tomorrow. Even if the store refused to refund her money, they could probably give her a credit. And so she carried her groceries into the house but left the doggy items in her car to be returned later.

Still feeling a bit silly, she stowed her groceries away—all except for the baking ingredients, which she lined up on the counter by the stove, just like she used to do before a full day of holiday baking. Then she stood there staring at the bags of chocolate chips, nuts, dried fruits, and powdered and brown sugar, and finally just shook her head. Had she lost her mind?

Did she really plan on making Christmas goodies to give to her neighbors—people she barely knew? And to share her homemade treats with the likes of Jack Jones? Was that even sensible? What if she were setting herself up for trouble? What if Jack Jones was a dangerous man? A criminal? It was one thing to love her neighbor, but what if her neighbor was a murderer, or a pedophile, or a sociopath? Should she take cookies to a man like that?

With a little more than a week still left until Christmas, she decided to think about these things later. Right now she was too tired to think clearly, let alone bake cookies.

Betty awoke to the sound of something knocking on the front door. She blinked and slowly pushed herself out of her recliner, thinking it must be that mongrel dog again. Why wouldn't he just leave her alone? Didn't he know where he lived? She groaned as she made her way through the living room. Her arthritis was acting up, probably as a result of this cold, damp weather.

But when she looked through the peephole, not expecting to see anyone, she saw what appeared to be an attractive, dark-haired young woman. A scarlet-red scarf was wound so high up her neck that it concealed the lower half of her face, so it was hard to tell who it was. Feeling slightly befuddled and not completely awake, Betty just stared at the person, thinking to herself that those dark brown eyes looked oddly familiar.

"*Avery!*" Betty fumbled with the deadbolt and opened the door so she could unlock and open the screen door. "Avery!" she cried again as she embraced the girl in a warm hug and pulled her into the house. "I almost didn't recognize you. It's been so long."

As Betty closed the front door and relocked the deadbolt, Avery began to unwind the scarf from around her neck. "Hi, Grandma," she said in a tired voice. "Sorry to bust in on you like this, but I was, uh, in the neighborhood . . ."

"I'm glad you came! I'm so happy to see you." Betty took the girl's slightly damp parka and hung it on the hall tree to dry out, along with the snagged-up scarf that appeared to be nearly six feet long. "How are you?"

"Oh, I'm okay . . . I guess." Avery pushed some loose strands of dark hair away from her face. The rest of her hair was pulled back into a long and messy ponytail. Her skin seemed pale, there were dark smudges under her eyes, and without her parka, she seemed very thin and waiflike.

"Come in and sit down and get warm." Betty motioned Avery toward the living room.

"Wow, everything looks just the same, Grandma." Avery

looked around the room with hungry eyes. "Nothing has changed."

Betty laughed. "I guess that's how it is when we get old. We're comforted by keeping things the same."

"I'm comforted too." Avery sat on the couch and picked up a pillow with a crocheted covering that Betty's mother had made for her years ago. Avery just stared at the pattern of colors—roses, lilacs, and periwinkle. "I always loved this pillow, Grandma."

Betty smiled. "I'll make sure to leave it to you in my will."

Now Avery looked sad as she set the pillow aside. "Don't say that. I'd hate to think of you dying. I don't want the pillow that bad."

"Don't worry, I don't plan on going anytime soon."

Avery nodded. "Good."

"So, what brings you into my neck of the woods?"

Avery sighed. "I don't know . . ."

Betty considered the situation. She didn't want to press too hard, didn't want to make Avery so uncomfortable that she'd be tempted to run off again. Better just to keep things light. "Say, are you hungry?"

Avery looked up with eager eyes. "Yes! I'm starving."

"Well, I just went to the grocery store today. And I haven't had lunch yet either. Why don't we see what we can find?"

Before long, Betty had grilled cheese sandwiches cooking on one burner, and Avery was stirring cream of tomato soup on another.

"This feels good," Avery said.

"Cooking?"

"Yes. Being in a real kitchen, smelling food . . . it feels kinda homey."

Betty had noticed how grimy Avery's hands and nails looked. Like she hadn't bathed in days, maybe even weeks. "Well, everything's about ready," she told her. "Maybe you'd like to go wash up before we eat."

Avery nodded. "Yeah, that's a good idea."

Soon they were both sitting at the kitchen table, and, as usual, Betty bowed her head to say grace.

"Just like always," Avery said after Betty finished. "You still thank God every time you eat?"

"I try to."

"That's nice." Avery smiled and took a big bite of her sandwich, then another, and then, in no time, her sandwich was gone and she was shoveling down her soup.

"I'll bet you could eat another sandwich," Betty said.

"Do you mind?"

"Not at all." Betty got up to fix another.

"Grandma?"

"Yes?" Betty paused from slicing the cheese.

"Why is it so dark in here? Why are the curtains all shut?"

"Oh." Betty frowned. "It's a long story."

"I've got time."

So, as Betty grilled the second sandwich, she began to explain about her unpredictable and somewhat thoughtless neighbor. She tried not to paint too horrible a picture of him. After all, she didn't want to frighten Avery. But she did want her to understand that the man was a bit of a loose cannon. "And now that he's got this crazy dog, well, it's getting to be even more complicated."

"What kind of a dog?"

"Who knows? A mutt."

Avery laughed. "Oh."

Betty reached over to open the drapes that had been blocking the view of the backyard. But to her pleasant surprise, the dog was not anywhere in sight. "Hopefully, Jack has enough sense to put his dog inside," she said. "Because it looks like it's about to rain again. And as cold as it is out there, I expect it might turn into a freezing rain by tonight."

Avery stood and began to clear the table. "I'll clean these things up."

"Thank you," Betty said. "I appreciate that."

"You go put your feet up," Avery said. "Leave everything to me."

"Now that's an offer I cannot refuse."

For the second time that day, Betty got into her recliner and put her feet up and was about to doze off when she heard something at the door. Avery was still in the kitchen, so Betty slowly made her way out of her chair, went to the door, and realized that this time it really was that dog again. In Betty's excitement over seeing Avery, she'd forgotten to lock the screen door, and now the dog had wedged itself between the loose screen door and the front door, almost as if he thought it was a place to seek shelter. Betty had barely opened the door and was about to shoo it away, but the dog shot between her legs and right into the house.

"No! No!" Betty waved her hands. "Out of my house, you mongrel! Get out of here! Get out! Get out!" But the dog ran down the hallway and headed back toward the bedrooms.

"What?" Avery came out holding a sudsy saucepan. "Do you want me to leave?"

"No, not you. That darn dog sneaked into my house. I was yelling at it to go away."

"Oh, I thought you meant me."

"No, of course not." Betty pointed down the hallway. "He went that way. Help me catch him."

They finally cornered the runaway dog in the bathroom, where it cowered on Betty's pale pink bath mat. Or what used to be pale pink before being spotted with muddy smudges.

"Bad dog!" Betty shouted.

But Avery knelt down beside the dog, holding its head in her hands and looking into its face. "Poor thing. Look how dirty and cold it is."

"Yes, Jack Jones is a very bad man. He should be arrested for pet neglect, among other things."

"Can I give him a bath?" Avery asked with hopeful eyes.

"A *bath*?" Betty gasped. "You mean right here in my bathtub?"

Avery nodded.

Betty wrung her hands. "But he's filthy. It will be such a mess, the whole bathroom will smell like a dog."

"I'll clean everything up when I'm done." Avery looked sad now. "Look, he's so cold . . . he's shivering." She touched his muddy brown coat. "And he's so dirty and matted and sad. Please, Grandma, we can't let him go back like this."

Betty got an idea. "Okay, you can bathe him, but not in here. You can put him in the laundry sink. That won't be such a mess."

"Okay!" Avery scooped up the dirt-encrusted dog and carried him through the house with Betty trailing behind her, carrying the half-washed saucepan in one hand and the soiled bath mat in the other. Betty deposited these items, then dug through her linen closet to find two old towels to give to Avery. By now the laundry sink was nearly full.

"Do you have any soap to use on him?" Avery asked.

Betty remembered her recent doggy purchases. "As a matter of fact, I have just the thing." She headed out to the garage to get the shampoo and returned with all the doggy items in tow.

Avery's eyes grew wide. "Where did you get all that stuff?"

"At the store."

"For *this* dog?"

"I wanted to be a good neighbor." Now Betty felt a little sheepish to admit this, since she'd just tried to chase the mutt out of her house. "I thought Jack Jones needed some help with his dog."

"I'll say." Avery reached for the bottle of shampoo and began to lather up the wet dog. "I have a feeling this is going to take awhile."

"I'll leave you to it," Betty said. She went to finish up the nearly cleaned kitchen, then on to the hallway and bathroom to mop up the dirt the dog had tracked in, and finally back to her recliner, where she collapsed in exhaustion and closed her eyes.

When Betty opened her eyes about an hour later, she saw a clean brown dog lying in the plaid bed, wearing a red collar and snoozing comfortably. But where was Avery? Surely she hadn't left. Not in this weather. And not after dark. Betty went down the hallway and noticed the bathroom door was shut with a light coming from beneath it, and she could hear water running. Avery had probably discovered that after bathing the filthy dog, she needed a bath as well. Hopefully, this meant she planned to stay awhile.

And if Betty had her way, Avery would at least spend the night here. Not that she could force her to stay longer than that. But Betty would certainly put her foot down if Avery made any attempt to leave this evening. And so Betty went to check on the guest room, the same room Avery had inhabited so many years before. She turned the baseboard heater up, fluffed the pillows, and added an extra quilt at the end of the bed. Avery hadn't brought any luggage with her, nothing besides an oversized bag. Was it possible she had only the clothes on her back? And if so, why?

Betty went to her own room and retrieved a pair of pretty pink pajamas that Susan had given her last Christmas. She'd never even worn them. Not because she didn't like them, but probably because she'd been saving them. But saving them for what? Well, she didn't know. It's just the way she was about some things. Perhaps she'd been saving them for Avery. Whatever the reason, she neatly refolded them and placed them by Avery's pillow. Then she turned on the small light on the bedside table and smiled in satisfaction. Very welcoming.

"I hope you don't mind that I took a shower," Avery said

when she emerged from the bathroom with wet hair. "But I was kind of a mess."

"You did a good job of cleaning up that dog." Betty nodded to where the mutt was still sleeping. Then she frowned at Avery's soiled T-shirt and jeans. "But why did you put on your dirty clothes again?"

"Because they're all I have."

"You don't have any other clothes?"

Avery just shrugged. "I'll be okay."

Betty shook her head. "No, you will not be okay, Avery. I know you're smaller than I am, at least around, and I think you might be a bit taller. But I might have something for you to wear while we wash your clothes."

"Okay." Avery smiled.

"And the guest room is all ready for you. In fact, if you like you can simply put on the pajamas I laid out for you."

"Okay," Avery said again.

"And then we'll sit down and talk."

Avery bent down to pat the dog, and he looked up with what almost seemed a grateful expression.

"He looks like he's got some terrier in him," Betty said.

"Yeah, that's what I thought too."

"Well, I need to figure out how to get him back to Jack now."

Avery frowned. "I don't think that horrible Jack person deserves to own this dog. He's got a really sweet disposition, and Jack sounds like a total monster. The poor dog's hair was so matted and filthy that it took a bunch of shampooing and rinsing to get him clean. And the whole time he was totally patient. I could tell he liked the attention. But I could feel his ribs. I think he hasn't been fed properly."

Betty nodded. "I'm sure you're right about Jack not being a fit pet owner, but I don't know what we should do about it."

"We should report him to the ASPCA."

"That thought has crossed my mind." Betty pressed her lips together firmly. She wondered what kind of a Christian witness it would be for her to turn in her neighbor. On the other hand, what kind of a Christian allows an innocent animal to suffer that kind of neglect?

She looked at Avery's dripping hair and dirty clothes. "We'll figure out the doggy dilemma later. In the meantime, why don't you change out of those dirty things and get your hair dried before you catch pneumonia."

Avery patted the dog one more time, then left the room. Betty sighed loudly as she sat back down in her recliner. Rocking back and forth, she pondered over what should be done—not so much about the dog as about her wayward granddaughter. Why had Avery shown up like this? And where had she been these past months? Should Betty call Avery's parents? Or should she simply encourage Avery to let them know she was okay?

Betty looked over to where the dog was sleeping again. What was her responsibility for that poor dog? Avery was probably right, he did seem like a nice dog. Not that Betty wanted or needed a dog—she most definitely did not!

And then there was Jack to consider. Betty leaned her head back and closed her eyes. Only yesterday, her biggest challenge was to stop envying her friend's new coat and to make an attempt to love her unlovable neighbor. But her problems seemed to have multiplied. Now she had not only Jack to contend with but a neglected dog and a troubled granddaughter as well. Oh my!

5

"It will serve him right," Avery said. They had just agreed to keep Jack's dog overnight. Perhaps he'd be worried about his animal and want to take better care of him. Or so they hoped.

"And when I return the dog to him tomorrow morning, I'll warn Jack that this neglect cannot continue." Betty stirred the simmering rolled oats, relieved that Avery didn't mind having oatmeal for dinner. It was one of Betty's favorites.

"Tell Jack that you'll report him if he doesn't treat his dog right," Avery said.

Betty nodded. "I'll try to make that clear. But I don't want to be too confrontational with him."

"Why not? He's a total jerk, Grandma."

"Yes, he is a jerk. But he's also my neighbor. And the Bible teaches us to love our neighbors." Betty turned off the stove and removed the pan.

"Even when they're jerks?"

"Even when they're jerks, and even if they're our worst enemies."

"That doesn't sound possible."

Betty smiled. "Yes, I've felt like that myself. It's a challenge."

Avery was studying the calendar that was taped to Betty's fridge. "Wow, is this what day it is?"

Betty looked to where Avery's finger was pointing and nodded. "That's right."

"It's like eight days until Christmas."

Betty spooned out the oatmeal and set the bowls on the kitchen table. She'd already put out brown sugar, raisins, walnuts, and milk to go with it. "I can hardly believe it myself," she said as she sat down.

"Whose fiftieth anniversary is this?" Avery asked as she continued to study the calendar.

"My good friends Marsha and Jim Deerwood."

"Oh, I thought maybe it was yours." Avery kind of laughed and joined Betty at the Formica-topped table. "But I guess you don't celebrate anniversaries if you're not both around."

"To be honest, I do." Betty bowed her head and said a quick blessing over their oatmeal. When she looked up, Avery had a curious expression.

"You celebrate your anniversary?"

"I know it sounds silly. In fact, I've never told anyone before. But yes, I do. I fix a special little dinner, set the table for two, and think about Chuck, and I remember our wedding day."

"What day did you get married?"

"June 20. Last summer would've been our fiftieth anniversary."

"Wow. That's a long time."

Betty nodded as she chewed a bite.

"Why didn't you ever remarry?"

Betty considered this. It was a question she used to get

asked a lot. But not so much as the years piled on. "I just never met the right man. It was hard to measure up to Chuck."

"But don't you get lonely?"

"I suppose . . . a little. Especially after I retired from the electric company. But I've had plenty of time to get used to being alone. Also I have my church, my friends, my neighbors."

"Some of your neighbors sound awful."

Betty forced a smile. "The neighborhood has changed over the years."

"So, are you going anywhere for Christmas?" Avery asked.

"No. I plan to stay home this year." Betty poured more milk on her oatmeal. "I offered to help with my friends' fiftieth anniversary, and it's just a few days before Christmas. Then I'm scheduled to go to Susan's shortly after the New Year."

"Oh."

"What about you, Avery? Do you have special plans for the holidays?"

Avery stirred her oatmeal without looking up.

"I know that you had a fight with your mother."

"Did they call you?"

"No . . ." Betty wasn't sure how much she should press Avery.

"Well, I guess I'm kind of like Jack's dog."

"How's that?"

"If you don't treat me right, I run away."

Betty chuckled.

"Do you know how many times my mom's been married?"

"I thought Gary was her second husband."

"That's what she *wanted* you to think."

"So, he's not?"

"Nope. She was married *three times* before Gary. He's her fourth."

Betty tried not to look too surprised.

"Gary knows about it now."

"But he didn't before?"

"Nope."

Betty wondered how Gary had reacted to this news but didn't want to ask.

"And I'm the one who told him."

Betty lifted her brows. "And how did your mother feel about that?"

"That's what started our big fight. Actually, the fight was already in motion, but that's what made it really take off. Mom told me to leave and never come back."

"Your mother said that?"

"Pretty much so."

"But she was probably speaking out of her emotions, Avery. I doubt that she really meant it."

Avery shrugged as she stuck her spoon back in her bowl. "I think she meant it."

Now Betty didn't know what to say. Really, what could she say? It wasn't as if this was her business. And she'd heard enough about Avery's adolescence to know there were probably two sides to this story. Still, Betty felt disappointed that Stephanie had deceived her as well as her son. She really was curious as to how Gary had reacted to this bit of news. She knew Gary loved Stephanie. But she also knew he had a strong sense of propriety. He would not like discovering he'd been lied to.

"Anyway," Avery continued, "I do not plan to be home for the holidays. I doubt that I'd even be welcome there."

"You're welcome to stay with me."

Avery brightened. "Thanks!"

"But on one condition."

Now she frowned slightly. "What?"

"Let your parents know where you are."

Avery seemed to be thinking about this.

"I realize you're not a child, Avery. How old are you now, anyway?"

"I turned twenty-three in September."

Betty shook her head. "And I completely forgot to send you a card."

"That's okay."

"But as I was saying, you're not a child. You're an adult, but that means you need to be responsible. And a responsible adult lets family members know that she's okay."

"Yeah, you're probably right."

"So if you take care of that, you're welcome to stay here during the holidays."

Avery nodded.

Betty wasn't sure what more she should say to the girl. She certainly had questions, but she didn't want to make Avery feel like she was participating in the Spanish Inquisition tonight. Nor did she want to lecture her or drive her away. Betty suspected that Avery was broke. And it appeared that she had nothing more than what was on her back and in the oversized bag she'd tossed into the guest room.

Betty knew enough about Avery's past to know that, much to her parents' dismay, she'd dropped out of college at the end of her junior year. Avery had claimed that a degree would not guarantee a job. But since leaving school, her employment history had been splotchy at best. According to Susan—Betty's best news source since Gary preferred to keep his mother in the dark—Avery had held a variety of low-paying and unimpressive jobs. And she seemed to bounce back and forth between living at home and staying with friends. Now she was here.

But the truth was, Betty was grateful for the company. And she didn't mind that Avery would be with her through the holidays. Just as long as she informed her parents of her whereabouts. Betty did not want to find herself in the center of a family feud.

Betty glanced at the kitchen clock to see that it was past seven. "I suppose you should wait to call your parents until tomorrow since it's pretty late where they live."

Avery looked relieved. "Yeah. I'll call in the morning."

Just then the dog wandered into the kitchen, going straight to Avery as if they were old friends. "I think we should set the dog's bed and things up in the laundry room," Betty said.

"Is it okay if I feed him again?" Avery asked. "He seemed pretty hungry."

"I'll leave that up to you. Just make sure he has a chance to go out and do his business before you tell him good night."

Betty awoke to a high-pitched whining the next morning. It took her a moment to figure out that the sound was coming from the laundry room, more specifically from the dog. And then she realized that the dog needed to go outside for a potty break. She let him out into the backyard and watched from the open doorway as the dog started to hike up his leg on the trunk of the dogwood tree again.

"No, no!" Betty yelled from where she was standing in the house. The dog looked at her but didn't seem to understand. She just shook her head, tightened the belt of her robe, and waited for him to finish his business.

Betty let the dog back in through the sliding door. "Don't get too comfortable here," she warned as she attempted to usher him back to the laundry room. But since he didn't seem very eager to go, she resorted to using an opened can of dog food to entice him. Holding it in front of his nose, she led him into the room.

"Now, as bad as your master may be, he's still your owner." Betty spooned some food into the bowl. "And like it or not, you're going back to him today."

Betty went to check on Avery, only to discover that she was still sound asleep. Probably exhausted from her travels or whatever it was she'd been doing. Betty decided to just let the girl rest. Besides, it might make it easier to return the dog without Avery around to stir things up.

Betty knew that Avery was outraged by Jack's attitude toward his dog. Perhaps it had to do with Avery's feelings about how her mother was treating her. Or maybe it was just empathy. Whatever the case, Betty knew this was something she should handle on her own. So she gathered up the dog things and put them in an oversized trash bag, then leashed up the dog and proceeded down the street and around the corner toward Jack's house.

As usual, his pickup was parked diagonally across the front yard, and the place still looked like a wreck. And just like yesterday, no one answered when she rang the doorbell. Then it occurred to her that the doorbell, like the rest of the house, could be out of order. And so she knocked loudly. But as she knocked, she noticed that the door was ajar. She pushed it open slightly and was tempted to peek inside, but she worried that she might be caught and accused of trespassing, so she controlled herself. Instead, she simply unlatched the leash from the little dog's collar and shoved the unsuspecting pooch through the open door, then closed it firmly. She left the leash and the bag of doggy things on the front porch. Resisting the urge to brush off her hands or shake the dust off her feet, Betty turned and marched away. Mission accomplished.

Betty went home and cleaned up the laundry room, trying to eradicate the damp doggy odor that seemed to permeate the tight area. She put in a load of laundry, including Avery's soiled clothes and the smelly dog towels, and then she straightened the house and gave the kitchen a good scrub down.

Eventually she went to check on Avery again. It was nearly eleven, and the girl was still fast asleep. But Betty remembered the dark circles she'd noticed beneath Avery's eyes last night. She probably needed a good rest. And Betty needed to put her feet up. But first she called Susan. When she got Susan's answering service, she left a message, explaining that Avery was safe and with her, and that she'd make sure Avery called Gary and Stephanie as soon as possible.

It was almost one by the time Avery made an appearance. By then Betty had enjoyed a short nap and come up with a plan for their day. She explained her idea to Avery as she set a peanut butter and jelly sandwich and glass of milk in front of her. That used to be Avery's favorite lunch, but that had been quite some time ago. She hoped it didn't look too childish now.

"I've got errands to run for my friends' anniversary party," Betty said as she refilled Avery's milk glass. "And then I thought we'd take you shopping for some clothes."

"Cool." Avery's eyes lit up like she'd just won the lottery or an all-expense-paid shopping trip.

Betty cleared her throat. "But since I live on a pretty tight budget, I'm taking you to a thrift store to shop. In fact, Goodwill is located in the same strip mall as the party store where I need to shop. We'll save on gas money as well. I hope you don't mind secondhand clothing."

"That's okay," Avery said with her mouth full. "I like retro clothes."

"Retro?" Betty thought about this. "Well, that's a good thing."

"You're probably wondering where my other clothes are." Avery took a long swig of milk.

"Yes, I suppose I was."

As Avery devoured the second half of her sandwich, she told Betty a crazy story about traveling with a friend named Kendra. They ran out of money and panhandled until they could afford bus tickets to L.A., where they planned to stay with a friend for a while, but there was some kind of disturbance on the bus during the night.

"It was all this old dude's fault." Avery shook her head as she set her milk glass in the sink. "He was like forty, and he'd been coming on to both of us, so Kendra got fed up and smacked him in the nose." Avery made a face. "So this jerk made a big fuss, telling the driver that we were propositioning him, which was so not true, and the driver put Kendra and me off the bus, right out in the middle of nowhere. So we hitchhiked, and the guy who picked us up offered to buy us breakfast in this little town. We left our backpacks in his car, and while we were using the bathroom, he took off with our stuff."

"Oh my." Betty just shook her head. "You should be thankful he didn't hurt you girls. Hitchhiking sounds very dangerous."

"I guess. After that, Kendra and I got in a huge fight and went our separate ways. Since I wasn't too far from your place, I caught a ride into town . . . and now here I am." She smiled. "I was so glad to see they still hang those candy cane decorations on the streetlights here. So old-fashioned and sweet."

Betty nodded. "Yes, that's one way to look at it. Some people just think it's because the city is cheap." She pointed to Avery's dirty dishes in the clean sink. "I'd appreciate it if you picked up after yourself while you're here, Avery. The dishes in the dishwasher are dirty."

"Uh, sure, okay."

"Thank you." Betty watched as Avery rinsed the dishes and put them in the dishwasher. She didn't want to sound like an old curmudgeon. But she didn't want to encourage laziness in the girl either.

"No problem." Avery closed the dishwasher and turned to look at her. "Now what?"

"Your clothes should be clean and ready for you," Betty said. "I heard the dryer buzzer a few minutes ago."

"Thanks."

Betty glanced up at the clock. "And if you don't mind, I'd like to leave by two. I want to get back home before it starts to get dark. That's around four thirty these days."

"No problem."

As Avery got dressed, Betty went to fetch her coat and purse but was interrupted by a banging on the front door.

And there on the porch was that dog again!

"What on earth are you doing back here?" she said. Naturally, the dog didn't answer, but his tail waved back and forth with canine enthusiasm. And there on a corner of her porch was the same garbage bag Betty had left at Jack's house. That's when Betty noticed a piece of paper taped on the dog's red collar. Stooping to examine it more closely, Betty saw some words scribbled in pencil: "Thanks, but NO thanks!"

She blinked and stood up. Well, it just figured. She must've insulted Jack Jones with her generosity. Fine, if he didn't want the doggy things, she didn't care. Why had she expected a normal reaction from the foolish young man in the first place? Still, it seemed irresponsible to send his dog like this to inform her. And it did seem a waste of money since she certainly couldn't return these used items to the store. Besides, it appeared obvious that Jack needed some help in the doggy department.

"Your owner doesn't have a lick of sense!" Betty frowned at the dog. His tail stopped wagging, and he looked somewhat confused by the tone of Betty's voice. "Oh, I'm not scolding you. It's just that your master is very stubborn." Betty thought for a moment. "But then, so am I."

Betty went into the house and dug out a small white index card, then wrote "Merry Christmas" in bold letters with a red felt pen. She stuck a hole in one corner and threaded a piece of yarn, then tied it securely around the dog's collar. "We'll see who wins this little battle of the wills."

She gathered up the bag containing the dog paraphernalia and threw it over one shoulder like a grumpy Santa. Taking the leash in her other hand, Betty marched back to Jack's house. His pickup was still there, but this time the door was firmly closed, and she could hear his power tools running inside. Just the same, she tried knocking on the door, then banging loudly, but to no avail. So she retrieved the plaid dog bed from the bag, shook it out, and set it on a protected corner of the porch. She tied the leash to the nearby post, leaving enough slack so the dog could move around a bit.

Betty did feel a bit sorry for leaving the dog like that, but it was better than him running loose in the neighborhood or being hit by a car. And she and Avery could check on his welfare when they returned from their shopping and errands in a couple of hours. Hopefully the dog would bark and make some kind of fuss to get his owner's attention before long. Betty just hoped that Jack would take the hint that the doggy goodies were intended to be a gift and simply keep them.

6

"What happened to the dog?" Avery asked as they got into the car.

"He went home."

"To Jack?" Avery's voice was laced with disgust.

"Yes." Betty slowly pulled out of the garage.

"Did you talk to him first?"

"The dog?"

Avery laughed. "No, Grandma. I mean Jack. Did you talk to the beast? Did you tell him that he needs to take better care of his dog?"

"Not exactly." Betty sighed. "Would you mind hopping out and closing the garage door, dear?"

"Where's your remote?"

"What?"

"For the door."

"This is a very old-fashioned door."

Betty frowned as she waited for Avery to close the door. She felt like she was in over her head. Not just with Avery, but with Jack and the dog and just everything.

"Thank you," Betty said as Avery hopped back in the car.

"So, was Jack happy to see his dog?" Avery persisted.

"I . . . I don't know."

"What do you mean you don't know?"

"I mean I didn't actually see him."

"But you took the dog back?"

"Yes. He didn't answer the door." Betty considered explaining how she'd taken the dog back twice but figured that would only muddy the already murky waters.

"How could you possibly give the dog back without seeing his lame owner, Grandma?"

Betty grimaced. Why was this so complicated? "Avery . . ." Betty suddenly remembered a good distraction technique. "Did you remember to call your parents?"

"No . . ."

"Well, you promised me you'd do that."

"Can I use your phone?"

"Of course you can use my phone. I already told you that."

"Okay." Avery held out her hand.

"What?"

"Your phone."

"But it's not here, Avery. We're in the car." Betty wondered if the girl had lost her senses.

"You mean you don't have a cell phone?"

"Oh." Betty shook her head as she stopped for a red light. "No, of course not. Why would I need one of those foolish things?"

Avery looked astonished. "Are you serious?"

"Of course I'm serious. I do not understand what all the fuss is about. We've all gotten along fine without those little phones for a long time. In fact, I think people who use their phones in public—in restaurants or movie theaters or even church—well, they are very inconsiderate."

"You really are old-fashioned, Grandma."

Betty peered at Avery. "Shall I assume you have a cell phone?"

"The light's green."

Betty pulled forward.

"I *had* one. But I lost it."

"Oh yes, the great hitchhiking heist."

Avery laughed.

"Well, you must promise me that you'll call your parents as soon as we get home, Avery." They shook on it.

Avery shadowed Betty as they perused the party store for golden anniversary items. Betty had offered in early November to do this for Marsha and Jim. And she'd meant to take care of it long before now, but she'd been hit with a nasty cold that had hung on much longer than usual. She just hoped that she hadn't waited too late. Fortunately, she'd had the foresight to order the napkins earlier. She just hoped there would be no shortage on paper plates and cups now.

"How about helium balloons?" Avery asked.

"Balloons?" Betty looked up at the gaudily decorated Mylar confections displayed along the wall and frowned. There were rainbows, kitty cats, dinosaurs, and cartoon characters, but nothing very appropriate for a golden anniversary. "I don't think so, dear."

"Why not?" Avery reached into a basket of regular balloons. The old-fashioned kind. "You could do the plain metallic-gold ones mixed with some pearly whites. Put a bunch of them together in balloon bouquets. It would be pretty."

Betty considered this, trying not to look shocked as Avery raised the balloon to her lips and proceeded to inflate it.

"And cheap," Avery said as she proudly held up the filled balloon. It was actually rather attractive, and it did look like gold.

Betty nodded. "Yes, I suppose balloons might be nice after all."

"Where are you having this little shindig anyway?" Avery let go of the balloon and it went flying through the store, making a long series of sputtering sounds.

Betty looked over her shoulder nervously. "The church."

"Down in the basement?"

"Yes, of course. That's where we have social functions."

"Then you'll need lots of balloons and all kinds of things to brighten it up."

"I've only budgeted fifty dollars for this," Betty said.

"Fifty bucks?" Avery frowned. "For how many people?"

"We've estimated around eighty to a hundred. Fortunately, I've already paid for the napkins."

They headed to the paper plate section.

"So what all do you need to get with your fifty bucks?"

Betty pulled out her list. "Paper plates, coffee cups, plastic punch glasses, and forks. Oh yes, and a few decorations."

Avery picked up a package of gold paper plates and shook her head. "I'm not a math whiz, Grandma, but these plates alone are going to eat up a big chunk of your budget."

Betty felt a headache coming on. Avery was probably right.

Oh, why hadn't she considered this earlier? "I suppose I'll just have to increase my budget."

"Or . . ."

"Or what?"

"Let me help you, Grandma."

Betty blinked. "That's very sweet, Avery. But how do you intend to help me?"

Avery got a sly look. "Back in high school, I loved doing set design in drama. I was always able to take a tiny budget and make it go a long way. Everyone was impressed. One year we did a pirate musical, and you should've seen how realistic it was."

Betty didn't know what drama or pirates had to do with golden anniversaries, but her head was beginning to throb more now. "I think I need an aspirin," she muttered as she opened her purse to peer inside.

"Are you sick?"

"Just a headache."

"I know," Avery said suddenly. "I saw a coffee shop next door. Why don't you go and sit down, take your aspirin, have a cup of coffee, and just relax. I'll do your shopping for you."

Betty knew this was a bad idea, but she didn't want to offend Avery. "Oh, I don't think that's necessary. I just—"

"No, Grandma." Avery snatched the list from Betty. "Let me do this for you. Just trust me, okay?"

Betty reached up and rubbed her temples.

"I promise you won't be disappointed."

"I just don't think it's a good idea, dear."

"You liked the balloon idea, didn't you?"

"Well, yes, but—"

"No buts."

Betty felt too flustered to think clearly. On one hand, it would be an enormous relief to hand this off to Avery, go and sit down, have a cup of tea, and take it easy. On the other hand, what if the whole thing turned into a complete mess?

"Really, Grandma, I *know* I can do this." Avery's eyes were so bright and hopeful that Betty decided she wanted to give the girl this chance. Really, what could it hurt? So she opened her purse, extracted the money she had put into an envelope marked "Deerwoods' Fiftieth," and handed the bills to Avery.

"And I can go to Goodwill too," Avery said. "You know, to pick up some clothes."

"Oh, yes." Betty had nearly forgotten that part of the plan. She reached into her purse again and took out her old, worn billfold. She pulled out two twenty-dollar bills. She knew that wasn't much for clothes shopping, but it was the remainder of her December grocery money. Still, she thought that perhaps this month's budget would need to be increased a bit. After all, she hadn't planned on having a houseguest. She could make adjustments for it later. It was always such a challenge living on a fixed and very limited income. But she had made it this far in life, and always the good Lord provided.

"Here you go, dear. I hope you can stretch this."

"Now you just go next door and relax, Grandma. Let me take care of everything."

Betty closed her purse and nodded. But the movement only made her head throb more. All she wanted was to sit down, take an aspirin, and sip a nice, hot cup of tea.

Before long, that was exactly what she was doing. And after about thirty minutes, she began to feel more like herself again.

"More hot water for your tea?" the middle-aged waitress asked.

Betty glanced at her watch. "Yes, I suppose that would be nice."

"Doing some Christmas shopping today?" The waitress refilled the metal teapot, snapping the lid shut.

"Not exactly." Betty smiled at her. She explained about her friends' fiftieth wedding anniversary and how her granddaughter had offered to help with the shopping.

"Your granddaughter must be delightful," the woman said. "What a relief when so many young people are so messed up. Did you hear the news today?"

"What's that?"

"Big drug bust over on 17th Street. Cocaine, meth, marijuana . . . there were even a bunch of firearms."

"In our town?" Betty clutched her coffee mug.

"Oh yeah." The waitress lowered her voice. "I actually recognized one of the young men. He'd been in here a number of times. I never would've guessed he was involved in something like that." She shook her head. "You just never know."

"No, I suppose not." Of course, this only made Betty think about Jack Jones again. Suspicions such as these had gone through her head more than once in regard to him. For all she knew, he could've ripped the house apart in order to grow marijuana inside. She'd heard of things like that before. And what if he had guns? Oh, it was too horrible to think about.

But what about that poor dog? Perhaps she'd been cruel to leave him there with Jack. She hoped that Jack wasn't cruel to the poor animal. And then she thought about her grand-daughter and how upset she would be if any harm came to that dog. What had Betty been thinking?

Betty looked at her watch again. She was surprised to see that an hour had passed with no sign of Avery. She finished the last sip of tea and wondered what she should do. The strip mall wasn't so large that Betty couldn't go look for Avery. But it was cold outside. And what if Betty went to the wrong place and Avery showed up at the coffee shop?

"Everything okay?" the waitress asked with a concerned expression.

"Yes. I just thought my granddaughter would be finished by now."

"Have you tried to call her?"

Betty frowned. "No . . . but I'm sure she'll be along any minute now."

"Yes, I'm sure she will."

But as soon as the waitress returned to the kitchen, Betty began to get worried. Really, what did she know about Avery? She hadn't spent time with her in years. Betty knew that she'd run away from home. And she hadn't even called her parents to say she was alive. Then she'd hitchhiked with a friend, gotten her things stolen, and eventually wound up on Betty's doorstep. Not exactly the profile of a responsible young woman. And not exactly like the picture Betty had concocted for the waitress.

For all Betty knew, Avery could be involved in something horrible. Something frightening like drugs. And hadn't Betty just given Avery a handful of cash? What if Avery was long gone by now? What if she'd simply pocketed Betty's money and run?

Betty sighed. It wouldn't be the money so much. But to think that Avery had tricked her, deceived her into believing that she wanted to help, when she was really taking advantage of her . . . Well, it wasn't only disheartening; it made Betty feel sick. She closed her eyes and took a deep breath, willing herself to relax, to let these worries go, and to put her trust in God. It was an old habit she'd adopted long ago—a way of dealing with life's stresses.

As she sat there with her eyes closed, she heard the familiar strain of Bing Crosby crooning, "I'll be home for Christmas, you can count on me . . ." Funny how the old tunes from her era were becoming popular among young people again.

She relaxed as she listened to the words, remembering how she and Chuck had been separated for one Christmas while he was serving in Korea. How many times had she listened to the song and cried? But then he'd come home, they'd gotten married, and she had never again expected to be separated from him during the holidays. Little had she known that they would have only a dozen Christmases to share. And then he'd be gone.

The song ended, and Betty opened her eyes to discover

that her cheeks were damp with tears. Embarrassed by this display of emotion, she quickly reached for the paper napkin and dabbed at her face. So silly, after all these years, to still be missing him like that.

She sighed and looked outside. It was starting to get dusky, and she had told Avery she wanted to be home while it was still light since she didn't see well after dark. She put out the money to pay for her tea and slowly stood.

"No sign of your granddaughter yet?" The waitress frowned.

Betty just shook her head and slowly walked toward the door. It felt as if someone had tied large rocks around her ankles. And she knew she was a very foolish old woman to have trusted Avery like that. At least she hadn't given her the car keys. That was something to be thankful for.

7

"Grandma!" Avery called. She rushed toward the coffee shop with what looked like dozens of shopping bags hanging from her shoulders, arms, and hands.

"Avery!" Betty couldn't believe her eyes. "Where have you been?"

"Shopping, of course."

"But you took so long." Betty peered at her. "How did you manage to buy so much . . . stuff?"

"Goodwill, the Dollar Store, and a craft shop around the corner."

"Oh?" Betty opened the trunk of her car, watching as Avery piled in her purchases.

"Yeah. I found all sorts of cool things, Grandma. It's going to be so awesome."

Betty blinked to see some magenta and lime-colored artificial flowers tumbling out of a large plastic bag. She couldn't imagine what those bright blooms might be for—perhaps a Mexican fiesta. But they certainly weren't appropriate for a dignified fiftieth anniversary party. Even so, she was so relieved to see Avery again, to know that she hadn't run off and that she actually had been shopping—well, Betty didn't even care what kind of frivolities Avery had wasted her money on. At least she was safe.

Avery was very secretive about her purchases when they got home. She asked if she could keep the decorations in her room while she worked on them. Betty had no idea what that meant, but she was too tired to protest, so she agreed.

"But don't forget your promise," Betty said. "To call your parents."

"Yeah." Avery nodded as she went into her room. "I'll do it."

"I'm going to begin fixing dinner. I have decided that I'll do the cooking and you'll be on cleanup. Does that sound fair?"

Avery grinned. "Sure. I love your cooking, Grandma."

Betty smiled. Maybe Avery hadn't changed that much after all. Still, it was a bit stressful having a young person suddenly thrust into your life. One didn't know what to expect, how to react.

Tonight Betty was making macaroni and cheese, but not the boxed kind that turned out orange and salty. Avery had talked her into getting some of the boxed kind at the store when she'd been visiting Betty one summer. One bite and Betty had decided that Avery needed to learn a better way. Avery had been cautious at first, complaining that Betty's macaroni "looked funny," but after she tasted it, she declared it to be the "bestest macaroni and cheese ever." Betty made it with real cheese and butter and cream, and she always baked it in the oven, removing the foil for the last few minutes so the bread crumbs turned crispy and golden brown. Betty hadn't made macaroni and cheese in ages, but her mouth was watering when she finally slid the heavy casserole dish into the oven.

She looked at her messy kitchen, then smiled to herself. This was one of the benefits of having Avery here. Betty could cook what she liked, and her granddaughter would clean up the mess. Not a bad little setup.

"Grandma," Avery said from the living room. "Someone's at the door. Want me to get it?"

"I'm coming." Betty untied her apron and went out to see who was there. It was nearly six now, and most respectable people would be having dinner.

"Oh!" Avery said. She opened the front door wide enough for Betty to see Jack standing there, a somber expression on his face and a familiar-looking garbage bag in his hand. The dog stood at his feet, wagging his tail and looking into the house like he expected to be invited in for dinner.

"What do you want?" Avery put her hands on her hips and scowled at Jack.

Jack studied her for a moment, then turned toward Betty. "I don't know what your game is, but I do not want a dog."

Avery stepped forward and stared up into Jack's face. "Seems like you should've thought of that sooner."

"Huh?" He frowned. "Who are you anyway?"

"This is my granddaughter, Avery," Betty said. "Avery, I'd like you to meet my neighbor Jack."

"I know all about you, Jack," Avery said. "I wanted to report you to the Humane Society, but Grandma wouldn't let me."

"What?"

Avery pointed down at the dog. "You're a grown man.

You should know better than to treat an animal the way you've treated him. He's a sweet dog, and you have totally neglected and—"

"You're crazy," he said. "This isn't my dog."

"He was filthy and cold and half-starved and—"

"And he's not my dog," Jack said. He looked over at Betty again. "I thought he was your dog. I saw him in your yard."

"And I saw him in your yard," Betty said. "I assumed he belonged to you."

"Looks like we both assumed wrong." Jack dropped the plastic bag in her house. "Here you go."

"What do you mean, 'here you go'?" Betty said.

"You got him this stuff." Jack glared at her. "I guess that means he belongs to you."

"He does *not* belong to me." Betty stepped closer, glaring back at him now.

"Looks to me like he does. You got him the collar and leash and—"

"But he is *not* my dog. I only got those things because I thought you were—"

"So you admit that you purchased the dog paraphernalia?"

"I felt sorry for the dog."

"And they say possession is nine-tenths of the law, right?"

Betty didn't know how to respond.

He kicked the plastic bag with the toe of his boot. "So this is your dog bed, and that must mean this is your dog."

"But I don't want a—"

"I'd appreciate it if you'd quit dropping your dog off at

my house." He narrowed his eyes at Betty. "And if you do it again, I will report *you* to the Humane Society. Do you understand?"

Betty was too angry to respond.

"We understand," Avery snapped, "that you are a selfish, mean man. And you don't deserve a dog like this." She reached down and picked up the mutt, holding him protectively in her arms. "He is lucky to escape you."

"You got that right!" Jack turned and slammed the door shut behind him.

"What a beast!" Avery said.

"Good riddance," Betty said.

"You poor thing," Avery cooed to the dog. "I'll bet you're hungry."

Betty just stared at her granddaughter and the dog. She wanted to tell Avery in no uncertain terms that the dog was not welcome in her home. But Avery looked so happy and hopeful that Betty just couldn't bring herself to say those words. Not yet anyway. Besides, there wasn't much they could do about the situation tonight. The animal shelter would probably be closed by now. And Betty didn't like to drive after dark anyway. She would deal with the dog tomorrow.

"Don't forget to call your parents," Betty said as she headed back to the kitchen to make a salad.

While Betty was in the kitchen, she overheard Avery talking on the phone. She could tell she was talking to her mother and that it wasn't an easy conversation.

"I want to stay *here* for Christmas," Avery said. There was a long pause, and Betty imagined what Stephanie was probably saying to her daughter. So often she had used accusatory words, negativity, blame, and guilt to pressure her daughter into complying with her wishes. Betty had witnessed these awkward conversations before. But because Stephanie wasn't her daughter and Betty had no actual blood relation to Avery, she had always kept her mouth shut. Still, it had troubled her. It seemed unhealthy. And sad.

"I'm a grown-up," Avery said. "And I can—" She was obviously cut off again. No surprises there. "I'm sorry you feel that way, Mother. Merry Christmas to you!" There was a loud bang as Avery slammed the receiver down. Good thing that old phone was tough.

"My mother is a moron," Avery said as she joined Betty in the kitchen. "Man, something smells really good in here." She peeked in the oven. "Mac and cheese?"

"Yes. I was hankering for some."

Avery smacked her lips. "All right."

"So . . . how are your parents?" Betty asked with hesitation.

"I don't know about Gary. But my mom is as messed up as ever."

"I'm sure they've been worried about you."

"My mom is more worried about how it looks to have a missing daughter." Avery began to imitate her mother. "'Oh dear, what *will* people think if Avery is still AWOL at Christmas? It will completely ruin our hallowed Christmas celebrations if Avery doesn't show up looking like the perfect little princess daughter. Oh my, we must keep up appearances.'"

Betty smiled. Avery actually did sound a lot like Stephanie. Not that Betty intended to say as much.

"I gave the dog some food, Grandma. But he hasn't even touched it. Do you think he's okay?"

"I have no idea. I've never had a dog before."

"Me neither. But he's so sweet. If he really doesn't belong to Jack, I think I'll keep him."

As they set the table together, Betty wanted to point out how unrealistic Avery's adopt-a-dog plan was, but she decided to hold her tongue for now. Of course, the dog would need to go to the animal shelter tomorrow. But Betty would see to that. In the meantime, it wouldn't hurt to postpone that conversation. And Avery seemed so happy tonight, chatting cheerfully as they ate dinner. Betty felt there was no sense in hurrying up what would surely come as a disappointment later.

While Avery was cleaning up the dinner things, the phone rang. Betty always had a tendency to jump when the phone rang. Maybe it was because she didn't get that many calls in the evening. Or maybe it was just an old reaction from a time when a ringing phone could bring bad news. But she hurried to pick up the extension in the hallway, out of the noise of the kitchen.

"Hi, Mom."

"Oh, Gary." Betty smiled as she sat in the straight-backed chair. "It's so nice to hear your voice."

"You too. I hear that Avery paid you a surprise visit."

"Yes, she's here. And I'm thoroughly enjoying her."

"I'm sure she's enjoying you too." There was a pause, and Betty thought she could hear another voice in the background. "But, uh, Stephanie is not too happy."

"Oh?"

"She really wants Avery home for Christmas."

"That's what Avery said."

"And she wants me to tell you that you should send her home."

"I should *send* her home?" Betty blinked as she imagined packing her granddaughter in a large cardboard box and shipping her out to Atlanta on a UPS truck.

"Naturally, we'll pay for her airline ticket," he said quickly. "But if you could just make Avery see that she needs to—"

"I doubt that I can *make* Avery do anything she doesn't want to do."

"Okay, Mom, *make* was not the right word. But I know that you could influence her. Avery would listen to you."

"Avery is an adult, Gary."

"An adult who can act very childish."

"Perhaps she acts childish because she is so often treated as a child."

There was a long pause. "You make a good point."

"Avery seems to want to stay here," Betty said. "She has offered to help me with the Deerwoods' fiftieth anniversary celebration."

"They've been married fifty years?"

"Yes." Betty wanted to point out that she and Gary's father would've been beyond that milestone by now if Chuck was still alive. But she realized there was no reason to.

"Tell them congratulations for me."

"I will. But, you see, Avery has helped me to get things. And she's going to work on them and—"

"Sorry, Mom," he said quickly. "But Stephanie wants the phone. Do you mind talking to her?"

"Not at all." But Betty wasn't the one to do the talking. When Stephanie got on the other end, she immediately began to rant and rave about how Avery needed to come home—right now. About how she'd been gone away too long. And about how it was wrong for Betty to keep her away from her family.

"Excuse me," Betty said. "I am *not* keeping Avery from anyone."

"You're making it easier for her to avoid facing up to her responsibilities."

"Her responsibilities?"

"To her family."

"What responsibilities does she have to her family?"

"To be here with us. To be with our friends. It's what we do every year. Avery knows that."

"But Avery is an adult," she said for the second time. "She should be able to make up her own mind about—"

"Avery has the mind of a child," Stephanie snapped. "She proved that by running off and doing God only knows what with God only knows who."

"That may be. But she's here with me now. She's in no danger."

"And I suppose you can promise me that, Betty? You're prepared to take personal responsibility for my daughter's welfare?"

"I'm only saying that she is just fine. And she's welcome to stay with me for as long as—"

"So you're choosing her side. You're taking a stand against me while you enable her."

Betty wasn't exactly sure what *enabling* meant these days, but the way Stephanie slung the term, like it was an accusation, worried Betty. Why didn't game shows like *Jeopardy* talk about words like this? Just the same, Betty decided to give it a try. "Wouldn't *enabling* mean that I'm *helping* a person to do something . . . as in making them *able*?"

Stephanie laughed so loudly that Betty's ear rang, and she had to hold the receiver away. "Of course that's what you'd think, Betty. But no, enabling is making it easy for a person to avoid what they really need to be doing. You enable them to fail."

"Oh." Betty had no response to that.

"But if you're determined to position yourself between us and Avery"—Stephanie made a sniffling sound, although Betty did not think she was really crying—"then I suppose I can't stop you."

"I'm not taking a position," Betty said.

"Oh yes you are."

"I've simply told Avery she can stay with me through the holidays if she wants to and—"

"Fine. Have it your way. I hope you both have a very merry Christmas!" Of course, with the tone of her voice and the way she said this, she could've been using foul language and the meaning would not have been much different. And before Betty could respond, she heard the dull buzz of the dial tone in her ear.

"Let me guess," Avery said as she appeared in the hallway with a dish towel hanging limply in her hand. "My mom?"

Betty just nodded as she replaced the phone.

"Now she's mad at you too?"

"I'm afraid so."

Avery grinned. "Well, join the club, Grandma."

"Apparently my dues are all paid up in full."

"My mother would've made a good dictator."

Betty stifled a smile.

"She wants to rule the world, you know."

"I just hope you're sure you're making the right decision to stay here for the holidays."

Avery frowned. "You don't want me?"

Betty hesitated. Of course she wanted her. But was she wrong to keep Avery from returning home? Was she an enabler—the bad kind?

"I'll leave if you want me to," Avery said quietly.

"No, of course I don't want you to leave." Betty put a hand on her shoulder. "I only want what's best for you, dear."

Avery nodded, but there was a flicker of hurt in her eyes. Betty wondered if she should say more to reassure her granddaughter. But what could she say? It was true that Betty only wanted what was best for Avery. The problem was that Betty didn't have a clue as to what that was. Should Avery stay here and risk angering her mother? Or go home and face whatever it was she needed to face? Really, what was best? And it seemed unlikely that an old woman like herself—living on a very frugal budget and on the verge of selling her home and fleeing from a questionable neighborhood—was truly the best resource for someone like Avery.

8

Then next morning, Betty got up at her usual time, just a bit past seven. But when she went to the laundry room to check on the dog, she was surprised to discover that he was not there. The door was firmly shut, just like it had been last night, and his bed and food dishes were still there, but the dog was missing. Betty checked around the house and even looked out into the backyard, but the mutt was nowhere to be seen.

Finally, worried that Jack had sneaked over and broken into her house in the middle of the night, she decided to check on the welfare of her granddaughter. And there, in the guest bed, were both Avery and the dog. The dog looked up from where he was comfortably curled up against Avery's back, but Avery continued to snooze. Betty just shook her head and quietly closed the door. She hoped the dog didn't have fleas.

Thanks to the dog's need to go outside, Avery got up before eight. Betty sipped her coffee, watching as Avery waited by the sliding door for the dog to finish up his business. To Betty's relief he had found another part of the yard—not the dogwood tree—to relieve himself this time.

"It's freezing out there," Avery said as she let the dog back inside. "Do you think it'll snow?"

"I'm sure it's a possibility." Betty set her coffee mug down.

"I've always wanted to see a white Christmas," she said dreamily. "Maybe this will be the year."

"Maybe." Betty smiled at Avery. "Now, if you don't mind, I'd like to hear more about what you got for the Deerwoods' anniversary party."

Avery's mouth twisted to one side. "But I wanted to surprise you, Grandma."

"Surprise me?"

"Yes. I have to work on everything. But I don't want you to see it until I'm done."

"That's very sweet of you, dear. But I'd really like to have some sort of an idea of what you're—"

"I used your list," Avery said. "And I can guarantee you that I got enough plates and cups and things for a hundred people. And I've got what I need for decorations too. So can't you just let me work on it and surprise you? I promise you it'll be awesome. You won't be disappointed."

Betty thought of those loud magenta and lime flowers she'd spied in the trunk and wasn't so sure. What if the Deerwood party turned into a luau or a fiesta or a pirate party? How would Betty explain it?

"Please?" Avery asked.

Betty remembered how many times Avery's mother had questioned Avery's abilities, belittled her skills, and treated her like a child. "All right." Betty nodded. "I will trust you with this, Avery."

Avery threw her arms around Betty. "Thank you, Grandma! I won't let you down."

After breakfast, Avery remained barricaded in her room. Occasionally, she'd emerge in search of things like glue, scissors, staplers, and tape. Sometimes she would carry plastic bags out to the garage, warning Betty not to come out and peek while she worked on something out there. Avery reminded Betty of some mad scientist, secretly creating . . . what? Frankenstein? A bomb? Hopefully the Deerwoods' fiftieth anniversary would survive whatever it was she was putting together.

To distract herself, Betty decided to proceed with her Christmas baking. Just as she was attempting to fit a pan of fudge into the fridge, she felt a nudge on the back of her leg. She jumped and nearly dropped the pan before she realized it was the dog.

"Oh!" she exclaimed. "You scared me."

The dog looked hopefully at her, wagging his tail, then he ran toward the sliding glass door.

"You need to go out?" she said as she slid the fudge pan onto the lower shelf. "I'm coming, I'm coming." She opened the door and let the dog out, but as she was waiting she heard the oven timer ring. She hurried back to the kitchen, worried that her walnut squares might be getting overdone, which would ruin them completely. But she removed the pan to see that they looked just about perfect. And smelled even better.

She got out the waxed paper, tore off a sheet, and laid it on the cutting board. Then she sifted a layer of powdered sugar onto this and went back to see that the pan had cooled just slightly, so she carefully turned it upside down and dumped the squares onto the waxed paper. She sifted more powdered sugar over the top while the squares were still warm.

Finally they were finished. She couldn't resist trying a square just to be sure. And then, of course, she needed a cup of coffee to go with it. She poured the last one from the morning pot, then sat down to enjoy this lovely little treat.

She had just finished it up when she looked out into the backyard to realize that the dog didn't appear to be there. She stood and looked more closely, peering to the left and the right. Then she went outside to call for him. But he didn't come. That's when she noticed the hole in the back fence. Had the foolish dog gone off and wandered into Jack's yard again? She peered into Jack's yard, which was just as messy as ever, but she didn't see any sign of the dog. Still, she felt certain that was where he had gone.

Betty returned to the house and wondered what to do. Really, the sooner she took the dog to the pound, the better they'd all be. Besides, it had occurred to her that it was entirely possible the dog already had an owner who was looking for him. In the meantime, she didn't want to give Jack enough time to follow through with last night's threat to call the Humane Society and turn her in as a negligent pet owner. Not that he could prove such an outrageous accusation, but even so, she didn't wish to invite trouble.

She got her walking jacket and the dog leash, and on her way through the kitchen she paused to look at the walnut squares. Suddenly she remembered what her daughter Susan had said: "Kill him with kindness." Fine, that was just what she would do. Or at least try.

Betty got into her holiday cupboard, dug out a festive plastic Christmas plate, and carefully arranged walnut squares and fudge on it. It would've been prettier with a few more kinds of cookies, but this would have to do. She covered it tightly with plastic wrap and hoped that this would do the trick. Then she slipped on her gloves, and armed with leash and cookies, she was ready for her mission.

Before she left, she knocked on Avery's door.

"Don't come in!" Avery yelled.

"I won't. I'm just going next door."

"Okay!"

Betty considered giving her granddaughter a fuller explanation about the missing dog but didn't want to involve her in what could easily turn into another nasty dispute. Who knew how Jack would react? Would he assume that Betty had purposely sent the dog to his house in order to harass him? Just what she didn't need right now. Hopefully her sugary peace offering would help to smooth things over.

As she walked to Jack's house, Betty wondered how she might use the dog's runabout habits to her advantage today. She was well aware that Avery wanted to keep the dog. But perhaps she could convince her that the reason the dog had run away was to search for its real owner. And that the responsible thing to do was to reunite the mutt with his family. Surely Avery would understand.

Today Jack's front yard was cluttered with what appeared to be the Spencers' old wall-to-wall carpeting. Betty frowned down at a strip of olive-green rug. Gladys had always kept her home immaculate, and Betty suspected that the carpet still had many years of serviceable use left in it. Not that Jack seemed to care about such things.

Not for the first time, Betty was curious as to the interior state of the house. She stepped over the carpet strip and rang the doorbell. She could hear a power tool running inside, whirring noisily. She rang the bell again and then knocked. But the sound of the machine continued steadily, and Betty knew that it was hopeless. She was tempted to try the door but knew that could easily backfire. The last thing she needed was for Jack to accuse her of breaking and entering.

She considered leaving the cookie plate behind, but Jack would probably assume it was one of his neighbors attempting to poison him and toss it into the trash. And she wasn't about to waste perfectly good cookies.

Why was this so frustrating?

She turned on her heel and marched back to her house. Really, why did she even bother? As for the dog, well, he was on his own as far as Betty was concerned.

"Where's Ralph?" Avery asked as Betty came into the house.

"Ralph?" Betty set the cookie plate aside and removed her gloves.

"The dog."

"You named him Ralph?" Betty blinked. "Why?"

"It was my grandpa's name."

"Oh. Well . . ." Betty hung up her coat.

"I looked in the laundry room and in the backyard, but I didn't see him anywhere. Do you know where he is?" Avery looked worried.

"I was looking for him myself. I thought maybe he'd gone to Jack's house."

"Did he?"

"I don't know for sure. Jack's not answering his door."

"But you think Ralph is there?"

Betty shrugged. "Or perhaps he ran away to search for his owner."

"His owner?" Avery scowled. "Do you really think Ralph has an owner, Grandma? He looked like he'd been abandoned or was a runaway."

"Or maybe he's just lost. It occurred to me that he could have a family who loves him. Someone might be looking for him."

"He didn't have a collar. And you said there'd been a string tied around his neck, almost like someone wanted to strangle him."

"We don't know that for sure, Avery."

"Well, I'm going out to look for him." Avery reached for the door.

"Wear a coat," Betty told her. "It's freezing out there."

So Avery grabbed her coat, took the leash, and then was gone. Betty stood by Avery's closed bedroom door and considered taking a peek, but she knew that would offend her granddaughter. Instead, she returned to her baking.

She was just rolling out sugar cookie dough when Avery appeared—with the dog. "I found Ralph!" she said.

Betty peered down at the dog. He was wagging his tail happily, sniffing the floor and eagerly licking up spilled crumbs from Betty's baking spree. "Where did you find him?"

"You were right, Grandma." Avery tossed her parka over a kitchen chair. "He was at Jack's house."

"Jack answered the door?"

"Nope."

Betty frowned.

"I rang the bell and knocked, and finally I just opened the door and went in."

"You went *into* Jack's house?" Betty's hand flew to her mouth.

"Yep. Walked right in. Man, what a mess."

"What was going on inside?"

"Major demolition."

"He's tearing the place apart?"

"It sure looked like it."

"Did you see anything, uh, unusual?" Betty wanted to ask specifically about dangerous things like drugs or firearms, but knew that sounded a bit paranoid.

"I didn't get far enough to see much."

"Jack stopped you?"

"Yeah. But not before I spotted Ralph."

Betty shook her head.

"So I snatched up Ralph and gave Jack a piece of my mind."

"Oh dear."

"I told Jack that he was rude and selfish and mean, and that you were a nice person and that he had no right to make your life miserable."

Betty held on to a kitchen chair to brace herself. "You said all that?"

"I sure did."

"Oh my."

Avery took a piece of cookie dough and popped it in her mouth. "Yum!"

"And what did Jack say to you?" Betty asked. "I mean in response to all you said to him?"

Avery laughed. "Nothing. I think he was speechless."

"Did you ask him why he let the dog in his house?"

"I accused him of dognapping."

"Dognapping?"

"Yeah. I told him since he'd made it clear that Ralph didn't belong to him, he had no right taking him into his house."

"I am curious as to why he'd do that. Especially after all he said last night. He seemed to genuinely dislike the dog."

Avery nodded. "Yeah. I think it's suspicious, Grandma. I don't trust Jack."

Now Betty remembered her previous strategy. "But I'm also curious as to why the dog took off like that, Avery. It makes me think that he could be looking for his family."

"We're his family now, Grandma."

Betty frowned. "But what if someone out there is missing him, Avery? Perhaps a family with children? What if they want their pup home for Christmas?"

Avery bit her lip.

"We wouldn't want to be responsible for someone's sorrow."

Avery nodded. "You're right. I'll make 'found dog' posters. I'll put them in the neighborhood and—"

"But I thought we should take him to the dog shelter."

Avery shook her head stubbornly. "No, that would be cruel."

Betty didn't know what to say.

"Let me handle this, Grandma. Please."

Betty looked down at the dog and sighed. "I'll tell you what, Avery. I'll give you until the weekend to find his owners."

Avery nodded. "Okay. I'll do my best."

"In the meantime, the dog—"

"Ralph."

"Fine. In the meantime, Ralph will be your responsibility."

"No problem."

"And I suggest you fix that hole in the fence unless you want to go looking for him at Jack's house again."

"I'll handle it." Avery reached for another clump of cookie dough and popped it in her mouth, then turned to the dog. "Come on, Ralph."

Betty watched as the dog, tail wagging, followed Avery out of the kitchen just like he'd been doing it his whole life. Still, this was not reassuring. Already it seemed that Avery had bonded with the dog. What would happen when she'd be forced to part with him?

9

Avery, true to her word, made "found dog" posters and hung them around the neighborhood. But, just to be sure, Betty called the animal shelter and local vets to let them know about Ralph as well. Naturally, she did this while Avery was holed up in her room, where she was working on the anniversary things and unable to hear. But so far there hadn't been a single inquiry about the dog. Betty didn't know what to make of it.

Then late on Thursday afternoon, the dog went missing again. Avery was fit to be tied, and Betty felt a mixture of relief and regret. On one hand, it would be easier for everyone if the dog simply exited their lives as quickly as he'd entered. Yet at the same time, Betty realized she'd grown a tad bit fond of the mutt. She didn't mind when he nestled down at her feet while she sat at the kitchen table. And she liked how nicely he would sit to wait for a treat—just like someone had taught him manners. Sometimes she thought he was a right nice little dog. This, of course, worried her—she had no intention of becoming attached to a pet.

"I'll bet Jack took him again," Avery said as she pulled on her parka. "I'm going to find out."

"I don't think you should go alone." Betty pushed herself up from her recliner.

"You sit tight, Grandma," Avery said. "I can handle this."

Betty wasn't so sure. "But Jack is a bit unpredictable, dear."

"I can deal with him."

"Wait," Betty said. "Why don't you take him a cookie plate?"

"A cookie plate?" Avery frowned. "Why would I want to do that?"

Betty took Avery by the elbow and walked her to the kitchen as she explained the "kill him with kindness" theory. "Your Aunt Susan reminded me of it a few days ago. And I think it's worth a try."

"I don't know."

But Betty was already loading up a Christmas platter. "I don't think it could hurt," she said as she wrapped it in plastic wrap. "And if it doesn't sweeten him up, well, at least we can tell Susan that we gave it a try."

"Okay." But as Avery took the plate, she still looked skeptical.

"Are you sure you don't want me to come along?"

"No, I'll be fine."

"Just be careful." Betty shook her finger in warning.

"Yeah, yeah." Avery was already halfway out the door.

Betty sighed as she returned to her recliner and the task of untangling an old string of Christmas lights. Earlier that morning Avery had decided to venture into the attic, then happily came down with two boxes of Christmas decorations. After that, she'd been determined that the house should be decorated to the hilt.

At first, Betty had opposed the idea. She had imagined being alone when it was time to take everything down, struggling to get it all put away before her trip to Florida. However, it wasn't long before the youthful enthusiasm infected Betty, and it was fun to see Avery enjoying herself. Betty watched with fascination as her granddaughter tried out new ways of using old decorations. For instance, Betty never would've hung her mother's old handblown glass ornaments on the dining room chandelier, but they actually looked quite lovely there, reflecting and refracting the light. Very clever indeed.

Betty set aside the hopelessly tangled lights and frowned out the front window. Had she been foolish to allow her granddaughter to go to that man's house? She got up and hurried to the kitchen, nervously staring at Jack's mess of a house as if she thought she could help Avery should trouble erupt. Just then the phone rang, and she was forced to turn away from the window.

She'd barely said hello when the female voice on the other end demanded to know if Avery was there.

"Hello, Stephanie," Betty said cheerfully, hoping she could warm up her daughter-in-law. "How are you doing, dear?"

"How do you think I'm doing when my only daughter refuses to come home for Christmas?"

"I really don't see why that should be such an—"

"That's just it. You really don't see, do you, Betty?"

"Avery is a grown woman, Stephanie. Shouldn't she be allowed to make her own choices about where—"

"Talk to your son," Stephanie snapped.

And then Gary was on the line. "Hi, Mom," he said.

"Hello, Gary."

"Stephanie wants me to persuade you to send Avery home."

"Is that what you want too?"

"I suppose." His voice sounded flat.

"But why? I don't understand why it's so important."

He didn't answer right away, and when he did, his voice was quiet. "Stephanie's mom is coming for Christmas. And, as you know, Evelyn is, uh, well, rather jealous."

"Oh?" Betty was well aware that Evelyn had often resented Betty's relationship with Avery in the past. But that was when Avery had been a little girl, a long time ago.

"I know it probably sounds silly to you."

"I just don't really understand."

"Well, Evelyn wants us to help her with her will. And Stephanie is worried that if Avery isn't here, and if Evelyn figures out that she's with you . . . well, Stephanie feels this could present a problem."

Betty was speechless. Did they plan to use Avery as some sort of bargaining chip, a form of insurance to assure them they would be properly compensated for in Evelyn's will? This just seemed so ridiculous.

"I know what you're thinking, Mom."

"Really?"

"I can guess."

"Well, I must admit that I'm a bit surprised."

"Anyway, I'm not telling you what to do." His voice was

gentle now. More like the old Gary. "I'm just telling you how it is here. Frankly, I'm glad that Avery is with you. I think you're a wholesome influence in her life."

"Well, thank you."

"I just wanted you to know that Steph is very determined."

"I see."

"So if Avery could give her a call, just talk things through, I'd appreciate it."

"I'll tell Avery."

"And I apologize for how Steph just spoke to you. All I can say is that she's very upset. And she's been hurt deeply by Avery's little disappearing act."

"I'm sure it's been difficult for her."

"But I realize Avery is an adult. At least according to her birth date."

"If it's any encouragement, Avery is acting very much like an adult." Betty described how Avery had taken full responsibility for the anniversary preparations and how she'd put up "found dog" posters. "And this morning she even got me to help in decorating the house for Christmas. I'd been feeling a bit like Scrooge. But she's so enthusiastic that I finally gave in. And she's actually quite clever." Betty rambled on until Gary said he needed to go.

"I'll tell Avery to call her mother," Betty said. Then she hung up and looked out across the backyard toward Jack's house. It was dusky now, and suddenly Betty felt concerned. How long had Avery been gone? Shouldn't she be back by now? Betty could see light coming from what had once been the dining room window. But there was something like a sheet draped over it, so she couldn't see inside.

Betty began pacing in the kitchen. Should she go and check on the girl? Or would that seem like interfering? Would it send the message that Avery wasn't mature? That she wasn't capable of taking care of herself?

Betty looked up at the clock. It was about four forty now. Perhaps she should wait until five. But what might happen in twenty minutes? And then, if something really was wrong, wouldn't it be foolish for Betty to go over there? Wouldn't it be better to call the police? But if she called the police, what would she say to them? That her grown granddaughter had been at the neighbor's house for more than thirty minutes? They'd probably just laugh or write her off as crazy.

She considered calling the Gilmores, but what would she say to them? Katie was already fearful about Jack. Why alarm them further? Or maybe Katie and the girls had fled to her mother's by now. In that case, what would Betty say to poor Martin? He'd already endured several confrontations with their contrary neighbor. Why would he want to have another?

Betty continued to pace, staring out the window and trying to replace her worry with prayer. But her prayers sounded feeble. "Protect Avery," she said again and again.

Finally, it was nearly five o'clock, and she could stand it no longer. She went for her coat and took off to discover what was wrong. If all else failed, she might be able to scream loudly enough to disturb a neighbor. But Betty had barely rounded the corner when she spied Avery and the dog strolling her way.

"What happened?" Betty said. "Are you okay?"

"Sure." Avery smiled.

"But you were gone so long." Betty realized that her hands were shaking. Perhaps it was from the cold, but she thought otherwise.

"You were right, Grandma."

"Right?"

"Jack seemed to appreciate the cookies."

"Really?" Betty wasn't sure how to respond. She should be happy about that, but instead she felt suspicious.

"And we had a nice talk."

"Is that so?" Betty imagined Jack's dark countenance as he eyed her granddaughter. Sizing her up, making his plans for evil. Avery was a beautiful young woman. And vulnerable too. What if Jack were a rapist, a serial killer, or both? Oh, why had Betty been such a fool as to let her go over there by herself?

"He's lonely, Grandma."

"Is that what he told you?"

"Yes, and—"

"I don't want you going over there by yourself again," Betty said quickly. "I'm afraid he could be dangerous and—"

"He's not dangerous." Avery laughed.

"You don't know that."

"Oh, Grandma, you're just being paranoid. Jack told me about the misunderstandings you've had and how he's tried to talk sense into you, but how you just won't listen, and now the whole neighborhood has turned against him."

"And you believe him?" Betty stopped walking and turned

to peer at Avery. Her face was illuminated by the streetlight, and she looked confused.

"Why shouldn't I believe him?"

"Because he's not trustworthy, Avery."

"But you're the one who said to be kind to him. And I think that's just what he needed."

Betty was too flustered to respond. So they both walked back to the house with only the clicking of the dog's toenails on the sidewalk to break the silence.

Why hadn't Betty seen the danger in this situation? Why had she allowed Avery to walk right into what could have easily been a trap? Wasn't that how criminals worked? They earned the victim's trust, and then they went to work. What would Avery's mother think if she knew?

"Your mother called," Betty said as they went into the house.

"So?"

"She wants you to call her back." Betty removed her jacket. "She said it's urgent."

"Big surprise there."

"But you'll call her, won't you?"

"I guess."

"I promised that you would."

Avery groaned. "I wish she'd just leave me alone."

"I'm going to start dinner," Betty said. She headed for the kitchen, but once she got there, she just stood and looked out the window toward Jack's house. As she looked, it appeared more frightening and sinister than ever. And so she prayed again. Only this time she prayed that somehow Stephanie would convince her daughter to come home for Christmas. And, as much as Betty would miss the girl, she felt certain that Avery would be safer there than here.

Because they'd had a good-sized lunch, with a snack of Christmas cookies and tea in midafternoon, Betty decided to fix oatmeal for dinner. This with whole wheat toast and home-canned peaches should be sufficient for both of them. She was just taking the oatmeal off the stove when Avery appeared.

"My mother is losing her mind." Avery sat down at the kitchen table, which Betty had already set for their simple meal.

"How so?" Betty avoided Avery's eyes as she spooned the hot cereal into the bowls.

"She says Grandma Evelyn is dying."

"Is she?"

"I seriously don't think so."

Betty sat down, bowed her head, and asked the blessing. Then she looked at Avery. "So why does your mother think Evelyn is dying?"

"Because she's old."

Betty nodded. "But what if your mother is right?"

Avery just shrugged and stuck her spoon into the brown sugar, dumping two heaping spoonfuls onto her oatmeal.

"Would you feel bad if you didn't get to see your grand-mother . . . if she were to die?"

"I guess."

Betty felt a stab of guilt. She knew she was being some-what insincere with her granddaughter. But she was doing it for Avery's own good. She wanted Avery out of harm's way. More specifically, out of Jack's way.

"I still regret not making one last trip out to see my own mother," Betty said slowly. "I knew she'd been having some health problems, but I just didn't believe it was terribly serious. I considered going out to visit in June. But then I changed my mind. I don't even recall why exactly. The next thing I knew, she was gone. I never got another chance."

Avery nodded. "I'm sorry."

"Thank you, dear."

"But that was your mother. Not your grandmother."

"That's true."

"And I assume you had a good relationship with her?"

"Yes, very good."

"Well, it's not like that with me and my grandmother."

"Perhaps that's an even better reason to spend time with her."

"So that she can torture me?"

Betty didn't know what to say.

"Grandma Evelyn and my mom will probably gang up on me, Grandma. They'll get on my case for taking off. They'll lecture me about going back to school. They'll remind me that I'm a failure, and then they'll rub my nose in it." Avery seemed on the verge of tears now. She set down her spoon with a clank. "And I just can't take that—that's not a happy way to spend Christmas." She scooted her chair back and ran out of the kitchen, slamming her bedroom door behind her.

Betty felt like a villain. And her few bites of oatmeal now sat like hard little stones in her stomach. She just sat there with her hands laid flat on the kitchen table and wondered how she had managed to make such a mess of things. How was it possible to hurt someone so deeply when you only wished to help them?

Betty realized she was crying for the second time in one week. The tears surprised her. She was a woman who usually kept her emotions in check. But what surprised her even more was the feeling of something warm pressing against her leg. She looked down to see the dog sitting right next to her, looking up at her with the most compassionate brown eyes she'd ever seen.

Reaching down, she stroked his smooth head. "You really are a good dog, aren't you?" She stood slowly. "But there is someone else who needs you more than I do right now. Come on, boy." He obediently followed as she walked to Avery's room and quietly opened the door. Betty let him into the darkened room, where the quiet sobs of a hurting girl cut through her like a knife. She knew the animal's presence would just be a Band-Aid—a temporary solution to a problem that was much bigger than a little brown dog. But at the moment, it was all Betty had to offer.

10

Avery's mother called again the next morning. Betty tried not to eavesdrop as she took over the chore of cleaning up the breakfast things, but she could tell that Avery was trying to be reasonable. She could hear the strained patience in Avery's voice. She had to give the girl credit—she was trying.

"I'll call you tonight," Avery promised. "Yes, Mom, I love you too."

Betty was just putting the last dish in the dishwasher when Avery came back to the kitchen. "Hey, Grandma, you weren't supposed to clean up."

"It's all right." Betty smiled as she gave the speckled Formica countertop one last swipe with the sponge. "I didn't mind."

"I told my mom that I'd make a decision by tonight."

Betty just nodded.

Avery looked at her hopefully. "What do you want me to do, Grandma?"

"I want you to do what's best for you."

"But you think I need to be with my family?"

Betty pressed her lips together tightly.

"You're not going to tell me, are you?"

"I think it's a decision you need to make, Avery."

"Well, I'm not going to think about it today." Avery brightened. "Today I'm going to go decorate the church basement for the Deerwood party."

Betty blinked in surprise. "Goodness, I'd nearly forgotten that today's Friday."

"And tomorrow's the big event," Avery said. "The church secretary told me that I could come anytime after eleven today to get everything all set up for tomorrow."

Betty tried not to look too concerned. But she was feeling more than a little worried that she'd still not seen what Avery had been secretly preparing in her room. "Do I get to have a sneak peek?" she asked.

"Nope."

Betty frowned.

"Don't you trust me?"

"Yes, you know I do, Avery."

"Do you trust me to drive your car today?"

Suddenly, Betty wasn't so sure.

"I'm a good driver."

"I'm sure you are."

"And I need to load and unload everything without you seeing it," Avery continued, "or else that'll spoil the surprise. So you'll have to let me use your car, Grandma."

Just then the dog barked from outside. "You'd better let him in," Betty said, "before he wanders off."

Avery went to open the door, then came back and asked again to use the car.

"Well, I suppose I don't have much of a choice," Betty finally said.

"No, I suppose you don't." Avery grinned. "You won't be sorry."

Betty wanted to say, "I hope not," but she knew that would sound rather pessimistic. And so she just smiled and tried not to think about lime- or magenta-colored flowers. She tried not to imagine piñatas or pirates or multicolored balloons. No, she trusted Avery with this. Her granddaughter would not let her down.

"I still have some things to get ready," Avery said.

"And I have a hair appointment at nine," Betty suddenly remembered. She had booked the appointment a month ago. Going to the beauty parlor was a luxury that Betty budgeted for only twice a year. One time before Christmas and again before Easter. The rest of the time, Betty tended to her own hair. Whether it was cutting or curling it, she'd become rather adept at it over the years. Still, it always looked nicer when it was done professionally.

For nearly two blissful hours, Betty sat and listened to the hairdresser talk about everything and nothing while she worked on Betty's hair. Betty welcomed this break from thinking about runaway dogs, mixed-up granddaughters, frightening neighbors, angry daughters-in-law, and circus-like anniversary parties. And when she left the salon, she told herself that somehow everything was going to be okay. She could just feel it.

But when she got home, she found a flustered and unhappy Avery. "It's after eleven," Avery said. "And I need to get the stuff to the church."

"I know, but you can use as much time as you like to do your decor—"

"And Ralph is gone again. I checked at Jack's, but his pickup is gone too."

"Now, don't worry," Betty said. "You just go ahead and pack your things up in the car and head on over to the church. I'll find the dog, and everything will be just fine when you get back."

Avery seemed somewhat relieved, and then she smiled. "Hey, your hair looks pretty, Grandma."

Betty patted her hair. "Why, thank you."

"So, do you mind waiting in the living room while I get things loaded into the car? So that you don't see anything?"

"I'll just go and put my feet up."

"Thanks. It should only take about fifteen minutes."

"That's fine."

"And then you'll go and look for Ralph?"

Betty nodded. "I will do my best to find him."

By the time Betty heard Avery backing out of the driveway, it was close to noon. And despite being on the verge of a nap, Betty forced herself up, put on her jacket and gloves, got the dog leash, and headed out to search for the dog. She called up and down the street but didn't see the dog anywhere. And Avery was right, Jack's pickup was gone.

Betty stood on the street, looking at Jack's house and wondering if he might've possibly kidnapped the dog and then dumped him somewhere. Perhaps he'd been irked at the dog for wandering into his yard and relieving himself on the grass.

"Hey, Betty," Katie called out as she took her mail out of the box.

Betty waved and smiled. "I thought you'd have taken the girls to your mother's by now."

Katie came down the walk toward her. "That was the plan. But then my mother came down with that nasty flu, and I didn't want the girls to be exposed to it."

"I understand." Betty nodded, then frowned as she glanced over at Jack's house again. Just what was that man up to anyway? Had he taken the dog? And, if so, how would Avery react?

"Is something wrong?" Katie looked worried. "Tell me, Betty, has Jack done something again?"

Instead of voicing her concerns about Jack's interest in her granddaughter, Betty quickly explained about the missing dog. "He's shown up at Jack's more than once, so I thought maybe he'd be there today."

"You still have that dog? I saw all those dog posters around, and I figured the owners must've called you by now."

"No." Betty shook her head. "And I'm not sure what to do about it. My granddaughter, who's staying with me right now, is getting very attached to the mutt, but we will most definitely have to find a home for him soon."

"You mean if you find him at all."

"Yes, I suppose that's true." Betty sighed. "He's a nice little dog, but he's also a bit of a nuisance with all this running-off business."

"I know what you mean." Katie pulled her knit hat down over her ears. "We had a runaway cat for a while—every time Fiona took off, the girls' hearts were just broken. I could hardly stand it. I'd waste hours on end just hunting all over for her."

"I remember," Betty said. "She was a little black and white cat. Sometimes she'd be in my yard."

Katie nodded. "We got her spayed and everything, but it made no difference. She had absolutely no sense of boundaries. She'd be gone for a week and we'd be almost ready to give up on her, then she'd come home again. Naturally, the girls would be deliriously happy, and for a while everything would be fine. And then foolish Fiona would pull her little disappearing act again. I finally decided it was in the best interest of the girls' emotional welfare if that crazy cat was gone for good." Katie had a sly expression now. "The next time she ran away . . . she never came back."

Betty blinked.

"I simply took her to the pound, Betty. And I told them that the cat needed to be out on a farm where she could roam freely."

"How did the girls feel about not seeing Fiona again?"

"Naturally, they were sad. But they got over it. In the long run, it was really the kindest solution. Better to deal with these things early on—less pain that way."

Betty nodded. "That makes sense."

"Anyway, I'll let you know if I see your funny little dog around," Katie said.

Betty placed a hand on Katie's arm. "Say, I'll bet your girls would love to get a dog for Christmas."

Katie just laughed. "A runaway dog, Betty? Weren't you listening?"

"Well, I thought it was worth a try."

"Thanks anyway."

They parted ways, and Betty made a mental note to take the Gilmores a cookie plate—a small consolation for being stuck in this neighborhood during the holidays.

Betty walked up and down the street one more time, calling and looking, but with no luck. As she walked, she replayed Katie's story about the runaway Fiona. Maybe Katie was right about this. Maybe it was better to just get it over with, get rid of the dog before anyone—specifically, Avery—had time to become too attached. Yes, it made perfect sense. And if she were lucky, the dog would go away and stay away on his own. Maybe that's what he had already done. He certainly seemed the type.

She was about to turn the corner to go home and forget all about the mutt when she saw that familiar red pickup coming down the street. She waited for Jack to slow down and then watched him drive right up on the curb, over the sidewalk, and park right in the middle of his brown yard. Such a lovely sight.

"Hey," he called out to her. "I got your dog."

Betty hurried over, ready to demand to know why in the world this thoughtless young man felt it was okay to nab someone's dog and then drive him around in his truck. Furthermore, if he thought that was acceptable behavior, where did he draw the line? Would he be kidnapping Avery next and—

"I found him out in the street," Jack said as he climbed out of the pickup. The dog hopped out behind him, looking none the worse for wear. "I drove by your house earlier to drop him off, but your garage was open and your car was gone."

"I was getting my hair done." She realized that this had probably come out sounding rather snippy. But she was angry and getting angrier.

"Yeah, well, it didn't look like anyone was home. So I decided to take Ralph to the lumberyard with me."

"Ralph?" Betty was surprised that Jack actually knew the dog's name.

"Yeah, that's what Avery said she's calling him."

"Avery can call him whatever she likes, but he'll be going to the dog shelter before the day is over."

Jack scowled at her. "Shouldn't that be up to Avery?"

Betty wanted to tell him to mind his own business but decided to go another route. "Avery will be returning to Atlanta for Christmas, and with holiday travel costs what they are these days, and this being at the last minute, I seriously doubt her parents will be willing to pay airfare for this stray dog as well." She bent down and clipped the leash onto his collar.

Jack's dark eyes felt like drills boring into her now. "Does Avery know you're taking Ralph to the pound?"

Betty blinked. "I told my granddaughter that I'd give the dog a few days to be picked up by his owners. Since that does not appear to be the case, she will surely understand about this."

Jack just pressed his lips together and shook his head.

"I am in no position to be adopting a pet," she said. Not that it was any of his business or that she needed to defend herself to the likes of him.

"I'm not suggesting you are." He just shrugged.

"Come on," she said to the dog, jerking firmly on the leash.

Jack watched her with obvious disapproval.

"Come on," she said again. Fortunately, this time the dog listened and began to move.

"Anyway," Jack called as she began to walk away, "thanks for the cookies."

She turned and looked back at him in surprise. "You . . . you're welcome."

Then he smiled. But, for the life of her, she could not read what was behind that smile. In some ways it seemed genuine, but the more she thought about it, the more convinced she became that it was a mocking smile. As if he knew something she didn't. And it was unnerving.

Betty took the dog into the house, put him in the laundry room, securely closed the door, and proceeded to look up the number for the animal shelter. As the phone rang, she reminded herself of Katie's story, of runaway animals and broken hearts. Really, it would be for the best.

Finally, a man answered, and she quickly explained her situation.

"We're pretty full up right now," he said.

"I'm very sorry about that," Betty said. "But this is not my dog. I've allowed him to stay with me, but I can't continue this. He had no ID or collar or anything. And it's been almost a week. I've already called the local vets and posted 'found dog' signs, and I even offered him to my neighbor as a Christmas present for her little girls."

The man chuckled. "That didn't go over?"

"Not too well." She almost told him about the runaway part but thought that might not present the dog in the best light. "So, you see," she said, "I really need to bring him in. Before the weekend, if possible."

"We're open until six."

"Thank you." Betty hung up and just hoped that Avery would get home from the church in time to make it to the shelter before six. She also hoped that Avery wouldn't be too upset or try to put the brakes on this solution. Because, really, it was for the best. It made no sense for either Betty or Avery to hang on to this mutt any longer.

And yet, if it truly was for the best, why did she feel so uncertain? Why did she feel somewhat guilty?

Just then the phone rang, causing Betty to jump.

"How are you, dear?" Marsha asked.

"Oh my! Do you really want to know?"

"Of course I do. What's the matter?"

So Betty poured out the whole frustrating story about the stray dog and the unexpected granddaughter and everything. Almost. The only part she left out was in regard to Jack. But that was only because she knew Marsha lived a protected life. With a gated neighborhood and a modern security system in her home, Marsha couldn't possibly understand a neighbor like Jack.

"Is there anything I can do for you?"

"As a matter of fact, yes." Betty told her about the need to take the dog to the shelter. "I'd drive him myself, but I let Avery use my car so she could set things up for your anniversary party tomorrow."

"Avery is setting things up?"

Betty could hear the concern in Marsha's voice. "Oh,

she's very talented," Betty said. "Much more creative than I am."

"Really?"

"She's been working on it for the past few days."

"The past few days?" Now Marsha sounded impressed, and Betty worried that she may have overstated things. "Isn't that nice."

"So, you see, I'm without a car. And I'm worried the shelter may close before Avery gets back. And then we'd be stuck with the dog all weekend, and I just don't know what to—"

"Well, I was just on my way out to pick up Jim's favorite suit at the cleaner's. How about if I come and pick you up?"

"Oh, I would be so grateful, Marsha. You're sure you don't mind?"

"What are friends for?"

Betty waited on pins and needles, watching eagerly for Marsha's silver Cadillac to pull up. She so wanted to take care of this business before Avery got back from the church. She'd already put on her coat, and the dog was on his leash. Her purse and gloves were ready to grab up in order to make her getaway.

It was nearly two when she saw Marsha's car coming down her street, and even before she pulled into the driveway, Betty and Ralph were out the door and heading toward her.

"My, but you are eager," Marsha said as Betty opened the door on the passenger side.

"I didn't want to waste any of your time."

Marsha frowned slightly. "I don't suppose you have a doggy carrier for him, do you?"

"I'm sorry." Betty bent down to pick up the dog, then eased herself backward onto the seat and planted the dog securely on her lap before turning her legs around. "But I'm sure he'll be no trouble."

"I just don't want him to scratch the leather upholstery. Jim wouldn't appreciate that."

"I'll be very careful."

"Very wise of you to take care of this doggy business before the holidays," Marsha said. "Pets can be such a nuisance, underfoot, breaking things."

Betty felt unexpectedly defensive of the little dog just then. And she almost told Marsha that this animal was different, that he didn't break things or get underfoot, and he certainly would not scratch up Marsha's upholstery. At least she hoped not. And he didn't disappoint her—he sat perfectly quiet as Marsha drove them across town.

"I'm so looking forward to the celebration tomorrow," Marsha said. "I can't wait to see who comes." She explained that her daughter Karen had let it slip that they'd received some unexpected RSVPs. "She wouldn't say specifically from whom, but I could tell by the way Karen said it that we'd be pleasantly surprised."

"How nice." Betty patted the dog on the head and tried not to feel guilty for what she was about to do. Surely the dog would find a good home. Besides, what choice did she have? Avery would be returning to Atlanta soon. Having the dog around would only make it harder on everyone. Betty was doing her granddaughter a favor. Not only would it please Avery's parents, but it would keep her out of harm's way where Jack was concerned.

"Here we are," Marsha said as she pulled up to a cinder-block structure that looked more like a prison than a shelter. "Would you like me to come in with you?"

Betty considered this. The truth was that moral support would be most welcome right now. But then she looked at Marsha's lovely leather jacket and considered the animal smells that would most likely permeate the building, combined with Marsha's general disapproval of pets. "No," she finally said. "I'll be fine. But thanks for offering."

Betty picked up the dog and set him outside the car, but she could tell by his quivering body that he was just as nervous as she. And he was probably even more frightened. Still, she suppressed these troublesome thoughts as she walked toward the entrance. This really was in the best interest of everyone, she told herself as she reached for the door. Katie had said as much, and so had Marsha. Betty was foolish to think otherwise.

As she entered the building, hearing barks and yelps of other dogs, she knew that she'd done Avery a big favor by handling this on her own. It took strength to do something like this.

"May I help you?" asked a young woman in blue jeans and a sweatshirt.

Betty quickly explained her phone call and how a man had told her she could bring the dog in. The woman asked her some questions and finally handed her a rather lengthy form. Betty carefully filled it in and gave it back to her.

The woman studied the form, then frowned at Betty. "You're sure you wouldn't want to keep this dog?"

Betty glanced down at the dog. He looked up with such trusting brown eyes that she forced herself to turn away. She shook her head. "No, no. I can't have a dog. You see, I go to Florida next month, and I don't have anyone to care for him . . ." She continued rambling about how she planned to sell her house and perhaps look into some kind of retirement home. Even to her own ears it all sounded rather lonely and sad . . . and perhaps a little bit phony.

The woman took the leash from Betty's hand. "It's not required, but we like to recommend that people who leave pets in the shelter make some kind of a donation toward the welfare of the animal."

Betty tried not to look too surprised as she opened her purse. "I live on a fixed income," she explained as she extracted a ten-dollar bill and several ones. "Will this be enough?"

"Thank you." The woman smiled. "That will help to buy pet food."

Betty nodded and backed away from the woman and the dog. "Yes . . . I suppose it will." She turned and made her way to the front door, realizing that everything looked blurry now. She reached for the doorknob but couldn't actually see it. She fumbled until it turned in her hand. Then, as she went out into the cold air, she realized she had tears running down her cheeks. She was crying again. The third time this week. And this time, she was crying harder.

She paused to reach for a handkerchief, drying her tears and blowing her nose before getting back into Marsha's warm car. *Goodness*, she thought as she tucked her hanky back in her coat pocket, *all this emotion—just for a dog?*

11

Betty was relieved to see that her car was not in the garage when Marsha pulled into her driveway.

"You seem very quiet today," Marsha said as she put her car into park. "Are you sure you're okay?"

Betty sniffed. "As I said, it's been a little stressful this week."

"I hope our anniversary party hasn't added to your stress."

"No, not at all. In fact, Avery seems to have thoroughly enjoyed helping."

"I'm so excited to see what she's done."

Betty nodded. "So am I."

"And now I better get over to the cleaner's." Marsha looked at her watch. "Can you believe that I'm still not finished packing yet?"

"Oh, I nearly forgot about the cruise Jim booked." Betty gathered her purse and reached for the door handle. "When do you leave again?"

"Sunday morning. We'll miss the Christmas service in church."

"I'll miss you too." Betty sighed as she opened the door.

"At least you'll have Avery to keep you company." Marsha reached over and patted Betty's shoulder. "That's a real comfort to me. I told Jim that I felt sad to think of you spending Christmas alone this year."

Betty forced a smile. She did not intend to tell Marsha that Avery might be going home after all. Why cause her concern? "Avery has decorated the house and wants us to cook a turkey. Do you know I haven't cooked a turkey in years?" Betty was out of the car now. "I'll see you tomorrow, Marsha. Thank you again for helping me with the dog."

Marsha waved as she backed out of the driveway.

Betty went through the garage into the house. She paused by the laundry room, where the dog's things were still in their place, as if the dog would be coming home any moment. Betty quickly gathered up the dog bed and bowls and stashed them on a low shelf in the garage. Out of sight, out of mind. Or so she hoped.

Then she made a cup of tea and sat down in her recliner to relax. But as she sat there, all she could think about was that silly little dog. And even when she closed her eyes, hoping for a nap, she felt as if those liquid-brown canine eyes were indelibly printed inside her head. Finally, she reached for the remote and turned on the TV, flipping through the familiar channels until a figure skater appeared.

"I'm home," Avery called as she came into the living room.

Betty opened her eyes, blinking into the light.

"Sorry, Grandma. Did I wake you?"

"It's okay." She smiled at her granddaughter, watching as

Avery removed her parka and unwound the bright scarf from around her neck.

"It's so cold out." Avery rubbed her hands together. "I really think it's going to snow."

"You might be right." Betty put the footrest down and sat up straight. "So, tell me, how did the decorating go?"

Avery's eyes lit up. "It was awesome, Grandma. It looks really, really cool."

"Cool?" Betty nodded, taking this in.

"Way better than I expected. No one will even remember they're in the church basement. It's like another world down there now."

"Another world?" Betty wasn't sure what to make of that. Was it another world like Mexico, or a pirate's cove, or Mars perhaps? Still, she was determined not to show the slightest sign of distrust.

"Where's Ralph?" Avery asked.

Betty stood slowly.

"Grandma?" Avery's voice sounded worried now. "Where is he? Did you find him? Is he okay?"

"Avery . . ." Betty looked into her granddaughter's eyes. "I have something to tell you."

"Has he been hurt?" Avery looked truly upset now.

"No, he's perfectly fine."

Avery looked relieved. "Oh, good. But where is he? Outside?"

"He's not here."

Avery frowned. "Where is he, Grandma?"

Betty walked into the kitchen. She knew she was stalling,

but she just hadn't thought this through properly. How was she going to explain to Avery what she'd done? How was she going to make her understand?

"Grandma?" Avery followed her.

"The dog had run away again," Betty began. "I looked all over the neighborhood for him, Avery. I was quite worried. Finally, I found him. It turned out he was with Jack, in his truck."

"Did Jack take Ralph?"

"No."

"Then what?" Avery said. "Where is Ralph?"

"I knew that you were considering going home for Christmas, Avery. In fact, I think that's probably just what you need to do, and—"

"What does that have to do with Ralph?"

"Well, as you know, I can't keep a dog. I'll be going to Susan's in January. And I may even sell my—"

"Please, Grandma, just cut to the chase. Where is Ralph?"

"I took him to the animal shelter."

"To the pound? You took him to the pound?"

"It's an animal shelter," Betty corrected. "They'll take good care of him and find him a home or perhaps his original own—"

"Unless the pound is overcrowded," Avery snapped. "And then they might just kill him."

"Oh, no," Betty said quickly. "They are good people. And I gave them money for dog food. They won't hurt him." But even as she said this, she didn't know it for certain. And the idea of those people hurting that dog, or that Betty was responsible, cut through her like a knife.

Avery was crying now. She sank down into a kitchen chair, holding her head in her hands and sobbing. "I love that dog, Grandma. I needed him."

Betty didn't know what to say. And when the phone rang, she was relieved for the distraction. Until she realized it was Avery's mother on the other end. She'd completely forgotten about Avery's promise to make a decision by tonight.

"Hello, Stephanie." Betty's voice was flat.

"May I speak to Avery, please?"

Betty glanced to where Avery was still sobbing at the kitchen table. "Avery is, uh, well, she's unable to come to the phone right now."

"Unable? Or unwilling?"

"She's a bit upset," Betty said.

"Upset? Why? What's going on there, Betty?"

"She's sad that I took a stray dog to the animal shelter."

"Is that all? Well, put her on the line, please. I need to speak to her."

Betty stretched the cord of the phone over to where Avery was sitting. Covering the mouthpiece, Betty said quietly, "It's your mother, dear. She wants to speak to you."

Avery looked up with watery eyes. "I don't want to speak to her." Then she stood, but before she left the room, she added, "Or you either."

Betty felt a lump in her throat as she put the phone back to her ear. "I'm sorry, Stephanie, but Avery really doesn't want to talk right now."

"Well, when does Avery want to talk?"

"I really can't say, dear." Betty heard the front door open and close.

"Because we need to figure this out. Gary just found an airline ticket online. It's not cheap, but it's better than we expected."

"That's good."

"That's only good if Avery is coming home."

"Yes, that's true." Betty looked out the kitchen window, peering out into the darkness and worrying about her grand-daughter being out on the streets alone on a cold winter night.

"And we don't know if Avery is coming home. There is no point in wasting good money on air fare if Avery has no intention of coming home. Do you understand what I'm saying to you, Betty?" Stephanie said as if she were speaking to a child.

"Of course."

"So, can you tell me what we should do? Should I tell Gary to get the ticket?"

"I really don't know."

"Can you promise me that you'll see to it that Avery gets to the airport and gets on the plane? It's a red-eye flight."

"A red-eye flight?"

"Yes. The plane leaves at 10:15 p.m. your time."

"At night?"

"P.m. means night, Betty."

"Yes, I know that." She imagined herself driving Avery to the airport at night. Betty did not see well after dark. And the airport was nearly an hour away.

"So, do we book the flight or not, Betty?" Stephanie's voice was sounding more and more impatient. She reminded Betty of a rubber band that was stretched too tightly.

"I just don't see how I can possibly make that decision," Betty said.

"Well, someone needs to."

"And I believe that someone is Avery."

"Then put Avery on the phone!"

"I can't."

"Why not?"

"Because she's not here."

"But you said—"

"She stepped out."

"But it's nighttime. Even in your time zone it must be dark out."

"Yes, it is. I'm sorry, Stephanie, but I really don't see how I can help you. You and Gary will have to make your own decision about the plane ticket."

Somehow Betty managed to extract herself from the phone conversation, then she hurriedly put on her coat and went outside to see if she could find Avery. She went up and down the street, looking this way and that, feeling foolish, old, and tired. Really, what chance did she have of catching up with a young girl?

Finally, she returned home in defeat. Out of curiosity, she checked Avery's room. It was something of a relief to see that Avery had taken nothing with her. Not even her purse. Perhaps she was just taking a walk to cool off. But with temperatures dropping below freezing tonight, she would cool off quickly.

It was nearly eight when Betty finally made some oatmeal for her dinner, but even then she didn't feel hungry. Where was Avery? Was she okay? Should Betty call the police and report her as missing? Would they even be concerned? Wasn't there some kind of rule about a person being missing more than one day before they would search? But perhaps Betty could explain that her granddaughter was distraught, possibly even depressed. Would they go and look for her then? If Marsha and Jim weren't busy packing and preparing for their big day tomorrow as well as their anniversary cruise, Betty would call them and ask for help.

After only a few bites, Betty dumped her oatmeal and began to clean the kitchen. By nine, she decided to call the local police. Really, what could it hurt? But as she expected, they did not want to file a missing persons report yet.

"Most cases like this resolve themselves," the woman told her. "Your granddaughter is probably on her way home right now."

"But—"

"If it makes you feel better, I'll let our patrolmen know that she's out there."

"Oh, yes, I would appreciate that." Betty gave her a description of Avery, thanked her again, and hung up. She looked out the living room window, staring out into the darkened street and hoping that, like the policewoman had assured her, Avery would suddenly show up at the door.

Finally, Betty attempted to watch some TV. And eventually she just went to bed, but she was too worried to sleep. And so she prayed. She prayed that somehow God would unravel this tangled mess that she felt responsible for creating. She prayed that God would somehow take what appeared to be evil and transform it into good.

At just a few minutes past eleven, Betty heard the front door open and close. She'd purposely left it unlocked in the hopes that Avery would return. But now she was worried. What if a perfect stranger had just walked into her home? Perhaps her strange neighbor Jack?

Betty remained motionless, almost afraid to breathe as she listened to quiet footsteps. Then she heard someone using the bathroom. And then going into Avery's room and closing the door. Of course, it had to be Avery. But just to be sure, Betty slipped out of bed and tiptoed to the living room. Hanging limply over the back of an armchair was Avery's parka and bright red scarf. She was safe.

12

Betty slept in later than usual on Saturday morning. Probably due to her late night and worries about her granddaughter. Still, she felt hopeful as she got out of bed. She was optimistic as she did her morning stretches, then pulled on her thick, quilted robe. Avery was home, and this morning they would talk. Betty would apologize for taking Ralph (yes, she was calling the dog by his name now) to the shelter. And perhaps she and Avery could figure this whole thing out together. Maybe there was a way that Avery could keep the dog. Even if it meant Betty had to use some of her savings to pay for the dog to fly to Atlanta with Avery. Oh, some might think it foolish on Betty's part, but maybe it was just what the girl needed.

Avery's bedroom door was open, but Avery was not in her room. Her bed was neatly made, and some of her clothes were folded and sitting at the foot of it.

"Avery?" Betty tapped lightly on the partially opened bathroom door. But Avery wasn't in there. Betty continued to look through the house, only to discover that Avery wasn't there at all. But where could she be? Suddenly Betty realized that she'd never gotten her car keys back from Avery last night.

But when she hurried out to the garage, she found the car parked there as usual.

As Betty made coffee—a full pot since she told herself that Avery had simply taken a morning stroll—the phone rang again. This time it was Gary, and all Betty could tell him was that Avery had come home safely last night but had gone out again this morning.

"This isn't helpful, Mother."

"I'm sorry, but that's all I know."

"Steph is really bugging me to get that ticket."

"Like I told her yesterday, that is up to you. I don't know how to advise you."

"Well, when Avery comes in, please ask her to call."

She promised to do that and hung up. A part of her was tempted to jerk the cord out of the wall, but she knew that wasn't a very responsible thing to do. Instead, she sat down and drank her coffee and prayed that Avery would come home soon. Surely she'd want to go to Jim and Marsha's anniversary celebration this afternoon. She had worked so hard on those decorations and had been so excited about everything. Betty remembered how her face had lit up while she was talking about it yesterday. Yes, Avery would certainly want to go to the party.

But at one twenty, Avery was still not back. The party was supposed to start at two, but Betty had planned to get there early to check on things. So she left Avery a note along with bus fare, saying that she looked forward to seeing her at the celebration.

Betty grew increasingly nervous as she drove toward the

church. Suddenly she was remembering those gaudy flowers again, those mysterious bags, and how Avery had holed up in her room. What if she'd actually created a monstrosity? What if Avery was too embarrassed to show her face at the church now? How would Betty explain it? How could she possibly apologize or make it up to her good friends?

Betty parked in the back, thankful that no other cars were there yet. It was barely one thirty now. If the decorations were truly a disaster, Betty might have enough time to make changes, to cover up for her granddaughter's lack of discretion.

She entered the church and headed straight down the stairs, bracing herself. She was about to turn on the lights when she realized there was already some light down there. Not bright, but enough to see.

Betty entered the room and was stunned to find that the basement had been transformed into a gold and white fairyland. So pretty it literally took her breath away. How was it possible that Avery had done this? And on such a frugal budget? It seemed nothing short of miraculous.

Betty walked through the room, admiring a concoction of gauzy white fabric that was hung like an arbor over the main table. The folds of fabric were sprinkled with gold sparkles and tiny stars and intertwined with small white Christmas lights. There were pearly white and gold balloons here and there, and an abundance of gold and white flowers artfully arranged. Upon closer investigation, Betty discovered that spray paint had been involved—Avery had used metallic gold and white spray paint to transform the previously bright-colored artificial blooms into something much more dignified and fitting for a golden anniversary.

Paper doilies were painted gold, arranged beautifully beneath small stacks of white paper plates and embossed napkins. If Avery had told Betty she was using plain paper plates, Betty would've been concerned. But the way Avery had placed and arranged everything—it was all perfectly elegant. It was truly a work of art. Betty wished she'd thought to bring a camera. But surely someone would have one.

Now Betty noticed a number of white candles that had touches of gold spray paint, like gilt, to make them lovelier. And nearby was a box of matches and what appeared to be a folded note with "Betty Kowalski" written on it.

> Dear Grandma,
>   I came by and turned the light strings on. All you need to do is light the candles and it should be all set for Jim and Marsha. I'm sorry to miss it. And I'm sorry I've been so much trouble for you. I know I need to figure out my own life, and that's what I plan to do. Thank you for putting up with me.
>   Love,
>   Avery

Betty refolded the note and slipped it into her purse. Avery must've stopped by here sometime earlier. Perhaps just to make sure that everything was still okay. But why hadn't she stayed for the party? What difference would a few more hours make? Why had Avery been in such a hurry?

Of course, Betty knew why. It was because of her . . . and what she'd done to Ralph.

Betty put her coat and purse in the closet and slowly went

about the room, lighting the various candles and pausing to admire the beauty of her granddaughter's handiwork. The flickering candlelight, which was reflected on surfaces of metallic gold, made the room even more magical than it had been before. It was a masterpiece. And Betty knew that Marsha and Jim would appreciate it.

As she stood off to one side, looking at the scene from a distance, she realized that once again she was crying. She went into the bathroom, blew her nose, and dried her tears, telling herself that she was too old for such melodrama.

And, really, shouldn't she be happy for her granddaughter? Avery's note had actually sounded very mature. As if she had finally decided to take responsibility for her own life. To stand on her own two feet. Yet Betty couldn't help but wonder how Avery would accomplish this with little or no money. How could Avery possibly take care of herself? What would she eat? Where would she sleep? How would she manage to get by?

Betty heard some young-sounding voices outside of the bathroom and suddenly felt hopeful. Perhaps Avery had changed her mind and come back. Maybe she'd give Betty a chance to start over again after all. Eagerly, Betty went out into the room to discover Jim and Marsha and their children and grandchildren. They were going around the room oohing and aahing, obviously pleased with Avery's creation. Betty forced a smile to cover her disappointment as she said, "Happy anniversary!"

"Oh, Betty," Marsha gushed, "it's so beautiful!"

"Did you do this?" asked Marsha's younger daughter, Lynn.

"No, not me," Betty said quickly.

"It was Betty's granddaughter, Avery," Marsha said.

"Well, it's incredible," Lynn said.

"Is your granddaughter an artist?" one of the grandchildren asked. Betty didn't recall the little girl's name.

Betty nodded proudly. "Yes, I think she is."

"Is she here?" she asked eagerly.

Betty sighed. "No, unfortunately, she had to leave."

"I want to get photos of this before anything gets messed up," Lynn said. "Mom and Dad, you go stand over there beneath that arbor thing, and let's get some shots."

Soon the cake arrived, and although Betty wasn't on the refreshment committee or the cleanup committee, she spent most of her time helping in the kitchen. Oh, she made an appearance now and then, smiling and visiting congenially, but mostly she wanted to remain behind the scenes, alone with her thoughts. She didn't wish to spoil her friends' fun, so she hid her broken heart behind busyness.

Finally, the party was winding down. Jim and Marsha came into the kitchen and thanked Betty again. "It was so beautiful," Marsha said. "I wish Avery had been able to come. I would've loved to tell her in person how brilliant I think she is."

"I'm sure Betty will pass that along," Jim said.

"Of course." Betty nodded.

"Will you join us for dinner?" Marsha asked. "Lynn surprised us by having it all catered at our house, and I know there's plenty for—"

"No thank you," Betty said quickly.

"Avery could come too," Jim said.

"Thanks, but we have other plans."

"Are you sure?" Marsha looked disappointed.

"Yes." Betty forced a smile.

Then Marsha and Jim hugged Betty and wished both her and Avery a merry Christmas. Betty told them to have a delightful cruise and to send a postcard.

"Count on it," Marsha said as she rejoined her family.

Betty remained in the kitchen just puttering around, wiping things that she'd already wiped, and waiting for everyone to depart on their merry ways. Finally, it was only the cleanup committee that remained, and they were getting right to work.

"Hey, Betty," Irene called out, "do you want to save any of these decorations?"

Betty went out and looked around the room. It no longer seemed magical with the harsh glare from the florescent overhead lights. Irene blew the last candle out, and others gathered up trash, plates with remnants of uneaten cake, plastic cups, and wadded-up napkins.

She was about to say no but then thought of Avery and all her hard work. She went to the main table and picked up a candle that was wreathed in gold and white flowers. "Yes," she told Irene. "I'll keep this as a memento."

"We'll put some of these other things in the wedding closet," Irene said. "You never know what might come in handy."

Betty nodded. "You never know." Then she got her coat and purse and went out to her car. It was just getting dusky out, and as Betty drove, she couldn't help but keep a lookout for Avery. How she longed to spot the girl, to pick her up, hug her tightly, and take her home. But there was no sign of her.

As Betty turned down her street, she saw that it was beginning to snow. Perhaps Avery's much-longed-for white Christmas was about to become a reality. But where was Avery?

Suddenly, Betty grew hopeful again. Perhaps Avery was at home. Maybe she'd realized that being broke and homeless on a cold day like this was not all she'd hoped it would be. Maybe she'd come to her senses.

Betty was tempted to drive fast, but she knew the streets were getting slick, and her night vision was lacking, so she went slowly and carefully. But when she got into the house, it looked just as it had when she'd left. Avery's clothes were still folded neatly at the foot of her bed. This had given Betty some hope earlier, thinking that Avery had probably planned to return. But as Betty looked more closely, it seemed that most of Avery's things, including her oversized bag and personal items from the bathroom, were missing. As if she had packed up and left for good. Those few items of clothing still on the bed had probably been too bulky to stuff into her bag.

Betty picked up a wooly sweater that Avery had purchased for two dollars at Goodwill, and held it to her chest. Why hadn't Avery taken this with her? If it was too big to pack, she could've at least worn it under her parka. It would've been much warmer than some of those other lightweight blouses Avery often wore. Why hadn't she taken it with her? And why had she left at all?

13

At five thirty, Betty put together a cookie platter for the Gilmores. She'd been meaning to do this for a couple of days, but what with Avery, the dog, and the anniversary party, she had forgotten. But now, despite the weather and the hour, she was determined to get it delivered. And her determination was twofold. Naturally, she wanted to be neighborly. But she also wanted to know if, by any chance, they had observed Avery coming or going today. Perhaps Katie had spoken to her. Although it seemed unlikely.

There was a dusting of snow on the sidewalk as Betty made her way down the street, then knocked on the Gilmores' door.

"Oh!" Katie opened the door, holding a roll of Santa wrapping paper in her hand. "What are you doing out in this weather?"

Betty forced a smile. "Wishing my neighbors a merry Christmas!" She held out the cookie tray.

"Oh, thank you!" Katie stuck the roll of wrapping paper beneath her elbow to receive the platter of sweets. "Won't you come in?"

"Perhaps for a minute."

"Martin took the girls out to get a Christmas tree," Katie

said as Betty came inside. "He grew up in a family that firmly believed respectable people never put up their trees *until* Christmas Eve. But the girls begged and begged, and he finally gave in. So this year our tree will be up two days before Christmas." She winked. "That's progress."

"Yes." Betty nodded and smiled.

Katie cleared away wrapping paper and ribbons to make a spot for the cookies on the dining room table. "Would you like some coffee or tea or—"

"No thank you. I really can't stay. I can see you're busy."

"And I know you have your granddaughter visiting . . ." Katie frowned slightly, as if something unpleasant just occurred to her.

"Yes? What about my granddaughter?" Betty leaned forward. "Have you seen her today?"

"I realize it's not really any of my business."

"What isn't your business?"

"Well, I did notice your granddaughter today. I was picking up the newspaper this morning, and I saw her."

Betty nodded. "And?"

"And . . . I couldn't help but notice she was with Jack."

"Oh?"

"Yes. I thought it was rather odd, Betty. I hadn't imagined that they'd be friends."

"Well, Avery has met Jack. And they actually had a nice little chat the other day. It seems he's lonely, and it's the holidays, and . . ." Betty didn't know what else to say. And despite her reassuring words, her heart was beginning to pound.

"Oh. Well, it just caught my attention to see her with him. They were getting into his truck."

"Jack's pickup?" For some reason, this struck Betty as strange. It was one thing to visit with a neighbor, something else altogether to let them take you somewhere in their vehicle.

Katie nodded. "Yes. And . . . I don't know how to say this, except to just spit it out in the open."

"Say what?"

"Your granddaughter seemed, uh, a little upset."

"Was Jack forcing her into his pickup?"

"I don't think so. But something about the whole thing just struck me wrong—I felt worried."

"Oh dear!" Betty's hand flew to her mouth.

"I'm sorry, Betty. I had meant to mention it to you earlier, just to make sure everything was okay. But then things got hectic, and Martin offered to watch the girls so I could do some last-minute Christmas shopping, and by the time I got back, you were gone. I got busy wrapping presents, and I guess I just forgot."

A rush of panic jolted through Betty. What if Avery, after a short conversation, had trusted Jack? And what if he'd turned out to be just the sort of person that Betty and everyone else in the neighborhood had feared? What if he had somehow tricked Avery? What if she was in trouble now?

"So, is everything okay? I mean with your granddaughter?"

"Actually . . . she's missing."

Katie's eyes grew wide. "Oh no! I'm so sorry, Betty. I knew I should've said something sooner."

"I'm sure everything is fine." But Betty could hear the tremor in her voice.

"Where do you think she is?"

Betty considered this. "I don't really know. But I know who I'm going to ask."

"Jack?" Katie looked slightly horrified.

"Yes."

"Oh, Betty, don't go over there alone. Not at night."

"I need to speak to him."

"Why don't you wait for Martin to get home? I'm sure he'd go over there with you."

"No, this can't wait." Betty's hand was on the door now.

"You can't go alone." Katie reached for her jacket. "I'm coming too."

"No, Katie." Betty shook her head. "You stay here."

"I can't. But wait and let me get my cell phone. I'll be ready to call 911 if it's necessary."

Betty decided not to argue, and they walked over to Jack's house. His pickup was there, and the lights were on inside the house.

"I'll knock on the door," Betty said.

"What if he doesn't answer?"

"I'll make him answer."

"I'm scared."

"You stay back," Betty said. "If anything goes awry, you make a run for it and call the police."

Katie just nodded. Her face looked pale in the street-light.

Betty turned, took a deep breath, and marched up to Jack's door. First she rang the doorbell several times, then she pounded loudly with her fist. Suddenly the door opened, and she nearly struck Jack in the chest with her final blow.

"What's going on?" he said.

Betty stepped back, then remembered her mission. "I'm looking for my granddaughter," she said.

"She's not here."

"But you were seen with her. You took her somewhere in your truck this morning."

He shrugged. "Yeah, I gave her a ride."

"But she's missing." Betty stared at him, trying to see if there was evil in his countenance.

"Missing?" He looked slightly confused now.

"Yes. She never came home."

He nodded as if he knew something. "Of course not."

"What do you mean by that?"

"She didn't come home because I took her to the bus station."

"The bus station?"

"Look." He rubbed his hands on his bare arms. "It's cold out here. Why don't you come inside and we can discuss this calmly?"

Betty glanced over her shoulder to Katie, who was now standing directly behind her on the porch.

"You can both come in," he said.

"Fine," Katie said. "But first I'm calling Martin to let him know where I'm at."

They waited for Katie to make her call, and then the two women followed Jack into his house. He took them past the foyer and into what had once been a formal living room, but because some walls had been removed, it now seemed to be part of the kitchen, and it was also connected to the small family room and dining room. Instead of four rooms, it was now simply one. Did he plan to knock out all the walls and turn the house into a big barn?

"You've made some changes," Betty said.

"Wow," Katie said as she looked around. "This is exactly what I've been telling Martin that I want to do with our house. Have a great room."

"A great room?" Betty was confused. "It looks like a great big mess to me."

"No," Katie said. "It's opened up so that a family can be together in one space."

"That's right." Jack nodded toward a couple of folding lawn chairs. "I don't have much furniture, but you're welcome to sit down if you like."

"No thank you." Betty turned her attention back to Jack. "Let's cut right to the chase, Jack. What have you done with my granddaughter?"

"Like I said, I dropped her at the bus station. Well, that was after I took her by a church."

"A church?"

"She needed to leave a note with somebody."

Betty nodded. "And after that you took her to the bus station?"

"That's what I just told you."

"What time was it then?"

His brow creased. "I'm not sure. But it wasn't noon yet. Maybe not even eleven. Avery had come over to my place fairly early."

"She came to your house?" Katie asked.

"Yeah. We'd arranged to meet here in the morning."

"You *arranged* to meet her?" Betty frowned. "Why?"

"She wanted my help."

"Why?" Katie asked.

"Because she'd been over the night before. She was upset about losing the dog. We spent a long time talking things out. She decided that it was time for her to move on with her life, so she asked me to help her."

"To help her?" Betty said.

Jack shoved his hands in his jeans pockets but didn't answer.

"How exactly did you plan to help her?" Betty persisted.

"She was broke. She wanted to get away from here." He scowled at Betty. "And she wanted to get away from you too. She wasn't too pleased with what you did to her dog."

Betty felt her cheeks flush. "Yes, I know."

He shook his finger at her. "She really loved that dog."

Katie looked at Betty with an alarmed expression. "What did you do to the dog?"

"I took him to the animal shelter."

"Oh, well . . ." Katie shrugged. "That was probably for the best."

"Unless you're attached to the animal and want to keep it," Jack shot back at her. "Avery didn't even have a say in the matter. That wasn't fair."

"I know." Betty nodded again. "Jack's right about that. I regret what I did."

"You do?" Jack looked surprised.

"Yes, I do. But back to Avery. You say you took her to the bus station. Do you know where she was going?"

He shook his head. "I assumed she was going home, to her family."

Betty felt a small wave of relief. And yet she wasn't sure. How could she trust Jack? What if he'd concocted this whole story, and in the meantime, Avery was tied and gagged back there in one of the bedrooms?

Betty frowned. "Do you mind if I use your restroom?"

He gave her a funny look. "Seriously?"

"If it's okay with you."

"Well, the powder room is torn out right now."

"I know." Betty nodded toward the backyard. "I've been privileged to enjoy the pink commode with my morning coffee."

He kind of chuckled. "Sorry about that. I guess it's time to make a run to the dump again."

"I know where the other bathroom is," she told him as she headed down the hallway. Fortunately, the doors to the first two bedrooms were open. Except for some random boxes and building things, the rooms appeared to be empty. Betty paused by the master bedroom and was relieved to see that, except for a mattress topped with a sleeping bag in the center of the floor, it too appeared vacant. And since all the closet doors had been removed, there was no place else to hide a captive.

She went into the bathroom, which was surprisingly neat considering the state of the rest of the house, and after a few seconds, she flushed the toilet. Then, satisfied that Avery was not in the house, she returned to find Jack and Katie discussing, of all things, remodeling.

"The trick is not to change the plumbing and electrical," he was explaining to Katie. "That helps to keep costs down." He eyed Betty. "Did you have a good look around?"

Betty just cleared her throat. "Did you stay at the bus station to make sure Avery got onto the bus safely?"

He frowned. "She's not a baby. I'm pretty sure she knows how to take care of herself."

"But did she have enough money for the fare?" Betty frowned. "Atlanta is a long way."

"She had enough fare money as well as money for food."

Betty felt her shoulders relax. "I really should thank you, Jack."

"No problem."

"And I'd like to pay you back."

"Avery promised to pay me back."

"Well, okay. Then I suppose we should go. I need to let her parents know that she's on her way."

"Don't you think Avery would have done that by now?" he asked.

"Perhaps, but they've been quite worried."

He nodded. "I guess you'd know best, Mrs. Kowalski."

Betty was suddenly seeing this young man in a new light. Why had she been so hard on him before? So suspicious?

She stuck out her hand. "Just call me Betty, please." As they shook, it occurred to her that, like her, Jack had some challenges. She also knew, better than some, how challenges sometimes led to grumpiness. Maybe everyone just needed to be a little more patient, a little more understanding. After all, wasn't it almost Christmas?

He released her hand and smiled. "Just call me Jack." His face was transformed by that smile. And for the first time, she realized that he was fairly attractive in a rugged sort of way. "Oh, yeah." He chuckled. "You already do call me Jack."

"Sorry to have bothered you," she said.

"It's okay."

"Thanks for the remodeling tips," Katie said as they went to the door.

"And thanks for the cookies, Betty," Jack called out. "They were great."

She turned and smiled at him. "I have more, if you'd like some."

He looked away and sort of shrugged, and suddenly she wondered if she'd stepped over some kind of invisible line again. "Thanks again," she said anyway. "I mean for helping Avery like you did."

Betty and Katie walked down the sidewalk until Katie finally spoke. "He seems kind of nice."

"Yes . . . perhaps we were wrong about him all along."

"Unless he's very good at covering something up." Katie lowered her voice. "I've read about serial killers, Betty, and some of them seem very nice on the surface. But they're actually coldhearted, psychopath murderers underneath."

Betty stopped walking and turned to face Katie. "Do you really think that Jack is a psychopath?"

"I honestly don't know . . . and I'll admit that sometimes I have an overactive imagination."

Betty shivered in the cold.

"But that's the problem with psychopaths, Betty. Most of the time people don't figure it out until it's too late."

Betty just shook her head and continued walking. Maybe it was a mistake to listen to Katie. After all, she was nearly a third Betty's age. What made her such an expert on anything?

"I'm sorry." Katie put a hand on Betty's shoulder as they paused by the Gilmores' house. "I'm sure Jack's not a psychopath serial killer. Like Martin says, I should quit reading those horrible books."

"Perhaps so . . ." Betty told Katie thank you and good night and hurried back to her own house, carefully locking the doors and the deadbolts once she was inside. She shuddered to think that she'd gone to bed with her front door unlocked last night. But that had been for Avery's sake. Surely there was no chance she'd try to slip in late tonight.

Betty still felt unsettled as she picked up the phone to call her son and daughter-in-law. But she was determined to remain calm and collected. Thankfully, it was Gary who answered, and she quickly told him what she'd just learned about Avery. Hopefully, it was the truth and not a cover-up.

"I can't tell you exactly when she'll get there," she said. "But the neighbor who told me made it sound as if she was heading your way."

"Well, that's a relief. That airline ticket didn't last long online, and I doubt that we'll find another one in time for Christmas now."

"So perhaps it's for the best."

"Maybe so. Thanks, Mom."

Betty controlled the urge to apologize. She longed to confess all and to tell her son that this foolish mess was all her fault. She wanted to admit how she'd failed Avery, how she'd betrayed her trust. But she suspected that would only make him feel more concerned for Avery's welfare. Better to wait until Avery was safely home, and then Betty would gladly take the blame. And hopefully, Avery would forgive her.

"I'll go online tonight and check the bus schedules from your town so we can have an idea of when to look for her," Gary said. "And we'll be sure to let you know when she arrives."

"Thanks, I appreciate that." But after they said good-bye, more doubts began to creep into Betty's frazzled mind. As much as she wanted to trust Jack, to believe what he had told her, how could she be certain? What if, like Katie had suggested, he really was a psychopath skilled at telling people what he thought they wanted to hear? What if Avery was actually in danger?

Once again, Betty knew her only answer, her only recourse, her only real lifeline, was to pray. And so she would pray and hope for the best.

14

Betty got up early on Sunday. But as she walked through her house, going through the paces of pulling on her old robe, slipping into her worn slippers, and putting on coffee, she felt more alone than ever. She looked at the Christmas decorations Avery had placed around the house. So jolly and festive just days ago, they seemed to be mocking her now. Who was she to expect a merry Christmas?

Betty looked out her kitchen window as she sipped her coffee. A white blanket of snow had turned her otherwise drab backyard into a winter wonderland. Avery's white Christmas was just two days away. Not that Avery would know or care now.

Betty looked beyond the fence toward Jack's house and was surprised to see that the pink toilet, as well as a few other things, had been removed from his backyard. Perhaps he had taken her comments to heart and made that trip to the dump after all. But when would he have done that? Last night? It seemed a little odd to make a trip to the dump on a dark, snowy night. Was the dump even open? And why the big rush?

Unless Jack had something else he needed to dispose of . . . something like criminal evidence.

Betty shook her head as if to shake away these horrible thoughts. She was being foolish. Katie's talk of psychopaths and murderers had poisoned her mind. Jack was a good man. He had befriended Avery when she had no one to turn to. He had helped her out of a crisis. Betty should be very grateful. Not suspicious.

Betty jumped when the phone rang. Her heart raced as she picked it up. *Please, let nothing be wrong.* To her relief, it was Gary. And he sounded cheerful. "I checked the bus schedules, Mom," he said. "And it looks like Avery will be here in time for the Christmas Eve party tomorrow night."

"Oh, that's good." Betty sighed. "Did she call you?"

"No, but Steph thinks she's probably planning to surprise us. You know how unpredictable she can be."

"Oh, yes . . . of course."

"So it looks like our Christmas won't be spoiled after all."

"Oh, I'm so glad." Betty tried to insert a smile into her voice.

"Thanks for your help with this, Mom. We're just going into church now, so I'll have to hang up."

"Thank you for calling, dear."

When they hung up, Betty just sighed. Why was she feeling so emotional these days? Was it old age? The time of year? Senility?

She went into her bedroom to get ready for church. She always looked forward to the Christmas Sunday service. Their church didn't have an actual Christmas Eve or Christmas Day service like some did. But the Sunday prior to Christmas, they always did up right. At least that was something to look forward to.

Betty put on her favorite winter skirt, a red and black tartan plaid that Marsha had gotten for her in Scotland many years ago. Perhaps that had been the Deerwoods' twenty-fifth anniversary trip. She topped the skirt with a black cashmere sweater that had seen better days, then went to the bureau and opened her old jewelry box. But instead of retrieving her pearls, she paused to pick up an old photo of Chuck. He'd just enlisted in the army when it was taken. As hard as it was to see him leaving for Korea, she'd thought he looked so devastatingly handsome in that uniform. And when he'd offered her an engagement ring and the promise of marriage upon his return, she couldn't resist.

She studied his gentle brown eyes now and sighed. All these years later, she still got a sweet, warm feeling just looking into those eyes. So much love, compassion, tenderness . . . Oh, how she missed him. But, she reminded herself, each passing year brought her closer to their reunion.

She replaced the photo on the lace runner and sighed. She picked up her pearls (the ones Chuck had brought her from the Orient) and put them around her neck, checking the clasp to make sure it was connected.

As she went to the hall closet for her wool coat, she was still remembering Chuck's eyes. For some strange reason—and it almost seemed disrespectful—something about her dearly departed husband's eyes made her think of that stray mutt, Ralph. Oh, she knew there was no real relationship between the two. But something about the mutt's eyes—maybe just the color or maybe even the warmth—reminded her of Chuck.

As she got into her car, she wondered what Chuck would think of an old woman who abandoned homeless dogs at the pound just days before Christmas. More than that, she wondered what she thought about such things herself—not that she cared to think about it anymore.

She drove slowly to church, relieved to find that the main streets had been plowed, and told herself it was ridiculous to think along these lines. Imagining that her dearly departed husband would want her to take in a stray dog was not simply ridiculous, it bordered on the verge of crazy. Perhaps even a symptom of early Alzheimer's or dementia, although she certainly hoped not. But silly enough anyway.

Betty arrived early for church. She knew that the sanctuary could be crowded during the holidays, and she wanted to be able to sit in her regular spot. But when she got to the third row, she was dismayed to see that not only was her place taken, but so were the places where Jim and Marsha usually sat. She knew her disappointment was childish, not to mention selfish, and that the fourth row would be just fine. But feeling displaced as well as old, she simply turned around, went to the rear of the church, and sat in the very back row. Alone.

She told herself she would not feel sorry for herself as the organ played Christmas hymns. She forced a smile, or what she hoped might pass as a smile. She leaned back and closed her eyes and just listened to the music. After a couple of pieces, the choir began to sing. And soon the seats around her filled up, and although she didn't know the people sitting next to her, there was a comfort in being invisible in the midst of strangers.

During the first part of the Christmas service, which was much the same as every year, she continued to feel distracted as she pondered over what it was in Chuck's eyes that had brought that silly dog to mind. Well, besides plain foolishness. She sat up straighter and forced herself to focus on the children, who were dressed for the nativity story and singing "Silent Night." She remembered when her own children did this very same thing during their grade school years. Gary had always wanted to be a shepherd, and one year, not long after Chuck had passed, their own Susan was chosen to play Mary. So long ago. So far away.

Betty used her clean hanky to dab her eyes. She had quit keeping count of how many times she'd cried this past week, and simply decided that it was just a new stage in aging. And that her best defense was to keep a handkerchief handy.

Pastor Gordon was at the pulpit now, and Betty willed herself to listen. He'd been the pastor of this church for more than two decades, and Betty had grown to respect him for both his biblical knowledge and his spiritual insights. She had missed the beginning of his Christmas sermon but was determined to listen carefully for the remainder.

"It was not so different then, more than two thousand years ago." He nodded toward the children dressed in their robes and angel wings, who now sat restlessly in the front row. "At the first nativity, the world was not expecting this holy guest either. They were not prepared to receive this heavenly visitor, this stranger who came in the form of an innocent child. A babe, a gift from God Almighty. And yet the world needed him. They needed this gift—desperately.

"We are no different today, friends. We get caught up in the season, busily making preparations for Christmas. We decorate, bake cookies, shop, and wrap presents, and yet we aren't truly ready. We aren't waiting with great expectations. Our hearts aren't prepared to receive this holy guest, this heavenly visitor. We have already settled into our preconceived notions. We have decided how this thing called Christmas is about to go down. We have our agendas, we've made our plans." He chuckled. "But you know what they say about the plans of mice and men."

Pastor Gordon leaned over the pulpit and paused, looking across the congregation as if he were about to disclose a great secret. "God's ways are higher than our ways, my friends." He held up a fist and raised his voice. "And God's love can come unexpectedly. It can rock your life and rattle your heart! Just like the world wasn't ready to receive God's love in the form of a child that was hurled from heaven to earth, we're not always ready to receive God's love. And we're not prepared to accept that it comes in a variety of ways. Often when we least expect it, God's love can show up in the form of something or someone we aren't happy to see—something or someone we want to push away or even run from. And, let me tell you, God's love can make us downright uncomfortable at times. Just like that newborn baby wailing in the night made some people in Bethlehem uncomfortable. And yet they needed him—desperately. And we need him. Desperately. Embrace God's love, my friends. Receive it. And then share it. Let us pray."

As Pastor Gordon prayed, Betty could think of only one thing. She had to get out of there. It wasn't that she wanted to escape her pastor or her friends or even the strangers sitting next to her. But what she wanted—what she truly, truly wanted—was to go straight to the animal shelter and get Ralph. Because it seemed entirely possible that God's love had come to her in the form of an unwanted little dog. And she had missed it. Oh, she'd probably missed lots of other things too. But she could do something about this. Ralph needed her, and she needed him.

When the service ended, she exchanged some hasty Christmas greetings and made her way to the exit, then left as quickly as she could. As she drove across town, she had no idea whether or not the shelter would even be open, but she was determined to find out. To her delight, the shelter was not only open, but Christmas music was playing and there were cookies out on the counter, and several people appeared to be shopping for pets. It was actually a very merry place.

Betty munched a sugar cookie as she waited for someone to help her.

"You're certainly busy," she said to the young man wearing a Santa hat who had just stepped behind the counter.

"That's because we had a spot on the local news this morning," he said. "We encouraged families to adopt unwanted animals rather than buying them from pet shops, which might support puppy farms where animals are not treated humanely."

"That's wonderful," Betty said.

"Except that we suggested they wait until *after* Christmas. But I guess we can't complain when our animals are finding good homes."

"No, of course not."

"So, what can we do for you? A cat perhaps? I have a nice tabby—"

"No thank you," she said. "I have something very specific in mind." She explained about dropping off Ralph recently. "It was a mistake, I'm afraid. And I'd like to have him back, if it's all right."

"Could you spot him?" the young man asked.

She smiled. "Of course."

He took her back to where dogs were barking and jumping in kennels. They walked up and down the aisle, and she studied all the dogs and finally shook her head. "I don't see him."

Just then the young woman who had helped her before walked by. Betty touched her arm and explained who she was and what she was looking for.

"Oh, that little brown terrier mix." The girl nodded. "Yes, he's been adopted."

Betty blinked. "Adopted?" Ralph had been adopted? How could this possibly happen?

The girl smiled. "Yes. He's such a sweet little dog, I'm not surprised someone wanted him. Now if you'll excuse me, I need to help this family with their paperwork."

"We have lots of other cool dogs," the young man said.

"Oh, yes . . . I see that you do." Betty just nodded.

"How about that schnauzer mix over—"

"No thank you."

"Are you sure?"

"Perhaps you're right about waiting until after the holidays . . ." She attempted to smile.

"Oh, yeah." He nodded. "It's better for the animal. So

much is going on at Christmas. Pets get sick eating rich food or ornaments, or they get neglected or handled too much by guests—all kinds of holiday things that can be a threat to a new pet. You're wise to wait."

She thanked the young man for his help and then walked slowly out to her car. As she drove home, she tried to understand this whole strange chain of events. To start with, a dog she had never wanted and did not need had sneaked into her life. She had made many attempts to get rid of him and finally was successful. Or so she had thought. But as a result of dumping the dog—and wasn't that what she'd done?—she had hurt and then lost her granddaughter. Of course, she had wanted Avery to go home to her parents. But she hadn't wanted her to leave like that—not without at least saying good-bye. And what was the reason Betty had wanted Avery to leave? Jack. She had been fearful of Jack. She'd felt Avery would be safer at home.

Betty just shook her head to think of what a foolish woman she'd been.

And then she thought she'd figured things out while listening to Pastor Gordon's sermon—she knew that what she really wanted, what she needed, was that little dog. But now Ralph was gone. Adopted by someone else.

Love had come scratching at Betty's door in the form of a little brown dog, and she had completely missed it. She'd had her chance to welcome it, to receive it, and she had slammed the door in its face.

15

Betty woke up on Christmas Eve morning to the jarring sound of the phone ringing. It wasn't even seven yet, but she reached for the phone and tried to sound somewhat awake. "Hello?"

"Mom, this is Gary."

"Oh, Gary." She blinked and sat up. "How are you?"

"Not very well."

"Oh dear, what's wrong?"

"Steph was worried about Avery coming on that bus, afraid she wasn't going to get here in time or miss a connection. So I gave the route and schedule information to a cop friend of mine, and he checked the passenger list just to make sure everything was okay. And guess what?"

"I can't imagine."

"Avery was not a passenger."

"Oh?"

"She never even bought a ticket."

Betty was out of bed now. On her feet and pacing. "How can that be?"

"That's what we want to know. Where is Avery?"

"Goodness, I have no idea where she is, Gary."

"When did you last see her?"

Betty replayed the last several days for him, finally telling him about Ralph and how Avery had been hurt when she'd taken him to the shelter. "I was going to tell you this earlier," she said, "but I didn't want you to worry."

"We're worried now."

"I'm sorry."

"So who is this neighbor who supposedly put her on the bus?"

"Well, he didn't actually put her on the bus—"

"Who is he, Mom?"

"He lives in the old Spencer house. His name is Jack, and—"

"Crazy Jack?"

"What?"

"Susan told me you had a nutty neighbor who was tearing up his house and that you planned to move as soon as possible."

"Susan told you that?"

"Well, I might be exaggerating. We talked before she and Tim left for the Keys. She seemed to think the whole thing was rather humorous. I thought it sounded pretty bizarre. And I think you should sell your house."

"But I was wrong about Jack."

"How do you know?"

"Because I talked to him on Saturday. He helped Avery."

"Helped Avery do *what*?" Gary's voice was loud now. And sharp.

"He loaned her money and—"

"How do you know that, Mom? Did you *talk* to Avery?"

"Well, no."

"I'm sorry, Mom. I'm not mad at you. I know this isn't your fault. I'm just very frustrated. And Steph is coming unglued."

"I'm sorry." Betty didn't know what more to say. "But as you know, Avery has a mind and a will of her own. And she's not a child, Gary."

"Yes, so you've told me before."

"And I'm sure she's perfectly fine."

"I wish I felt as sure as you do." He sighed loudly. "My cop friend is going to help me figure out a way to look for her. We'll let you know if we find anything out. You do the same."

They said good-bye, and as she hung up, Betty felt her legs shaking as if they were going to give way. She sat down on her bed and just shook her head. What was going on? Where was Avery? And why didn't she get on that bus? Nothing made any sense. And now Betty was feeling frightened—and guilty. If anything had happened to Avery, if Jack was somehow to blame, Betty wouldn't be able to forgive herself.

She quickly got dressed, then pulled on her jacket and snow boots and walked toward Jack's house. But as she turned the corner, she saw that his pickup was gone. She stood there for a couple of minutes wondering what to do, and then she realized there was really nothing more she could do right now. Except pray.

As she trudged back to her house, she prayed for Avery—that she would be safe and that she would reveal her whereabouts to her family. Next she prayed for Ralph—that he'd found a good home and people who would love him. And finally she prayed for Jack. Or maybe she prayed more for herself. She asked God to show her how to be a good neighbor to Jack. Then, as if adding a postscript, she said, "And, dear Lord, if Jack is a dangerous criminal, please show me the best way to inform the authorities so that he might be arrested. Amen."

Now she realized that sounded like a doubtful sort of prayer. How could one pray to love her neighbor with one breath and then pray about turning him in with the next? She just hoped that God would understand.

Betty went into her house and sat down at the kitchen table to make a grocery list. It wasn't that she wanted to go to the store, but she was out of necessities like bread, milk, eggs, and even coffee. And although she didn't feel the least bit hungry, she knew the responsible thing was to take care of this chore.

But after the sparse list was made, she just sat there staring at it. She felt as if all energy had been drained from her, as if it were an enormous chore simply to stand. Yet somehow she forced herself up. Then she stood there for a moment, feeling disoriented. Finally, she went into her bedroom and climbed into her bed, fully clothed, then pulled the covers up and slipped into a deep sleep.

"Grandma!"

Betty looked up and blinked. There before her stood Avery. At least Betty thought it sounded like Avery. But this girl was dressed in white and hovered over her like . . . like an angel. Was it an angel? Or was it Avery? Betty squinted her eyes, but the bright light behind the girl framed her head like a halo and made it hard to see. "Avery?"

"Are you okay, Grandma?"

Betty nodded and sat up. "Avery?" she said again.

"I'm sorry if I scared you." Avery sat down on the side of Betty's bed and reached for her hand. "Actually, you scared me. I knocked on the door and no one answered. And then I saw it was unlocked, which made me really worried, so I came in. And then I found you in bed like this and I thought . . ." Avery shook her head. "I thought you were dead."

Betty smiled and squeezed Avery's hand. "Not quite dead—just a little rattled and tired I suppose. But I'm better now."

Avery hugged her. "I'm so sorry I was such a spoiled brat."

"You?" Betty held on to the girl. "I'm the one who should be sorry."

Avery released Betty and studied her face. "Why should *you* be sorry?"

Betty reached out to touch Avery's cheek, wanting to make sure she was real and not just a dream. "I have so many reasons to be sorry, Avery. Where do I begin?"

"With a cup of tea?" Avery suggested.

Betty nodded. "Yes, that sounds perfect."

"I'll go get it started."

"I'm right behind you." Betty stood and slipped on her shoes, then hurried into the kitchen, where Avery was already filling the kettle.

"I still can't believe it's you," Betty said. She watched Avery turn on the stove and reach for the tea mugs and tea canister. "I saw a girl dressed in white . . ." She chuckled. "And I thought that God had sent an angel to get me."

Avery laughed. "I'm hardly an angel. And this ugly white blouse is my uniform."

"Uniform?"

"Yeah. I got a job at the bus station café."

"The bus station café?" Betty sat down in a kitchen chair.

"Yes. It's a long story. I was so furious at you for giving Ralph away that I ran off to Jack's house and unloaded on him. I told him I was leaving that night, but he talked me into waiting until morning."

"And then he loaned you money and took you to the bus station?"

"Did you talk to him?"

"Yes. I was worried."

"He's really a sweet guy, Grandma. He even tried to talk me into staying with you. But I told him I was done with you." Avery made a sad smile. "I'm sorry."

"Don't worry, I understand. I've been a bit fed up with myself too."

"So anyway, I was at the bus station and about to get a ticket to take me home, but I just couldn't stand the idea of going back there. So I got a cup of coffee."

"At the bus station café?"

"Exactly. This girl was the only waitress there. And she was in the weeds."

"In the weeds?"

"You know, too many customers, too many orders, over her head."

"Oh. I see."

"And everyone was complaining, and this one dude was being really rude to her because his cheeseburger was probably getting cold, and she was about to start crying."

"Poor thing."

"That's what I thought, so I walked right past her and got his cheeseburger and handed it to him. And then I started taking orders and getting stuff and filling coffee cups, and the girl never even questioned it."

"Really?" Betty tried not to look too stunned. What nerve!

"Finally, it kind of slowed down, and the girl asked me who I was and if I'd come about the job." Avery put the teabags in the mugs.

"And so she hired you?"

"Her dad did. He's the cook and the manager. They'd just lost two waitresses earlier that week. And with holiday travelers, they were getting desperate."

"But how did you know how to do all that?" Betty studied Avery. "Taking orders and getting food. Don't you need to be trained or licensed or something?"

"Waitressing is waitressing. I've done it a lot of times." She filled the mugs with hot water and brought them over to the table.

"But it's been two nights since you left. Where did you stay?"

"Abby and Carl let me sleep on their couch."

"The waitress and the cook?"

"Yeah. But that couch was getting uncomfortable. And Abby's sister Laurel was coming home from school today, so the apartment was going to be crowded. They gave me tonight and tomorrow off since Laurel will help them out. So I thought I'd come check on you. Then you scared me half to death by playing possum in your bed. Were you feeling sick?"

"Just very tired." Betty took a slow sip of tea.

"Hey, how did you like my decorations for the anniversary party?"

Betty gushed about how much she loved them and how everyone else was extremely impressed as well. "Marsha and Jim were completely overwhelmed with how beautiful it was, and their grandchildren thought you must be a professional artist."

"I wish."

"So, do you want to continue with the waitress job?" Betty asked.

"Yeah. For a while. Until I figure something else out."

"Would you like to stay here?" Betty asked. "The city bus stop is only—"

"Two blocks from here." Avery grinned.

"You know that you're welcome."

"Thanks. I'd appreciate it."

"Would you mind calling your parents?"

Avery frowned.

"Or, if you don't mind, I can call them—just so they'll know you're safe."

"That's okay. I'll call them. I'm trying to act more like a grown-up. That's what Jack told me I should do."

"He told you that?"

"And a lot of other things. He's been through a lot, Grandma. You should get to know him better. I think you'll like him."

Betty nodded. "I'm sure you're right."

They finished their tea, and Avery, true to her word, called her mother. Betty could hear the tension in Avery's voice, and not wanting to eavesdrop, she hurried back into her bedroom and closed the door.

"It's safe to come out now," Avery called after a few minutes.

"I take it your mother wasn't too happy."

"That's a pretty safe guess."

"But she was relieved to hear you're okay?"

"I suppose."

"It's not easy being a parent, Avery."

Avery just shrugged with a hurt expression, and Betty decided to change the subject. "You'll never guess what I did yesterday."

"Let's see. It was Sunday . . . did you go to church?"

Betty smiled. "Yes, as a matter of fact, I did. But after that I went to the animal shelter. I wanted to get Ralph."

Avery's eyes lit up. "You got him back?"

Betty sighed. "No. I was too late. Someone else adopted him."

Now Avery looked sadder than ever.

"I'm sorry," Betty said quickly. "Maybe I shouldn't have

told you that. But I just wanted you to know that I had a complete change of heart. I realized that Ralph was a wonderful, sweet little dog. And that I needed him. It almost seemed like God had sent him to me, and then I'd stupidly turned him away. I can't even describe how sad that made me feel." She put a hand on Avery's shoulder. "Almost as sad as losing you."

"But I'm back."

"Yes, you are." Betty smiled. "And I need to go to the grocery store. I made a short list, but now that you're here, I think it's time to kill the fattened calf."

Avery looked confused.

"Or roast a turkey."

So they went to the grocery store, and since Betty had already spent her December budget, she decided to dip into January's. Of course, this would blow her grocery budget to pieces. But she didn't even care.

16

"This is a lot of food, Grandma." Avery surveyed the bags now lined up like soldiers on the kitchen counter.

Betty chuckled. "Well, yes, I suppose it is. We better get those cold items in the fridge."

"Can we invite Jack for Christmas dinner?" Avery handed Betty the turkey. "I mean, if he doesn't have other plans, which I'll bet he doesn't since he has no family around here anymore."

"Anymore?" Betty adjusted the lower shelf to make room for the turkey.

"Yeah. Jack's grandparents used to own his house."

"Jack's grandparents?" Betty scowled. "The only people who've ever lived in that house were the Spencers."

"Yeah. They must've been Jack's mom's parents. He said she grew up here. He even showed me her room. It's still painted pink."

"Donna Spencer is Jack's mom?" Betty dropped the package of celery in the vegetable bin and turned to stare at Avery. "Are you sure?"

"You know Jack's mom?"

"I knew her. Donna was a sweet girl. As a teenager, she used to babysit my children during the summers when I worked at the post office. Then she got married and moved away. Last time I saw her, she was on her second marriage." Betty strained her memory. "It seems to me that she had a little boy in her second marriage, but they only came out to visit a few times. And I think his name was Johnny."

"Jack."

"Jack is Johnny?"

"Yeah. I guess he switched over to Jack while he was in Afghanistan."

"He was in Afghanistan?"

Avery nodded and handed Betty a bag of potatoes. "He said it was pretty rough over there. But it sounds like it's been almost as rough being home. He told me he has horrible nightmares, and that's why he likes to work on his house at night sometimes."

"Oh." Betty still remembered how Chuck had had bad dreams after he'd come back from Korea, but he'd never wanted to talk about his experience there. And to think Jack had been suffering too. Making noise in the night, with his neighbors all thinking the worst of him. She shook her head. "Poor boy."

"Anyway, his mom gave him that house," Avery said.

"Donna gave him the house?"

"Yeah. She and her brother inherited it. Only her brother didn't want it."

Betty just shook her head. "I still can't believe I didn't know that Jack was Gladys and Al's grandson. I wish he would've told me sooner."

Avery shrugged. "It sounds like he never got the chance."

"I suppose I never gave him the chance."

They were done putting things away now. "I think it's a lovely idea to invite Jack for Christmas dinner," Betty said. "How about if we invite the Gilmores too, unless they're busy. It's about time neighbors started getting acquainted."

"And we can serve dinner in the dining room," Avery said. "We'll use your pretty dishes. I'll get it all set up and—" Avery paused. "Can you hear that, Grandma?"

Betty stopped folding the paper bag and listened. "My old ears aren't too sharp."

"It sounds like someone at the door."

Betty tucked the bag into a drawer, then looked up in time to see Avery dashing out of the kitchen. "Grandma!" she screamed. "Com'ere quick!"

Frightened that there was an armed gunman at the door, Betty hurried to see Avery squatting on the floor with a familiar little brown dog licking her face.

"It's Ralph!" Avery said. "He's back!"

Betty couldn't believe her eyes. But it certainly did look like Ralph. "How on earth?"

"He found us, Grandma!" Avery scooped the dog into her arms. "He's home!"

Betty considered this. On many levels she wanted to agree with her granddaughter and say, "Yes, he's home, and all will be well." But at the same time, she was concerned. "But the people at the shelter said he'd been adopted, Avery."

"Maybe he didn't like his new owners."

Betty nodded. "Maybe."

"Can we keep him?"

"You know I want to keep him, Avery. But what if his new

owners are looking for him right now? I'm sure they paid good money for him. He was probably meant to be someone's Christmas present. And certainly there's some kind of record at the shelter—"

"So what are you saying?"

"I'm saying that I'd better call the shelter. I'll explain everything to them, and I'll ask if we might possibly purchase Ralph back from his new owners. The shelter people care about animals, and I'm sure they'll understand that Ralph came looking for us, not the other way around. Ralph is more than welcome to stay with us, Avery, but I do think we need to go about this the right way."

Avery looked disappointed, but at least she agreed. Betty went to make the call. She carefully explained everything right from the beginning until how the dog had shown up of his own free will this afternoon. "I'm sure his new owners must be worried," Betty finished. "If I knew their phone number, I could give them a call." Betty decided not to mention her ulterior motive about wanting to purchase Ralph back from his new family.

"I can understand your problem," the woman said. "We're a little shorthanded here today. But if it will help to reunite the dog to his family, I think it's okay for me to give you the name and phone number of the dog's owner."

"Thank you so much!"

The woman shared the information, and Betty thanked her and hung up.

"So?" Avery was waiting expectantly.

Betty just stood there, staring first at the dog and then at Avery.

"What's wrong, Grandma?"

"The owner . . ." Betty shook her head. "It's Jack."

"Our Jack?"

Betty nodded.

Avery sighed. "Oh."

"I had no idea Jack wanted the dog."

"He didn't."

"Well, to be fair, neither did I." Betty sighed. "Not at first."

Avery was clearly disappointed, but she just nodded. "Fine. I'll take Ralph back to Jack. Just let me run and use the bathroom first."

Betty reached down and patted Ralph's head. "It was nice of you to pop in to say hello," she said. "At least we're neighbors. And you're welcome to visit—"

Just then there was a loud knock on the door. Betty opened it to see Jack standing there. "Come on in, Jack."

He came in hesitantly. "Sorry to disturb you, Betty, but I'm, uh, looking for—" His brows lifted slightly when he noticed the dog. "Looks like Ralph decided to drop by."

Betty nodded. "And I just found out that he belongs to you now."

Jack looked slightly sheepish. "I just couldn't bear to think of him at the pound."

"He's a good dog."

Jack actually smiled now. "He is a good dog. But he seems a little confused about where he lives today."

Avery came into the room with her parka and bag over one arm. "Jack!"

"Avery!" Jack looked even happier to see her than she was to see him. "What are you doing here?"

With half sentences tumbling over each other, Avery explained about not going home, her new job, and her decision to stay in town. "Which reminds me, I want to pay you back the loan now."

He waved his hand. "That's okay, you—"

"No way," she said quickly, reaching for her bag. "I'm trying to do the grown-up, responsible thing. Remember?" She counted out the money into his hand. "Sorry about all the change, it's from tips. And you'll have to trust me for that last twenty. I had to use it for a city bus pass."

"Well, I better get out of your hair." Jack reached down to pick up Ralph. "Sorry to have bothered you."

"It's no bother," Betty said quickly. "In fact, we wanted to invite you for Christmas dinner tomorrow."

"Grandma got a turkey and all the trimmings." Avery smiled. "And I'm going to make a pumpkin pie."

"Do you have plans?" Betty asked.

"No . . ."

"Then we'll expect you at two."

Jack nodded. "All right then."

"And bring Ralph too," Avery said.

Jack chuckled. "My guess is that he'll beat me over here."

17

Jack guessed right. Shortly before noon on Christmas Day, Ralph came over to visit them again. "He must've smelled the turkey cooking," Avery told Betty. She led the little dog into the kitchen, then returned to where she'd been rolling out pie dough.

"Merry Christmas, Ralph." Betty plucked a turkey giblet out of the dressing she was mixing and tossed it to him.

"You're too early for dinner," Avery told him.

"Should we take him back?" Betty asked.

Avery paused with the rolling pin in her hand. "I suppose that's the right thing to do, Grandma. Although I'll bet Jack can guess where he is."

"How about if I take him," Betty offered as she wiped her hands on her apron. "That way you can finish the pie crust before it dries out. And I wanted to give Jack another cookie plate anyway."

Betty put together a generous goodie platter, but instead of putting the red bow on the plastic wrap like she usually did, she stuck it on Ralph's head. "Come on, boy," she called as she went for her coat. Acting as if he'd received top honors at doggy obedience school, Ralph stuck to her heels as she led him out the front door and down the walk.

Betty smiled as the little dog took the lead, trotting about a foot in front of her like he knew exactly where he was going and why. He turned the corner and headed straight to Jack's house just like he lived there. And, well, didn't he? Still, as Betty followed him, she couldn't help but wonder how a little stray dog like that had wandered into their lives, or how he had attached himself to not just one person in need, but two. Make that three. And she considered how this little dog had brought them all together. Really, in some ways, it seemed nothing short of a miracle.

"Merry Christmas," she told Jack when he opened the door.

"Hey, I was just looking for you, Ralphie." Jack grinned to see the red bow on his dog's head. "You're like a real party animal."

"He's a very special dog," Betty said. She handed Jack the cookies. "I think he just likes bringing people together."

"I guess so." Jack's expression grew thoughtful. "You know, Betty, I was wondering if it would be okay for me to give Ralph to Avery for Christmas. I know how much she loves him and everything. But then I got worried that you might not appreciate that—you might not want a dog in your house. And I sure don't want to rock your boat again."

Betty just laughed. "You know what I think, Jack?"

He looked slightly bewildered now. "What?"

"I think Ralph is a Christmas dog, and I think he's going to give himself to whoever he feels needs him the most."

Jack nodded. "I think you're right. Kinda like share the love?"

"And maybe we'll just have to share him too."

"Tell you what, Betty." Jack nodded toward the backyard. "I'm going to rebuild that fence—right where it's standing now, where my grandparents built it—but how about if we put a gate between the two yards?"

"And a doggy door too?"

"Absolutely." He stuck out his hand. "Deal?"

"It's a deal." Betty firmly shook his hand, then opened her arms to hug him, nearly toppling his cookie platter. "Welcome to the neighborhood, Jack!"

"Thanks, Betty. I think I'm starting to feel at home."

Betty patted Ralph's head again. "I thank you, little Christmas dog, for bringing us all together. And now I have a turkey to baste."

"We'll see you at two," Jack called. "Merry Christmas!"

"Merry Christmas," she called back. As she walked toward home, it occurred to her that her old neighborhood—which looked more spectacular than ever in its clean white blanket of fresh, fallen snow—was getting better all the time.

The
CHRISTMAS
PONY

1

December 1937

Lucy Turnbull knew better than to wish for a pony for Christmas this year. Besides receiving the upsetting news that Santa Claus was only make-believe (Tommy Farley had popped that beloved bubble several weeks ago), Lucy had been assured by Mama in no uncertain terms that she was not getting a pony—and furthermore, Lucy had no business asking for such nonsense. "You might as well ask me to buy you the moon," Mama firmly told her at the dinner table.

"Ponies are expensive," Grandma added. "Only rich people can afford those luxuries these days."

Really, Lucy should have heeded their warning. But at bedtime, after she'd finished her prayers, Lucy noticed that the corners of Mama's mouth were turned downward. Lucy pulled the covers to her chin, cringing to realize she was to blame for the two deep creases in the center of Mama's forehead. Lucy should not have asked God for a pony. Not tonight. And especially not after what Mama and Grandma had told her at dinnertime.

As Mama put an extra quilt on the bed, Lucy craned her neck, straining to see the picture she'd pinned above the metal head-board earlier. She'd drawn her dream pony on the blank side of the November calendar sheet that Grandma had nearly used as fire starter. Then, using her best penmanship, Lucy had written "Pony for Sale or Trade" across the top of her drawing—just like the sign she'd noticed this afternoon. The wooden sign had been nailed to a fence post by the Greenburg field, and Lucy knew that meant that Mr. Greenburg was selling Smoky. She'd admired the little gray pony for as long as she could remember. Seeing he was for sale had sent her running home to tell Mama and Grandma the good news.

"You know that I can barely afford to keep food on the table." Mama sighed as she leaned over to kiss Lucy's forehead. "Heaven knows I cannot afford to feed a horse as well."

"Smoky's not a horse," Lucy pointed out. "He's a pony."

"Ponies . . . horses . . . they still eat food, don't they?" Mama tucked the quilt more snugly around her. "The only extra mouths we need around here are the paying kind, Lucy. Instead of praying for a pony, why don't you ask the Good Lord to send us some boarders?"

"Yes, Mama." Lucy burrowed deeper into the covers as Mama pulled the string on the overhead light. "I *will* pray for that," she promised. Lying in the darkness, she listened as Mama's footsteps went down the hallway toward the kitchen. She heard the squeaking of the woodstove door and the clunk of a heavy piece of firewood being set inside, followed by the clanking sound of the heavy door being closed and, after a bit, the reassuring creak of the old rocker as Mama sat down.

Grandma was already in bed, but Mama always stayed up late. She was probably reaching for her knitting basket now. Lucy didn't know how it was possible, but sometimes Mama could knit a whole sock in just one single night. The socks were all made out of worsted wool, a fine black yarn that Mama said was hard on her eyes. But when Lucy suggested she use another color, a prettier one like sky blue, Mama had explained that the store would only sell her socks in black. Lucy knew that ever since Daddy died, back when she was just five, they needed Mama's socks to trade for groceries. Just like they needed paying boarders to fill the three upstairs bedrooms of the old farmhouse, because even though they earned extra money by taking in people's laundry, Lucy knew that it was never quite enough. She'd heard Mama and Grandma speak of this very thing often enough. Mostly when they didn't realize she was listening.

"We just have to make ends meet," Mama would tell Lucy sometimes, especially when Lucy couldn't have something she wanted. Usually it was something she didn't really need, like candy or toys or pretty hair ribbons. Always it was something much smaller than a pony.

Lucy was only eight years old, but she was old enough to know that times were hard. Grandma said that often enough. "Times might be hard, Lucy," she'd say in her slow, quiet way, "but you can still be thankful for what you've got—a roof over your head and food to eat." Of course, Lucy didn't think too much about those things. She was more thankful for the long rope swing over the creek, or the bird's nest she found after last week's windstorm, or getting to play an angel in this year's Christmas pageant. Those things were easy to be thankful for.

Sometimes Lucy would overhear Mama and Grandma having conversations they didn't want Lucy to be privy to, but the solemn, serious tone of their voices always made her ears perk up, and she would listen harder than ever. Like when the Saunders family lost their farm last spring and had to move away. Lucy wasn't quite sure how their neighbors "lost" their farm since, as far as she could see, it was still there. Sure, it was overgrown with blackberries and weeds and the slumping fences needed fixing, but when she walked past it on her way to school every day, it never looked lost to her. The only thing that seemed to be missing was the Saunderses themselves. Lucy missed her best friend Clara Saunders and wondered where the Saunderses' dusty green farm truck had carried Clara and her family off to and whether or not Clara was happier there.

True to her promise, Lucy closed her eyes now and, with genuine faith, prayed for God to bring them some paying boarders. Mama had just said that this time of year, with Christmas around the corner, not many travelers would be stopping in Maple Grove to stay. The best time of year for boarders always seemed to be summer. Just the same, Lucy knew that God could do anything. At least that was what Pastor McHenry liked to say. Sometimes she wasn't too sure Mama believed that exactly.

Otherwise, why would she be so worried about Lucy's prayers for a pony?

After Lucy finished praying for boarders to come and stay in the upstairs rooms, she got a brand-new prayer idea. Instead of simply asking God to give her a pony, she would ask him to give her what the pony would need to eat as well. Surely Mama wouldn't be opposed to that sort of prayer.

"And please, dear God," she said finally, "help Mama to find her smile again." Lucy could remember when Mama had the prettiest smile ever. Back when Daddy was still alive. But like Lucy's memories of her father, Mama's smile had faded some over the last few years. If Lucy couldn't have a pony for Christmas, she would settle for Mama's smile instead.

After Lucy said amen, she began to imagine what it would be like to ride Smoky to school each day. The trip to town was almost a mile, and without Clara and her sister to walk with, it had felt longer than ever this year. Lucy imagined how she'd tie her gray pony to the willow tree by the creek, close enough so he could get a cool drink to refresh himself with and where he could feed on the grass that grew lush and green there—and it occurred to her, the grass food would be free. Maybe other kinds of pony food would be free as well. She would gladly collect the mushy windfall apples for Smoky in the fall, just the ones that were too wormy for cider or anything else, although she might slip him a good one now and then too. She'd sneaked him apples before. Just the memory of the fuzzy feel of his warm muzzle on the palm of her hand made her smile, and thinking these lovely thoughts, Lucy drifted off into a sweet pony dream.

The next morning, after Lucy tended to the chickens and collected the eggs and did her other usual Saturday chores, Mama held up a small package wrapped in brown paper. Lucy knew it held this week's socks and, judging by the size, contained four pairs.

"Do you have the list ready?" Lucy pulled on her winter coat, buttoning it up to her chin. She was accustomed to doing their Saturday shopping by now. She and Grandma used to go together, but the cold, damp weather was aggravating Grandma's arthritis something fierce this year. So for the last several weeks, Lucy had been doing the Saturday errands on her own. She liked doing it herself too. Knowing Mama trusted her and that she was old enough to help out like this, well, it just felt good.

Mama handed her the sock package and a small slip of paper, and Lucy read over the list with disappointment. Only three items were on it: yeast, coffee, and baking powder. "This is *all* you need?" She tucked it into her coat pocket.

Mama shrugged. "For today, it is."

Lucy suspected that meant it was all they could afford today, but she just smiled as she pulled on her knit hat. "Well, it's not much to carry back. I guess I won't need to take my wagon."

Mama tugged the hat down over Lucy's ears. "Don't forget your mittens. It's cold out there. But at least it doesn't look like rain today. Now, be on your way and don't dillydally in town."

Lucy considered telling Mama that a pony would come in mighty handy for doing errands in town, especially on a cold day like this when she could cling to his furry coat for warmth, but she stopped herself. She might be just a kid, but she knew enough to understand how that kind of talk would simply aggravate Mama. There was no sense in doing that. Even so, she would walk quickly to town and complete the errands and still have enough time to stop to visit with Smoky, and if she was lucky, maybe Mr. Greenburg would be around and she could ask him about the pony's price or inquire as to what he would consider for trade. Not that Lucy had much of anything of value to trade. But it couldn't hurt to ask. With a spring in her step, she hurried toward town.

Walking past the Saunderses' old farm, Lucy tried not to think about Clara. As she passed the Greenburg place, she waved and called out to the pony. "Hello, Smoky! I'll stop by to see you on my way home."

She was about halfway to town when she heard a car coming down the road behind her. It was making a lot of noise, and when she looked, smoke was billowing all around it. She stepped to the side of the road, watching as the pale yellow car slowly sputtered and clunked past her. Despite the cloud of smoke, it looked like a pretty car. Too bad it didn't work right.

When Lucy got to the edge of town, she noticed the pale yellow car parked in front of Hempley's Garage, and a man in a brown suit was talking to Mr. Hempley. But it was the lady getting out of the passenger side of the car who really captured Lucy's attention. Wrapped in a royal blue coat with a big silver fur collar, she had shining hair almost the same color as the pale yellow car and cut short with bangs that curled like a fringe around her pretty face.

As Lucy got closer, she could see the lady's rosy cheeks and lips of scarlet red. Lucy stopped walking, staring openly at this fancy lady. She looked just like a real movie star! Lucy had seen only a handful of motion pictures in her life, mostly the ones with Shirley Temple in them, and only during the summertime or when Mama had paying boarders and money was not so tight, but Lucy had seen enough to know that this lady looked just like the pretty actresses on the silver screen. Gripping the package of socks tightly in her arms, Lucy just stared without moving.

"Hello, doll." The lady smiled down at Lucy.

"Hello," Lucy managed to say back to her.

"Is there a place I can buy a soda around here?" Her voice sounded as sweet as sugar and honey and something else too. Maybe spice.

Lucy blinked and tried to gather her thoughts. "There's the mercantile right there." She pointed across the street. "They sell sodas in there. They have a big Coca-Cola cooler right by the front door." Then Lucy realized this lady probably meant the kind of soda that comes in a glass with a straw and ice. "But there's Ruth's Café too," she said quickly. "Down on the other end of town."

The lady hooked the handle of her shiny black handbag over her arm as she gazed across the street. "I'll be over there in the mercantile," she called out to the man in the brown suit.

"That's where I'm going too," Lucy said as she walked with the lady. "I'm doing my mama's errands today."

"Well, isn't that nice." The lady pulled her fur collar more tightly around her neck and shivered. "Brrr . . . it's cold here."

"My grandma said it might snow," Lucy said cheerfully.

"Snow?" The lady's thin eyebrows went up. "But this is Arizona. I thought it was supposed to be warm here."

"In the wintertime?" Lucy frowned.

"Oh, yes." The lady nodded as if remembering something. "George did mention the high altitude here. That probably explains it."

Lucy wasn't sure what it explained, but she couldn't think of anything else to say as they went into the store together. Even so, she watched curiously as the lady walked over to the big red cooler and selected a bottle of orange soda. Lucy knew it was impolite to stare, but she couldn't help herself as she watched this lady walking—or was she floating?—around the store, looking at the candy case and then the sundries section and finally stopping at the magazine rack.

"Hello, Lucy," Mrs. Danson called out with unusual friendliness. "Can I help you, dear?"

Lucy went over to the counter, setting her package of socks in front of Mrs. Danson. "I only need a few things today." She peeled off a mitten and reached into her coat pocket.

"Who is that with you?" Mrs. Danson whispered as she opened the package of socks, examining them closely before setting them aside.

Lucy shrugged. "I don't know."

"She's not from around here, that's for certain."

Lucy told Mrs. Danson the items on her list, and while the storekeeper went to the back room to get some yeast, the man in the brown suit came into the store. "Bad news," he told the blonde lady. "The mechanic just told me that the engine overheated."

"What does that mean?" The lady looked at him with big blue eyes.

"It means I should've stopped driving before the radiator boiled dry." He ran his hand through his short dark hair with troubled eyes. "The mechanic says he can order parts, but it will take a few days, maybe even a week, depending on how bad the damage to the engine is—and it doesn't look good."

"*Oh, dear!*" Her jet black eyelashes fluttered. "What on earth will we do, George? Can you get another car to get us out to California?"

He let out a big sigh, then shook his head. "I need to stick around long enough to get this car fixed."

She plunked her bottle of soda on the counter with a thud. "Do you think there's anyplace to stay in this one-horse town?"

Lucy's ears perked up now. "My mama runs a boarding house," she quickly told the lady. "We've got room."

The lady's fine brows arched. "Really?"

"It's about a mile out of town," Lucy explained. "We have three upstairs rooms and my mama is a good cook and—"

"A mile out of town?" the lady frowned.

"But it's real pretty and quiet out there," Lucy said hopefully, "and lots cheaper than the boarding house here in town." She refrained from mentioning that the place in town was said to have bedbugs since Mama would not approve. "The food is lots better at my mama's boarding house too. It's not bragging 'cause everyone says so."

"That sounds good to me." The man's brown eyes lit up.

Just like that, Lucy was explaining to them where the house was located and what color it was and that she'd run on home ahead of them and inform her mama that they were coming. "If you get there in time, you can have lunch with us too. Grandma's making chicken and dumplings today."

"I like the sound of that." The man looked at his watch and grinned. "My mouth is already starting to water."

"But a mile from town?" The lady's red lips puckered as she stuck out a shiny black shoe. "How on earth do we get there?"

The man just laughed. Meanwhile, Lucy scrambled to gather up the package that Mrs. Danson had readied for her, bidding everyone good-bye before she hurried on her way outside. Heading down the road for home, she partly walked and partly ran, but she realized that her plans for stopping by to talk to Mr. Greenburg about Smoky would have to wait for now. However, if God had already answered her prayers for paying boarders, maybe that meant he would answer her prayers for a pony as well.

2

W ho are these people?" Mama asked after Lucy had breathlessly told her the good news.

"I don't know their names," Lucy gasped as she peeled off her coat, "but they look like rich people." Now she described the yellow car and the lady's fine clothing. "I think I heard them saying they were on their way to California."

"With half of the rest of the country," Grandma said from where she was tending a pot on the stove.

"Passing through." Mama hung Lucy's coat on a peg by the door. "Everybody is just passing through Maple Grove."

"Did you get the yeast?" Grandma asked Lucy. "I'll need it to bake bread for tomorrow. Especially if we're having guests."

"It's in there," Lucy told her.

"You run on upstairs and check the rooms," Mama said to Lucy as she reached for her good apron. "Open the doors to let some heat in, and take the feather duster with you and make sure everything looks tidy and fresh. I expect they'll want the front room since it's bigger and the sun comes in so nice in there, but we'll let them take their pick."

Lucy scurried up the stairs, opening all the bedroom doors and even checking the bathroom to make sure there were no spiders or webs in the sink or the big claw-foot bathtub. Everything seemed to be in good order, but she wished it was summer so she could gather some pretty flowers to put in a vase. She thought the movie star lady would like that.

She stooped to straighten out the colorful braided rug that ran down the length of the hallway. She and Grandma had made that rug from long strips of old fabric last winter. Lucy did the braiding and Grandma did the sewing. It was supposed to keep the sounds of footsteps quieter up there, but Lucy thought it mostly looked pretty and festive.

She was just coming down the stairs when she heard someone at the front door. Lucy rushed to answer it. "Hello," she said eagerly. "I forgot to tell you, I'm Lucy."

"Pleased to meet you, Lucy. My name's Veronica." She jerked her thumb toward the man behind her. "And this is George."

"Pleased to meet you, Lucy." He leaned down to shake her hand.

Lucy was leading them into the front room just as Mama came through the dining room. She still had on her working clothes, and Lucy could tell she was uncomfortable. Probably even more so when she saw how fancy Veronica looked.

"This is George and Veronica," Lucy told Mama.

"Lucy, where are your manners? You don't call grown-ups by their first names."

"That's my fault," Veronica said. "But, really, I like to be called by my first name. It makes me feel like an old schoolmarm to be called ma'am or missus." She elbowed George.

"George is fine for me." He smiled down at Lucy. "Since we're among friends."

"Mama's real name is Miriam," Lucy told them. "Isn't that a pretty name?"

"It's very nice," George said. "Nice to meet you, Miriam."

"Aren't they nice?" Lucy looked at Mama and could tell that something was bothering her. Maybe it was that this couple was nothing like their usual boarders.

"Mr. Hempley from the garage gave us a ride here," Veronica said. "He left my other suitcase on the porch for me."

"I hope we're not imposing on you." George removed his hat. "We met Lucy in town and she said you had rooms available."

"We have plenty of room." Mama made her polite face— not exactly a smile, but not unpleasant either. "I hope you'll make yourselves at home. Lunch will be ready in about half an hour . . . if you'd like to freshen up a bit. There's a guestbook in the dining room for you to register in." Now she nodded toward the stairway where Lucy was waiting. "Lucy can show you where the rooms are located, and you can take your pick." Mama stepped back. "Now if you'll excuse me, I need to help my mother prepare lunch."

As the man went out to fetch the other suitcases, Veronica patted Lucy on the head and smiled. "This is a nice little place you got here, doll."

The man returned with two more suitcases. They were tan and white and matched the smaller one that Veronica carried in one hand. Lucy wished she could see what was inside those pretty bags and wondered what Veronica might say if Lucy offered to help her unpack.

"I hope you both enjoy your stay here." Suddenly Lucy felt as if she were playing a part in a movie. Perhaps like Shirley Temple in *The Little Colonel*. "Now I will show you to your room." Holding her head high, she led them up the stairs, taking them from room to room and explaining every single detail, including how the pipes might sometimes rattle if air got trapped inside. "You just give it a good whack like this"—she hit the exposed pipe that went to the bathtub—"and it should quiet right down for you."

"I've known plumbing like that before," George told her.

"We have an outhouse too," Lucy explained. "Sometimes it comes in handy, but it can be awful cold this time of year." She stopped by the front bedroom now. "This room is really the best one." She proudly pointed to the large window. "Mama says it gets the best light in here."

"Why don't you take this room," George said to Veronica.

"Thank you." She rewarded him with a pretty smile as he set her suitcase next to the door.

"I'll take the one in the back," George told Lucy. "I like the way it looks out over the apple trees."

Lucy tried not to show her surprise, but she hadn't expected them to want *two* rooms. Most married couples shared a room together. However, she knew that Mama should be pleased by this arrangement because it meant more money, since they charged by the room as well as the meal. Lucy had imagined these people were rich. It seemed she was right. She just hoped they'd stay for a whole week or even more.

"You make yourselves comfortable," Lucy said, imitating Mama. She considered offering to help Veronica unpack but was afraid that might sound too nosy. "I should go down and set the table now."

But by the time Lucy reached the dining room, Mama was nearly finished setting the table. To Lucy's surprise, she'd put out the good china dishes—the ones with the gold and black design around the edges. "The table looks real pretty," Lucy told her. "George and Veronica should like it a lot."

"That's all?" Mama frowned as she adjusted a teacup. "Just *George* and *Veronica*?"

"Yes." Lucy nodded. "George and Veronica."

Mama looked doubtful. "Didn't they tell you their last name, Lucy?"

"I guess I forgot to ask," Lucy admitted, "but you heard them tell me to call them by their first names. Is that all right, Mama?"

"Well, I suppose so. If that's what they want. However, I don't generally care for you calling adults by their first names."

"I know." Lucy was about to tell Mama how George and Veronica were using two rooms upstairs, but Grandma stuck her head in the swinging door that led to the kitchen. "Miriam," she said, "I need your help in here, please."

"You go wash up," Mama told Lucy. "Then you can fill the water glasses for me."

Before long, the new boarders had returned downstairs and everyone was seated around the dining room table where Mama bowed her head to say grace. They made small talk about the weather and traveling as the food was passed around, but the conversation grew quiet as they ate. Lucy was seated across from George and Veronica so she had a good view of their exciting new guests. Veronica had removed her fur-trimmed coat and now wore a shiny dress that was almost the same color as purple irises in the springtime. She also had on a necklace and earrings that looked like real diamonds, but Lucy couldn't be sure about that since she'd never seen real diamonds before. No matter, Veronica was still the most glamorous person Lucy had ever seen in real life. Lucy wished that Clara still lived down the road so she could see her too.

Lucy glanced over to where Mama was sitting in her usual spot at the end of the table closest to the kitchen. She liked to sit there so that she could fetch things more easily. Lucy knew it was probably wrong to compare Mama to Veronica, but she just couldn't help herself. Mama looked kind of washed out today. Sort of like when Lucy's favorite red gingham blouse got left in the sun too long and the color got drained right out of it. Even Mama's dress looked more faded and worn than usual. Plus Mama's light brown hair, pulled back in its usual bun, seemed sadly drab too. Still, Mama's eyes were pretty—and even bluer than Veronica's— although Veronica's eyelashes were much blacker, more fancy somehow. But, Lucy reminded herself, mothers weren't supposed to look like Veronica—and Mama was simply Mama. And really, she was a lot prettier than all the other mothers in Maple Grove.

"This is about the best chicken and dumplings I've ever had," George proclaimed. "My compliments to the chef."

"Grandma does most of the cooking," Lucy told him. "But Mama can cook too," she added quickly.

George told them about his car and how he felt like a fool to have let the radiator boil dry like he did. "My father used to warn me about that very thing. I really should've known better. That's what comes of driving too many hours, but I'd really hoped to make it to Los Angeles before nightfall."

"What takes you to Los Angeles?" Grandma asked.

"I hope to find work there," he told her.

"What sort of work?" she asked.

"That's a good question." George's mouth twisted to one side as they waited for him to answer. "You see, I'd been in college back east . . . back before Black Friday. I'd been in law school, but like a lot of other students, my family's funds ran out before I could finish my degree. So I took a clerical job in an insurance firm and worked there for the past six years, finishing my schooling and trying to save enough to take my bar exams and get a practice started. As luck had it, the insurance company went under last spring, and I haven't been able to find work since. I've heard that California has more job opportunities."

"Not to mention more sunshine," Veronica added. "Did you know that California is so warm and sunny that you can actually grow orange trees right in your own backyard?" She sighed dreamily. "Imagine that."

"That does sound lovely," Mama said. "I'm sure you'll be very happy there."

"If I can ever get there." George dismally shook his head. "I'm afraid my car's engine is going to take nearly until Christmas to get fixed. And the holidays aren't a good time to go job hunting."

"You can stay here for Christmas," Lucy said suddenly. "We have plenty of room."

George laughed. "I appreciate the offer, little lady. I just hope I don't have to take you up on it."

"I don't *want* to stay here until Christmas." Veronica made a pout toward George. "Surely it won't take that long to fix your silly old car, will it?"

He shrugged, but the look on his face was hard to read.

"Well, one way or another, I plan to get myself out to California," Veronica proclaimed. "There must be a train station nearby."

"Of course." Grandma reached for the butter. "Flagstaff has a perfectly good train station."

"How far are we from Flagstaff?" Veronica asked.

"It's about twenty miles," Mama told her.

"Surely I could get a train to California from there." Veronica made a long sigh. "That is, if I could get myself to Flagstaff."

Lucy stared at her. "You'd go to California by yourself?"

Veronica just laughed. "Well, of course."

"Would you care for more chicken and dumplings?" Mama asked George in a stiff-sounding voice.

"Don't mind if I do."

As Mama quietly ladled out another helping, Lucy could tell by the firm set of Mama's mouth that she was upset about something.

"I have to get to Hollywood," Veronica explained, "because

I plan to become a movie actress. You know, like Jean Harlow . . . Myrna Loy . . . Barbara Stanwyck."

"Is that so?" Grandma adjusted her glasses, peering more carefully at Veronica.

"You're pretty enough to be an actress," Lucy said shyly.

"Well, thank you very much." Veronica rewarded her with a shining smile.

"Do you know how to act?" Mama asked her. "I mean, have you participated in dramatic productions or theater before?"

Veronica waved her hand. "Oh, sure. I've done a few things. Nothing terribly impressive. But that doesn't matter so much in the motion picture business. Most of all the directors are looking for the right kind of face." She turned her head to one side and tipped her chin upward. "I've been told I'm highly photogenic and I'd look good on the big screen."

Lucy nodded eagerly. "I think you'd look just fine in a movie."

Veronica began to talk about a motion picture she'd recently seen. "Clark Gable and Claudette Colbert were in it," she explained with wide-eyed enthusiasm. "It was called *It Happened One Night*, and it was about a couple who were taking a road trip." She giggled. "Kind of like George and me." She went on to say how everyone got very confused, and then the woman was going to marry someone else, and Veronica chattered on and on until Lucy felt lost—happily lost. She thought she could listen to Veronica talking about movies forever.

"Well." Mama said this in a way that suggested she'd heard enough. "That is all very interesting, but if you'll excuse me, I have some work to attend to now." She scooted back her chair and stood. "Lucy, you will help your grandmother clear the table, please." Mama left, and the meal and the interesting conversation seemed to be over too.

"I'm plumb worn out from all the traveling I've been doing." Veronica set her napkin on the table. "I do believe I'll catch up on some beauty rest this afternoon."

George thanked Grandma for the delicious meal and excused himself as well. Grandma reminded them both to sign in at the registration book on the buffet table, and then she and Lucy began to clear the table and wash the dishes.

"I 'spect your mama won't be using the good china for the next meal," Grandma said in a funny-sounding voice.

"Why not?" Lucy asked.

Grandma just chuckled.

Lucy held up a delicate teacup and nodded. "I guess I don't mind if she uses the everyday dishes. I don't worry so much about breaking those."

"Everyday dishes are more practical."

"Do you think Veronica is pretty, Grandma?"

Her brow creased. "I suppose some people might think a woman like that is pretty . . . if you like that sort of thing."

"I think Veronica is about the prettiest person I've ever laid eyes on," Lucy confessed.

"I don't know as I'd go as far as all that."

"I think she'll probably become a real movie star too," Lucy continued with enthusiasm. "Can't you just imagine seeing Veronica's face at our movie theater in town?"

"You know I don't care much for motion pictures, Lucy. The

truth is, I'm rather surprised that George is agreeable to that kind of nonsense for his wife. He didn't strike me as that sort of fellow." Grandma made a tsk-tsk sound through her teeth. "But young people nowadays . . . I 'spect times are changing."

After the dishes were washed and dried and put back in the china cabinet, Lucy decided to take a peek at the registration book. She was curious about where George and Veronica had come from. But to her surprise, they had written down different last names. George's last name was listed as Prescott and Veronica's was Grant. Not only that, but George had written that he'd come from Chicago, Illinois, and Veronica had written St. Louis, Missouri. Lucy knew enough about geography to know that those places were a ways apart.

"Did our guests sign in?" Mama asked as she laid some freshly ironed table linens in the drawer at the bottom of the china cabinet.

"Yes . . ." Lucy gave her a quizzical look.

"Is something wrong?"

Lucy shrugged, then closed the guestbook. If something was wrong, she wasn't sure she wanted Mama to know about it. Not just yet anyway. Already Mama seemed slightly disturbed by their new guests. Lucy suspected that Mama might not be too happy about renting rooms to movie stars, or *almost* movie stars. But Lucy thought it was terribly exciting. It was also an answer to her prayers. Besides that, didn't they need the money?

Fortunately, Mama didn't question her further. Instead she asked Lucy to bring some firewood out to the barn where she was working on laundry this afternoon. Some people might think it strange to do laundry in a barn, but their barn wasn't used for animals anymore. The only livestock they had these days was old Beulah the milk cow, who mostly lived in a loafing shed near the barn, and the chickens. The barn had long since been cleaned and swept and was where Mama kept their wringer washer and ironing board as well as several clotheslines that were strung back and forth. During the winter, a woodstove was kept burning to warm the barn enough for the laundry to dry.

As Lucy piled firewood into her wagon, she daydreamed about Veronica Grant starring in a motion picture playing at the Maple Grove movie theater. It would be so exciting to stand in the ticket line and tell everyone within earshot about how the famous actress had actually slept at their house.

Lucy wished that school wasn't already let out for Christmas vacation, because she wanted the chance to tell Helen Krausner all about it. She wouldn't brag, exactly, since bragging wasn't very nice. But she would happily tell Helen all about the almost movie star who was staying at their house. She would carefully describe just how beautiful and well dressed Veronica was and how she let Lucy call her by her first name and all sorts of things. Not to be mean, but just to show Helen that she wasn't the only one with interesting things to talk about. Helen always acted like she was better than everyone else, but Lucy was certain that Helen had never had someone as glamorous as Veronica Grant stay at her house. Really, it was almost as good as having a pony!

3

"Do you need some help with that?"

Lucy looked up from where she was using both hands in an attempt to tug her heavily loaded wagon out of a muddy rut in the middle of the driveway. George peered down at her with a curious expression. He'd changed out of his brown suit and was now wearing gray corduroy trousers and a dark green sweater. Without waiting for her to answer, he picked up the back end of the wagon and helped her to move it past the rut.

"Thanks." She smiled at him.

"Where are you taking that wood?" he asked as he walked alongside her.

She explained about Mama's laundry setup in the barn.

"No kidding?" He scratched his head. "Your mother is a very enterprising woman."

Lucy frowned. "Enterprising?"

He grinned. "That means she's a hard-working business-woman."

"Oh." She nodded. "My daddy used to take care of everything. But when he died, Mama had to work harder than ever."

"I'm sorry to hear about your father, Lucy." Now he reached down and took the handle of the wagon from her. "Why don't you let me help with that?"

Lucy didn't protest as he continued pulling the firewood toward the barn. "Can I ask you a question?" she said quietly.

"Sure." He paused to look at her.

"Why do you and Veronica have different names?"

He looked somewhat bewildered.

"I peeked at the guestbook," she confessed. "Veronica's last name is Grant and yours is Prescott."

He still seemed slightly confused, almost as if he was surprised by this himself. But then his eyes lit up like someone turned the lights on. "Oh, I think I understand. You must have assumed that Veronica and I were husband and wife."

Now Lucy felt confused, but she just nodded dumbly.

"Veronica and I aren't married, Lucy. We simply met on the road."

"You met on the road?" Lucy tried to imagine them meeting on the road, shaking hands, exchanging names.

"It's a long story, but Veronica needed a ride and I was going her way. That's how we met."

Lucy didn't know what to say as she slid open the barn door and waited for George to pull the loaded wagon inside before she slid it closed again.

"Oh?" Mama looked up from her ironing board in surprise.

"George is helping me," Lucy explained as she pointed over to the big old woodstove.

George rolled the wagon over and started unloading the wood onto the nearby pile.

"Well, thank you," Mama told him in a stiff voice.

"This is quite some setup you've got here." George looked around the barn with an approving expression. "What a great idea for drying laundry in the wintertime."

"Yes, well, we don't usually have our guests out here." Mama pressed her lips together as she smoothed the front of her old apron.

"I'm sorry to intrude." George stepped back as if he were feeling uncomfortable. "I was just out for a walk, and it looked like Lucy needed a hand."

"George said you're *enterprising*," Lucy told Mama, trying out her new word and hoping to put things more at ease. Why was Mama acting so contrary today?

"Enterprising is one way of putting it." Mama was using a tight-sounding voice. "I just do what needs to be done." She turned her attention back to where she was ironing a man's white shirt. "So if you will kindly excuse me."

"Sorry to bother you, ma'am." George tipped his hat, then made a quick exit.

"*Mama.*" Lucy went over by the ironing board after the door was closed. "Why are you being rude to our guests today?"

Mama used the back of her hand to push a wisp of hair off her damp forehead. "Was I being rude?"

"It seemed like it to me." Lucy peered curiously at her.

Mama sighed. "I suppose it's because I don't completely approve of our guests, Lucy. I don't like the idea of a man letting his wife run off to Hollywood to become a movie actress. It just doesn't sit well with me, and I think—"

"But Veronica's *not* his wife," Lucy clarified.

Mama looked at her with startled eyes. *"What?"*

"George just told me that they met on the road. They're not married at all." Lucy thought that this should fix everything in Mama's mind.

"They're *not* married?" Mama set her iron down with a thud.

"No, Mama."

"Well!" And just like that, without even moving the iron from the shirt it was still resting on, Mama stormed out of the barn without even bothering to close the door.

Feeling alarmed and somewhat responsible for whatever was about to happen, Lucy set the heavy iron upright, then trailed after her angry mother. "What's wrong, Mama?" she called, but Mama was walking fast, and in a moment they were in the kitchen where Mama was talking quickly to Grandma, using words like *morals* and *scruples* and *conscience* and *ethics* and saying how nobody seemed to have them anymore and what was the world coming to anyway.

Mama threw her hands up in the air. "They are not even married," she proclaimed as if it were a crime.

"Oh my!" Grandma looked alarmed now. "What are you going to do about it, Miriam?"

Mama was pacing back and forth in the kitchen now, wringing her hands and shaking her head. "I don't know. I just don't know."

"You could throw them out," Grandma said.

Lucy bit her lip. *"Throw them out?"* she repeated. "Why would we throw them out?"

Mama's frown lines deepened. "They are a bad influence on you, Lucy. As your mama, I can't let them stay here like this."

"Why?" Lucy asked. "Is it because Veronica wants to be a movie actress?"

Mama knelt down now, looking Lucy directly in the eyes. "No, that's not the reason. Oh, I don't really approve of that exactly, and certainly not under these circumstances. But it's not a reason to throw them out."

"Then *why*, Mama?" Lucy felt close to tears now. "I prayed for boarders, just like you said, and God sent them to us. Why would you throw them out?"

Still down at Lucy's level, Mama pressed her lips together and looked up at Grandma, as if she thought she might have the answer.

"It's complicated, Lucy," Grandma said slowly. "Your mama and I don't approve of a couple sharing a room together if they're not married, and it's just—"

"But George and Veronica aren't sharing a room together," Lucy exclaimed. "Veronica is staying in the front room and George took the one in back."

"Oh." Mama stood back up, folding her arms across her front.

"So . . . can they stay?" Lucy asked hopefully.

Mama and Grandma looked at each other, but they still looked uneasy. "I don't know for sure, Lucy."

"But we need the money, Mama. You said we do."

"Why don't you go speak to them?" Grandma suggested to Mama. "Get to the bottom of it."

Mama firmly nodded. "I'll do that."

Lucy started to go with her, but Grandma put a hand on her shoulder. "You stay here with me," she said quietly. "This is grown-up business."

Lucy stayed in the kitchen, helping Grandma to make piecrust while Mama was gone. But as Lucy was rolling out the dough, she noticed George outside. It looked like he was coming back from his walk. "I guess Mama hasn't talked to George yet," she told Grandma, pointing out the kitchen window.

"That might be easier." Grandma shook her head. "She and Veronica can talk woman to woman."

Lucy wished she could overhear the conversation. More than that she hoped Mama wasn't saying anything rude to Veronica. Even if Mama didn't approve of movie actresses, it seemed wrong to be mean to her. What if Veronica took offense and decided to leave? Besides them needing the money, Lucy didn't want Veronica to go.

"Well, that's all settled," Mama said as she rejoined them in the kitchen.

"What did you decide?" Grandma asked.

Lucy stayed quietly put, hoping she might go unnoticed as she slowly moved the rolling pin across the dough on the kitchen table. Like Grandma sometimes said, Lucy just wanted to be like a fly on the wall as the grown-ups talked.

"Lucy was right," Mama told Grandma. "George and Veronica are not married. And they are not sharing a room. Veronica claims that they met while traveling. It seems Veronica needed a ride and George offered her one. Apparently there was no romance involved." Mama made an exasperated-sounding sigh. "At least not yet, anyway. But when I voiced my concerns, Veronica assured me there would be no"—Mama cleared her throat—"no degeneracy going on. And I made it perfectly clear that I will tolerate none."

Lucy wasn't sure what degeneracy meant and had no intention of asking, but based on the tone of Mama's voice, she suspected it was not a good thing. Mostly she was relieved that Veronica Grant was being allowed to stay on with them.

"Are you going to speak to George?" Grandma asked quietly.

"I don't think that will be necessary." Mama was halfway out the back door now. "I have the woman's word."

"Well." Grandma slapped the flour off her hands. "I guess that takes care of that."

After the pies were in the oven, Lucy slipped upstairs. She knew she was supposed to go up there only to replace linens or tend to the needs of guests, but she told herself that it was possible the towels needed freshening by now. Mostly she was hoping that she'd get a chance to say something to Veronica. Just in case she was feeling bad about what Mama had said.

"Hello, doll," Veronica called out as Lucy walked quietly down the hallway. "What are you up to?"

Lucy smiled at her. "Just checking to see if you need anything. Towels or soaps or anything? Or if you'd like a cup of tea?" They didn't usually bring tea to their boarders, but Veronica seemed special.

"Tea?" Veronica's blue eyes sparkled. "Yes, that would be lovely, thank you. I take just a spoonful of sugar, please."

Excited at the prospect of delivering a cup of tea to Veronica, Lucy scampered downstairs and explained her plan to Grandma.

"Tea?" Grandma scowled. "She expects you to serve her tea in her room?"

Lucy shrugged. "It was kind of my idea."

Grandma's scowl was replaced with amusement. "Oh, it was, was it?"

Lucy grinned and nodded.

"Well, just this once. No need to tell your mama about it." She nodded to the stove. "The kettle is hot, and you know where the tea is."

"I'll use an everyday cup and saucer," Lucy promised.

"That would be wise."

Before long, Lucy was carefully going up the stairs with the steaming cup of tea in both hands, trying to keep the amber liquid from slopping over the sides. "Here you go," she said as she carried it into Veronica's room.

"You are an angel." Veronica took the cup and saucer from her with a grateful smile. "I was just feeling plumb worn out from all the traveling and everything I've been through these past few days. I'd say you're just what the doctor ordered, doll."

Lucy smiled happily. "Was it exciting traveling?"

"Oh, it was exciting at first." Veronica sat down on one of the chairs flanking the window and tipped her golden head toward the other. "Do you want to sit with me?"

Lucy nodded eagerly and sat down. She didn't want to be rude, but Veronica's silky, lilac-colored dressing gown and matching bedroom slippers were so elegant and glamorous looking, it was hard not to stare. Outside of the movies, Lucy had never seen anything like them before. She wondered what Helen Krausner would say.

"You see, I started out my trip with a friend." Veronica reached for a strand of shining hair and twisted it around her finger so that it curled just like a perfect C beside her dainty pink ear. "At least I *thought* he was a friend. Marshall told me that he was going to manage my acting career, and that he had connections in Hollywood, and that he was going to make me into a star." She looked upward and sighed. "But he turned out to be a dirty rotten scoundrel—a liar and a thief."

Lucy's eyes grew wide. "A liar and a thief?"

Veronica nodded as she sipped her tea. "Yes. He stole money from me. We got into a big fight over it, and I told him I no longer wanted to travel with him." Her thin eyebrows arched high. "So he pulled over—right in the middle of nowhere—and he threw me and my luggage out! Right along the side of the road! Can you believe that?"

Lucy shook her head. "What did you do?"

"I was in shock at first. I mean, what was I supposed to do? Out there in the middle of nowhere with not a car in sight. But then I remembered a scene from that movie—you know, the one I told you about earlier. I was just about to do what Claudette Colbert did, when along came this pretty yellow car. The nice driver stopped and asked if I needed help. And that is how I met up with George." She giggled. "In fact, I think George looks an awful lot like Clark Gable. Don't you think so too?"

Lucy shrugged. "I don't know who Clark Gable is."

Veronica laughed. "Well, you will, doll. Believe you me, that man will be around for quite some time. And I'd wager that someday you'll see Clark Gable and me right up there on the silver screen together."

"I can't wait!"

"Anyway, back to my story. After he rescued me out on the open highway, George and I traveled for nearly two days straight just to make it this far, and then his silly old car had to go and break down on us this morning." She frowned. "I still don't know what I'm going to do about that."

"About what?"

"About getting myself to Hollywood, of course."

"Maybe you can just stay here for a while," Lucy suggested hopefully. "You said you were tired and needed your beauty rest. Why not get some beauty rest right here?"

"For a little girl, you're a smart one, aren't you?"

Lucy smiled.

"Now that your mother understands that"—she giggled in a nervous way—"that there is no sort of impropriety going on here, well, maybe I'll do just like you said. I'll get myself all rested up and refreshed real nice. Then I'll be at my very best when I head off to Hollywood. Perhaps we'll get lucky and George's pretty car will get its motor fixed sooner than they expected."

"Hempley's Garage is a very good place to get cars fixed." Lucy declared this as if she were an expert in such things, but mostly she just wanted to be sure Veronica stayed with them for a while. It was almost like having a motion picture right in their own house, and Lucy wanted to hear more of Veronica's interesting stories.

"Well, it's not like we had a choice in garages." She chuckled. "Don't take this wrong, but Maple Grove is a real hole in the wall."

"But it is nice and quiet here," Lucy pointed out. "A good place to rest up."

"Yes. And I can't really complain about the company either." She made a dreamy looking smile. "Besides . . . you never know . . . there's that old saying about the best-laid schemes of mice and men . . ."

"What's that mean?" Lucy asked.

"Just that . . . well, sometimes things have other ways of working themselves out, if you get my drift."

"Oh." Lucy nodded as if she understood.

Veronica yawned and stood. "Thanks for the tea, doll. It was *delish*."

Lucy jumped up to take the dishes from her.

"Now I think I'll catch a few more winks of beauty rest."

With the empty cup and saucer in hand, Lucy tiptoed from the room, closing the door quietly behind her. *Delish?* Was that short for delicious? Lucy would have to remember to use that word sometime. And maybe she'd try to make her bangs curl around her fingers the way Veronica did. There was so much she could learn from someone like Veronica. As she quietly walked down the stairs, she wondered what Veronica thought about sweet gray ponies and if she'd like to take a walk down the road with Lucy in order to see one.

4

To Lucy's dismay, Veronica did not emerge from her room until dinnertime. George had helped Lucy to pass the time with a couple games of checkers. He claimed not to be any good at checkers, and after the first game, she nearly believed him. But after the second game, she wasn't so sure. She would've challenged him to a third one, but it was time to help Grandma in the kitchen.

When they sat down to dinner, Mama was acting very prim and proper, and Lucy knew this was Mama's way of showing she was not entirely pleased with her boarders. If Mama was enjoying the boarders, she usually made cheerful small talk with them, going out of her way to make everyone feel comfortable. Tonight she was about as warm as the duck pond in January.

Fortunately, Grandma was in a talkative mood and asked George and Veronica a number of questions about themselves. But it was Veronica who kept the conversation rolling along.

She didn't mind talking about herself one bit. So far, Lucy had learned that Veronica's parents had owned a music store when Veronica was a girl. "But they had to give up the store in '31," she said sadly. "Just when I was getting good at the piano too. After the store was gone, I didn't have a piano anymore. But I can play well enough to act like I'm a pianist in a movie." With her eyes partially closed, she held her hands up over her plate and wiggled her fingers as if playing on a keyboard.

"That looks very real," Lucy told her.

"What do your parents think about your aspirations of becoming a motion picture actress?" Grandma asked as she served dessert.

"Well, my daddy threw a horrible fit. But my mother kind of likes the idea. She's a real good singer, and she used to do some acting too, back in her day. She told me if I make it big, she'll come out to California and live with me." Veronica giggled. "I don't think Daddy would much like that, though."

After dessert was finished, Lucy helped Mama to clean up the dinner things while Grandma sat in the front room with George and Veronica. Lucy wished she could join them, especially when she heard sweet ripples of Veronica's laughter floating toward the kitchen. It seemed like Mama was doing all she could to keep Lucy contained in the kitchen. Finally, after the last dish was dried and put away, Lucy was about to slip out to the front room, but Mama insisted they needed more firewood first.

Lucy considered protesting since the firewood box was nearly half full, but she realized it would probably save time (and trouble) to just hurry and fetch it. She pulled on her coat, then turned on the back porch light, hurried across the yard toward the woodpile with her wagon in tow, and started to load it up.

"Need a hand?" George asked as he joined her.

She looked up in surprise. "I, uh, I don't think Mama likes our guests to help with chores."

But he was already putting pieces onto the wagon. "I like making myself useful." For every piece she put in, George stacked several. Then he grasped the handle of the wagon. "Let me take that."

"Were you smoking out here?" she asked as they walked back.

"Just my pipe," he confessed. "Is that not allowed?"

"No, it's allowed," she said quickly. "I was just curious. My daddy used to smoke a pipe too."

"I don't smoke it a lot," he told her as they reached the back porch. "But sometimes it's a comfort." Already he was unloading the wood, stacking it onto his cradled arm. She wanted to tell him that he didn't need to do this, but it seemed too late. Instead, she opened the back door and, carrying the few pieces that were left, followed him into the bright, warm kitchen.

"What?" Mama looked at Lucy with wide eyes.

"I insisted on helping your daughter," George told her as he unloaded the wood into the firebox. "I hope you don't mind."

"Well, I . . . it's just that you're our guest." Mama hung her apron on the peg by the stove and stepped back. "We don't expect you to help."

He nodded, standing up straight. "I know you don't, ma'am. It's just that it looks like I'll be here a few days, and I find it hard to just sit around and do nothing. If I can do something to keep myself busy, well, it just passes the time a little easier. That is, unless you have objections."

Mama shrugged as she folded her arms across her front with a slightly aggravated expression. "No objections, Mr. Prescott. If it helps you to pass the time, feel free."

"Like I told you earlier, please, just call me George."

Mama simply nodded, but those two creases had reappeared in her forehead again. Lucy knew what that meant.

"Maybe you'd like to play some more checkers?" Lucy suggested to George as she pushed open the door that led to the dining room. Mostly she hoped to get George out of harm's way since it looked like Mama was about to give him a piece of her mind.

"That sounds like a good plan," he told her.

Before long, Lucy and George were happily playing checkers. Veronica moved to a chair next to George, looking on and making comments in a way that made Lucy think she was trying to get George's attention. After a bit, Grandma excused herself to bed. But Mama never stepped a toe into the front room, not until it was time to announce that Lucy needed to get ready for bed too.

"We have church tomorrow," Mama announced. "As always, the guests here are invited to attend with us. Our neighbors, the Brewsters, are always happy to give us a ride."

"Church?" Veronica's brows arched high. "Well, I haven't been to church in ages."

"We have to leave by ten to make it on time," Mama told her. "Breakfast is at eight on Sundays."

"Eight?" Veronica sounded surprised.

"It's at seven on the other days," Mama told her.

Veronica laughed. "Well, don't worry about me. I rarely eat breakfast on any days."

"I wouldn't mind going to church," George said quietly. "If it's not a problem."

"It's not a problem at all," Mama said in a terse tone, "as long as you're ready to go when the Brewsters get here."

Veronica looked as if she was having second thoughts. "Perhaps I'll come too," she said. "You say we need to be ready by ten?"

"That's right," Mama told her as she took Lucy by the hand. "Good night, everyone."

It wasn't until Mama and Lucy were in Lucy's room with the door shut that Lucy decided to take a chance and speak her mind. "Mama," she began carefully as she unbuttoned her dress, "it seems that you're not being very *hospitable* to our guests." Although she didn't use the word a lot, Lucy knew what hospitable meant.

Mama blinked as she handed Lucy her nightgown.

"You and Grandma always tell me that I'm to treat our boarders with respect," she continued, "because they are our guests and we want them to feel special here."

Mama pressed her lips together but said nothing as she helped Lucy pull the flannel nightgown over her head. Lucy shivered as the cool fabric brushed against her back. She knew that eight years old was more than old enough to get ready for bed by herself, but this was always the one part of the day when she and Mama spent time together, so she never complained about Mama's help. As usual, she sat down on the hard-backed chair, waiting as Mama reached for the hairbrush and began to undo Lucy's braids, slowly brushing the hair out and then re-braiding it into one braid down Lucy's back.

"I suppose you're right, Lucy. I have been acting inhospitable."

"Why, Mama?"

"Well, as I already told you, I'm not that comfortable with our boarders."

"I think they're nice."

Mama didn't say anything as she set the brush down.

"And isn't it nice they want to go to church with us in the morning?"

"I suppose so." Her voice sounded tired.

Lucy turned around and hugged Mama tightly. "I'm ready to say my prayers," she whispered.

Mama nodded, waiting as Lucy knelt down on the rag rug next to her bed. Tonight Lucy didn't ask God to give her a pony. Instead, she thanked him for bringing their boarders to them, and then she asked God to bless everyone in their house. It wasn't until Mama had kissed her good-night and turned off the light that Lucy silently continued her prayer—and now she did ask God for a pony . . . and to bring back Mama's smile.

It was just a little before ten o'clock and as the Brewsters' big old Ford pulled up that Veronica made her appearance downstairs. Lucy was relieved that she was dressed—beautifully dressed in a scarlet red dress—and ready to go to church. George helped her into her fur-trimmed coat, and they all went outside to pile into the car. Usually Mama, Grandma, and Lucy sat in the backseat, but today Grandma sat in front with the Brewsters and Lucy offered to sit in the rumble seat. It was chilly back there, but it was well worth it for the joy of having Veronica Grant (soon-to-be movie star) in their company. Hopefully Helen Krausner would be in church today to see this.

Lucy looked over to Mr. Greenburg's field as the car rumbled past, making sure that Smoky and the "For Sale or Trade" sign were still there. To her relief, they both were. Hopefully she'd get a chance to pay him a visit tomorrow. Maybe she could talk Veronica into walking down there with her to see him too. The Greenburg farm was only two farms down, really just a nice walk if the weather was favorable.

As it turned out, the Krausners weren't at church, but Veronica Grant got plenty of curious looks from the congregation anyway. Lucy proudly took Veronica by the hand, leading her to the pew where they always sat, and then she squeezed down close to the end to be sure there was plenty of room for everyone in their row.

Lucy always enjoyed the singing part of church the best, and she was happy to share her hymnal with Veronica. She wasn't even too surprised to hear that Veronica had a pleasant soprano voice. No doubt that would be useful in the movie-making business too. Lucy tried to pay attention to the sermon, but instead she was distracted by staring at the beadwork on Veronica's gloves and found herself daydreaming about glamorous things like fancy dresses and sparkling jewelry. When it came time for the final prayer, Lucy was thankful that Pastor McHenry wasn't able to read her mind. She told God that she was sorry and she would try to pay better attention next Sunday.

After the final hymn, Pastor McHenry reminded the congregation of the upcoming events pertaining to Christmas, a little less than two weeks away. "For the children in the Christmas pageant, there will be rehearsals on Thursday and Saturday afternoons at two o'clock. Mrs. Babcock wants to remind everyone not to be late."

As they walked out to the car after greeting and visiting with friends, Veronica inquired as to whether anyone cared to stay in town to attend a matinee.

"On Sunday?" Mrs. Brewster sounded alarmed.

"No, dear," Grandma told her. "None of us will be seeing a motion picture today. Of course, you and George might have other ideas."

"Not me," George said as he opened a car door for the ladies.

"I'd be happy to go," Lucy said, knowing full well that this could get her into hot water with Mama. But the idea of seeing a movie with Veronica was too tempting.

"Not on a Sunday," Mama said sternly.

Veronica leaned over and patted Lucy's cheek. "Then we'll simply have to go another day. Maybe next Saturday."

Lucy smiled up at her. "I'd love that."

The perfectly delightful idea of going with Veronica to the movie theater, where Helen Krausner might see them together, was almost enough to keep Lucy warm all the way home. Although her nose did feel like an ice cube by the time the car rumbled up to their house.

"Let's get you inside," Mama said as she took Lucy by the hand, leading her directly to the kitchen where the fire was still burning in the stove.

"It almost feels like it could snow out there," Grandma said as she closed the door and began peeling off her heavy winter coat.

"*Snow?*" Lucy began to dance around the kitchen. "Snow for Christmas—do you really think so, Grandma? Oh, I can't wait!"

"Don't count your snowflakes before they fall," Mama warned her.

"Which reminds me . . ." Grandma looked at Lucy. "Did you tend to the chickens this morning?"

Lucy nodded. "I did. But there were no eggs today."

Mama blinked as she hung her coat by the door. "No eggs?"

"It's nearly winter solstice." Grandma moved the cast iron pot to the hottest part of the stove. "The shortest day of the year."

"That's right!" Lucy remembered from last winter—shortly after they'd purchased the laying hens from a neighboring farm. "The chickens need more sunlight to want to lay eggs. That's why there were no eggs this morning."

"You probably won't find eggs again for a while." Grandma shook her head. "Fortunately we still have a couple dozen in the cooler. I'll have to tell Mrs. Brewster that we can't sell any to her after all. I should've remembered that this always happens at Christmastime."

"Just one more reason I'll be glad when Christmas is over and done with this year." Mama reached for her apron.

"*Mama.*" Lucy let the disappointment show in her voice. "How can you say that?"

Mama looked somewhat contrite. "I'm sorry, Lucy. I know you love Christmas. It's just that . . . well, when you're a grown-up . . . things change."

"Then I *never* want to grow up," Lucy declared.

Grandma patted her head. "Then how about if you go set the table?"

As Lucy set the table, she decided that even if she had to grow up, she would never be like Mama. Not about Christmas, anyway. No, Lucy told herself as she set the plates down, she would rather be like Veronica Grant. Surely Veronica still liked Christmas. And Veronica liked going to movies—even on Sundays—and Veronica liked wearing pretty clothes and laughing and all sorts of exciting things. Veronica probably even liked sweet gray ponies!

5

After Sunday dinner, Lucy announced that she wanted to take a walk later, after she finished helping to clean up the dishes. Her intention was to stroll down to the Greenburg farm and check on Smoky. Maybe she'd even chat with Mr. Greenburg if he was around. "Would anyone like to join me?" She looked longingly at Veronica.

"Not me." Veronica stifled a yawn. "All that good food and getting up early has made me very sleepy. I think I'm going to take a little nap."

"I'd love to go stretch my legs," George said. "That is, unless I can do something to help out around here." He looked at Mama and then Grandma. "Need any firewood chopped?"

"No. No, thank you," Mama said quickly. "You go ahead and take a walk with Lucy if you like."

"Just make sure you bundle up," Grandma told them. "It's getting mighty cold out there."

"Grandma said it might snow," Lucy told George as she started to help clear the table.

George peered out the front window, then shook his head with a frown. "Well, I sure hope it holds off some. At least until my car gets fixed."

Lucy carried the dishes to the kitchen, but then Grandma shooed her out. "Go ahead and take your walk, Lucy. I'll get the dishes washed, and you can dry them when you get back."

Lucy found George and they layered on coats, scarves, and hats, then headed on down the road toward town. As they were walking, Lucy confessed her real reason for wanting to take a walk. "He's the most beautiful pony in the whole wide world," she told George. "Smoky's got the prettiest coat you've ever seen—dapple gray. And it's already soft and fuzzy. Nice and warm for winter. His eyes are big and brown. And he's very smart too. He'll come over to the fence when I call him. You'll see."

"He sounds like a great little pony. I'm surprised the owners want to sell him."

"I'm surprised too," Lucy admitted. "But I know times are hard. We had to sell almost all of our livestock."

"You had livestock?"

She nodded as she stuck a mittened hand into a coat pocket, checking to see that the big end of a carrot was still safely there. "Before my daddy died, we had cows and horses and pigs. Now we just have the chickens and one milk cow."

"Was it too hard to take care of all those animals?"

"I guess so. Mama said that someday we might get them back, though. That is, if we get the rest of our farm back."

"The *rest* of your farm?"

Lucy explained about how some of their land was being farmed by the Farleys now. "The Farleys have six boys to help out with farm chores," she told him. "For a while Mr. Farley paid us every year at harvest time for using our land. But he can't do that anymore. Mama says we're just lucky he's working it at all. Otherwise it would just go back to weeds." She pointed at the Saunderses' neglected farm. "Like that farm." She told George about Clara and her family moving away and how much she missed them. "Clara was my very best friend."

"Are there any other girls living nearby?" he asked.

"No." She sadly shook her head, explaining that the Brewsters never had children and that the Greenburg children were all grown up.

"Maybe that's why Mr. Greenburg wants to sell his pony," George suggested.

She nodded. "Maybe so." She pointed at the sign still on the fence post. "That's for Smoky," she said happily. "That must mean no one bought him yet." She ran up to the fence, climbed onto the bottom rail, and called out. Just like that, Smoky left where he'd been standing in the trees, trotting over to see her.

"Don't tell anyone," she said as she extracted a slightly fuzzy-looking carrot stub from her pocket. "But I sneaked this from the kitchen."

George chuckled. "Your secret's safe with me."

"Hello, Smoky," she said happily. "How are you doing today?"

He shook his mane as if to greet her, and she peeled off her mitten and held out the carrot stub in the palm of her hand. "It's not much," she told him. "But I hope you like it." She giggled as the warm, fuzzy muzzle tickled the palm of her hand and just like magic the carrot disappeared. She patted the broad side of his cheek. "Isn't he just the most beautiful pony you've ever seen?"

George reached out and stroked Smoky's mane. "He's a very nice-looking pony, for sure. And he seems healthy too."

Lucy looked all around the field behind Smoky, hoping to spot Mr. Greenburg. But all was quiet and still today. Maybe the Greenburgs were in town. She looked up at the sky now, noticing that it was almost exactly the same color as Smoky, and then to her delighted surprise she spotted a snowflake fluttering down right in front of her. "Look at that!" she cried, pointing upward. "It's starting to snow!"

George looked up and chuckled. "You're right about that."

"Maybe we will have a white Christmas," she told him.

"Maybe so." He slowly nodded.

She remembered his concerns about getting to California in the snow. "Or maybe it's just fooling us," she said quickly. "Sometimes our weather is tricky like that. It looks like snow is coming, but then it waits a few days."

"Well, just in case, I suppose we should turn back and get home. I wouldn't want to get caught out here in a blizzard."

She climbed down from the fence. "Good-bye, Smoky," she said sadly. "I'll come back and see you again as soon as I can. Please don't let anyone buy you."

Smoky tipped his head up and down as if agreeing to this. Lucy reluctantly turned away, and she and George headed back toward home. They walked quietly for a ways before Lucy spoke up. "Please don't tell Mama that I took you to see Smoky," she said suddenly.

"Why not?"

Lucy considered this. "Well, Mama doesn't want me to keep wishing for a pony. She thinks it's impossible. And Grandma says ponies are only for rich people. But I've been praying for a pony, and Pastor McHenry says God can do impossible things." She peered up at George. "Do you think God will answer my prayer?"

George's mouth was in a firm line now. "Yes . . ." he said slowly. "I definitely think God will answer your prayer, Lucy. But sometimes God's answer isn't the answer we want. Sometimes God's answer is no . . . or wait."

Lucy kicked a stone on the road and sighed. "I know. Grandma says that exact same thing sometimes. But maybe God will say yes."

"Maybe so." George pointed up at the sky. "It looks like this snow is really coming now. Maybe we should walk faster."

By the time they got home, everything, including Lucy and George, was spotted in white snowflakes. Pausing on the front porch to brush the snow off, Lucy suddenly remembered Smoky. "Do you think he'll be okay?" she said quietly to George.

"Who?"

"Smoky." She imagined the pony coated with snow, shivering in the wind.

George got a thoughtful look, then nodded. "Yes. Smoky has a thick wooly coat. I'm sure he'll be just fine."

Lucy hoped that George was right. She'd never worried about

farm animals being out in the cold like that before, but she knew that she wouldn't want to have to live outside when it was snowing and blowing like it was starting to do now. And even though Mama used most of the barn for her laundry business, there were still some nice warm stalls in the back. Surely it would be all right for a pony to use one of them . . . just to come in from the cold. Lucy would keep it nice and clean.

Lucy was pleased to wake up to a white, wintry world on Monday morning. It was only a few inches so far, but it was beautiful. Like a gigantic frosted cake.

"Sit still," Mama said as Lucy kicked the heels of her boots against the kitchen stool. "Let me get this last braid finished."

"I just can't wait to go outside," Lucy said happily. "I'm going to make a snow angel first thing. Then a snowman if the snow is sticky enough."

"Just make sure you see to the chickens first. And bring in some more wood."

"Yes, Mama." Lucy pulled on her coat, searching her pockets for mittens. Before long she was bundled up and on her way outside with a bucket of chicken food. The air was crisp and cold, and the sound of snow crunching beneath her boots filled her with high hopes. She always felt excited over the first snow, and to have it before Christmas was a real treat.

"Good morning, Lucy."

She jumped to see George coming around the corner of the barn. "What are you doing out here?" she asked.

"Just taking a walk." He jerked his thumb behind him. "I broke the ice in the chickens' water trough. I hope that's all right."

"Sure." She grinned. "Thanks. I'm just on my way to feed them now."

He turned around and walked back with her. "I noticed an old Model T back behind the barn."

"That was my daddy's car." Lucy opened the gate to the chicken yard and went inside. George hadn't just broken the ice; he'd refilled the water and even cleaned the snow out of the food trough so it was all ready for her to dump the kitchen scraps. The hungry hens gathered around her feet as she spread the food out for them. "You girls need to start laying eggs again," she told them.

"Why aren't they laying eggs?" George held the gate open for her, then securely latched it closed after she came out.

Lucy explained about the winter solstice, and he rubbed his chin with a thoughtful expression. "So they need sunlight to lay eggs?"

"That's what Grandma says. It always happens right around Christmastime."

"What if we rigged up a light bulb inside their coop?"

"A light bulb?" She giggled as she tried to imagine a light bulb in the henhouse.

"You could turn it on just before the sun sets. Leave it on for an hour or so. Maybe the chickens would think it was still daytime and reward you with some eggs."

"Do you really think that would work?"

"It might be worth a try." He pointed to the barn. "I noticed there's electricity running from the house to the barn."

"Mama had the electric put in so she could do her laundry out there."

"Well, it wouldn't be hard to run a cord from the barn to the chicken coop and get a light set up. I could give it a try if you think it's a good idea."

She nodded eagerly. "It's a swell idea."

"Would your mother mind if I poked around to find what I need for the light?"

"I think Mama would be real happy if we started getting eggs again."

"About that car," he said as they walked back to the house. "Does it run at all?"

"No, it's been broken down for a long, long time. Mr. Brewster offered to buy it once, but Mama said no. Now she'd gladly sell it, but he can't afford to buy it anymore. And no one else wants a car that doesn't run." She stopped walking and set the chicken bucket down. "I'm glad because sometimes I like to sit in it and I pretend like I'm driving." She flopped down on her back, and George's eyes nearly popped out.

"What's wrong?" He bent over and stared. "Are you okay?"

"I'm making a snow angel," she explained as she flapped her arms and legs.

With a quizzical expression, he pulled out his pipe and watched her.

"See?" She stood, proudly pointing to the angelic image in the snow.

"Very nice." He lit his pipe and smiled.

She went over to where the snow angel head was and drew in a halo. "There. Perfect."

"Do you think your mother would mind if I took a look at the old car?" He let out a puff of sweet-smelling smoke. "My dad used to have a car almost exactly like it, and if I'm lucky, I might be able to get it running again."

"*Really?*" She brushed the snow off her coat sleeves.

"It's a possibility."

"I sure wish it could run again." She sighed. "I remember how I used to ride to town in it with my daddy . . . back when I was a little girl."

His pipe slowly moved up and down like he was thinking hard.

"Maybe we shouldn't tell Mama about it, though." She glanced over to the house. "Just so we don't get her hopes up. You know, in case you can't fix it."

He removed his pipe, placing a forefinger over his lips. "I won't tell if you won't tell."

She nodded. "It's a deal."

As they were finishing lunch, George announced that he planned to walk to town to check on the progress of his car's repairs. "Let me know if there's anything I can bring home for anyone."

"No, thank you," Mama primly told him. "Lucy did the shopping for us on Saturday."

"But you might let George drop off your laundry parcels," Grandma suggested to Mama. "That would save you a—"

"Oh, that's all right," Mama said. "I don't mind the walk."

"I'd be pleased to deliver your parcels for you," George told her.

"But I wouldn't want to bother you with—"

"It's no bother," he assured her. "Just write down the addresses for me, and I'll gladly drop them off. I plan to leave around two."

Mama started to protest again, but this time Veronica interrupted. "Why don't you just use the telephone, George?" she suggested. "Simply call the garage and check on your automobile. Save yourself a senseless walk."

He shook his head. "I'd prefer to walk. I need the exercise."

"Do you want any company?" Lucy offered hopefully.

"I need you to stay home and help Grandma and me," Mama told her.

Lucy frowned but didn't say anything.

"Maybe next time," George said gently.

"Yes, maybe next time." Mama's voice was firm.

"You didn't invite little old me to go to town with you, George," Veronica said in a sugary voice.

George looked taken aback by this. "Well, I—I suppose I assumed you wouldn't want to walk out in the snow."

"You know me too well." She made a pouting face. "You're right about walking in the snow. I don't have the right sort of shoes."

"Mama could loan you her work boots," Lucy suggested.

Mama looked as if she was about to choke, but Veronica just laughed. "Really, now, Lucy, can you imagine me in your mama's work boots?"

"Of course not." Mama began clearing the table. "What a ridiculous idea."

"Well, I'm sure they're just fine for you," Veronica said apologetically. "You need sturdy boots to work on a farm."

Mama excused herself. As she went through the swinging door, Lucy felt pretty sure she wouldn't come back out again.

"I do wish there was some other way to get to town," Veronica said to George. "Do you suppose there's a taxi that could come and fetch us?"

Grandma chuckled. "Not in Maple Grove." She picked up the bread basket and butter dish and excused herself to the kitchen too.

"If I had a pony," Lucy told Veronica, "I'd let you ride it to town."

"Me on a pony?" Veronica giggled. "Now *that* would be a sight to see. I've never been on a horse in my entire life."

"What if you needed to ride a horse to be in a movie?" Lucy asked.

"Well, then I wouldn't be in that particular movie." Veronica nudged George with her elbow. "I'll bet you don't know how to ride a horse either, do you?"

"Now there's a bet you would surely lose," he told her.

"Well." She looked impressed. "You are just full of surprises, aren't you, Georgie Porgie?"

Lucy pressed her lips together as she remembered his ideas for fixing the old car. That would probably surprise Veronica too. Instead of saying anything about this, Lucy began to help clear her side of the table.

"She just gets to me," Mama was quietly saying to Grandma as Lucy came in. But seeing Lucy, Mama stopped talking.

"Did I say something wrong, Mama?" Lucy set the dishes by the sink and peered up into Mama's face.

"Oh, it was silly of you to think Veronica would wear my old boots . . . that's all."

"And to think she'd walk to town," Grandma added with a half smile. "Well, that's not very realistic."

Lucy shrugged. "She might walk to town . . . if it wasn't so cold and snowy out." The dining room was empty when she went back to get the last of the dishes. She was just about to return to the kitchen when she overheard Veronica talking to George in the front room.

"Oh, come on, George," Veronica was saying sweetly. "Just use the telephone to call and find out about your silly old car. That way you can stay here and keep me company. We can play games or listen to the radio or just visit."

"I'm sorry. I already planned to go to town."

"But it's so quiet and lonely when you're not in the house," she protested.

"Like I said, you're welcome to join me."

"You know I don't want to do that. Oh, Georgie Porgie, you're just a big meanie," she teased, "but I'll come up with a way to get back at you. You know I will."

"I'm sure you will."

"Will you bring me back something?" she pleaded in childlike voice. "A candy or some kind of special treat?"

"Sure. Tell me what you want and I'll bring it back."

Feeling guilty for eavesdropping and just a little bit jealous that George was going to bring Veronica a treat, Lucy made her way back into the kitchen. Mama had gone out to get the laundry parcels, and Grandma had already started on the dishes.

"Do you think Veronica and George are falling in love?" she asked Grandma as she set the cups and saucers on the counter.

"Falling in love?" Grandma peered curiously at Lucy. "What put that kind of an idea in your head?"

"Helen Krausner is always talking about falling in love," Lucy confessed. "But I don't think I've ever seen it happen. Not for real."

"I suppose they could be falling in love." Grandma squeezed soapy water out of the dishrag. "Although I think George is too sensible for that flibbertigibbet."

"Flibbertigibbet?" Lucy was surprised.

Grandma chuckled. "I suppose that's not very nice to say about our guest, Lucy. I hope I don't hear you repeating it."

"I'd never say that about Veronica," Lucy assured her. "I like Veronica." But even as she said this, Lucy wasn't so sure. She didn't think she liked Veronica quite as much as when she'd first met her. She wasn't even sure why.

6

After helping in the kitchen, Lucy went to her room to work on this year's Christmas presents. She'd started crocheting the potholders for Grandma in October. Made from various colors of yarn that she'd found in a box in the attic, their colorful stripes reminded her of rainbows. At first she thought she only had enough yarn for two potholders, but to her surprise there was enough for a third.

For Mama, she'd made a picture frame out of sticks and pinecones that she'd gathered out in the woods. Inside the frame was a pencil drawing that Lucy had made of a cactus wren. The small, spotted wren was the Arizona state bird, and Lucy had meticulously drawn it from a picture she'd found in a bird book at school. She'd also embroidered a white linen handkerchief with birds for Mama. One was a beautiful red cardinal and the other a bluebird. Mama loved birds of all kinds, and Lucy couldn't wait to see her face when she opened these presents on Christmas morning.

But with George and Veronica staying with them, hopefully until Christmas, Lucy had decided to make some more Christmas presents as well. For Veronica, she was making a pincushion. Oh, she knew that Veronica probably didn't know how to sew, but she had some beautiful brooches that she liked to wear, and Lucy thought perhaps she would use the pincushion for those.

For George she had started to make a pipe holder. Of course, she had no idea if he would have any use for such a thing or even if there was such a thing as a pipe holder, but it seemed like a good idea. She'd started with an old wooden cigar box she'd found in the attic. First she took it apart, and she was now trying to transform some of the pieces into a rack of sorts. Plus she'd found a picture of a handsome black racehorse in an old magazine and carefully cut it out and glued it to the back of the holder. Now she was gluing some sticks around the horse like a little frame, and really, it was becoming a rather handsome piece.

It was just getting dusky when Lucy remembered she hadn't fed the chickens this afternoon. Pulling on her boots and coat, she grabbed the bucket by the back door and hurried outside. As far as she knew, George hadn't returned from town yet. But when she reached the chicken coop, she was surprised to see that light was coming from the coop area. Filling the food trough, she heard the sound of crunching snow coming from around the backside of the barn. Worried it might be a wild animal, she lifted up the bucket, ready to throw it if needed. But to her relief it was only George.

"You scared me," she said as she lowered the bucket.

"I'm sorry. But I thought I heard someone over here. What do you think of our light?"

"I think it's great. I hope it works."

"I figure we should only leave it on for an hour. So they can get used to it."

"Do you think it'll work?"

He tipped his head sideways. "I have no idea, but I guess we'll find out. We just need to remember to come out here to turn it off after dinner. How about if I take care of that while I'm here? I'll just say I'm going out to smoke my pipe."

"Sounds good to me." She looked toward where he'd come around from behind the barn. "What are you doing back there?"

He held up a wrench with a sheepish grin. "Working on your dad's car."

"Really?"

He nodded. "Picked up a couple things at Hempley's Garage and couldn't wait to see if they worked."

"Do they?"

"We'll see."

"You sound like Mama."

He chuckled. "I'll take that as a compliment."

"Speaking of Mama, I'd better get back inside and set the table."

"Not yet." He came over and opened the gate to the chicken yard, waiting for her to come out before he closed it. "I have something for you first." He reached in his pocket now and pulled out something wrapped in brown paper.

"What?" she said eagerly.

"Just some peppermints." He held up his forefinger. "But not until after dinner."

"Thank you!" She stuck it in her coat pocket, then hurried back into the house to help with dinner. But Mama was already helping Grandma, and once the table was set, they didn't need Lucy anymore.

"Why don't you go visit with Veronica?" Mama suggested. "She's sitting by herself in the front room."

"All that woman does is sleep and listen to the radio all day," Grandma said quietly as Lucy was leaving.

"Hello, Veronica," Lucy said pleasantly. She sniffed the air, noticing a strange smell. Kind of like the chicken scraps starting to go bad on a hot summer's day.

"There you are, doll." Veronica gave a pretty smile as she set a small bottle of red fingernail paint on the coffee table. Lucy hoped there were no drips on the bottle since Mama loved that table. "I was just wishing for something to amuse myself with."

"Want to play checkers?" Lucy offered.

Veronica wrinkled her nose. "I don't like board games. Besides, I just did my nails."

"Oh." Lucy sat down on the chair across from her.

"What I wouldn't give for a ride to town to see a movie tonight."

"That would be fun." Lucy nodded.

"I am hopelessly bored." Veronica blew across the tops of her blood red fingernails. "I cannot comprehend how on earth you country people manage to live like this. So isolated . . . and now all this horrid snow. I feel as if I'm trapped." She sighed.

"How I miss the city lights, the nightclubs, the glamour, the music." She made a groaning sound. "I feel like I shall start climbing the walls."

"Oh . . ." Lucy smiled to herself as she imagined Veronica in her elegant, pale blue dress climbing up the front room walls.

Veronica looked hopefully at Lucy now. "Listen, doll," she began quietly. "Maybe you can help me."

"Help you?"

Veronica leaned forward. "You're on pretty good terms with old Georgie Porgie, aren't you?"

Lucy wasn't sure how to answer, so she shrugged. "I guess so."

"Maybe you can do some sweet-talking for me."

"Sweet-talking?"

"It sounds like Georgie's car might be fixed by Wednesday."

Lucy felt a wave of disappointment. "Wednesday?"

Veronica nodded eagerly. "I plan to be dressed in my traveling clothes with everything neatly packed so that I'm ready to hit the road as soon as that sweet yellow roadster rolls up to the house. And I'd like Georgie to be on the same page."

"On the same page?"

Veronica laughed. "I want Georgie all packed and ready to go too. My thinking is that we could make Los Angeles by midnight." She sighed happily. "Imagine that. Hollywood . . . sunshine . . . orange trees. It will be like heaven."

"Oh . . ." Lucy looked down, picking at the beginnings of a hole in her work trousers. She must have caught it on the chicken wire.

"Here's what I want you to do for me." Veronica began to

map out a plan for Lucy to hint to George that he and Veronica should be on their way . . . the sooner the better for everyone. "Maybe you can let him know that Christmas is a time for families to be together and that your family won't be wanting any strangers around during the holidays."

"But you and George aren't strangers," Lucy protested.

Veronica laughed. "Well, that's real sweet, doll, but a few days from now George and I will be living a completely different life in a completely different place, and you'll still be here. In a way we'll be like strangers."

Lucy felt a lump in her throat.

"So will you do that for me?"

Lucy nodded sadly. "I guess so."

"Don't worry, doll, we won't really be strangers. I'll always remember you and how your family took me in."

"Really?" Lucy blinked at her.

"Sure. And when I'm famous, you'll go see me at the movie theater, won't you? You can tell all your friends that you're a friend of Veronica Grant." She tipped her head back and smiled as if someone were taking her photograph.

"I guess that means we won't get to go to the picture show on Saturday."

Veronica gave Lucy a sympathetic look. "I'm sorry, doll. But you understand . . . if I'm going to become a star, I must get to Hollywood."

Lucy told Veronica that she understood and that she would do what she could to help, but she didn't tell her that her heart would not be in it.

The next morning, Lucy was surprised to see nearly a foot of snow on the ground. At this rate, they really would have a white Christmas this year. Of course, she realized this could present its own set of problems. For one thing, Veronica wouldn't like it one bit. It might put the brakes on their trip to California. Although when Lucy had raised the subject last night, hinting about Veronica's plans, as George smoked his pipe on the porch, he had seemed unconcerned about whether they left for California on Wednesday or next week. Lucy had been relieved, but she knew Veronica would not be pleased.

Besides the snow being a problem to George and Veronica, Lucy knew it meant there would be more work to do—snow shoveling on top of all the other chores which grew more difficult in wintertime. Still, she was happy about the snow and the idea of having a white Christmas, and she hurried to get dressed and because she was anxious to check on the chickens. Maybe George's light idea had worked and the hens had laid some eggs last night. She zipped out through the kitchen and nearly collided with Mama on the back porch.

"Oh!" Mama balanced the pail of milk in her hand, managing not to spill a drop. "Careful there, Lucy."

"Sorry. I was on my way to the chickens."

"In an awful hurry too." Mama peered curiously at her. "By the way, I noticed that someone ran electricity out to the chicken coop."

Lucy bit her lip and looked down at her boots.

"Do you know anything about that, Lucy? Or did the chickens decide that it was about time they lived like the rest of us?"

Lucy looked up and grinned.

"Tell me, what's going on?"

Lucy quickly explained George's idea. "We were going to surprise you with it . . . I mean, if it turned out that it worked."

With a bewildered look, Mama just shook her head.

"Is it all right? I mean, that we did it without telling you?"

"Yes. It's fine. It actually sounds like a good idea." Mama reached for the door. "I'll be curious to see if it works or not."

"I'm on my way to check right now." Lucy picked up the chicken bucket, then hurried on her way. It wasn't until she was halfway to the barn that she realized someone had plowed a path through what otherwise would have been knee-deep snow. Mama must have gotten up really early this morning. To Lucy's delight, the path went all the way to the chicken coop. Not only that, but the chicken yard had been shoveled as well.

Feeling optimistic, Lucy checked the hen nests, but to her dismay there were no eggs yet. "Come on, girls," she told the sleepy hens. "If you like having your own light at night, you need to thank us with some eggs." Lucy filled their trough, but like yesterday their water had already been tended to. Surely that was not Mama's doing. Lucy rubbed a wooly mitten across her dripping nose and wondered what it would be like if George lived with them all the time. Winters could be hard in this part of the country. Last year had been bitter cold, and it hadn't taken long for Lucy's enthusiasm over the first snow to grow thin. She latched the gate closed and sighed. Well, with Christmas only a week away, she was not going to worry about that now. Maybe she would secretly pray that this weather would keep George and Veronica here until New Year's!

As usual, Veronica slept in during breakfast. The first day this happened, Lucy had felt disappointed. She never wanted to miss an opportunity to be around the glamorous Veronica Grant. But this morning she realized that meals felt more pleasant when Veronica wasn't there. It seemed that everyone at the table was more cheerful and the visiting sounded cozy and natural . . . and nice.

"Thank you for shoveling snow this morning," Mama told George as she passed him the bowl of applesauce.

"So that *was* you!" Lucy said. "I thought so."

"Unless it was your snow angel . . ." His eyes twinkled with mystery as he spooned some applesauce onto his hotcakes. "I think I saw her dancing about in the twilight this morning."

Lucy laughed. "Today I plan to make a snowman," she told everyone. "I'll sit him in front of the house, right next to the porch. I want him to be really tall too." She pointed at George. "Even taller than you."

"Need any help?"

"Sure." She took a big bite of her hotcake, eager to finish her breakfast and get outside.

"Chew your food," Grandma told her. "The snow isn't going anywhere."

True to his word, George helped her make what turned out to be the best snowman ever. Not only was he taller than George, but Mama brought out one of Daddy's old work hats and a knitted scarf to dress him with.

413

"Now wait," George told Lucy. "I'll run and get my camera and take a photograph of you and Mr. Snowman together."

"I want you in the picture too," Lucy exclaimed.

"But I need to take the photo—"

"Let Mama take it," Lucy said.

After George returned with his camera and explained to Mama how to use it, Lucy and George posed on either side of the giant snowman as Mama took the photograph. "When I get the film developed, I'll send you this picture," George promised.

Lucy felt sad now. "You mean when you and Veronica are in California?"

"Here." Mama handed George his camera, pausing to look at him with a funny expression, almost as if she was trying to figure out a problem. Then, just like that, she thanked him and turned away. But it was the look in George's eyes that made Lucy wonder. As he watched Mama going into the house, it almost seemed as if he had a hopeful look in his eyes.

At lunchtime, Lucy carefully watched George and Mama every time they spoke to each other, which wasn't often since Veronica was there and doing most of the talking. But unless it was Lucy's imagination, there seemed to be some kind of invisible conversation going on between Mama and George. It was the way their eyes seemed to light up, the slight lilt in Mama's words, the way George smiled.

As Lucy helped Grandma in the kitchen, she decided to mention it. "Do you think Mama and George are falling in love?" she asked quietly.

Grandma dropped the pan she was scrubbing and turned to stare at Lucy. "What?"

"Do you think—"

"I heard you perfectly fine, Lucy. I just cannot believe you would say such a thing."

"Why?"

Grandma slowly shook her head. "I think you're awfully eager to see someone falling in love. First it was Veronica and George. Now Mama?" Grandma chuckled. "Next thing I know you'll be having George and me falling in love. No, Lucy, I do not think your mama is falling in love with George." Grandma returned to scrubbing the pot.

Lucy wanted to ask Grandma what made her so sure but knew that would only invite more trouble. Besides, Grandma was a grown-up . . . she was probably right.

"Why don't you go visit with Veronica," Grandma suggested as they were finishing up.

Lucy almost admitted to Grandma that she'd rather work in the kitchen, but she knew this would only bring unwanted questions, and when it came to Veronica, Lucy felt more and more confused. As much as she had liked Veronica to start with, she didn't trust the pretty lady too much now.

7

So, doll, you haven't told me how our little scheme is going," Veronica said as Lucy sat down in the chair in the front room. "Did you manage to convince Georgie that he and I should be hitting the road tomorrow?"

Lucy felt confused. "But you were at lunch," she reminded her. "You just heard George telling us that there's too much snow in the mountains to travel right now."

Veronica scowled. "Yeah . . . but I had hoped you would work your magic on him."

"My magic?"

Veronica rolled her eyes. "I think you could wrap old Georgie Porgie right around your little finger."

"Huh?"

Veronica smiled in a way that reminded Lucy of Helen Krausner after she'd said something mean or the way a cat might look after eating a pretty bird. "Not that it's a bad thing. I happen to find that to be a rather attractive quality in a man."

"What?" Lucy was hopelessly lost.

"Oh, *never mind!*"

Lucy stood now. It seemed clear her company was not wanted here anymore, but she still needed to remember her manners. "Excuse me, please."

"Wait." Veronica's voice warmed up. "I'm sorry, doll. I suppose I'm in a bit of a snit today, but I shouldn't take it out on you. That's not fair."

Fingering the scratchy fabric of the chair behind her, Lucy waited.

"You see, I'd gotten my hopes up, you know, that George and I would be leaving tomorrow and we'd make Los Angeles by midnight. I even got my bags nearly packed. And now this. I'm severely disappointed."

"Oh . . ."

"But it's not your fault."

There was a long silence with only the sound of the mantel clock ticking, and Lucy was thinking hard. Surely there was some way out of this. Then it hit her. "What about the train in Flagstaff?" she said suddenly. "It might be slow, driving in the snow and all, but I'll bet George could get you that far, Veronica. Then you could get a train ticket and—"

"But what about George?" Veronica's eyes grew wide.

"He could come back here and stay with us until Christmas . . . or until the roads get better." Lucy was smiling now, pleased that she, all by herself, had come up with such a perfect plan. "If you want, I'll even go ask George about this for you. I know where he is and I'm sure he'll—"

"*No.*" Veronica's pale blue eyes turned as frosty as a January morning. "That's not necessary."

"But you could be in Los Angeles soon," Lucy told her. "With all the sunshine and orange trees and Hollywood and everything."

Veronica let out a sad sigh. "Can I tell you a secret, doll?"

Lucy twisted her mouth to one side. On one hand, it was always delicious getting to hear a secret. On the other hand, she felt wary of Veronica. "All right . . ."

"Remember I told you about my bad friend, the one who was taking me to Hollywood to make me a star?"

Lucy nodded. "The man who left you on the highway?"

"Yes. And I told you how he took my money." Veronica held out her hands with palms up. "I am broke."

"Broke?" Lucy thought about Veronica's fine clothes and jewelry and shoes and suitcases. She looked like a rich lady.

"Penniless."

Lucy blinked. "Oh."

"You promised to keep my secret, doll."

Lucy swallowed hard. "So you can't afford to buy a train ticket?"

"No, I can't." She sadly shook her head. "I need George to get me to Hollywood. And since I told you that secret, I might as well tell you another." She peered at Lucy. "Can I trust you?"

"I guess so."

"The truth is, I think George fancies me as much as I fancy him. I think that when we get to California, we will continue getting acquainted, and, well . . ." She giggled. "If George should come to his senses and propose to me, well, I might just forget all about becoming a famous movie actress and star as his wife instead."

"What?" Lucy could not believe her ears.

Veronica shrugged. "I don't know for sure . . . but I might enjoy being married."

Lucy didn't know what to say, and manners or no manners, she suddenly felt the need to get outside and breathe some fresh air. Maybe it was the strong smell of Veronica's flowery perfume or stale fingernail paint or just Veronica herself, but Lucy felt like she was suffocating. Without saying another word, she turned and dashed from the room, grabbed her coat and boots, and, thankful that Grandma wasn't in the kitchen, streaked outside and toward the barn.

The next thing she knew, she was in Mama's arms with tears streaming down her cheeks. "What is it?" Mama demanded as she stroked Lucy's hair. "What happened?"

"Oh, Mama!"

"What? Lucy, please, talk to me. Is it Grandma? Do I need to—"

"No, no, it's not Grandma." Lucy stepped back, wiping her nose with her sleeve right in front of Mama.

"What then?" Mama put a warm hand on Lucy's cheek. "Talk to me."

"It's Veronica," Lucy sputtered. "She—she's going to—to marry George!"

It was almost as if some kind of light went out of Mama's blue eyes. Although she wasn't frowning, her mouth looked sadder than ever, but she simply shook her head. "Oh, Lucy," she said quietly. "Is that what's troubling you?"

"But it's all wrong, Mama. All wrong."

Mama knelt down, looking intently into Lucy's eyes. "It's not your decision to make, Lucy. I know you admire George greatly. But it's not your decision. Everyone has to live their own life. Someday when you're a grown-up you'll understand that better."

"I don't want to be a grown-up," Lucy said stubbornly. "Not ever." She wanted to add that all grown-ups were stupid, but she stopped herself because Mama wasn't stupid. There was no reason to make Mama feel worse. Lucy could tell that she wasn't happy with this news either.

Mama stood, pushing the loose strands of hair away from her flushed face. "Well, someday you will be a grown-up, Lucy. But right now, you're a child. So why don't you go out and play or something?"

"Do you need any help?"

Mama just shook her head, turning back to where she was pegging up a sheet. "Thanks anyway, Lucy. I'm almost done out here."

As Lucy walked back to the house, she decided that Mama was right. Everyone did have to live their own life. She realized that the sooner George and Veronica were able to be on their way, the better it would probably be for everyone.

On Wednesday afternoon, George's big yellow car parked in front of the house, and George came into the front room where Veronica, Grandma, and Lucy were listening to a program on the radio. "Anyone care to go for a ride?" he asked cheerfully.

"I do! I do!" Veronica stood up. "I'll get my coat."

George looked at Grandma and Lucy. "How about you two?"

"Not this time." Grandma stood, making her way toward the kitchen. "I need to get dinner started."

"Lucy?" His brown eyes lit up. "Want to come?"

"No, thank you." She looked down at her lap, picking at the hole in her trousers that was getting bigger.

"Come on, George," Veronica urged as she returned with her fur-trimmed blue coat. "Let's go. I want to go to town. Maybe you can take me to dinner. Or we can go to a movie or—"

"Lucy," George interrupted Veronica, "I thought you might like to drive by and check on Smoky."

Lucy felt her heart lurch. "Smoky?"

"Don't you want to see how he's doing in all this snow?"

She stood and nodded. "Yes. I'll get my coat."

George was waiting outside for Lucy. Veronica was already in the passenger's seat, but George led Lucy to the driver's side. "Slide on into the middle," he told her.

Sitting between George and Veronica, Lucy looked straight forward as George's car headed down the snowy road. She couldn't wait to see Smoky. Usually she stopped and talked to the pony every day on her way home from school. But it had been days since she'd seen him.

"There he is," she said eagerly, pointing to where Smoky was standing beneath the shelter of the trees in the middle of the field. "Do you think he's cold?"

"He's a horse," Veronica said sharply. "He's supposed to be cold."

"He's a pony," Lucy corrected.

"He's probably not too cold," George assured her. "Do you want to get out and say hello?"

"If you don't mind."

"Not at all." George reached behind the seat to pull out a bag, removing a whole apple. "I got these at the store in town. Want to give Smoky one?"

Her eyes grew big. "A whole apple?"

George laughed. "Sure."

"Thanks!"

Before long, Smoky was happily crunching on the apple, and Lucy giggled as his whiskers tickled her palm as he sniffed around for more. "Sorry, Smoky," she told him. "That's all for now."

George held out another apple. "You sure about that?"

"Is it all right?"

"I don't see why not."

Feeling extravagant and happy, she fed Smoky the second apple, petting his head and telling him not to get too cold. "Go on back to your spot by the trees," she said as she climbed down from the fence. "I'll try to come back as soon as I can."

He raised and lowered his head as if he understood. Then George and Lucy headed back to the car, where Veronica was sitting with her arms folded across her front and a slightly sour-looking expression on her face. "Is the horsey happy now?" she asked after George started the car.

"He's a pony," Lucy said. "And yes, he is happy." She turned to George. "So am I. Thank you, George."

"Now that everyone else is happy, do you think we could go to town and have some fun?" Veronica said hopefully.

"We can't stay in town for long," George told her as he drove.

"Why not?" Veronica demanded. "What about taking in a movie? Or dinner?"

"Because we're expected back at the house," George said.

"I need to set the table," Lucy added.

Veronica let out a disgruntled sigh, and Lucy and George exchanged glances.

"I don't know why I even bothered to come then," Veronica said. "I thought we were actually going to have fun."

"I just wanted to take a ride," George told her. "I thought you understood that."

"Then maybe I should ask you to drive me to the train station in Flagstaff," she said in a grumpy tone.

"I'm more than happy to do that," he told her.

She leaned back and made a *humph* sound.

"Would you like me to take you there tomorrow?" George offered.

"No, thank you," she said tersely.

Lucy remembered the secret—that Veronica had no money. Lucy wished she could confide in George. Maybe he could loan Veronica some money, and that would get Veronica on her way . . . and everyone would be happy. But Lucy had promised.

"Why can't you just drive us to Los Angeles?" she asked.

Just then the car slid slightly and George turned the steering wheel, guiding it back to the center of the road. "It should be obvious why I don't want to drive to Los Angeles," he said. "It's slick enough on flat ground. The mountain pass would be treacherous."

"All right." Veronica sat up straighter. "Then we will just have to make the best of it, won't we?"

They were slowly driving through town now, looking at the stores and businesses. Some of them were decorated for Christmas, and with the dusky blue blanket of snow outside, the warm yellow lights coming out of the windows, and the lamplights glowing, it looked like a completely different town.

"It's so pretty," Lucy said slowly. "I never saw town looking so pretty. It's like a picture book."

"Or a Christmas card," George added.

"Look at that sign." Veronica pointed to a poster on a window. "A Christmas dance on Saturday night. Oh, George, can we go? Can we? Can we?"

"I, uh, I don't know."

"Please, George. If we have to be stuck in this little one-horse town, we should at least get to have some fun. Please, say you'll take me to the Christmas dance."

He glanced at Lucy. "Let me think about it."

Using a little girl sort of voice, Veronica begged him a while longer, but George didn't answer one way or another. Even so, all the way home, she continued to chatter on and on about how much fun the dance would be, and what she would wear, and how it would make her time in this "one-horse town" a little more bearable. Lucy wanted to point out that their town had a lot more than just one horse. Although it was possible there was only one pony in Maple Grove. At least only one that Lucy knew about.

By the time they got home, Lucy couldn't wait to get away

from Veronica, but first she spoke politely to George. "It's a very nice car," she told him. "And it was fun to see Smoky today. I know he liked the apples. Thank you very much." Then she hurried into the house and started setting the table.

"We have good news." Grandma set the butter dish on the table.

"What?" Lucy paused with the soup spoons in her hand.

"One more room will be filled starting tomorrow. And for more than a week."

"During Christmastime?"

Grandma explained how the Farleys already had a houseful of people coming to visit. "Their second boy, Howard, is getting married right after Christmas. So Mrs. Farley called to ask if her elderly aunt and uncle could stay here."

"That is good news." Lucy carefully set a soup spoon down.

"Naturally, they'll spend the holidays and whatnot at the Farley house, but we will have them the rest of the time." Grandma smiled as she adjusted a place setting. "Four paying guests during Christmas. It's a real windfall."

Lucy suspected there might not be *four* paying guests. She'd given it some thought, and if Veronica was truly penniless, how would she pay her bill when it came time for her to check out? Not that Lucy planned to mention this to anyone—not after she'd been sworn to secrecy. Even so, Lucy knew that three paying guests were better than none. Unfortunately, it wouldn't be the first time someone had been unable to pay the bill.

8

Mr. and Mrs. Dorchester arrived not long after Lucy and Grandma had cleaned up lunch on Thursday afternoon. "If you're hungry," Lucy said as she showed the older couple to their room, "my grandma will fix you a snack."

"We haven't eaten since breakfast on the train," Mrs. Dorchester said as she set her handbag on the dresser. "And that wasn't anything to speak of. Goodness knows, with the price of train fare these days, one should be able to find something decent to eat on the train."

"Was it exciting traveling by train?" Lucy asked.

"Heavens no!" Mrs. Dorchester unpinned her hat with a sour expression. "I wouldn't wish train travel on my worst enemies."

"Oh." Lucy was surprised since it always looked glamorous in the movies.

"We would've come by automobile except for this horrid snow. Why on earth Howie wanted to get married in the middle of winter is a mystery to me."

"Maybe the bride picked the date," Mr. Dorchester suggested.

She glared at her husband, then looked back at Lucy. "Please tell your grandmother that we would appreciate something to eat as soon as possible," Mrs. Dorchester instructed. "And tell her that I have sensitivity to onions and raw vegetables."

Lucy nodded.

"And if she could please hurry it a bit." Mrs. Dorchester held the back of a plump white hand against her forehead. "I am feeling a bit faint."

"I'll go down and set the table," Lucy told her as she rushed from the room. It seemed like Mrs. Dorchester was going to be what Grandma called a *dingdong fussbudget*. Naturally Grandma hadn't said this knowing that Lucy was listening, and as far as Lucy knew, she'd only said it about that one guest, but Lucy felt certain that Mrs. Dorchester was one of those.

Grandma was warming some leftover stew, which unfortunately had onions that Grandma had tried to pick out, and Lucy was just finishing up the table when George came in, stomping the snow from his boots. "Are you ready to go to town for your Christmas pageant practice?" he asked her.

"Oh, yes!" Lucy looked at the clock. "I nearly forgot."

She set down the last cup and called out to Grandma that George was taking her to town now.

"Did I hear someone say they're going to town?" Veronica said as she came down the stairs. "Any chance I could come along too?"

"We have to get going in the next few minutes," George told her, "in order to get Lucy to the church on time. I'm already warming up the car, so you'd better hurry."

"I won't be but a minute," she chirped as she headed back up the stairs.

Lucy got her coat and things and went outside with George. "Thank you for giving me a ride," she told him.

"It's my pleasure." He grinned as he opened the door for her. "Besides, I need to pick up a little something at Hempley's Garage."

Once they were in the car, she asked how his mechanical work on their old car was coming along. "I haven't told Mama or Grandma anything," she said quietly, as if someone might hear her, although Mama was doing laundry and Grandma was in the kitchen.

"It's coming along just swell," he said. "I expect to have her up and running by Christmas."

"So you *will* stay with us until Christmas?" she said hopefully.

"As long as this weather keeps up, I don't have much of a choice."

She told George about the dingdong fussbudget guest, and he threw back his head and laughed. "They'll be here until after Christmas?"

"Yes, but her husband seems real nice," Lucy assured him. "And I could be wrong about Mrs. Dorchester. Maybe she was just tired. Please don't tell anyone I told you that about her."

"No worries, Lucy. Your secret is safe with me."

Lucy looked back at the house, wondering where Veronica was.

"I told her to hurry," he said. "Maybe we should just leave without her." He put the car into gear, and just as the tires moved, out came Veronica with her coat flapping behind her.

"Wait!" she cried as she hurried down the steps, tugging on her gloves.

The car took off as she closed the car door. "Now I'll need to drive faster than I like," George said.

"I was moving as fast as I could," she told him.

"Remember the reverend said the children aren't to be late." George's car tore through the snow of their driveway and onto the road.

"Well, please excuse me for being a bit slow." Veronica used a sharp-sounding voice. "But if you'd given me a little more notice . . ."

Lucy pressed her lips tightly together and slumped down into the seat. She didn't like to be the reason for their fight, but she couldn't think of anything to say to make things better. The three of them rode in silence, but as they got closer to the Greenburg farm, Lucy sat up tall, hoping to catch a glimpse of Smoky. What she saw sent a cold chill down her spine.

"The sign is gone!" she cried out.

"What sign?" Veronica demanded. "A stop sign? George, do you need to stop?"

"No, not a stop sign." Lucy leaned forward, peering out the windshield, hoping to spy Smoky beneath the trees. "The pony for sale sign."

"Oh, is that all?" Veronica leaned back and chuckled. "I thought for a moment we were going to be in a smash-up."

"I don't see Smoky anywhere," she said to George. "Do you?"

He shook his head. "Can't say that I do, Lucy."

"Do you think someone bought him?" she asked in a small voice.

"Maybe Mr. Greenburg changed his mind about selling him," George suggested.

Lucy just nodded, but deep in the pit of her stomach she didn't think so. No, something told her that Smoky had been sold . . . and taken away.

As a result, she felt less than enthusiastic when she went into the church, where the other children were already up in front getting ready to rehearse. "You're late, Lucy Turnbull," Mrs. Babcock said, frowning.

"I'm sorry," Lucy told her as she peeled off her coat and mittens.

"You can't expect to be late and still have a good part in the pageant," Mrs. Babcock scolded as Lucy went up front to stand with the others. "You asked to be an angel, remember?"

"I really am sorry," Lucy said contritely.

"Never mind." Mrs. Babcock loudly clapped her hands. "I need everyone's attention." She began to instruct them on what they were to do, telling them who was to stand where and when they would come out in front. Lucy tried to pay close attention, but she was distracted by thinking about Smoky. She'd known it was unrealistic to put her hopes on getting a pony for Christmas, but when God had answered her prayers by bringing boarders—and now all the rooms were full—it had seemed like a possibility.

"What's wrong with you?" Helen Krausner asked as the angels were herded to the back of the church to wait for their turn to proceed forward in song. The fact that Helen was playing an angel seemed odd to Lucy. Then again, they were only acting.

431

Lucy shrugged. "Nothing."

"You look like you just lost your best friend." Helen made a catty smile. "Oh, that's right, you already did."

Lucy frowned at her. "That's not why I'm sad, Helen."

Helen leaned forward, looking slightly concerned. "What is it then? You can tell me."

For whatever reason, maybe just to make her stop asking, Lucy decided to tell. "I'm worried that Mr. Greenburg already sold Smoky, the pony . . . and, well, I was hoping to get him for Christmas." As she said this, she knew how ridiculous she sounded, at least to her own ears, since there was no way Mama could afford a pony. Not that Helen needed to know that. "It was silly, I suppose," she continued. "But I really did like the pony."

"That is very interesting." Helen's eyes twinkled in a mischievous way.

"Why?"

"Because I asked my father to get me that pony for Christmas too."

Lucy felt horrified. "You did?"

Helen nodded. "I have a feeling that is exactly what's happened. Father went out yesterday morning to see about something, and he was gone for most of the day. My mother was not the least bit pleased about it either." Her lips curled into a smug smile. "I'm sure that's what he was doing."

"Girls!" Mrs. Babcock called out. "No talking back there!"

Lucy felt sick inside. It was one thing for Lucy not to become the new owner of Smoky, but it was unbearable to think that someone like Helen was going to have him. Helen didn't even like animals. Lucy remembered the time Helen threw stones at a stray dog. She told everyone that the dog had rabies, but Lucy could tell he was only hungry.

It was time for the angels to march forward singing "Angels We Have Heard on High." Lucy tried to follow along with the words, but her heart was no longer in it.

Lucy was relieved when practice ended and she could make her way to the front door with her coat and mittens in hand.

"Do not forget," Mrs. Babcock called out. "I want you all here on time for Saturday's practice at two in the afternoon. We will have costumes here, and it will be a dress rehearsal."

Lucy nodded and waved, then hurried outside to see that George's yellow roadster was already waiting. She knew she should have enjoyed this moment, being picked up like a princess. She should've taken her time and made sure that Helen Krausner noticed her getting into the fancy car as well as the glamorous Veronica Grant sitting beside her in the front seat. But Lucy felt so downhearted, she didn't even care. As they rode home, she realized she'd completely forgotten to brag about the almost movie star who was staying at their house.

"How did it go?" George asked.

"It was all right," Lucy said glumly.

"After we dropped you off, I thought maybe I should've come inside," Veronica told her.

"Why?" Lucy turned to look at her.

"To help with the acting."

"Oh." Lucy nodded. "Maybe you can help on Saturday."

Veronica began to talk about some of the acting she'd done

back in St. Louis, and how she couldn't wait to get to Hollywood and try it out again, and on and on and on. Lucy resisted the urge to cover her ears with her hands. Instead, she leaned back into the seat and closed her eyes, trying hard not to think about anything. Unfortunately, all she could think about was that Helen Krausner was going to have her pony!

Lucy got both George and Veronica's word that they would not mention the pony to Mama. "It will only make her feel bad," Lucy told them as they neared home. "We couldn't afford a pony anyway. And Mama told me she didn't want me putting my hopes into something that was impossible. No sense in telling her about it now."

"You can trust me with your secret," Veronica assured her as George parked in front of the house. She winked like this was a fun game, then hopped out of the car and hurried up to the house, as the snow was coming down hard again.

George helped Lucy out of the car. Once they were on the porch he leaned over, placing a hand on her shoulder. "You know you can trust me too, Lucy. I just hope you're not too terribly disappointed."

"It's probably for the best," she told him. "Ponies are for rich people. Mama said it was like wishing for the moon." Of course, that was not how Lucy felt. But she'd learned long ago . . . maybe when Daddy died . . . that you didn't usually get what you wished for. She should've known better than to wish for a pony.

With more guests in the house, including the dingdong fussbudget and the rather spoiled almost-actress, life became noisier and busier than ever. Lucy didn't mind the extra activity and responsibilities, though, because it took her mind off of Smoky. Before bed, she removed the picture she'd drawn from her wall, tucking it into the bottom of a drawer. If Mama noticed as Lucy said her prayers, she didn't mention it.

As usual, of late anyway, some of the grown-ups stayed up in the front room talking. Sometimes Lucy tried to understand their words, but she was just far enough away that although she could make out who was speaking, she couldn't quite make out what they were saying. Tonight it was all four of their guests and Mama. Grandma must have gone to bed already.

After a while the Dorchesters made their way upstairs, leaving just George and Veronica . . . and Mama. Lucy was surprised that Mama was staying up so late, but from the gay sound of their voices, they were enjoying each other's company. Naturally, that made Lucy curious. Despite knowing that Mama would not approve, Lucy sneaked out of bed and down the hallway to where she could hear them plainly.

"I'm sure you'll make a fine movie actress," Mama was saying. "I honestly hope to see you in our little theater someday."

"Oh, do go on," Veronica crooned.

"You're very beautiful," Mama continued. "My own daughter told my mother that she thinks you're the most beautiful person she's ever laid eyes on."

"But surely she thinks you're beautiful too," Veronica said. "All little girls think their mothers are beautiful."

Mama laughed, but it didn't sound like a real laugh.

"Of course Lucy thinks Miriam is beautiful," George said. "Anyone can see that just to look at her."

"To look at whom?" Veronica asked.

"Miriam, of course." George chuckled. "Wouldn't you agree that she's a beautiful woman?"

"Oh, I wouldn't—"

"I was talking to Veronica." George cut Mama off. "You consider yourself an expert on beauty, Veronica. Look at Miriam's fine skin, those topaz blue eyes, her straight nose and—"

"That's enough," Mama said in a voice that Lucy didn't recognize. Was she mad, or embarrassed, or something else? "If you will excuse me, I would like to—"

"I'm sorry, Miriam," George said gently. "I didn't mean to offend you. But you were so complimentary to Veronica, it seemed only right that—"

"No apology needed," Mama said crisply. "Now if you will excuse me, I need to tend to some things in the kitchen for breakfast."

"Yes, we should all call it a night," George said. There was the sound of movement, and Lucy scampered like a mouse back to her room, leaping into her bed and pulling the covers up to her chin, worried that Mama might check on her. But after a bit, once her breathing evened out, Lucy heard talking again. This time it came from the kitchen and was only the sound of George and Mama's voices. Once again, Lucy tiptoed out to listen.

"I really am sorry," George was saying. "I know I made you uncomfortable, and that wasn't my goal at all."

"Never mind," Mama told him.

"I only wanted to put Veronica in her place," he said. "She sets such high stock on appearances, and she spends so much time worrying about her own. Yet you go about your business, you take care of everyone and everything, and in my opinion you are much more beautiful than Veronica. Not in a painted flashy way, of course, but in a lovely womanly way. I just hope you don't mind me saying so."

"Thank you, George." Mama's voice sounded stiff as the stove door clanked closed.

"I can tell I've offended you now."

"No . . . I'm not offended. Just uncomfortable."

"I suppose I've stuck my foot in my mouth again. Sometimes that got me into trouble at law school. On the other hand, I think a good lawyer knows how to speak his mind, even if no one else wants to hear the truth."

"I suppose the truth . . . like beauty . . . can be in the eye of the beholder."

He chuckled.

"Now, really, George, if you will excuse me, it's getting late."

"I will excuse you only if you promise that you'll forgive me for offending you."

"You did not offend me."

The kitchen was quiet for what felt like several minutes.

"Good night, George." Mama's voice sounded just a tiny bit more gentle, and now her footsteps were coming Lucy's way.

"Good night, Miriam," George called. Lucy was already making a beeline for her bed again. This time she stayed put. But what she heard in the kitchen did get her mind to wondering. Now that she knew she wasn't getting a pony for Christmas, maybe she should consider praying for something else—like a daddy!

9

After lunch on Friday, George invited Lucy to take a ride in his car, but once she was inside, he told her his real purpose. "Your house needs a Christmas tree," he said as the car took off over the snowy road. "You and I are going to find the perfect one."

As they drove, they talked. Mostly it seemed that George wanted to know more about Mama, and since Lucy thought she knew why he wanted to know more, she was happy to oblige him. Unfortunately, his questions only revealed that she did not know as much about her mother as she thought she did. Oh, she knew that Mama liked birds and growing flowers in the springtime. She knew that Mama was a good cook but that it made Grandma feel important to handle the cooking, so she stayed out of the kitchen most of the time. She knew that Mama took care of the laundry and sewing and some of the housekeeping and most of the outdoor chores and that Mama was kind and good and sometimes stern. Finally she thought of something she hadn't told him.

"Mama used to have the prettiest smile," she said as he parked the car near a grove of ponderosa pine trees. "But after Daddy died, it just seemed to go away."

"That's understandable."

"I prayed that God would give Mama her smile back," Lucy confessed as they got out of the car. "For Christmas."

George had a real thoughtful look as he reached for his pipe. "Maybe God's going to answer that prayer for you."

"You know what?" She felt a rush of excitement.

"What?"

"I'd rather have Mama's smile back than a pony."

George looked shocked. "No kidding?"

"It's true." She nodded eagerly.

That night the Christmas tree, which reached clear to the ceiling, was in place. "I've never seen a Christmas tree quite like this one." George touched a long-needled bough. "But I think it might be the most beautiful tree ever."

"It's certainly the biggest tree this house has ever seen," Mama told him.

"It didn't look that tall in the woods."

She shook her head. "I know I won't have enough ornaments to fill it."

"We can make some more," Lucy suggested.

"We can string popcorn," Grandma told her.

"Yes!" Lucy exclaimed. "Let's do that now."

"Not tonight, we won't," Mama said. "It's already past Lucy's bedtime."

Lucy groaned.

"We'll do it tomorrow night," Mama said gently.

"That reminds me," Veronica said suddenly. "Tomorrow night is the Christmas dance. Remember, George? You promised to take me."

"What?" George frowned. "I don't recall making—"

"Remember, we saw the poster in town," she reminded him.

"George didn't promise," Lucy pointed out. "He only said he'd think about it."

"Oh, please, George," Veronica pleaded. "Take me to the Christmas dance, I'm begging you. *Please.*"

"That must be the grange dance," Grandma said. "They have it every year."

"I remember hearing about a Christmas dance up north some-where, in a barn as I recall," Mrs. Dorchester said. "Horrible tale about how the whole place caught on fire and everyone was trapped inside. Nearly half the town was burned to death, and just before Christmas."

"Oh, dear!" Mama's brows lifted.

"Good heavens!" Grandma let out a loud sigh that sounded like *fussbudget* to Lucy's ears.

"Well, that's silly," Veronica told her. "People don't die at dances."

"Just the same, you won't catch us going to any Christmas dance at a grange." Mrs. Dorchester grimly shook her head.

"No, sirree. Now, come on, Fred, it's time you and I turned in for the night. My back is starting to ache something fierce."

"Time for me to call it a day too," Grandma said. "I'll say my good-nights now."

"And so will Lucy." Mama put a hand on Lucy's shoulder, guiding her out.

"Good night, everyone, sleep tight," Lucy called out, refraining from adding "don't let the bedbugs bite" like she sometimes did, since she knew Mama wouldn't approve. Not with paying guests in the house.

It wasn't until Lucy had finished quickly saying her prayers and was tucked snugly in bed that she knew she had to say something before it was too late. "You can't let Veronica talk George into taking her to that dance," she proclaimed just as Mama pulled the string on the overhead light.

"What?" Mama stood in the doorway, her silhouette framed in light.

"Veronica will just keep pestering George," Lucy explained. "And he's so nice, he might give in."

"Give in to what?"

"You know what, Mama. He'll take her to that dance."

Now Mama came back in, closing the door behind her and sitting down in the chair again. "What difference would that make, Lucy?" Her voice was soft and quiet in the darkness.

"The difference would be that George is falling in love with you."

Mama laughed in an odd way. "Oh, Lucy, your imagination is running away—"

"It's not my imagination. It's true."

"How do you know it's true?" Mama was whispering now, as if worried that someone might be listening.

"Because he kept asking about you when we got the tree." Lucy thought for a moment, trying to recall if George had asked her not to mention this, but she couldn't remember anything quite like that.

"What was he asking?"

"Just *stuff*, Mama." Lucy felt anxious. "But you can't waste time. You need to go out there and make sure Veronica doesn't talk him into it. She can be awfully persistent when she wants something."

"So I've noticed."

"Please, Mama. You have to trust me on this."

Mama slowly stood. "I can't make any promises, Lucy."

"Just try. *Please*."

"Good night, Lucy." Mama opened the door again. "I love you."

"I love you too, Mama—now hurry!"

Lucy could hear the sound of their voices in the living room, and to her surprise it all sounded quite pleasant again. There was even laughter. Then, just as she was considering sneaking out of bed again, it sounded as if they were all saying good night. This was followed by the sounds of footsteps and doors closing, and Lucy knew that everyone had gone to bed and she'd have to wait until morning to find out how it went. Hopefully Mama had managed to prevent what could be a disaster from happening.

On Saturday morning, Lucy was surprised by two things. First of all, she was surprised that Veronica was up in time to sit with them at breakfast. Dressed in an elegant green blouse and matching trousers, Veronica seemed fully awake and more intent than usual on keeping and maintaining George's attention. The second surprise was discovering that George had pulled a fast one last night.

"George told me that the only way he'll take me to the Christmas dance tonight is if Miriam goes too," Veronica announced. "I'm not sure if he thinks we need a chaperone or if he just wants to walk in with two women on his arm, but he made it clear that it's the only way he'll go." She turned to Mama, and Lucy waited hopefully. "You promised to sleep on it, Miriam. Have you made up your mind?"

Mama placed her napkin in her lap. "I'm afraid I have to decline."

"Oh, Miriam." Veronica pursed her lips together.

"Why, Mama?" Lucy asked. "You should go to the dance and have fun."

"I agree," Grandma said. "You should go to the dance. It's been years since you've been to a dance." She gave George a sly look. "Miriam used to be one of the best dancers in these parts."

"Oh, Mother."

"Is that true, Mama?" Lucy asked eagerly.

"No, of course not. Your grandmother is exaggerating."

Grandma shook her finger. "It is so true." She winked at Lucy. "Your mama and daddy used to go to the grange dances, back before you were born, and the word around town was that those two could really cut the rug." She laughed.

"Then you really should go to the dance," George urged her.

"Yes," Lucy chimed in. "Say you'll go."

"But I . . . I don't know." Mama slowly shook her head.

"Come on, Miriam," Veronica urged with a bit less enthusiasm. "Just do it for me. I've been so bored, and a dance sounds like such fun."

"Come on, Mama," Lucy tried. "Just go with them."

"You might enjoy the music," George added.

"And the dancing." Grandma grinned at her.

"Unless the whole place goes up in flames." Mrs. Dorchester grimaced as she reached for a second helping of fried potatoes. She must not have noticed the onions Grandma put in them.

Mama looked caught now. "Well, I suppose it wouldn't hurt to go."

"Of course it wouldn't hurt." Grandma cut off a piece of butter.

"Unless you all burned up."

Mama looked directly at Mrs. Dorchester now. "I really don't think that's a possibility. The grange has been having dances since I was a girl, and I've never had any reason to worry."

"Then come to the dance," George said happily.

It seemed settled. As odd as it was, Mama and George and Veronica were all going to the dance together. Lucy wondered if he would take turns dancing with them or attempt to dance with two partners at the same time.

After breakfast, alone with Mama and Grandma in the kitchen, Lucy asked Mama what she was going to wear.

"Oh, I don't know." Mama scrubbed a dish. "My Sunday dress, I suppose."

"What about that pretty blue shiny dress," Lucy said. "The one in the back of your closet. You never wear it."

"The topaz silk," Grandma said. "You should wear that, Miriam."

"I doubt it will even fit." Mama wiped her damp hands on the front of her stained apron and frowned.

"I don't see why it won't fit," Grandma told her. "And if we need to, we could make some alterations."

"But why go to such trouble?"

"Lucy?" called Veronica from the dining room. "Are you busy, doll?"

"Why don't you go see what she wants," Grandma said. "We'll finish up in here."

Lucy removed her apron and went to see.

"I nearly forgot that I made a promise to you."

"A promise?" Lucy followed her into the front room.

"I told you we'd go to the movie theater on Saturday. Your mother even agreed to it. Remember how I wanted to go last Sunday, and she said that was unacceptable?" One of Veronica's thin eyebrows arched higher. "So . . . what do you think, doll? Do you want to see a picture with me or not?"

Lucy felt a rush of excitement at this unexpected offer. "You mean it?"

"Of course. In light of your disappointment over that horse

yesterday, it seems like a good idea. You need a little pick-me-up." Veronica ran her hand over Lucy's hair.

"How will we get there?"

"George said he'd be happy to take us if you want to go. I told him I was absolutely certain you'd want to go. You do, don't you?" Veronica smiled hopefully. "I'm just dying to see a picture today."

Suddenly Lucy remembered today's Christmas pageant rehearsal. Disappointment seeped in as she reminded Veronica that she had to be at the church by two. "Maybe it's not such a good idea after all."

Veronica waved her hand. "Oh, don't you worry about that, doll. We'll go to the early matinee, and you'll be out in plenty of time to make it to your dress rehearsal. The church is only a couple of blocks from the theater. If George isn't back by then, we'll just walk over."

"George doesn't want to go to the picture with us?" Lucy asked.

"Not this time, doll. He says he has something he's working on." She rolled her eyes. "I told him that all work and no play makes George a dull boy, but he didn't seem to care."

"At least he's taking you and Mama to the Christmas dance," Lucy pointed out.

"Yes. This is going to be a red-letter day. Now you go and get yourself dolled up, and I'll speak to your mother about our plans."

Lucy was a little unsure about this but decided not to protest. By the time she emerged, dressed in her best school dress with ribbons tied on her braids, Veronica seemed to have smoothed everything over with Mama just fine. "Just be sure and mind your manners," Mama told her. "And don't be late for pageant practice. You know how Mrs. Babcock can be."

"Yes, Mama." Lucy blew her a kiss as they went out, and soon they were on the road. Today Lucy tried not to look at Mr. Greenburg's farm, but she did notice the sign was still gone. It wasn't long until George was dropping them in front of the movie theater and her sadness was replaced with anticipation as she followed Veronica to the ticket booth.

As she waited, she felt concerned. Hadn't Veronica said she was penniless? And didn't it cost a nickel to see a motion picture? Just the same, Lucy stood back, watching as Veronica consulted with the man in the booth. Lucy could tell by his expression that he was quite taken by Veronica Grant's exotic beauty. Perhaps he thought she was a film star and would let them in for free.

"The movie doesn't start for a while," Veronica explained. "Do you want to walk around town for a bit? Maybe we could get some soda or an ice cream."

Lucy wasn't going to argue with that plan either, although she wondered how they would pay for such things if Veronica was truly broke. But she watched with wide eyes as Veronica extracted a dollar bill from her shiny black purse. Lucy gratefully thanked her, feeling like she was someone else, or starring in a movie, as she strolled through town with Veronica Grant, sipping on her cherry soda. When they stood in line at the theater, she felt people watching them curiously, probably wondering who this elegant person was and why she was here. Lucy just smiled to herself, wishing that Helen Krausner was around to see them together but knowing she would hear all about it eventually. Word traveled fast in their town.

The movie playing was called *Beg, Borrow or Steal*, and it was unlike any other film that Lucy had ever seen. A bunch of men made a business of lying and tricking everyone in order to get money. The actress in it, a blonde lady playing Joyce, was very nice and her clothes were pretty. Still, Lucy was disappointed that Shirley Temple wasn't in it as well. That would have made it lots better. Lucy supposed it was a grown-up movie, and there were a number of parts she didn't quite understand. However, she was amazed at the ending of the movie by Joyce's wedding dress. It was the most beautiful gown Lucy had ever seen. Unfortunately, Joyce was about to marry the wrong man. But the good guy (who also turned out to be a wealthy count) showed up at the right time, and Joyce married him instead. Whew!

"Did you like it, doll?" Veronica asked as they went out into the bright daylight where the sunshine shimmered on the brilliant white snow.

"Yes." Lucy blinked. "Thank you for taking me, Veronica." She almost questioned Veronica about being "broke" but decided not to say that because it sounded ungrateful. Perhaps Veronica had gone to a bank or something. She knew that grown-ups sometimes went there to get money, although Mama had told Lucy they couldn't do that anymore. "Do you know what time it is? I don't want to be late for rehearsal."

Veronica looked at the watch George had loaned her to keep track of the time. "Oh dear, I completely forgot about that. We'd better hurry." She took Lucy by the hand and partly walked and partly ran down the boardwalk toward the church. "Now remember, Lucy, the best part of acting happens *inside* of you. You must think that you are an angel, and then you will act like one."

Lucy laughed. "I don't think I'm much of an angel."

When they reached the church steps, Veronica paused to catch her breath. "Here we are!" she puffed. "Now go—and be the most beautiful angel, doll."

"Do you want to come in?" Lucy asked hopefully.

"Not this time." Veronica patted her hair. "I think I'll call George to come pick me up. It's time for my afternoon nap."

"I better go in." Lucy grabbed the door handle, hoping she wasn't late. But once inside the church, she saw that the other children were already wearing their costumes and getting in their places, and Mrs. Babcock did not look the least bit pleased to see her.

"Lucy Turnbull, you are *twenty minutes* late," she scolded. "I've given your part of an angel to Molly Price. Now you will have to be a sheep." She pointed to a heap of wooly sheep-colored blankets, just like Lucy had worn when she played a sheep last year. "Hurry and get ready now." Mrs. Babcock clapped her hands to get everyone's attention.

Feeling a mixture of shame and deep disappointment, Lucy picked up a grayish and slightly musty-smelling blanket and threw it over her head and back like a cape. With burning cheeks and teary eyes, she walked over to join the other sheep, three slightly unruly boys who didn't even want to be in the pageant.

Knowing that she probably deserved this punishment, she got down on her hands and knees with the snickering boys, and hanging her head low, she wondered how she would explain this to Mama.

After practice ended, Helen Krausner came over to Lucy. "That's just terrible that you have to be a sheep again this year. It's so much more glamorous playing an angel. The angel costumes are even prettier this year than last year."

Lucy didn't know what to say, but she was determined not to let Helen make her feel any worse than she already felt. "Well, they can't be as glamorous as the movie actress who's staying at our house."

Helen looked doubtful. "You have a movie actress staying at your house?"

"Well, she's not a star yet, but she's on her way to Hollywood. Her name is Veronica Grant, and the reason I'm late is because she took me to see *Beg, Borrow or Steal* at the theater today."

"You saw *that* movie?"

Lucy nodded. "With Veronica. Wait until you see her, Helen. Veronica Grant is the most glamorous person that's ever been in Maple Grove."

"When will I see her?" Helen demanded.

Lucy thought. "Well, if you're in church tomorrow."

"I don't know about church." Helen frowned. "My father doesn't want to go . . . sometimes."

"Oh . . ." Lucy nodded, trying to figure this out.

"But at the pageant, for sure."

"I promise to introduce you to her."

"She's really going to be an actress?"

Lucy nodded eagerly. "I think she'll be really good too."

As the girls parted ways, Lucy wondered why she'd gone to such efforts to impress someone like Helen Krausner. Really, what did it matter what Helen thought?

10

You're being awfully quiet," George said. Long blue shadows cut into the white snow as he drove Lucy away from town after the dress rehearsal. "Anything wrong?"

Lucy felt her chin trembling as she shook her head no.

He gave her a concerned look. "You sure about that?"

She bit into her lower lip, feeling hot tears burning in her eyes. But she was determined not to cry.

"Did something bad happen today? At the movies? Or at pageant practice?"

The caring tone in his voice broke her, and suddenly she was sobbing. George pulled the car over to the side of the road, right next to Clara's old house, which looked even sadder and lonelier in this dusky blue light. George reached into his pocket, then handed her a handkerchief. "Want to talk about it?"

She wiped her eyes and nose and slowly nodded. Then, as if someone had popped the cork off a bottle, it all came pouring out—how she'd been late and demoted from an angel to a sheep. "The sheep are the worst roles to get in the whole pageant."

George reached over and patted her on the shoulder. "I'm sorry," he told her. "Is there anything I can do? I'd be happy to go explain to Mrs. Babcock that it's not your fault and—"

"No," she said quickly. "It's too late to fix it."

He slowly nodded, rubbing his chin like he was thinking. "You know the real reason we celebrate Christmas, don't you? I mean, beyond Santa Claus and jingle bells and Christmas trees?"

"You mean because Jesus was born?" she asked.

"Yes . . . but did you ever think about *how* Jesus was born? I mean, have you considered how it was such a humble birth, in a small barn . . . how he was laid in a hay trough . . . how the Son of almighty God humbled himself to be born in such lowly conditions? Have you thought about it like that?"

She shrugged, unsure of what George was trying to say. Of course she knew all about the stable and the manger. Wasn't she playing a sheep in the pageant?

"Jesus could've been born in a fine palace, Lucy. After all, he was the Son of God. But for some reason God chose humble beginnings for his Son. Do you ever wonder why?"

Lucy shook her head.

"I think it's because God wanted to show that his love could reach to everyone, no matter who they were, from the poorest of poor to great kings. Remember the three wise men who brought treasures to Jesus?"

She nodded. "Some of the older boys are playing the wise men. They're singing the three kings song."

"Here is what I'm thinking, Lucy. You getting to play the lowliest of animals is a little bit like Jesus must have felt by getting to be born in a stable."

She tilted her head to one side as she thought about this.

"Not only that, but do you know what animal Jesus is sometimes called?"

"An animal?" She frowned. Surely no nice person would call Jesus an animal.

"He was called the Lamb of God, Lucy."

"Oh . . . yeah . . . I do remember that now."

"If Jesus, the King of Kings, was called the Lamb of God, maybe it's not so bad being a sheep in the Christmas pageant . . . don't you think?"

"I'm not sure, George. The truth is, I still want to be an angel." She forced a little smile. "But that does make me feel better."

He grinned. "Good. Now we'd better get home. Your mother said dinner will be early tonight in order for us to get to the Christmas dance on time."

"The Christmas dance!" she exclaimed. "I completely forgot about that." The sky was dusky periwinkle now. "You better hurry, George!"

The house seemed busier than ever when Lucy went inside. Mr. and Mrs. Dorchester were sitting on the couch as a radio program with Christmas music played loudly. Veronica was all dressed up in a shiny red gown which seemed to match her painted nails and lips. Lucy blinked to see how low it was cut, both in the front and in the back. Wouldn't she get cold in it? However, her cheeks looked more flushed than usual as she danced around the front room as if to entertain the elderly guests.

"You look beautiful," Lucy paused to tell Veronica. "Like a real movie star."

"Thank you, doll." Veronica rewarded her with a flashy smile. "I feel like a real movie star tonight."

Lucy excused herself as she rushed toward the dining room where Mama was placing food on the already set table. "Sorry I'm late," she told Mama.

"That's all right. Hang up your coat and see if Grandma needs help in there. We're eating early tonight because—"

"I know," Lucy called as she pushed through the swinging door. "George told me all about it."

"There you are," Grandma said with a flushed face. "How was the motion picture, Lucy?"

"It was wonderful." Lucy peeled off her coat. "Well, maybe not exactly *wonderful*, but I did enjoy it."

"Here," Grandma set a bowl of cream on the table, handing Lucy the eggbeater. "Can you whip this for me?"

"Sure."

"What was the title of the picture you saw?"

"*Beg, Borrow or Steal,*" Lucy told her. Then as she turned the handle on the beater, trying to keep it balanced on the bottom of the slippery bowl, she told Grandma a bit about the movie.

"Goodness," Grandma said. "It sounds like a bunch of crooks and tricksters to me."

"They weren't all bad," Lucy said defensively. "The father learned his lesson by the end of the movie. And the wedding was absolutely beautiful." As she was describing the gown, Mama came in.

"Speaking of gowns . . ." Grandma frowned at Mama. "Why aren't you dressed for the dance by now? Veronica is out there parading around in her fancy finery."

Mama sighed as she held out the skirt of her stained apron. "Because I'm still working. Why would I want to take the chance of soiling my silk dress?"

"That's what aprons are for." Grandma handed her a bowl of green beans.

"Oh, Mother, that blue silk is not the kind of dress one wears an apron with."

"Did you try it on?" Lucy asked eagerly. "Did it fit right and look pretty?"

"I had to make some alterations," Mama told her, "but I think it will be just fine, Lucy."

Soon it was dinnertime, and it seemed everyone had something to talk about. Mrs. Dorchester had spent the afternoon helping with wedding preparations at the Farleys', which, according to her, were frivolous nonsense. "I did enjoy seeing my niece, but why she wants to make such fussy little decorations is beyond me."

Veronica began to tell about the wedding scene in the movie, describing in detail the preparations for that lavish wedding. "Of course, these were very wealthy people," she said, "not just simple farm folks."

Lucy wanted to point out that they weren't as wealthy as they were pretending to be and that their wealth was wrongfully gained, but by then Veronica was so caught up in describing the bride's costume that Lucy couldn't help but listen.

"It really was beautiful," Lucy told them. "She looked like a fairy princess."

"Someday I'd like to have a wedding like that." Veronica looked longingly at George, as if she wanted him to participate in it.

"I'm sure that all girls dream of weddings," he said. He tipped his head to Lucy. "How about you? Do you dream of a wedding?"

Lucy giggled and looked down at her plate.

The conversation continued, moving faster than usual, and Lucy felt lost through most of it. That was because she was still trying not to feel bad over losing her part as an angel . . . and trying to decide when it would be best to tell Mama. Before she knew it dinner was over, it was time to clean up, Mama went off to get dressed for the Christmas dance, and Lucy was carrying dishes to the kitchen.

She was just starting to dry dishes when Mama came into the kitchen. Lucy almost dropped the saucer in her hand as she stared at the woman in the silky blue dress. "Mama, is that really you?"

Mama laughed as she did a little turn that made the skirt swirl out at the bottom. Lucy dried her hands and went closer to see better. Mama's light brown hair was piled higher than usual on her head, and holding it in place was a shiny pin with white and blue jewels. "Are those real diamonds?" Lucy asked in wonder.

"No, of course not. They're rhinestones."

"And that pin?" Lucy pointed to the smooth white brooch on the front of Mama's dress.

"That was mine," Grandma said proudly. "Your grandfather gave that to me on our wedding day. It's a moonstone."

"A moonstone," Lucy said slowly. "It does remind me of a moon." She threw her arms around Mama. "Oh, Mama, you are beautiful."

Mama smiled down at Lucy—*really smiled*—and Lucy thought her heart was going to burst just to see that smile. "Thank you, Lucy."

"You are the most beautiful lady in the whole world," Lucy told her.

Mama's smile got bigger. "You don't think my shoes look a bit silly with this dress?" She held out a foot.

"Those are your good Sunday shoes," Lucy reminded her. "I think they look just fine."

"So do I!" Grandma reached over and pinched Mama's cheeks.

"What are you doing?" Lucy asked.

"Just giving her a bit of color."

Lucy laughed. "I think she's already got lots of color."

Mama glanced at the kitchen clock. "Well, I feel a little nervous about this, but I suppose I should go out and tell them I'm ready."

"I'll get your good coat and your black leather gloves for you," Lucy offered.

"And my wool scarf," Mama said. "It will be cold tonight."

When Lucy joined the others in the front room, Veronica already had on her fur-trimmed coat and was looking at Mama with a curious expression. However, it was George's face that really got Lucy's attention. His eyes were fastened on Mama, and his mouth was smiling. "Here you go, Mama." Lucy started to hand Mama her things.

"Let me help with that," George offered as he reached to take Mama's black coat. Lucy waited as he helped Mama into it.

Feeling more happy than she had imagined possible considering all that had gone wrong in her life recently, Lucy handed Mama her gloves and scarf. "I hope you have a real fun time at the dance tonight."

"Oh, I'm sure I will," Mama told her. "Now don't you stay up late, you hear?"

Lucy nodded obediently, and just like that, they were off. Lucy wondered what their evening would be like. Judging by the look in Veronica's eye, it would be interesting at least. Hopefully Mama would tell Grandma about it in detail . . . and Lucy would be close enough to listen.

True to her promise, Lucy went to bed on time. Grandma walked her to her bedroom and offered to help her get ready for bed, but Lucy could tell she was tired. "That's all right." She hugged her tightly. "I'm a big enough girl to get myself to bed. I just let Mama help me because she likes to so much."

Grandma chuckled as she gently tugged one of Lucy's braids. "I just hope your mama is having a good time tonight."

"Me too." Lucy sat down to unlace her shoes. She wanted to ask Grandma if she thought George was in love with Mama, but she remembered how Grandma had responded to that last time. Besides, Grandma hadn't been in the front room to see how George's eyes had lit up when he was looking at Mama in her fine blue dress.

"Good night, Lucy." Grandma bent down to kiss her cheek.

"Good night." Lucy pulled off a shoe. "Sleep tight and don't let the bedbugs bite."

"Lucy!" Grandma put a forefinger over her lips. "Don't let the guests hear you saying that."

Lucy giggled. "Sorry. Good night, Grandma."

"You will say your prayers, won't you?"

Lucy nodded . . . but in her heart, she wasn't so sure. What if God was mad at her for being late to practice and then not telling Mama about it? Despite George's encouragement, Lucy felt worried. By the time she was in her nightgown, her feet were cold as ice, so she hopped into bed and tried not to think about anything at all. Not angels or sheep or even ponies. But Mama's sweet smile stayed fixed in her memory, and if she'd been of a mind to pray, she would've prayed that Mama and George were having a really great time at the dance and that they would fall truly in love with each other. As it was, she felt too guilty—and sleepy—to pray at all.

To Lucy's surprise, Veronica made an appearance at the breakfast table on Sunday. But something told Lucy that she was not in a very happy mood. For that matter, neither were George or Mama. In fact, everyone seemed quiet and subdued, especially after the joviality of their last meal together. In between feeding chickens and filling the wood box, Lucy spent much of the morning trying to pin down Mama in regard to last night's festivities, but Mama had been tight-lipped and something else too. Lucy thought perhaps Mama was *distracted.* That's what Mama said about Lucy sometimes, when her mind was somewhere else. Before she could get to the bottom of it, it was time to go to church.

As usual, the Brewsters stopped by to offer a ride. George also planned to drive. However, his roadster only had one seat, so Grandma and the Dorchesters decided to go with the Brewsters, and Mama was about to join them when George stepped in.

"Why don't you ride with me, Miriam?" he said cheerfully.

Mama looked somewhat surprised but pleased. "Well, I suppose—"

"But there won't be room in the roadster," Veronica said quickly. "Not if Lucy is coming with us, George."

Now Lucy stepped back. As much as she liked riding in George's nice car, she wanted Mama to ride with him. "I'll ride in the Brewsters' rumble seat," she said. "That's fun."

"But it's so cold," Mama told her.

"That's all right." Lucy smiled as she moved toward the Brewsters' car. "I don't mind. I just pretend it's a sleigh ride." Satisfied that she'd secured Mama a snug spot next to George, Lucy waited for Mr. Brewster to open the rumble seat. But as she got into the outdoor seat, she noticed Veronica's feathered hat ducking into George's car, and then Veronica slid to the center of the seat so that Mama had to sit by the door. Still,

Mama seemed fine, holding her head high as George headed the big yellow car down the snowy lane.

Lucy tried not to fume at Veronica as they rode to church. It was bad enough that she hadn't said her prayers last night, but to go to church angry . . . well, that just didn't seem right. Especially on the Sunday before Christmas.

The Brewsters' car pulled up by the church just as George was hopping out of his parked car. Lucy watched as George ran around to the passenger side and, with a flourish and a bow, opened the door, offered Mama his hand, and helped her out of the car. Completely ignoring Veronica, George led Mama up the church steps.

Lucy restrained herself from letting out a victory whoop as Mr. Brewster parked directly behind the yellow roadster, but she couldn't help but feel this meant that George was choosing Mama over Veronica. Feeling just a little sorry for Veronica as she crawled out of the car, adjusting the shiny purple feather on her hat, Lucy jumped down out of the rumble seat, made a sprint toward Veronica, and took her by the hand. "Did you have a nice ride?" she asked as they walked together into church.

Veronica made a stiff smile, holding her coat closed against the wind. "It's colder than the dickens today. I don't know how you could stand riding in that rumble seat, doll."

"It wasn't so bad." Even so, Lucy shivered as they went inside.

"Oh, to be in California," Veronica said dramatically.

Lucy nodded as if she agreed—and in truth, she did. If a genie appeared right now, offering her one magic wish today, she would ask that Veronica be whisked off to California immediately, or at least before sunset. (Or else she would do the smart thing and wish for three more wishes!) But as the congregation began to sing, Lucy realized that daydreaming about genies and wishes probably wasn't the best use of one's time during church. When it was time to silently bow her head before God, Lucy told him that she was sorry about being late for pageant practice and promised to tell Mama the truth at her first opportunity. After that, singing the hymns and Christmas songs felt so much better. Lucy felt certain she'd be able to say her bedtime prayers properly tonight. At least she hoped so.

11

The rest of Sunday passed in a flurry that started when Mrs. Dorchester tripped while going up the stairs shortly after their midday meal. It took Mama, Grandma, and Mr. Dorchester to get her safely down the stairs and onto the front room sofa, and the whole time she was howling in pain. Mama called Dr. Mickelson, who came by to see what could be done.

"It looks like a bad ankle sprain," he proclaimed. "Best thing you can do is to stay off of it for a couple of weeks."

"How am I supposed to do that?" she sputtered. "There's my nephew's wedding to attend to, and then I need to get home, and good grief, our room is up those doggone stairs." She pointed to the staircase as if it were to blame for her clumsiness.

Dr. Mickelson shrugged as he wiped the lenses of his glasses. "I'll have someone drop some crutches and other things by." He wrote something down in a little black book. "I've got something in my satchel for your pain." He glanced over at the stairs. "But you won't be going up those stairs for some time." He turned to Mama. "Is there a room down here that she can use?"

Mama frowned. "There are only two rooms down here. My mother and I share one, and Lucy is in the—"

"She can have my room," Lucy offered.

So it was that George spent a couple of hours helping Lucy to switch things from her room and the bedroom upstairs. It took lots of trips up and down the stairs, but George never complained once. Meanwhile Mama did her best to make Mrs. Dorchester comfortable and happy . . . which was not easy. Grandma tended to her usual chores in the kitchen.

Shortly before dinnertime, everything was set. Lucy was settled in the middle room upstairs, and Mr. and Mrs. Dorchester were down in her room. "Will you be comfortable up here?" George asked.

She grinned. "This used to be my room."

"Really?" He looked around the small room with interest.

"When my daddy was alive. He and Mama had the big front room and I slept right here." She patted the bed, which now had her crazy quilt spread over it. "After Daddy died, Mama and I moved our bedrooms downstairs. She said it was warmer down there in the wintertime. Then Mama started renting rooms up here. When Grandma came to live with us, she and Mama decided to share a room."

"Things changed a lot when your father died."

Lucy nodded.

"I'm sure you must miss him still."

She nodded again.

"Well . . ." He shoved his hands in his trouser pockets. "I'll leave you to it. I'm sure it must be just about time for dinner."

It wasn't until Lucy was seated at the table, where Mrs. Dorchester's chair was vacant, that she remembered she still hadn't told Mama about being late for the pageant practice and consequently losing her angel's wings. Lucy considered making this announcement now, but she couldn't quite think of the right way to say it.

"Who all wants to go to the Christmas pageant tonight?" George asked everyone at the table.

"Not Mrs. Dorchester, that's for sure." Mr. Dorchester shook his head. "Not me either."

"I want to go," Grandma said. "I'm sure Miriam does too." Mama just nodded as she reached for the salt shaker.

Lucy wanted to say she wasn't terribly eager to go but knew that would require a full explanation and wouldn't get her out of her responsibilities either.

"I'd like to go too," Veronica said. "I've been giving Lucy dramatic advice, and I'm most curious to see how well she performs."

Lucy felt her stomach twisting.

"I have an idea," George said. "Since my car holds only two passengers at the most, how about if I make two trips to town. I can drop Lucy and one other person earlier. Then I can take two others for the second trip." He pointed to Veronica. "Since you've been helping Lucy, maybe you'd like to be in the first trip."

Veronica looked uncertain. "Well . . . I suppose that would be all right. I could always walk around town a bit, just to kill time. It might be better than being stuck out here in the middle of nowhere."

It was settled, and Lucy knew there was no way out of it. She would've told Mama the whole story, but Mama was busy running back and forth for Mrs. Dorchester. Grandma had given her a bell to ring when she needed something, and it seemed the bell rang about every other minute.

"Time to go," George told Lucy and Veronica. "Are you ladies all ready?"

"Ready when you are." Veronica reached for her fur-trimmed coat.

Lucy grimaced. "Yes. I'll get my coat."

George wasn't even on the main road before Veronica began giving acting tips and advice to Lucy, telling her how to hold her chin high and to look directly out over the audience. Lucy exchanged glances with George, and it looked like he was suppressing laughter, although Lucy didn't see any humor in it.

"Remember what I said about thinking of yourself as an angel, Lucy. Think heavenly thoughts and put a sparkle in your eye and you'll be the—"

"*Stop!*" Lucy held up her hands. "Please, stop!"

"Well!" Veronica scowled at Lucy. "That's the thanks I get for all my help and advice. Humph!"

"I'm sorry," Lucy told her. "It's just that I don't get to play an angel after all."

"What?" Veronica looked surprised. "Why ever not?"

Looking down at her lap, Lucy explained that being late had cost her the role of angel. "I really wanted to be an angel this year."

"Well, that's too bad." Veronica made a tsk-tsk sound. "What are you playing then? A shepherd?"

"No . . . it's worse than that," Lucy admitted. "A sheep."

"A sheep?" Veronica made a snorting sort of laugh. "Are you kidding me?"

Lucy shook her head.

"What do you do? Say baa, baa?"

Lucy barely nodded.

Veronica laughed harder. "They are not going to believe this!"

"Who?" George asked.

"The people in Hollywood . . . I mean, when I get there. They are not going to believe I rode through a snowy night to see my little friend here playing the role of a farm animal." She threw back her head and laughed loudly.

Lucy felt that lump growing in her throat again. "I'm sorry," she said quietly.

"What?" Veronica turned to her. "I couldn't hear you over the engine, doll."

"I just said I'm sorry," Lucy repeated. "I can understand why you don't want to go now. Maybe you can ride back home with George or something."

"Hmm . . . not a bad idea."

George scowled at Veronica. "I'm looking forward to seeing Lucy as a sheep."

"I'm sure she will make a perfectly charming sheep," Veronica said lightly.

For the rest of the drive, the only sound was the motor rumbling and the crunching of snow beneath the tires. Lost in her thoughts, Lucy wondered how she would manage to find Mama and Grandma and explain everything . . . all before the pageant began.

"Here we are," George said as he pulled up in front of the church. As he helped her out of the car, he smiled. "Remember what I told you, Lucy. About the Lamb of God and his humble beginnings."

Lucy held up her chin and nodded. "I'll try to keep that in mind."

"Break a leg," Veronica called from the car.

Lucy frowned. "You mean like Mrs. Dorchester? But she only sprained—"

"No, silly." Veronica laughed. "It's a show biz saying. It's like good luck."

"Oh . . . thanks." Lucy waved to both of them, then hurried into the church. At least she wasn't late tonight. In fact, she was early. She slipped into the back of the sanctuary and into the last row, slumping down into the polished wooden pew and wishing she could think of a reason not to play a sheep tonight.

Before long, other children were coming in. Some were already in costume, and some went back to change. Lucy didn't need to worry about changing much since her costume was just the scratchy, smelly blanket. Even if she didn't grab it until the last minute, it would probably go unnoticed. Just like she would go unnoticed. Most of all, she wanted to keep a close watch on the door. She wanted to explain this business to Mama and Grandma.

Other parents and family members began filling the church pews, and Lucy was just getting worried that she wouldn't get a chance to speak to Mama when she and Grandma came in. "Oh, Mama," Lucy said as she jumped up from her seat.

"Lucy? What's the matter? Is something wrong?" Mama looked worried.

"Shouldn't you be in your costume?" Grandma asked.

"I have to tell you something first." Right in the aisle, with others looking on, Lucy spilled out the whole humiliating story of how she'd been late because of the movie. "Now I'm a sheep instead of an angel," she said breathlessly.

Grandma grinned. "Better a sheep than a goat."

"Why didn't you tell me this yesterday?" Mama asked.

"I wanted to, but—"

"Lucy Turnbull," Mrs. Babcock called from up front. "What are you doing down there? Come on, come on." She clapped her hands. "Front and center."

"I'm sorry, Mama," Lucy blurted. Then she turned and hurried up front.

All in all, it wasn't that bad playing a sheep again. Lucy put her heart into it as she thought hard about how a sheep might act. She bent down her head and pretended to eat grass, she said an authentic-sounding "baa" at appropriate times, and she even moved her body like she thought a sheep might do as she followed the shepherd up to the manger to see the baby Jesus, which was really Helen Krausner's old baby doll wrapped in a shredded sheet. Really, she thought, she was doing a much better job than the boys.

Even so, she was thankful when it was over. It was a relief to toss off her "costume" while other children struggled to peel off layers of cloaks and belts and headdresses. She hurried down to the church basement where the audience was to gather for holiday cookies and punch. She spotted George's tall head on the other side of the room, and as she made her way toward him, she spied Mama and Grandma too.

"Nicely done," George said as he patted her on the head.

"Thanks." She smiled. "I did my best."

He held up a frosted cookie shaped like a Christmas tree. "I saved this for you . . . in case you were interested. They were going fast."

"Thanks."

Mama gave Lucy an uncertain look but said nothing. Lucy supposed that Mama might be upset at her for keeping something from her. Still, Lucy wasn't sure what to do about it. Helen Krausner was coming her way. She motioned with her fingers for Lucy to come over and talk to her. Lucy wanted to turn and run the other way, but she went reluctantly.

"Where is your movie star friend?" Helen demanded. "You said she'd be here tonight."

"She decided not to come," Lucy told her.

Helen looked doubtful.

"She was disappointed when she found out I was only playing a sheep."

"Or else you just made her up."

"I didn't make her up," Lucy insisted. "She's real."

Helen rolled her eyes upward. "Says you."

"It's true. If you ask around town, I'm sure you'll hear that other people have seen her."

Helen shrugged. "I didn't think she'd really come. I could tell you were lying."

"I wasn't lying," Lucy protested. "Honest, Helen, Veronica is real."

Helen tilted her nose up, just the way Veronica sometimes did. "Well, I'll believe it when I see it." She turned and walked away.

"We'll have to pile into the car on the way home," George said as he led them outside. "It'll be cozy."

"Lucy can sit on my lap," Grandma offered.

Before long, they were all piled into the car with Mama in the middle and Lucy sitting on Grandma's bony knees. "Am I too heavy?" Lucy asked.

"No, dear, you're fine. Just lean back and relax." She wrapped her arms around Lucy's middle. "I'll pretend like you're my little Baby Lucy again."

Lucy giggled as she leaned back. "This is cozy," she said, "but I like it."

"How about if we sing Christmas carols," George suggested.

All the way home, they sang carols, laughing as one or the other stumbled over the words or the music. All in all, it was fun.

"That was almost like a sleigh ride," Lucy said as they got out.

"If it wasn't so late, I'd make us all some hot chocolate," Grandma said.

"I'm full of cookies and punch," George assured her.

"And I'm tired," Mama said. "Mrs. Dorchester is a demanding patient, and I suspect tomorrow won't be much easier."

"Too bad she can't stay with her niece while she's recovering," George said as they went inside.

"Hopefully she'll heal quickly," Mama whispered.

Inside the house, everyone said quiet good-nights, going their separate ways. To Lucy's surprise, Mama didn't even come up to her new room to help her get ready for bed or listen to her prayers. Perhaps she really was tired. Or maybe Grandma had told her what Lucy had said—that she was too old for bedtime help. Maybe Lucy was. Or perhaps Mama was embarrassed that Lucy hadn't played an angel tonight. Especially since the pageant program had mistakenly listed Lucy as an angel. More likely, Mama was just disappointed that Lucy hadn't told her the whole truth sooner.

Whatever it was, Lucy felt too tired to figure it out. Besides, it was well past her bedtime, and today had been a busy one. If Mama was up here, she would probably tell Lucy to go to bed! She climbed under the covers and made an attempt at her usual prayer, but before long, she felt herself drifting.

Lucy woke to the sound of voices just outside her door. Sitting up in bed, it took her a moment to remember where she was—in her old upstairs room. She saw a slit of light under her door and could tell it was George and Veronica who were talking in the hallway. Curious as to why they were still up and conversing, she tiptoed out of bed and put her ear to the door.

"I want out of here, George," Veronica was saying in an emotional voice. "I swear I cannot abide another day out here—in the middle of nowhere."

"Then you should leave," he calmly told her.

"*How?*" she demanded.

"Keep your voice down," he warned.

"Fine, but how can I possibly leave unless you go with me?" she hissed at him.

"Take a train," he suggested in a firm but quiet tone. "Like I've told you to do dozens of times already. Trains pass through every—"

"I know, I know. You keep saying that, George. But I—I just can't." She made a sniffing sound, like she was crying.

"Of course you can." His voice grew more gentle. "Lots of trains pass through Flagstaff on their way to Los Angeles, and I can—"

"Don't you understand?" Her voice turned small and sweet, like a little girl. "I can't take a train, George. I just can't. Why don't you understand that?"

Lucy pressed her ear closer to the door, causing a board to creak. George cleared his throat, and Lucy heard the sound of shuffling feet. "Maybe we should go down to the front room to talk about this," he whispered. "We might be disturbing Lucy."

Just like that, they were gone. Lucy stood there a bit longer, straining her ears to hear, but all she could pick up was a muffled conversation, and only just barely. Tempted to tiptoe down the stairs to hear the rest of their conversation, she remembered how several of the steps had loud squeaks and would probably reveal her spying ways, which might prove embarrassing. Still extremely curious, she went back to bed and wondered what was going on down there.

12

Lucy felt excited when she woke up the next morning. Today was Christmas Eve! Just the same, she knew there were chores to do and the chickens needed tending. Even though it was before dawn, she crawled out of bed, dressing quietly since she remembered she was upstairs with the guests now, then tiptoed down the stairs, where the third step from the top loudly creaked, and hurried to put on her outer clothes. Grandma wasn't in the kitchen yet, but there were still some red coals in the woodstove, which meant Mama or Grandma had fed it in the middle of the night. Lucy paused to load some more wood into it, then headed outside.

As she carried the chicken bucket across the yard, she was surprised to see that fresh snow had fallen during the night. A half moon, still hanging on the western horizon, was illuminating everything in a magical way. As she trudged through the crunchy snow, where no footprints showed and no shoveling had been done, she realized that she was the first one up this morning. For some reason that filled her with a feeling of high anticipation. Christmas Eve morning, and Lucy was the first one up to enjoy it!

She broke the ice and filled the water and food troughs. The chickens were still sleeping on their roosts in the henhouse, and she knew that during winter they could be deep sleepers. In fact, she'd heard some chickens could sleep so soundly that a fox could slip in and snatch them unawares. Thanks to the sturdy fence around the chicken yard, that had not happened. She crept quietly over to the nesting boxes, peeking inside just like she always did, and to her delight discovered seven eggs. Since she'd forgotten to bring the egg basket, she carefully slipped some of the eggs into her coat pockets, carrying the rest of them in her hands.

As she walked toward the house, she noticed that the eastern sky was turning pink, casting a rosy light over the snow. It was so beautiful that Lucy had to just stand there and look. Then she saw that the lights were on in the kitchen, and realizing she was hungry, she hurried inside to find Grandma, still wearing her housecoat, putting a pot of water on the stove.

"Eggs!" Lucy exclaimed as she burst into the warm, bright room.

"Oh, my!" Grandma examined the three eggs in Lucy's hands. "George's light trick worked. And just in time because I wanted to do some baking today and the recipe calls for three."

"There are more." Lucy handed over the precious treasure. "*Seven!*"

"Not enough to serve all the guests." Grandma set the eggs

in a blue bowl. "But I don't see any reason why you couldn't have one, Lucy, if you'd like."

"*Yes!*" Lucy smacked her lips as she peeled off her coat and mittens.

"Your mama is tending to Mrs. Dorchester," Grandma said as she cracked the egg and dropped it onto a cast iron skillet.

"Poor Mama."

"I've a mind to call up the Farleys and tell them to come get their relatives." She sighed. "Except that we need the money."

Lucy nodded. "I know. I can help with Mrs. Dorchester too," she offered as she washed her hands at the sink.

"We should charge the Dorchesters for nursing care too," Grandma said a bit tersely.

"The sunrise is so beautiful this morning." Lucy gazed out the window as she sat at the kitchen table. "Look, Grandma, all the snow is turning pinkish red now."

Grandma came over to peer outside, then shook her head in a dismal way. "You know what they say about a red sunrise."

"What?"

"Red sky at morning, sailors take warning; red sky at night, sailors delight."

"What does that mean?"

"It means if there's a red sunrise, the weather will be bad. But if there's a red sunset, the weather will be good."

"But there aren't sailors in Arizona," Lucy pointed out.

Grandma laughed. "That's true enough."

Mama greeted them as she came into the kitchen. "Is that an egg I smell, or am I dreaming?" She peered at the stove.

"Lucy found seven eggs," Grandma proclaimed. "So I figured it wouldn't hurt to reward her with one. However, we won't have enough for the guests."

"Hopefully they won't smell it cooking."

"Oh, dear." Grandma slid the sunny-side up egg onto a plate and set it in front of Lucy. "You'd better hurry and eat that."

"Maybe we could spare an egg or two for Mrs. Dorchester," Mama said. "Since she eats in her room. It might improve her spirits."

"I'm sure they can use some improving too." Grandma patted Mama on the back. "I don't envy you, although Lucy has offered to help with her."

Mama bent down to kiss Lucy on the top of the head. "You're a dear, Lucy, but I think we should leave Mrs. Dorchester to me. In some ways I feel sorry for her. She would really rather be at home with her injury. I can't blame her."

"I wish she were at home too," Grandma added.

Lucy beamed at Mama. Maybe she wasn't angry at Lucy after all.

"I realized after I went to bed that I completely forgot to tuck you in and hear your prayers," Mama said contritely. "I'm sorry, dear."

"It's all right, Mama." Lucy smiled. "I know you were tired and I was—" She was interrupted by the tinkling of a bell.

"Oh, dear." Mama sighed. "Time to fetch the bedpan."

"What's a bedpan?" Lucy asked as Mama left.

Grandma chuckled. "Don't ask."

Lucy shrugged and returned to eating her delightful egg. No

matter what Grandma said about red skies and sailors, Lucy felt certain that this was going to be a good day.

She had just finished up the egg and was setting the breakfast table when Mama returned, passing through the dining room with a perplexed expression. "I cannot believe it!" she exclaimed as she went into the kitchen.

"Believe what?" Grandma asked.

"What they have done," Mama said in a hushed tone.

Lucy paused now, holding a plate in her hand, straining to try to hear each word.

"They have left."

"Who has left?" Grandma demanded.

"Veronica and George."

"*What?*"

"On my way from the bathroom upstairs, after taking care of the bedpan, I noticed the front bedroom door was open and the sunrise was streaming in the big window, and I happened to glance inside the room."

"*And?*"

"And the room had been vacated. The bed was unmade, so it appears it was slept in, but all of her luggage—everything—was gone, Mother. The closet was bare."

"George too? You're sure he's gone?"

"His door was closed, but I knocked quietly, and when he didn't answer, I peeked in his room to see the bed was neatly made as usual, but it looked as if he'd cleared out as well. Then I came downstairs and looked out the front room window to discover that his car is gone too."

"What does this mean?"

"It means that they sneaked out in the middle of the night, Mother." Mama let out a low groan. "And they stiffed us on the bill."

"Oh, my! I simply cannot believe it, Miriam. George did not seem like the type to do something—"

"Well, he did, Mother. We might as well get over it."

"Oh, Miriam."

"Don't waste your pity on me, Mother. I'm going out to the barn now."

Lucy was still frozen in place, the plate in her hand. How could this be true? George wouldn't do something like this! She set down the plate and dashed upstairs, peeking into the rooms to see it was just as Mama had described. She looked out the window, and sure enough, George's car was gone. How could this happen?

As Lucy went downstairs, she remembered the conversation she'd overheard last night and how Veronica had sounded so unhappy and wanted to leave. Maybe George had driven her to the train station this morning! With this hope in mind, she hurried to finish setting the table, then grabbed her coat and dashed out to the barn. "Mama," she cried as she went inside to find Mama fueling the woodstove. "I think I know where George is!"

"What?" Mama turned to look at Lucy.

"I think I know what happened, Mama." She noticed that Mama had tears on her cheeks. She'd only seen Mama cry a few times, and it always felt horrible. Feeling a lump in her own throat, Lucy went over and put her arms around Mama's waist, looking up and explaining about the conversation she'd over-heard last night. "Maybe George took Veronica to Flagstaff," she said eagerly, "to get on a train."

Mama knelt down now, looking directly into Lucy's eyes. "I had thought the same thing, Lucy. But I looked outside to see there weren't any car tracks in the fresh snow."

"But maybe the snow fell this morning," Lucy suggested.

"I got up around two in the morning to get a bit of milk and to load up more wood on the fire," Mama told her. "It was already snowing then."

"Oh . . ." Lucy tried to grasp what this meant.

"They must have left shortly after you heard them talking, Lucy. Maybe around midnight." Mama sighed. "That was about eight hours ago. Even in the snow, it would take only an hour or so to reach Flagstaff."

Lucy felt tears filling her eyes now. Was it true that George really was gone? Gone for good?

"We'd better go back inside and help Grandma with break-fast." Mama stood, using the bottom of her apron to wipe her eyes. "How many places did you set on the table?"

"Oh, that's right." Lucy nodded. "I'll run back and remove two."

Mama nodded sadly. "Tell Grandma I'll be in shortly."

Lucy felt like her feet were weighted down with lead as she trudged back through the snow to the house. Maybe Grandma was right. Maybe red sky in the morning really was a bad sign after all.

Breakfast was a somber affair. Fortunately, the usually quiet

Mr. Dorchester didn't inquire about the missing guests, so no explanations were needed. He seemed to have plenty on his mind as he shoveled in his oatmeal. Perhaps he was worried about his wife. Lucy just hoped he wasn't planning a way for them to leave too. Because right now they needed the room and board money more than ever.

As Lucy helped with the breakfast dishes, she decided that she would do whatever she could to make Mrs. Dorchester as comfortable and happy as possible. Not only would it lighten Mama's load, but it might encourage the Dorchesters to remain here. However, it didn't take long before Lucy agreed with Grandma that perhaps it would be best if Mrs. Dorchester went to stay with her relatives nearby. Of course, she kept her thoughts to herself. Today was not a day for complaining. Grandma was in a foul mood, and Mama was keeping herself busier than ever.

"This tea is cold," Mrs. Dorchester told Lucy in midafternoon.

Lucy touched the outside of the teacup to feel that it was quite warm. "It feels hot to me."

"You are a child. Naturally, it would feel hot to you." She tipped the cup to her thin, pale lips to try it again and then made a face that looked as if she'd been stabbed with a pin. "But it is most definitely cold! Please tell your grandmother to make me a fresh cup." Before Lucy could take the tray away, Mrs. Dorchester snatched up the three ginger cookies.

As Lucy set the tea tray in the kitchen, she moaned. "Mrs. Dorchester said the tea is cold and to make another cup."

"Apparently she liked the cookies." Grandma slid the tea kettle to a hotter spot on the stove.

"How's Mama doing?"

"She's shoveling snow . . . again."

"Oh . . ."

Grandma peered curiously at Lucy now. "Why do you ask?"

"I know all about it, Grandma," Lucy confessed. "I know Mama's sad because George left . . . and all that." She didn't really want to go into it, to hear the awful story rehashed again. She just wanted to know that Mama was going to be all right.

Grandma tossed a dirty spoon into the sink and shook her head. "It's just a shame . . . a doggone shame! He seemed like such a nice fellow too. And to do that . . . and at Christmas! Well, I can hardly speak of it."

Lucy felt the lump returning to her own throat now. "I know."

"All I can say is good riddance." Grandma frowned as she reached for the flour canister, dipping in her measuring cup. *"Good riddance."*

Lucy went to look out the window. The sky was getting darker, heavy and gray. "Do you think it's going to snow again?" she asked quietly.

"Probably."

Lucy looked over to where George's car used to be parked, to where he had snuck away in the middle of the night. Suddenly she remembered something. "The old car!" she cried as she ran to the door, grabbing her coat.

"What?" Grandma called.

"I'll be right back." Lucy ran outside and through the snow and around the barn, back to the lean-to garage her daddy had built when she was little. There was their old car, all cleaned up and looking surprisingly nice. She got inside of it and wondered if the engine worked. Of course, she had no way of knowing. But it sure looked promising, cleaned up the way it was. She considered telling Mama about it but then realized that it would only get her hopes up . . . and what if it didn't run? Maybe it was best to wait a while. Still, it was nice to see.

"What was that all about?" Grandma asked when Lucy returned to the kitchen.

"Oh . . . nothing."

Grandma filled a teapot with steaming water, put the lid on, then slipped a crocheted tea cozy around it. "Well, here's a whole pot of very hot tea," Grandma told her. "Get it directly to Mrs. Dorchester. She's been ringing that bell almost nonstop for the last few minutes, and my nerves are wearing thin."

Lucy glanced at the loaf of pumpkin bread fresh out of the oven. "Should you send her a slice of that too?"

Grandma frowned, then nodded. "You're probably right, Lucy. It might help to keep her quiet for a spell. At least long enough for me to get dinner ready."

"Do you think we can still string popcorn tonight?" Lucy asked a bit timidly.

Grandma's face softened as she set two slices of pumpkin bread on a saucer. "Of course we can, Lucy. We'll have hot cocoa too." She patted Lucy's head. "You'll have to forgive me for being out of sorts."

"I do, Grandma." Lucy picked up the tray. "I understand."

"Yes," Grandma said sadly. "I'll bet you do, dear."

After dinner, Mr. Dorchester turned in early, so only Mama

and Grandma and Lucy remained in the front room with the oversized and sparsely decorated Christmas tree. True to her word, Grandma made hot cocoa, and they sat around listening to the Christmas songs on the radio and stringing popcorn. Lucy thought that in spite of all that had gone on today, they were having a pretty good time.

But sometimes, as she was reaching for more fluffy white pieces of popcorn to slip onto her sharp needle, Lucy would glance at Mama. If Mama didn't know Lucy was looking, the sadness would show in her eyes. Lucy didn't know if Mama would ever smile again, and it cut Lucy to the core. Plus, she couldn't help feeling somewhat responsible for this pain. After all, hadn't she encouraged Mama to put her hopes in George? Talking him up and telling Mama how she thought he was falling in love. Had Lucy imagined these things? Now she blamed herself for Mama's broken heart. Because that's what Lucy thought it was—a broken heart.

Lucy wished she'd never seen George and Veronica in town that day, never invited them to stay at the house, never welcomed them into her life . . . and never trusted them with her secrets. Maybe this was what Mama was talking about when she said that Lucy would see things differently when she was a grown-up. Maybe Lucy was closer to being a grown-up than she realized. However, she would follow Mama and Grandma's example. Lucy would keep up a brave front. After all, it was Christmas Eve.

13

Although Mama had told Lucy she could stay up past her bedtime tonight, Lucy wasn't so sure she wanted to. After she'd finished her last garland of popcorn, one that was taller than she was, she admitted that she was tired and happy to go to bed at her usual time.

"I'm with you, Lucy." Grandma stood and stretched her back. "It's been a long day, and I'm plumb worn out."

"Goodnight, Grandma." Lucy went over and kissed her cheek. "Goodnight, Mama." Lucy was ready to give her a kiss too, but Mama stood.

"Do you mind if I help you get ready for bed tonight?" she asked Lucy hopefully. "Or are you really too big?"

Lucy smiled. "I was hoping you'd ask."

Just like old times, Mama helped Lucy out of her clothes and into her nightgown. She brushed and rebraided Lucy's hair and listened to her prayers. But she didn't turn the light off right away. Instead she reached over for Lucy's hand, giving it a warm squeeze in her own.

"I know something is wrong," she told Lucy. "I can see it in your eyes."

Lucy swallowed hard, looking away.

"I suspect it has to do with George," Mama said quietly, "and the way he left so suddenly."

Lucy just nodded.

"I know George was a very good friend to you while he was here, and I suspect it's been hard on you and that you're feeling sad and—"

"I'm not sad for me," Lucy said suddenly. "Not really." She considered this. More than anything she wanted to be completely honest with Mama. "Oh, I guess I'm a little sad for me. Maybe even a lot. But most of all I'm sad for you, Mama."

"Oh . . ." Mama just nodded. "Well, you probably have figured out that I'm a little sad too."

"I feel like it's all my fault." Lucy started to cry now. "I did everything all wrong. I invited George and Veronica into our house. I trusted them. I thought they would pay for their rooms and they didn't. And I made you believe George loved you and—"

"Wait a minute, Lucy." Mama pointed a forefinger in the air. "You did *not* make me believe anything. If I believed something, it's because I chose to believe it."

"But I saw how he looked at you. I told you things that—"

"I'm a grown woman, Lucy. I have eyes to see with."

With tears pouring down her cheeks, Lucy sat up and wrapped her arms around Mama's neck. "I'm just so sorry, Mama. I wish

I could go back and change everything back to how it used to be. If I found a genie in a lamp, I'd make a wish that George and Veronica never came to visit us. That I'd never seen them in town that day."

Mama stroked Lucy's hair. "But maybe it was a good thing they came."

Lucy leaned back to look into Mama's face. How could she possibly think that? George and Veronica had brought nothing but pain—and they didn't even pay their bill.

"Maybe it showed me something . . ." Mama sighed. "Something about myself . . . something I needed to be reminded of."

"What?"

Mama made a smile—or maybe it was just half a smile, but it seemed genuine to Lucy. "Maybe it showed me that it might be possible to fall in love again, Lucy. Someday . . ."

Lucy blinked. "Really, Mama?"

Mama nodded. "Maybe so."

"But does it hurt to feel like that?"

Mama shrugged. "Some kinds of hurts can be good for us." She helped Lucy lean back into her pillow, tucking the covers snugly back around her chin again. "Remember that time you got a bad splinter in your thumb and how much it hurt to pull it out? But when it was done, you knew it was a good hurt because the sliver was gone and the wound would get better. So it was a healing kind of hurt. Does that make any sense?"

Lucy nodded, although she wasn't sure she really understood. Mostly she was just relieved to see that Mama wasn't as sad as Lucy had imagined.

"Don't feel bad for my sake. And please, do not blame yourself." Mama leaned over and kissed Lucy's forehead again. "Because, really, I am fine."

"I'm fine too, Mama."

"Don't forget, tomorrow is Christmas day. I'm sure we'll all have a very good day now, won't we?"

"Yes." Lucy smiled as she remembered the presents she'd made and wrapped. "Yes, we most certainly will!"

Mama stood and pulled the string on the light. "Good night, darling."

"Good night, Mama."

Lucy closed her eyes and let out a long sigh of relief. Oh, she still felt a little bit sad and sore inside . . . kind of like her thumb had felt before it got well again. But she did feel hopeful. Mama was going to be all right. And she'd almost smiled again tonight.

Lucy was just starting to drift off to sleep when she heard the sound of clumping and thumping and then footsteps in the house. She sat up in bed and listened hard—if Tommy Farley hadn't ruined her childish hopes of Santa Claus visiting on Christmas Eve, she might have actually thought that he'd come to her house after all. As it was, she wanted to find out what was going on. Silently slipping out of bed, she tiptoed to the head of the stairs and, clinging to the stair rail post, she listened.

"*George?*" Mama's voice sounded shrill with surprise. "What on earth are you doing here?"

"I thought I was staying here," he told her. "But I'm terribly sorry to get in so late. I was hoping everyone would still be up . . . since it's Christmas Eve."

Unable to believe her ears, Lucy ran down the stairs and into the front room, nearly crashing into Mama. *"George!"* Lucy exclaimed. "You came back!"

He gave her a sheepish grin as he removed his snow-coated hat. "I hadn't meant to be so late and to wake up the entire house. But yes, like a bad penny, I'm back."

"Where on earth have you been?" Mama asked. "And where is Veronica?"

"It's a long story." George started to peel off his coat, taking it over to the hall tree by the door to hang it up.

Mama frowned at Lucy. "You were in bed, young lady."

"But you told me I could stay up past my bedtime tonight," Lucy reminded her.

Mama nodded. "I suppose you deserve to hear this too." She reached for the crocheted afghan blanket on the back of the sofa. "Wrap up in this if you plan to stay and listen."

Lucy draped herself in the blanket, and soon they were all seated as George explained what had happened. "Veronica decided that she had to leave here," he began. "Unfortunately she made this decision shortly after midnight. It seemed a little crazy, but I was so relieved that she wanted to go that I finally decided to accommodate her. So I drove her to the railway station in Flagstaff."

"In the middle of the night?" Mama seemed a little doubtful.

"And you took your things," Lucy added.

He looked confused. "My things?"

"Your room was cleared out, George." Mama frowned at him.

He gave her a bewildered smile. "Did you check the closet and the drawers?"

"Well, no . . . but all of Veronica's things were gone . . . and your room looked vacated, and—"

"I just like to put my things away," he told her. "If you'd looked a bit more, you would've seen that everything, including my suitcase, was still here."

"Oh . . ." Mama's brow creased. "So you took Veronica to the Flagstaff train station . . . and then?"

"As you know, it was late at night. As it turned out, the next westbound train didn't leave until six in the morning. So I gave Veronica enough money for a ticket and a room for the night, and then I dropped her off at a nearby hotel."

"She really was penniless?" Lucy asked.

"That's what she told me," he said. "Just last night, in fact. Before that I had no idea she was broke."

"That's what she said to me too," Lucy confessed. "But she had enough to take us to the movies."

"Veronica Grant had *no* money?" Mama looked somewhat suspicious now. "Even though she dressed so finely, had so many expensive things?"

Lucy explained about Veronica's movie friend who'd taken all her money and dropped her off on the side of the road. "That's when George gave her a ride."

"Then how did she plan to pay for her room here?" Mama asked.

George held up his hands. "I have no idea. But don't worry. I plan to cover that for her too."

"But why *should* you?" Mama demanded. "Furthermore, why are you buying Veronica Grant train tickets and hotel rooms and paying her room and board, George? What do you owe her?"

"I don't owe her a thing." George held his hands palms upward, with a puzzled and somewhat tired look. "I suppose it was to get her out of your hair and on her way, Miriam."

"I heard Veronica talking last night," Lucy told Mama. "She sounded really eager to get out of here. She'd told me lots of times before that she wanted to leave and go to Hollywood. But she had no money." Lucy glanced at George. "I think she had another reason for staying too."

"What was that?" George asked.

"I think she wanted George to marry her." Lucy directed this to Mama.

"What?" Mama's brows lifted.

George laughed. "Well, trust me, there was never the slightest chance of that happening, Miriam. Not a snowball's chance in Tahiti."

"Why not?" Mama folded her arms across her front with her head tilted to one side.

His eyes twinkled. "Because Veronica is *not* the kind of woman that interests me."

"Even though she is so beautiful?" Lucy asked him.

He looked directly at Lucy now. "I'll be honest with you. When I first saw Veronica standing alongside the road, she did turn my head somewhat. For a moment I actually thought I was seeing things. But after she got in the car and as I got to know her—and, believe me, that didn't take more than a few hours—I knew without a shadow of doubt that Veronica Grant, as pretty as she might be, would never be the one for me. But by then I couldn't manage to shake her off. I tried to drop her off a number of times, but she kept making excuses to travel with me. I had no idea she was broke." He rubbed his chin. "Come to think of it, that explains a lot."

Mama stood now, pacing back and forth across the room as if she was trying to grasp all this, as was Lucy. Then Mama went over to look out the big front window. "I didn't hear your car drive up, George. Where is it?"

"That's part of the reason I'm so late."

"What happened to your car?" Lucy asked with concern.

"It broke down again." He chuckled. "I'm starting to think that it's not just lemon yellow but a lemon as well."

"Huh?" Lucy had no idea what he meant.

"How did your car break down?" Mama asked. "And where is it?"

"It happened last night. I was on my way back here, hoping that I'd slip back into the house and into bed and no one would be the wiser. Then I'd be the hero at the breakfast table when I announced to everyone that Veronica was on a train to Los Angeles. It seemed a good plan to me."

"That would've been nice," Lucy told him.

"Instead, I was stuck in a broken down car, just outside of Flagstaff, and just as the snow was starting to fall. It was coming down heavy and I wasn't sure if I was going to be buried alive in a snowdrift. But I pulled out the car robe and wrapped myself up in it and said my prayers and fell asleep. Well, I slept off and on. I did a lot of praying and thinking too."

"Weren't you scared?" Lucy asked.

"To be honest, I was. But I also had a sense of peace too. Somehow I knew everything would work out. Finally, about an hour after sunrise, which was one of the most beautiful sights I've ever seen, a farm truck happened along, and the good man gave me a ride back into Flagstaff."

George explained how he had to wait several hours in a Flagstaff coffee shop for a tow truck. "Being that it was Christmas Eve, not everyone was eager to work." Then he told how his car was towed to Hempley's Garage, but due to a couple of slippery incidents, it took nearly three hours.

"Why didn't you just go to a Flagstaff garage?" Mama asked.

"Because I was staying here," George told her. "And Hempley's is nearby. I tried to call the house this afternoon, but no one answered."

"It's been a very busy day," Mama told him. "We had Christmas songs on the radio, and we might not have heard the phone ringing."

"Well, anyway, I had dinner at the café, and after Hempley finally had a chance to look under the hood, he told me that it was only a broken belt. He offered to fix it, but I felt bad for taking him away from his family. I told him it could wait until after Christmas, and then I walked on out here." He shook his head. "Thanks to the snow, I somehow wandered down the wrong driveway, so it took even longer than expected." He sighed. "It's been a very long day."

"At least you're back." Lucy threw off the afghan now and ran over to hug him. "I'm so glad you didn't stiff us on the bill, George."

"*Lucy!*" Mama looked aghast, but George just laughed.

Lucy grimaced. "That's what Grandma said."

"Well, I don't want to hear you repeating everything your grandmother says."

"Sorry." Lucy turned back to George. "Still, I'm so glad you're back."

"Perhaps you should go to bed now," Mama suggested.

George nodded. "Especially if you expect Santa Claus to show up."

Lucy gave him a tolerant smile. "That's all right. I'm old enough to know that Santa Claus isn't real."

He looked surprised. "What makes you so certain?"

"Tommy Farley told me."

"And Tommy Farley is an expert on such things?" George asked. "Has he been to the North Pole and done investigations?"

"No. He's only ten."

"Ten years old and you listened to him?"

Lucy felt a bit foolish now. Come to think of it, Tommy wasn't right about a lot of things.

"If I were you, I would get myself to bed and to sleep as quickly as possible." George went over to look out the window. "Just in case Santa is passing over your house right now and deciding not to—"

"I'm going!" She made a beeline for the stairs. "Good night, Mama. Good night, George." Faster than lightning, she zipped up the stairs, leaped into bed, closed her eyes, and tried her best to go to sleep. But first she told God thank you for bringing George back to them. She didn't know how long George would stay or if he loved Mama, but at least he hadn't run out on them like they'd thought.

14

Once again, Lucy woke up before the sun. But since it was Christmas morning, she couldn't stay in bed a minute longer. She still had her doubts about Santa Claus visiting last night, but she was so glad George was back that she didn't even care. She dressed as quietly as she could and tiptoed out to see that George's door was still closed. She hoped he was sleeping in since he must have been tired after his long day yesterday.

When she got downstairs, it appeared as if no one else was up down here either. She silently gathered the chicken bucket and egg basket and went outside. By the light of the moon, which was nearly down to the western horizon, she made her way out to the chickens. Just like yesterday, her footprints were the first tracks in last night's snow. She tended to the chickens, tossing out some extra grain since today was Christmas. Before she left, she checked the nests and was delighted to find nine eggs! Carefully loading them into the wire basket, she could see the sky lightening in the east and knew it wouldn't be long until the sun was up.

With lighthearted steps, she was just heading back to the house when she noticed what looked like smoke coming from the back porch. Alarmed that something was on fire, she nearly dropped the egg basket and bucket, but then George stepped out and waved his pipe at her. "Merry Christmas," he called out in a quiet voice.

"Oh!" She let out a relieved sigh as she went onto the porch. "Merry Christmas, George. My goodness, when I saw the smoke, I thought the house was on fire."

He frowned at his pipe. "Oh, maybe I shouldn't be—"

"No, no," she told him. "It's all right. It just surprised me." She held up her egg basket. "The hens are laying eggs again!"

His eyes lit up. "The light trick worked!"

"Seven eggs yesterday and nine today. That's sixteen total!"

"Your math is good, Lucy." He grinned. "Now, how about if you put the eggs in the house and then come help me with something?"

"Sure." She opened the door, and seeing that the kitchen was still semidark, she quietly set the eggs on the table, then returned to see what George wanted.

"Come with me," he said as he led her toward the barn and then around behind it. "I have something to show you."

"I think I know what it is," she confessed. "I saw the car yesterday, George. I couldn't believe how good it looks. But does it run?"

He grinned. "You'll see."

Sure enough, the car did start and it did run. George even took her for a little ride. "Just to get the engine warmed up," he told her. "Then we'll surprise your mother."

"She'll be so happy." Lucy looked out the window as the sun crested the horizon. Today it was golden and bright . . . almost like a promise that things were going to get better.

"This is a good old car," George told her as he turned around to head back for home.

"It sure is." Lucy beamed at him.

"I think it's a better car than my roadster."

Lucy was surprised. "But your car is so fancy and nice, George. I'm surprised you'd say that."

He shrugged. "Fancy and nice doesn't always get you where you want to go, Lucy."

She remembered him telling about being stuck on the side of the road and nodded. "I guess not."

"Anyway, I told Mr. Hempley that I might be interested in selling my roadster to him."

"You'd sell your car?" She turned to stare at him. "How would you get to California?"

He made what looked like a nervous smile. "Maybe I won't go . . ."

"Won't go?" She tried to grasp what this meant. "Do you mean you'd stay here with us in Maple Grove?"

"If your mother would let me."

Lucy didn't know what to say.

"What do you think? Would your mother be interested in a

503

new husband? For that matter, Lucy, would you be interested in a new daddy?"

Lucy swallowed hard. This seemed too good to be true.

"Maybe I'm rushing things," he said now.

"No," Lucy said quickly. "No . . . I was just thinking, George. I do think Mama would be interested in a new husband. I know I'm interested in a new daddy." She turned and smiled at him. "As long as it's the right one . . . someone just like you!"

He grinned and drove the car a little faster. Soon they were parked in front of the house. "Why don't you go see if your mother is up yet and if she wants to come out and—" But Lucy was already jumping out of the car and running into the house.

"Mama, Mama," she cried out as she went inside.

"Lucy!" Grandma looked alarmed. "What's wrong?"

"Nothing's wrong," Lucy exclaimed. "Where's Mama?"

"She just went out to the barn. But what's this excitement? I heard George is back, but what are you carrying on—"

"I'll explain it all later," Lucy said breathlessly. "First I need to find Mama." She ran for the back door. "Merry Christmas, Grandma," she called over her shoulder as she shot out. She spotted Mama coming out of the barn now. "Mama," she cried out, pointing to the car in front of the house. "Look!"

Mama's face was full of wonder. "Who is that and what's going on?"

Lucy grabbed Mama's hand. "Come and see."

"Merry Christmas," George said as he hopped out of the car.

"Is that our old car?" Mama asked with wide eyes.

"And it runs, Mama!" Lucy pulled her over to the passenger side. "Get in! George will take you for a ride."

"Just a minute." Mama held up her hands with a troubled look. "I have some questions first."

"What's wrong?" Lucy felt worried now. "I told George it was all right to work on the car. I didn't think you'd mind. You're not mad, are you?"

Mama shook her head with a perplexed expression. "No, I think it's just fine—it's wonderful—that George fixed our car." She looked at him with glistening eyes. "Thank you very much, George."

"Then what is it?" Lucy demanded

Mama pointed back to the barn. "Have you been in the barn this morning, Lucy?"

"No, but I did feed the chickens. Do you want me to bring in some wood and—"

"That's not what I meant, Lucy." Mama glanced at George. "I just wondered if you'd gone into the barn at all."

"No, Mama." Lucy was confused now.

"Maybe you should."

Lucy nodded. "All right. I can do that. But will you go for a ride with George now? He really wants to show you how the car is working so nicely, don't you, George?"

He grinned. "I most certainly do." He made a slight bow in front of Mama. "It would be my pleasure. That is, if you would care to join me, Miriam."

Mama looked from George to Lucy, then smiled. "I would love to take a ride with you, George."

Lucy felt a wave of relief rushing through her. "Good. I'll go to the barn," she promised. She watched as George helped Mama into the car, then got in and drove slowly down the driveway toward the road.

Confused as to why Mama wanted her to go to the barn, Lucy trudged across the yard again and slid open the big door. Mama had already started a fire in the stove, but it didn't look as if she was doing any laundry this morning. Why should she do laundry on Christmas morning? Lucy was about to leave when she heard a shuffling sound. She jumped. What was that? Had a wild animal gotten trapped in here somehow? Carefully backing toward the door and getting ready to make a run for the house, she heard another sound . . . like a nickering, followed by more shuffling and then a clunk.

"*What?*" Lucy stopped backing up and instead walked slowly toward the box stalls in the rear of the barn. As her eyes adjusted to the dim light, she couldn't believe what she was seeing. In fact, it took her breath away. "*Smoky!*" she cried as she ran to get a better look at the pony. "What are you doing here?"

He moved his head up and down and let out a little neighing sound as if he was glad to see her, and she let herself into the stall and began to stroke his mane.

"Oh, Smoky," she said gently. "How on earth did you get here?" She pressed her face into his neck, smelling his horsey smell and feeling his soft, fuzzy coat against her cheek. Tears of joy filled her eyes. "This really is the best Christmas ever," she whispered to him. "The best Christmas in the whole wide world." Lucy wrapped her arms around his neck and closed her eyes, whispering a prayer of thanks to God. He had answered every single one of her Christmas prayers—and then some!

Now she noticed a bridle hanging on a peg. Over one of the stall walls was a small, nicely worn saddle and blanket. "Come on, Smoky," she said as she slipped his bridle onto his muzzle. "We should take a little walk." She thought she remembered how to do this from spending time at Clara's farm and working with their old, slow plow horses, back before the Saunders family moved away, but it took a few minutes to get it in place and secured.

Feeling happy and proud, she now led Smoky out of the barn and over to the house. "I'm going to get you a treat," she told him as she walked him up to the porch and tethered him there. "You be a good boy and wait."

She ran into the house and making a frantic attempt to pour out her jumbled story to Grandma, she grabbed an apple from the cooler and was heading back out the door.

"What on earth?" Grandma stopped her, putting her hand on Lucy's forehead as if she thought she had a fever.

"Come and see for yourself," Lucy called as she dashed back outside to make certain she wasn't imagining the whole thing. But Smoky was still there, patiently waiting by the porch.

"*My word!*" Grandma exclaimed as she came over to peer at the pony.

"Here you go, Smoky." Lucy held the apple out in her open palm, grinning at her bewildered grandmother. "*See!*"

"What in the world?" Grandma ran her hand down Smoky's fuzzy back. "Where did *that* come from?"

"He was in the barn, Grandma!"

"But how in tarnation did he get there?"

"I'm not sure." Lucy considered this. "There weren't any tracks in the snow this morning. I know because I was the first one up." She laughed as she stroked Smoky's mane. "Maybe Santa Claus brought him."

Grandma shook her head. "Well, I'll be. I'll be." She came around to get a better look at Smoky's face. "I know you're over the moon about this, Lucy. But what will your mother say?"

Lucy pointed to where the old Model T was rumbling toward them. "I'm sure you'll find out soon enough."

"*What?*" Grandma pulled her cardigan around her more tightly as she leaned forward to squint at the road. "Who is that?"

Lucy quickly explained how George had fixed their old car. "It was our secret," she divulged. "Now George says he might sell his roadster to Mr. Hempley."

"Whatever for?" Grandma put her hand to her cheek as if she was completely befuddled.

Lucy giggled. "Maybe George thinks one car is enough for one family."

Grandma's eyes got very wide now.

Lucy continued to pet and calm Smoky as the car pulled up and George turned the motor off. Then she and Grandma watched as George helped Mama from the car . . . and they watched as George pulled Mama into his arms . . . and they watched as George kissed Mama—right on the mouth. And they watched, and giggled,

508

as Mama looked at both of them with flushed cheeks and the biggest smile Lucy had ever seen.

Oh, yes! Lucy knew without the slightest shadow of doubt that this was the very best Christmas ever—the best Christmas in the whole wide world!

Melody Carlson is the author of more than two hundred books, including fiction, nonfiction, and gift books for adults, young adults, and children. She is also the author of *Three Days*, *The Gift of Christmas Present*, *The Christmas Bus*, *An Irish Christmas*, *All I Have to Give*, *The Christmas Dog*, *Christmas at Harrington's*, and *The Christmas Shoppe*. Her writing has won several awards, including a Gold Medallion for *King of the Stable* (Crossway, 1998) and a Romance Writers of America Rita Award for *Homeward* (Multnomah, 1997), and she was nominated for a *Romantic Times* Career Achievement Award in the inspirational market. She lives with her husband in Sisters, Oregon. Visit her website at www.melodycarlson.com.